TOP
HOOK

TOP HOOK

Gordon Kent

DELACORTE PRESS

Published by
DELACORTE PRESS
Random House, Inc.
1540 Broadway
New York, New York 10036

Copyright © 2002 by Gordon Kent

Book design by Virginia Norey

Delacorte Press® is a registered trademark of Random House, Inc.,
and the colophon is a trademark of Random House, Inc.

LIBRARY OF CONGRESS CATALOGING IN PUBLICATION DATA
Kent, Gordon.
    Top hook / Gordon Kent.
        p.   cm.
    ISBN 0-385-33627-6
    1. United States. Navy—Fiction.   2. Intelligence officers—Fiction.
    3. Military intelligence—Fiction.   4. Married people—Fiction.
    I. Title.
    PS3561.E5185 T67 2002
    813'.54—dc21   2001058161

Manufactured in the United States of America
Published simultaneously in Canada

June 2002

BVG   10   9   8   7   6   5   4   3   2   1

To those who drive the ships

TOP HOOK

PART ONE

Betrayal

1

Venice.

THE STREETS WERE A RIVER OF COLOR IN THE DARK, sequins and silks swirling around bare flesh. Masks and cloaks fought the assault of the rain and the splashes of the sea underfoot. Costumes flowed toward San Marco, just as the tide of the Adriatic ebbed away, leaving salt puddles to reflect the glare of carnival.

The pounding music from the palazzi and the manic orchestration of voices, Italian and foreign, stunned Anna's senses as she ran. Her masculine costume had saved her in the seconds when the meeting had gone bad, and now it freed her to move, thrusting through the tangle of the crowd. The sword at her side caught at passersby until she took the sheath in her left hand and lifted the hilt off her hip.

She stopped with her back against a medieval shop at the base of a bridge. Music pulsed through the stone at her back, and her lungs burned as she peered around the corner at the arch of the footbridge. Two lovers embraced against the stone railing; a reveler in a black cloak and white Pantalone mask strode past her toward the bridge. At the top of the arch stood another of the Serbs who had tried to kill her, talking into a cellphone, his head moving like an owl's. None of the Serbs had bothered to wear masks or costumes; all had leather jackets and mustaches. High on adrenaline, she drew the sword and shrugged off her cloak in one unconsciously dramatic motion. She gathered the cloak in her left hand and risked one glance back into the thick of the crowd. Then she drew herself up and flung herself around the corner at the bridge.

Because the Serb was talking, he was slow. She rushed past the Venetian in the white mask, his dignified walk and cloak screening her for an extra second. She threw her own cloak with both hands, and the Serb shot at it on instinct. His second shot buzzed in her ear as she took a last step and leaped, lunging forward, her whole weight driving the point of the smallsword through his neck. The blade grated against the vertebrae and she rolled her wrist and used the speed of her rush to tear the blade free. Momentum carried her past her victim, and she stumbled, caught herself on the railing, and leaped to the parapet of the bridge.

The reveler's white mask turned to the movement, black eye sockets locked on her. One of the lovers had been hit by a shot, and the Serb's open throat pumped red blood on the gray stones. A second's balance on the parapet as her mind recorded the copper scent and the sheen of blood, and she dove into the canal. The unwounded lover screamed.

The shock of the water cut off the screams, and she swam, eyes and mouth shut tight. She stayed down, lungs bursting from the run and the adrenaline, until her hands found the opening and she thrust herself through and up into the tiny space of a partly submerged chapel, lightless, silent. For an entire minute, she could do nothing but breathe, supporting herself on a stone that had been the base of the altar.

She snapped on a tiny flashlight whose glow reflected off gold leaf and mosaic.

Anna rolled into her waiting canoe, half filling it with water, and sat up. Her right hand still clutched the sword, and she pushed it under the bag in the front of the boat and played the tiny beam of light around her. The chapel had been a military one, eight hundred years ago; she hadn't noticed it when she had entered at low tide. Now, she watched the ceiling as the tide ebbed and her escape route cleared. A Byzantine Saint Michael held aloft a sword of light and threatened Satan; a figure in armor at the far end looked to her like Saint Maurice—or was it Saint George?

She shivered. She had never killed before. She didn't like it.

She pulled a travel book from her pack and opened it to the last page.

She had written four names there in Arabic script, in an old Persian language that was better than a code. She studied them in the flashlight's inch-wide beam.

Her lips thinned and she shook her head at the first name—*George Shreed.*

Suburban Virginia.

Sitting in his house alone, George Shreed stared at a dead computer screen and listened to the absence of his wife. She was dying in a hospice, and the house was dying with her, devoid now of her voice, of the smells of her cooking, of her off-tune singing. Thirty years of marriage create a lot of sound, and now it had all drained away, and he was alone.

He booted up one of his computers. Three monitors sat on tables in the small "study." He could communicate directly with his duty officer at the Central Intelligence Agency, or with several distant mainframes on which he kept coded and secret files, or with the vast world of electronic magic that a few years before had hardly existed.

"Janey," he murmured. It was not as if he meant to call her back from the edge of death, but only that he had to say her name sometimes, as if, left unsaid, the name too would disappear and he would have nothing.

"Oh, God," he muttered.

Shreed was frightened. Horrors never came alone: first, his wife's cancer; now, the woman in Venice. He had just learned that his people hadn't caught her, so she was still out there, still running around with evidence that could send him to prison for life.

Two weeks ago, she had made her first contact: an e-mail with a photograph that he had first sent two years before, encrypted, to an Internet address where it could be accessed by Beijing. Shreed had been stunned to get it back—a hand reaching out of the past to strangle him.

Ten days ago, the woman had e-mailed him a page of classified material about a project called Peacemaker—classified material that Shreed himself had covertly sent to his Chinese control in 1997. The Agency would have him for treason if they knew he had transferred it. With it had been a curt message: "Venice—Old Ghetto memorial—16 March—one million dollars."

Then he had sent people to find her, and she had escaped.

And she had sent him a second message: "Now the price is two million."

The computer screen was bright. He punched keys, and icons and prompts flew by. He moved out into cyberspace, entered a mainframe on a university campus two thousand miles away and called up a file that appeared as random symbols and letters on his screen. He keyed in a password, then another, then empowered an algorithm that ran in tandem with a checker within the file itself, and then he was in, and the symbols in the blink of an eye became words.

Project Peacemaker.

Janey didn't know about this part of his life. Nobody knew, in fact. Not true—some people in China knew. But Janey and his colleagues at the CIA didn't know. He didn't give a shit about the colleagues, but he was deeply guilty that he had hidden part of his life from Janey, who *was* his life, for so many years. He would have to tell her, he knew. Tell her the way people tell a priest, there in the humming silence of her hospice room, tell her as she lay full of painkillers, needles in her arms, tell her as if she were the wall with the little wicket of the confessional. And say, *Forgive me, Janey—forgive me before you go.* Even though she wouldn't have heard him, most probably.

Shreed went through the Peacemaker file. He needed a fall guy, or at least a diversion—somebody to take the heat of an investigation if this damned woman in Venice decided to go to the Agency.

He needed time.

Peacemaker had failed two years ago, a very promising project that hadn't worked right, in the end. He had backed it as a weapon with real potential, and he had leaked data about it to Beijing, and the Chinese had made too much stink about it, and Peacemaker had been aborted by the White House as "destabilizing." The Agency had been nosing around ever since about how the information had leaked, and if the finger ever pointed at him, there would be a disaster.

He needed a scapegoat.

He had to find somebody likely. He was not, himself, likely—that was the good part. He had been too visible in the project, one of its main sponsors. What he needed was somebody who had not been quite so visible, somebody about whom you could say after the fact, Oh, sure, now I see what that guy was doing—he was spying for the Chinese the whole time. Somebody who would have had to exert a little extra to find things out. Not quite a munchkin, but not quite a master of the universe, either. He began to go down lists of names. *No, no, no—maybe— no.* He smiled, a somewhat wolfish expression on his lean face. He had just come to the name of his own personal assistant, Ray Suter. Assistants were expendable, and Suter was a real bastard, but he was too closely associated with Shreed himself. Suspicion, like tar, sticks to everybody in the vicinity.

Who, then?

Name after name. *Not quite right. Completely wrong. Impossible. Maybe.* And then—

Shreed grinned.

Rose Siciliano.

She'd been the Seaborne Launch Officer on the project. Walled off from the Eyes-Only stuff but very much in on all the computer magic, the trajectory and targeting data. If she'd actually been the spy, she could have, with some snooping and some late hours and a certain amount of risk, busted the security and reported the deep stuff to Beijing. She'd even had a computer geek, an EM named Valdez (a name he'd already dismissed) whom she was always quoting about the data stream and stuff she wasn't being allowed to see. Perfect behavior for a spy.

Or at least the CIA investigators would see it that way.

And she was Alan Craik's wife. And he owed Craik one—the little shit. They'd hated each other for years. His grin widened as he thought about it: if the wife was accused of passing secrets about Peacemaker, the husband was sure to be suspected, too. Tar sticks.

Shreed glanced at his watch. He was due at the hospice to sit with Janey.

He hit a button and highlighted the name.

Rose Siciliano.

Newport, Rhode Island.

The Cessna 180 held steady at 5,600 feet. At the controls, Rose Siciliano flew with the unconscious ease of a seasoned pilot—helicopters, now heading for astronaut training. Next to her, her husband glanced over the gauges and listened briefly to the Quonset tower. That was mostly the way it went—she flew and he kibitzed and ran the radio. Now, he put his hand on her knee, and her hand came down to cover his, and she flashed him a grin.

"It's been a great couple of years," he said.

She nodded, looked aside. Below, the Rhode Island coast was spread out for them on a sparkling day, Quonset Naval Air Station in her near foreground as they came around for their approach. They had been here two years and now they were leaving—both lieutenant-commanders, both at the Naval War College, both taking a quiet tour after some very hairy sea duty. And in two weeks it would be over.

"Gonna miss it," he said.

"You bet." Her normally husky voice was even a shade raspier. She had had their second child here. They had been happy. "Like real people," she growled. *Like civilians,* she meant. Now, it was off to the CIA's "Ranch" for him, astronaut training for her. Great moves for both of them, exactly what they wanted, but— She squeezed his hand. "We'll look back on it," she said.

"Hey!" He squeezed her leg, laughed. "Come on! Life is good. What can go wrong? We're *us.*"

She grinned again, then leaned way over to kiss his cheek.

But what could go wrong? He was LCDR Alan Craik, off to the Ranch, the CIA's arduous school for spies; she was LCDR Rose Siciliano, off to conquer the stars. What could possibly go wrong?

He got on the radio, and she banked the plane and descended, and then both of them were absorbed into the routine of headings and altitudes, and they went down and down and around and she brought it in on the center line of the runway, the wheels touching with a bump and squeal, and the ground raced along under her, and she was happy.

ROSE LEARNED how fast things could go wrong when they got home. He was already indoors; she had put the car away and gathered up their stuff, and she was standing in the front door of their rented house, looking down the long central corridor at his study. He stood there, back to her, telephone at his ear. She knew that stiff posture and long neck and what they meant: rage.

Mikey, their seven-year-old, knew it, too. And he knew the Navy "His detailer," he said, with the wisdom of a child who had grown up in the Navy. The baby-sitter, also a Navy child, nodded.

Rose started down the hall. Calls to your detailer were life-changing; your detailer helped plan your career, generated your orders.

Alan hadn't said a word yet. She had almost reached him when she heard him say, "Understood," and he slowly hung up and then gathered the cordless phone and its cradle in one hand and threw it across the study. It smashed against the far wall; Rose flinched as bits of plastic flew.

"Those bastards!" he shouted. His face was contorted with anger. "Those bastards have changed my orders!"

Going to the Ranch had been a big deal. Their pal Harry O'Neill had urged it. It was a logical step for a hotshot whose squadron days were over, he said—move into the covert world and go where the action was.

"Why?" she said.

"How the fuck do I know why? They won't tell me why!"

"But—honey—"

He came down a little, his anger never hot for long. "They're sending me to some rinky-dink experimental project. Month at sea then—the detailer doesn't know."

"Tell them you won't accept the orders!"

He blew an angry sigh through puffed mouth. "The detailer doesn't advise it." He bent to pick up the telephone and tried to fit two broken pieces of plastic together. "Not going to the Ranch, Rose— It's as if they don't trust me all of a sudden." He stood there, holding the pieces as if they were emblems of his helplessness. "All of a sudden, I'm a pariah." He looked up at her in anguish. "Why?"

Tar sticks.

"Oh, shit." He sat on the stair. "I've got to be in Trieste, Italy, in four days. I'm going to miss my own fucking graduation from the War College!"

Venice.

Efremov was dead.

Anna had awakened to feel his body cooling in their bed, the bed she had shared with him for five years. She had checked for a pulse, respiration, but they were last acts of friendship, quite separate from hope. He was dead. She had left Tehran the same day.

Now, his death would be known throughout his world. As he had prepared her for so many things, so he had prepared her for this, with suggestions and instructions, a locked box, passports—and computer disks. She had begun the contacts with his former agents even as she had fled Iran.

She had found safety and anonymity in a youth hostel in Istanbul. She was twenty-six and beautiful, but she looked a mature twenty, and she had bought a passport and a student card from Israel to have a twenty-year-old's identity. In Istanbul, she had used the cyber-cafés around Hagia Sophia to contact a man who was only a name on a secret file, George Shreed. Shreed had hired the Serbs to kill her in Venice.

Now, one of them was standing under an arch outside her window. They had found her.

She was sharing a room, a very expensive room, with a stewardess from Lufthansa. Greta was on vacation and avoiding airlines, and they had met at the Hermès shop near the Doge's Palace, not entirely by accident—Anna had been looking for cover. Greta wanted adventure, a little romance, a man to last a few days. Anna made herself the ideal companion, which included listening to Greta's complaints about the man she had picked up.

"American?"

"Australian, *ma chérie.* Rude and a little unwashed. Too rude, in the end."

"Mine never made the assignation."

"Cowards, all of them."

Greta emerged from the shower wearing nothing but a towel on her head. Anna admired her candidly; Greta lacked Anna's legs and hips, but she was striking, and her breasts were enviable. Greta seemed unaware of Anna's gaze and collapsed theatrically on her bed.

"Shopping will cure it. And I want to go to the Rialto."

"Is the Gap in Venice any different from the one in London?" Anna had never been to London, but her passport said she had.

Greta laughed, a silly girl's laugh. "I know where to shop, here."

"You'll get me in trouble."

"Probably." They both laughed. Greta was very easy to like, Anna thought. She had confidence and enthusiasm that went deeper than the automatic smile of the airline employee. Anna pulled on a top, glanced out the window, half pulled the heavy green drape, and moved from her own bed to the room's desk with her laptop. Greta began rifling her purse, throwing her passport and wallet on the bed. They caught Anna's eye, like a signal. She glanced out the window again.

"Do you have a laptop? Mine keeps freezing on the keyboard." Actually, it was working quite well. Anna just didn't want to be tracked.

"Of course, *ma chérie*. It is there, by the television. But it is probably the phone lines. They are antique, like everything else in Venice."

Anna found the case, slipped down behind the chair next to the television, and connected to the net. The machine was very different from the succession of IBM laptops Efremov had always acquired for them. It had a fashion edge to it. The case was an after-market replacement, a deep, velvet blue.

"The case is wonderful!"

"It is, isn't it? A boy gave it to me." Greta's voice suggested a deep satisfaction with the case, or the boy. Perhaps both.

Online connection. All the directions in German, but her German was up to the task. Greta spoke a movie-star English, but Anna's stilted German had started the hasty friendship and established her bona fides as the child of Austrian Jews.

Search engine. The second name from her list. *Alan Craik*. Several hits. A Navy locator address. Anna flicked her eyes over the street outside; the watcher had a cellphone out. She read two short bios of the man Craik—service, medals, marriage. Naval War College.

She searched again on some ship names: Alan Craik was going next to an aviation detachment, that much was clear. She tried "Ombudsman" and "USS *Thomas Jefferson*." Seven hits. The Americans continued to pretend that their naval movements were classified, even as their wives posted lists of ports of call on the Internet. She used the unfamiliar finger pad to scroll through the seven hits.

Exactly. Liberty ports.

Movement on the street outside. A second man, a lit cigarette. Anna scooped Greta's documents off the end of the bed and put them in her bag without hesitation. Then she took her own expensive forgeries and dropped them on the telephone table, never taking her eyes off the street. Greta prattled on, and Anna made noises—*yes, no, interesting*—to suit Greta's noises. Greta knew nothing of the men outside the window or of the sudden loss of her identity.

One last bit of information from the laptop: Alan Craik would be in Trieste, Italy, in two days.

Anna closed the laptop and returned it to its case, running her fingers over the blue. Anna loved the best things, and so did Greta. On that ground, they truly met. Greta was applying her makeup, and their eyes met in the mirror.

"I have to run out, Greta." Anna waved her handbag. "I'll be back in a few moments."

Greta nodded in the mirror. Anna bit her lips in regret. Greta did not deserve what was to come, but no one did. Anna headed for the elevator.

The antique elevator was the only way she knew of getting to a lower floor. Even in Iran, there would have been fire stairs, but not in Venice. She thumbed the button. She had no gun and she feared what would emerge from that elevator.

Abruptly, while she was still trying to devise a plan to meet a rush of armed men, the door opened. One elderly woman emerged. Anna had the elevator to herself. She took two deep breaths before she thumbed the button for the first floor.

The Serbs would be in the main lobby by now.

The elevator crept down three floors, her heart hammering in time to the gentle sway of the old car within its track, and stopped with arthritic slowness. The door attempted to compensate with a harsh crash that could be heard throughout the building. They would hear that, know that someone had used the elevator to the first floor above the lobby. Anna fought down panic. They could not know it was she. Not yet. Not until they found Greta. If they could tell the difference between Greta and Anna, she was dead. She hoped they only had a description. In her experience, all desirable women looked alike to most men.

She walked to the room that corresponded to her own on the fifth floor. She had no reason for this choice, only a certain blind superstition. She breathed and knocked.

A middle-aged man in a dressing gown opened the door. Anna smiled, her body swaying with relief. "May I come in?" she asked. The man, a North American, appeared flabbergasted. His mouth moved, but no words emerged. Anna heard the elevator going up—and up, past this floor. Up to her room on the fifth?

She slipped past him into his room. Same layout as her room above, two beds, even someone in the bath. She walked to the window, moved the blinds. Empty. She pushed the window open. The man was saying something, and the sharp retort of a gunshot came from above them. She ignored both, letting the surge of adrenaline carry her out the window. She hung from the sill and dropped. One of her stupid heels broke, but her ankle held and she stumbled away. She pulled her shoes off, threw them in the canal, ran to the corner, began planning her movements off the island of Venice and up the coast to Trieste.

Planning it in her head as she ran barefoot—*Trieste . . . Alan Craik. . . .*

Trieste.

Alan joined his new command, an airborne detachment testing a new imaging system called MARI, while it was moving from Pax River via NAS Norfolk and Aviano, Italy, to join the USS *Thomas Jefferson* at Trieste. At first, it was like flying with strangers in a commercial jet; he was CO in name only, the movement already organized by the acting CO, a lieutenant-commander named Stevens. He was still in a rage over the change of orders, so his mood was not charitable, and he found himself making harsh judgments about the unit. Movement planning seemed to him substandard, the preparations made to work only because the junior enlisted worked their butts off and the senior enlisted were pros. The officers remained an unknown quantity—faces and handshakes at Pax River, and little else—and most of them had flown off with the det's two aircraft and would be waiting on the *Jefferson*.

By the time they had reached Aviano, he had at least gotten control of the anger, and he knew many of the faces, if not the names. He had made common cause with the senior chief, and they had agreed on how to improve the last leg to the ship. Then he saw to it that he was the last man to leave Aviano; that way, he knew that everything was in train, and the senior chief would get everything to the *Jefferson* on schedule.

He showered for the first time in two days, changed into civilian clothes at the NATO bachelor officers' quarters, and rented a car, which he drove a little too fast into Trieste before walking down to fleet landing. The *Jefferson* was anchored out beyond the main harbor entrance, washed by hazy sun and a faint Mediterranean mist that gave the port a friendly look and gilded the harshness of the modern waterfront.

Now almost resigned to the change of orders and buoyed by seeing a ship he knew and felt great affection for, his mood was raised further by seeing a familiar face: Chris Donitz, an F-14 jock who had been the senior LSO on his last tour.

"Hey, Doughnuts!"

He smiled because it was obvious that Donitz was glad to see him. In an instant, shipboard camaraderie embraced him, and he listened with a smile as Donitz told him that he was heading shoreward for two days of liberty and a meeting with his wife. Donitz was just beginning to rhapsodize about meeting her in Venice when Alan heard a voice at his shoulder.

"Sorry to interrupt, sir—are you Lieutenant-Commander Craik? Message at the SP shack, sir."

He thought, *Oh, shit, trouble with the det.* He shook Donitz's hand. "Better catch your train. Give my regards to Regina."

"You bet. But Al, listen, uh—"

Alan waited, literally balanced on one foot to walk away.

"Uh, watch your step, okay?"

That got Alan's attention, and he swung back. "What's that supposed to mean?"

Donitz flicked a glance at his watch and shuffled his feet. "Just some scuttlebutt about why you're here."

"An intel guy commanding a bunch of aviators? I can deal with it."

"Uh—sure. Hey, take care of yourself."

If Alan had been in less of a hurry, he would have known that Donitz had more to say. As it was, Donitz gave a quick hand gesture, part salute, part wave, and hurried through the shore-patrol sentries and down the pier toward the railway station.

Alan strolled over to the shore-patrol office. A well-turned-out jg stood inside, his creased whites gleaming. He was from the ship's company and didn't recognize Alan in his civilian clothes, but as soon as Alan introduced himself, the man snapped to attention.

"Sir, the previous DO left a message that your wife came by about an hour ago and said she'd wait for you in, uh, Lettieri." He had trouble with it, and the name came out as Letty-air-yury.

"My *wife*?" Rose was supposed to be in Newport, getting ready to graduate.

"That's what the message says, sir. 'Mrs. Craik waiting for her husband at the Letty-air-iery.' "

"Lettieri?" Alan asked. Rose had never mentioned coming out. Of course, she wasn't above surprising him—maybe even skipping her own graduation because he had to miss his, and they'd spend it together? Pick up a quickie flight from some friend in Transport— The thought of seeing her made him grin.

"Lieutenant, can you call the boat?"

"Yes, sir."

"Get CVIC on the line and tell them that LCDR Craik is going to miss the 1700 brief, okay? Ask my det NCOIC to see that my stuff gets to my stateroom."

"Aye, aye, sir."

"Now, where is the Lettieri?" He realized that he wanted to see his wife a lot more than he wanted to see his new command.

ALAN'S EAGERNESS to see Rose saved his life.

He followed the first part of the directions from fleet landing to the Riva Del Mandrachio, which ran along the waterfront, but the next turning eluded him. The landmark for this turn had been hotly debated by two sailors of the shore patrol, one arguing for a small church, the other for a bar, both making marks on the back of an advertising flier for a rock club. Alan saw several bars, but no church. He turned southeast, away from the waterfront, and headed into town, following the crude map and asking his way in his Neapolitan Italian, to the amusement of the Triestini.

The first local he asked pointed silently up the hill and waved Alan on. The second, as if to make up for the reticence of the first, offered to take him to a much better café, with a beautiful waitress, where the man himself was headed. Alan declined with courtesy, and the man shrugged. He gave directions rapidly, insisting that the Caffe Lettieri was on the Via San Giorgio. Alan followed the new directions as best he could.

Ten minutes later, he was deep in the old part of the city. He passed two of the city's foremost Roman attractions and stopped, his temper flaring. The anger about his changed orders was just below the surface again, ready to flare at any provocation. He took a deep breath, looked at his map, and began to doubt that any members of the shore patrol had got this far from the fleet landing. Then, deliberately calming himself, he walked slowly until he found a cross street whose name appeared on his map and moved briskly south toward the Via San Giorgio. By then, the sunny day had turned gray, and thin Adriatic drizzle had begun to fall, and he was hurrying because he was afraid he would miss Rose.

He had to walk for more than five minutes to reach San Giorgio, and he realized by the time he reached it that he was directly above the fleet landing; indeed, the shore patrol post was almost at his feet. The Caffe Lettieri was just ahead of him, a new, prosperous place with gold lettering on its façade. Rose's choice of a rendezvous now made sense. He hurried to meet her, overtaking what he took to be a local man talking on a cellphone.

And then something struck him as out of place. A car had pulled up ahead of him, a big Audi 5000; the doors opened even before it had stopped, and as the doors popped feet and heads and hands appeared, fingers gripped around door frames, tension in eyes that darted back and forth at him and at the man with the cellphone. He knew those eyes, those tense hands: *anticipating violence.* That was his reaction, irrational, atavistic: memories of Africa and Bosnia, men going into action, high on it, super-alert.

And the man ahead of him was speaking Serbo-Croat, not Italian.

The man closed his cellphone with a snap and drew a pistol from his backpack, his eyes fixed now on the Caffe Lettieri. He looked just like the men coming out of the Audi. Almost dancing on the pavement in his anticipation.

They were going to hit the café.

The café in which his wife was waiting.

Alan lengthened his stride and stepped up behind cellphone man and took a last, careful look up the street at the car, his mind stretching the milliseconds as he tried to read what he was seeing. Weapons were appearing now from black leather jackets. One man was checking his fly, the second time he had done that: *When did I see him do it? How did I notice?* Another licked his lips. Looking here, there—predators' eyes—

He took a deep, silent breath, gathered his anger and frustration, and threw himself on the man with the pack, pinning his arms to his sides. His weight carried the man to the ground and the man's head hit the pavement with a hollow thump, like a gourd meeting a cleaver. He heaved at the man, flipping him face up, gaining control of his limbs and taking the gun, a wrestling move that flowed from his past without conscious thought. He worked the slide on the pistol and rolled away, covering the head of the street, where one of the men from the Audi was opening fire into the front of the café.

Alan centered the sight picture on the man's chest above the machine pistol he was using and fired twice, knocking the shooter back over the hood of the Audi. One of the other leather jackets fired back at him, walking the stream of bullets over the man he had tackled. Alan felt a blow to his leg and fired back without any attempt to aim. He raised his head and shot again on reflex, but the man who had fired at Alan had thrown himself into the car.

All Alan could think was that if it was a terrorist attack they still had time to throw a bomb, that Rose was still in danger. The car shrieked away from the curb, hitting the mirror of a parked van.

Two men were down.

Alan stumbled forward, his left leg striking oddly on the street. As he came to the corner, he saw that the whole front of the café had been shattered by bullets, and he threw himself forward into the café. He bellowed, *"Rose!"*

Two young men were bent over a body. Alan leaned past them, saw that the body was a man's, and realized that he was still holding the gun. He shoved it in his waistband and went to the second body, clearly a corpse and with a pool of blue-black blood all around it. An older woman. *Not Rose.* Three other victims were on their feet, one staring at a bloody arm; a woman screamed and screamed; somebody slumped to the floor, his back tracing a red smear down the wall. He smelled gunpowder, blood, excrement.

Then his senses began to return from the overload of the shooting, and he heard the hooting of police sirens and more screaming.

"Alan Craik?" A woman's voice behind him.

"Rose?" He turned and saw a woman who was definitely not Rose, a tall blond woman with a straight nose and Asiatic cheekbones.

"You are Alan Craik, I think."

His leg was numb, and he looked down. The heel and sole of his left shoe had been shot away. He sat heavily on the floor, in a litter of broken glass. Reaction, fatigue. The sirens got closer. His foot had been cut by glass, otherwise was untouched, but his whole lower leg was numb. He focused on the woman in front of him. She looked like a wild animal caught between a need for food and a need to flee. His brain seemed to have been numbed, too: "Are you a friend of Rose's?" he said, hearing the stupidity of it.

"I told them I was your wife so you would come." Alan's head snapped back to her, and his right hand moved toward the butt of the pistol in the small of his back. *A trap? But the shooters are gone. What is she telling me?*

"I must meet with you."

Alan looked at her. She had neither blood nor glass on her and she looked like the cover of a glamour magazine, except for the fear in her eyes. She seemed to have no reaction to the screaming or the sirens or the blood, as affectless as a photograph, except for those eyes. He pulled himself up by grabbing a table that was puddled with coffee. His brain still seemed unable to make good sense. "Who are you?"

The sirens screamed outside. "Your next liberty port is Naples. Meet me there."

"Why?"

She was already moving away into the crowd in front of the café. For the first time, she seemed at a loss. Once at the edge of the crowd, however, she stopped, now part of it, not part of the attack.

"Bonner," she called. Then she was gone.

Bonner? He had to focus. Bonner was the name of the traitor who had got his father killed. Bonner was in a US prison. What did she mean, *Bonner?*

Police poured into the ruined café. He could make no sense of it, but his brain was clear enough now for him to know that what the woman had said had flung him back into a security investigation he had believed closed, and there was no way he could tell the Italian cops about it.

Newport and Utica.

FOR ROSE, THE NEW LIFE STARTED WHEN SHE CLOSED their rented house. She had loved living there, but now she was ready to go to the life she had dreamed of and worked toward for six years—Houston, the Space Center, astronaut training.

"Ready to go?" she said to Mikey, their seven-year-old.

"Let's go!"

"You ready?" she said to the dog. The big tail banged against a wall.

"Well—let's go!"

And without a backward glance she piled them into the 4Runner and started for her parents' house in Utica, New York. The kids and the dog would be left there while she drove to Houston, then camped out in the house they had already bought there. Her children would adapt. They belonged to a happy family, except that every two or three years, one or both parents went to sea. Or into space.

"You feel abused?" she said to Mikey.

"I'm busy." He was playing a computer game.

"That's what I thought."

The dog put his head over the seat from the back and licked her hair.

"You feel abused?" she said.

The dog wiggled all over.

"That's what I thought."

The trip was long, and Mikey got cranky, then slept; the baby howled; the dog threw himself on the floor and panted and gasped and whimpered. On and on, through Massachusetts and into New York, stopping to buy junk food and to piss and to walk the dog, then west along the Thruway and at last, as it was getting dark, to the little house in the Italian streets where she had grown up. Mikey, awake again, was eager.

"The first thing your grandmother will say is, 'You're later than you said.' "

"Grampa will tell her to shut up."

Kids hear a lot.

"You're late," her mother said. "You said seven o'clock." They kissed. "Dinner's ruint," her mother said.

"How's my girl?" her father shouted, embracing her. He was a small man, wiry even in old age, a fair singer and a great ballroom dancer. "Shut up, Marie, she drove all this way, she done great." He began to sing, *Rosie, she is my posy*—

"I'm starved, Ma," she told her mother. "Just starved." She wasn't, but she knew her mother wanted to feed her. Singing, her father took her in his arms and began to dance her around the driveway. *Rosie, she is my joy*—

Rose winked at her father, and they went into the house with their arms around each other's waist, Mikey holding his mother's hand. It was only after another ten minutes of shouting and trading news that her mother said, "Oh, your father forgot, you got a phone call! It's his business to tell you, I guess, but he forgot." She drew herself up. "Not bad news, I hope."

"Nah, nah, Jesus H. Christ, Marie! Give her a break, she just drove three hundred miles!" He turned to Rose. "It's some goddam military Mickey Mouse, I'd of told you tomorrow. Probably you didn't dot the i on an exam paper."

"She better call," her mother said.

"Call tomorrow. Tonight's for fun!"

"I'd of had her call the moment she got here."

"Goddamit, Marie—"

Rose was laughing at them, because nothing bad could happen and she knew her father was right; it was some Mickey-Mouse nothing. Still, she knew her mother wouldn't let it go until she called, so she asked where the number was and her father said by the phone. As soon as she saw the number, she knew it was her detailer's, and her confidence that nothing bad could happen gave a little hiccup. There was a second number, as well, with "home" written next to it in her father's precise writing.

Her confidence stumbled. Why did he want her to call at home? Or was that simply something that her father, a thorough man who had been a machinist and always worried about details, had asked for?

There was no privacy in that house. Even her father believed that if you needed privacy, you'd done something bad. She walked out to her car and got her cellphone from a box of office stuff that she'd shoved in the back, and she dialed the detailer's home number from there, leaning her buttocks against the back end of the car and looking up and down the twilit, familiar street.

"Anders," the male voice said.

"Hi, uh—this is Lieutenant-Commander Siciliano. You called me?" Letting her voice go up in that crappy, little-girl way that women affected now. Christ, what was wrong with her? "Something wrong?" she said, not able to keep from saying it, not even able now to keep the anxiety out of her voice.

"Oh, yeah." He sounded as if she had ruined his evening. "Thanks for calling." She could hear papers moving, an insect sound. He had her file next to the phone! "Your orders have been changed."

It made no sense to her. Then it made only trivial sense—the reporting date had been changed, or the time. Or she should go to a different office. But a warning voice was murmuring, *Just like Alan, just like Alan—*

"Your orders have been changed from Houston," he said. He was going slowly, but she said, her voice steely now, "Give it to me."

"The Houston orders were changed, I don't have the reason here—now don't shoot the messenger, okay, Commander—"

"Cut the crap. What are you trying to tell me?"

She heard a sigh, then words spoken to somebody on his end, something like *I'll be there in a minute.* Then he said, "The orders to the space program have been canceled. You have a new set of orders to a command in West Virginia. The, uh—Inter-Service Word Processing Training Center. As XO. Look, I had nothing to do with this; I just got a priority message—"

She stopped listening.

Her life stopped.

She wasn't going to astronaut training.

But why?

They had loved her in Houston. Her fitreps were great. Her physicals were perfect—the doctor's own word, "perfect," "You're a perfect type for space." She was perfect for space from the Navy's PR viewpoint, too—combat experience, a mother, attractive.

The detailer was asking her a question. Fax—did she have a fax?

"No. No, they don't have a fax here." Her voice surprised her with its steadiness.

"Well, get a fax number there someplace so I can send you the orders. The reporting date's been put back, so you've got a couple of weeks to, you know, adjust things."

Adjust things? That did it!

"Like my household goods, which are all on the way to Houston?" She was angry now—her one great failing. Was that it, they'd washed her out because she got angry? "I just bought a fucking house in Houston, and my household goods are going there, and I've got two kids and a dog and nowhere to live!"

"Look, I'm sorry, I'm sorry, this isn't my doing—!"

"Well, who the fuck's doing is it?"

"I don't know. This came from CNO's office."

What the hell did the Chief of Naval Operations care about her astronaut training? Jesus Christ! *Just like Alan, and they didn't explain to him, either*—

"This isn't fair. I want to appeal. This isn't the way the Navy does things! Goddamit, I've followed the rules; I believe in the system; they can't just—just— They've ruined my fucking career!"

He spent a minute or two talking her down, and the anger ebbed, turned into that steely calm again. Her mind was racing on, however, leapfrogging over anger and fear and hatred of the Navy, already seeking explanations, because there had to be an explanation, and when she found what it was, blood was going to flow.

"Okay," she said. "Don't jerk me around. I want answers."

"Absolutely." He wasn't a bad guy. He knew that something, somebody, had decided to destroy her.

She turned the phone off, then back on, and tried to call Alan at the BOQ at Aviano, but he wasn't there. Already on his way to Trieste, she thought, kicking ass as he went. Just as well—he had enough problems already.

She put the phone away and slammed the tailgate and stood there. It was so dark now that she hardly noticed her father at the corner of the car. How long had he been there?

"Rosie—what're they trying to do to you? I'll kill 'em, no kidding."

She laughed. "Oh, Dad—" Then she threw herself on him and wept.

Suburban Washington.

The corridors of the hospice smelled of potpourri and soap, with the scents of the dying only vagrant hints, an occasional whiff of antiseptic or bleach. The bowels loosen before death, but the system that transported air through the building was brilliant and powerful, and the grosser reminders were sucked away. It was an expensive place.

Heartbreak Hotel, he thought. He was even humming it to himself, not the Elvis version but Willie Nelson's: *I get so lonely, baby/ I get so lonely I could die.*

Heartbreak Hotel with a dedicated staff. George Shreed was a tough man, utterly unsentimental, but he knew when he had fallen among saints. If what they gave her was not love, it was such a counterfeit of love that it was, he thought, worth any price.

Shreed used two metal canes to walk. He heaved himself along on powerful shoulders and arms so ropy with muscles he might have been an iron-pumper. Thirty years before, he had crashed a jet in Vietnam, and he would have died there if his wingman hadn't stayed overhead, calling in the medevacs and taking AA fire and keeping the Cong off him. Now, planting his canes and pushing himself up on them and dragging his legs along, he thought grimly of that day when he thought he was going to die, and of that wingman of long ago—Alan Craik's father. Now Mick Craik was dead and he was still alive, and his wife, who was ten years younger than he and whom he loved to distraction, was almost dead.

"Oh, Janey," he muttered with a sigh. There he went, saying it aloud again.

"Hi, Mister Shreed!" The night nurse smiled, truly smiled, not a plastic smile but a real one. The smile slowly cooled, and she said, "You may want to stay with her tonight."

"Is it—? Is she—?" *Is she going to die tonight?* he meant. These people knew when death was waiting.

"You maybe just want to be there with her."

Janey lay on sheets from her own house, wearing a nightgown she had bought at the old Woodie's. The room had a real chair and a decent imitation of a Georgian chest of drawers, and one of her own paintings hung on a wall. *Der Rosenkavalier* was playing on her portable CD—the music she said she wanted to die to. It was on a lot.

No tubes and no heroics, she had said. She had a morphine drip in one arm and a Heparin lock in the other; she was dying of hunger now as much as of cancer.

She looked like a baby bird. Janey Gorman, who had been the prettiest girl at Radford College, had a beak for a nose and a scrawny neck and curled hands like claws. Shreed rested his canes against the chest of drawers and pushed the armchair over to the bedside, leaning on it for support, and he took one of her hands, and her eyelids fluttered and for a moment there was a sliver of reflection between the still-long lashes.

"Janey, it's George." He kissed her, feeling the waxy, faintly warm skin, then squeezed her tiny, bony hand. "Here again." The unsentimental man felt constriction in his throat, heat in his eyes. "Janey?" *Der Rosenkavalier* swelled up, that incredible final duet. Once, she had played it as they had made love, whispering *Wait* and *Wait*, and then as it rose toward its final too-sweet fulfillment, she had laughed aloud as they all reached it together. He listened now, let the music die, let silence come.

"Janey, I have to tell you something." He could see a pulse beating in the skinny neck, nothing more. "Before—you know." He stroked her hand. "I want to tell you something about myself. You never knew all about me. You didn't want to; we agreed on that right at the beginning. But it's not—not what I did for a living." The word *living* stuck a little in his throat, in that place. And, anyway, he hadn't done it for a living; he'd done it for a passion. "Janey—listen. Janey, a couple of years ago, you came into my study and you saw that there was—" He sighed. "Some pornography on my computer screen. You turned around and walked out and we never talked about it." Her cancer hadn't been identified then, but aging had made sex difficult for her despite the hormones that helped to kill her, so sex was not an easy subject between them. "You see, the truth, Janey, was worse than what you thought. And—" He sat.

"I want you to forgive me, Janey. Not for the porn—that was nothing—but for what I was really doing. I was sending classified information to a Chinese case officer. We used pornographic photos to embed the data in so we could send it over the Internet." He sighed. "I'm a Chinese agent." He waited. There was only the hum of the air-conditioning.

"I had a reason, Janey—I *have* a reason, I'm not just some goddam two-bit traitor! I have—my own goal."

He put her hand down on the flowered sheet and sat back.

"Remember the first tour in Jakarta? I was running agents against the Chinese mostly. I had a guy I called Bali, he was Straits Chinese, he was one of those foot-boxers. Tough. I found he was a double; he was being run from the Chinese interest office, so I played him for a year until I got a line on his control and I busted him. It was one of those macho things to do—guy who walks on two canes muscles a Chinese case officer, pretty stupid now that I think of it, but at the time I was a high flier, remember?

"I picked up his control in the apartment of one of Sukarno's buddies. He had the place wired like a concert hall. So I scoped it out and had a techie blank the mikes and play dead sound, and I went in and told him he was going to work for Uncle or he was going to be one dead Chink when Sukarno's buddy came home."

He looked at her. Was there something like a smile? "Remember Jakarta? The first time? Fantastic fucking. We were young." Her eyelids trembled.

Shreed sighed. "So— The guy's name was Chen. Bao Chen—Zhen, we'd say now. I was going to recruit Chen, and he recruited me. Not the way you think, though. He made me a deal. We'd trade. I'd give him stuff, he'd give me stuff. We were on the same level in our agencies; we'd help each other up the ladder. We'd both know the stuff wasn't first-class, not the stuff that would really hurt, so we wouldn't be traitors. More like scratching each other's back."

Shreed made a face—mouth opened in a snarl, tongue pressed first against the inside of an upper molar, then against the teeth in front, like a chimpanzee. His head went back and he breathed in and out. "I knew when he made the offer that it was really why I'd busted him—so he'd recruit me. You see, I didn't care about going up the ladder that much. What I cared about was becoming a Chinese agent! Because I knew that the Chinese were my real enemies—the fucking Soviets were on the ropes, I knew it even back then—and I knew that if they made me an agent and trusted me, I could fuck them good!" He closed his eyes, then popped them open. "It disgusted me then. It disgusts me now. *But I had to do it. Do you see? Do you see, Janey?*"

RAIN WAS FALLING on the streets outside the hospice. The night was warm; few people were out, yet one man had walked by the building three times. He had a dog with him, perhaps the reason for his walking, but the dog, a long-haired mutt, was miserable and was being dragged on its leash now. Still, the man walked.

He was Ray Suter, George Shreed's assistant. He was not there out of concern for his boss or his boss's wife. He was there to listen to the monologue being radioed to him from a microphone hidden in Jane Shreed's room. What he was hearing so excited him that he had forgotten the dog, and, hands plunged deep in raincoat pockets, he was striding along with the leash looped over a wrist and the dog trying to keep up on its short legs. The dog had given up sniffing bushes and posts and was simply trying to survive.

Suter was stunned by what he heard. All he had wanted was "something on his boss"—the words he had used in getting somebody to plant the bug. What he had expected was something ordinary perhaps sordid but not monumental—a confession to his dying wife of a woman on the side, or maybe office gossip, inner resentments of people above him, or ways he had screwed other people in the Agency. Something you could turn to good account when you wanted more power for yourself, more money, a leg up.

And now this. Suter was in a kind of shock—oblivious to the dog, the rain. *The man was talking about treason.*

From time to time, Suter pressed his right ear. He had a hearing-aid-sized speaker there; the sound varied as he walked by the building and was sometimes so faint he lost it. At last, when there was no sound at all, he hurried away to the next street, where a closed van with a neighborhood parking permit stood among the bumper-to-bumper cars.

"I've lost him!" he snapped to the man who huddled in the back. A rich odor of pizza, doughnuts, coffee, and flatulence filled the van.

"It comes and goes." The man was sitting in the dark with a cassette recorder and a couple of serious-looking electronic boxes. Suter could hardly see him in there, and he wanted to see him right then because he was thinking, *He's heard everything I've heard.* The full impact of that made it hard for him to speak, and he had to draw a deep breath to say, "He just fades away sometimes."

"What'd I just say?"

"Goddamit, this is important! Shreed's spilling his guts! Move the van closer."

"No way. I tole you, there's no place over there the cops won't notice me. Here, I'm golden."

"I want you to move the van." He didn't really care about the van; what he cared about was that suddenly he feared and therefore hated this man, this on-the-cheap private detective.

"You want me to get the goods on your boss. Well, that's what I'm doing. Djou feed that dog?"

Suter glanced at the cassette recorder. He had wanted a tape so that if there was something good, he could lay it on Shreed's desk if he had to, even play it for him. Now, the tape was like a bomb. "You're making only the one tape, right?"

"I promised my neighbor I'd feed the dog at eight. Gimme the can-opener."

"I said, you're making only one tape! *Right?*"

"What'd I just say? I promised to feed the fucking dog, now gimme the can-opener. It's right under your ass."

Suter had left the driver's-side door open, and the dog was sitting on the pavement in the rain. When it heard the can-opener start to operate on the can, it wagged its tail and then vaulted into the back seat, using Suter as a platform. He took a swipe at it with a hand and disentangled his wrist from the leash.

"Keep the fucking dog! Nobody's out there, anyway. We never should have brought it."

"So whose idea was it? 'Get me a dog for cover,' you said. Looka her eat! She's fucking starved."

"Tony, I don't want a word of this getting out of that mouth of yours. You understand me?"

"What'd I tell you when we joined up? 'I hear, I don't listen. Absolute confidentiality is my stock in trade.' Looka that doggie eat."

Suter looked into the darkness at the sound of the dog's slurping. "If any of this gets out, you're dead." The word boomed in Suter's mind like a low-pitched bell: dead, dead, dead—

"What'd I just say?" In the dark, the other man patted the dog. "What'd you do, try to drown her? She's fucking soaked. My fucking neighbor'll have a cow, I bring her back like this. You're a cruel guy, you know that, Suter?"

Suter lit a cigarette, inhaled, sighed. "Yeah, I know that. Make sure you know it too."

The car was silent. The smell of wet dog and cigarette smoke joined the other smells. After several minutes, Tony said, "Your boss's talking again."

"Christ!" Suter was out in the rain within seconds, pushing at his right ear and splashing away through the puddles. The bell kept tolling: dead, dead, dead—

Trieste.

"As soon as he drew a gun, I tackled the man in front of me and brought him down. Then I began to fire at the ones shooting into the front of the café. They returned fire and killed the man I had tackled."

"You had a gun, Commander?" The Italian cop smelled strongly of cologne and leaned forward across the desk every time he spoke. Alan couldn't decide whether it was a very polite interrogation or a very thorough witness examination.

"No, *signore,* I did not have a gun. I took it from the man who was standing in front of me."

"You are a commando? A specialist?"

Alan was now going over this ground for the third time. "I took him by surprise."

"You overpowered one terrorist, took his gun, and shot a second."

"Yes."

The cop watched Alan with a kindly look of disbelief. Another investigator entered the room, a razor-thin man in a very nice suit.

"Why were you there at all, Commander?"

"I wanted a cup of coffee." The name, Bonner, and all its implications hung before him. He wasn't ready to give them the woman yet. "*Signorini,* may I remind you that I'm an officer in the US Navy and that under international agreements I have the right to representation by my service and to have them informed? Am I a suspect in this?" He wanted to say as well that his foot hurt like hell, but he didn't think they'd be sympathetic.

"It would be easier for all of us if you would simply aid our investigation, Commander. Are you uncomfortable?"

"I have a detachment to command."

"You shot two men in our city, Commander. That causes us huge concern. You understand that since the recent unfortunate incident with the US plane and the cable car, Italians are very touchy about Americans killing people in Italy."

Alan spread his hands in an engaging, almost Italian way, as if to say, *What can I do?*

"I do understand that, but I also understand that you're keeping me without a charge, and I would like my command to be notified. I have cooperated. And I didn't kill both of them. I shot *one.* The other was shot by his own people. And they weren't Italians, they were Serbs."

"Italy is not at war with the Serbs, Commander." He put an index finger, pointed upward, beside his temple, as if he was signaling an idea. "I wonder if you did not come to Italy to execute these men." He raised his eyebrows: *Good idea?* Getting no response, he looked for the fifth or tenth time at Alan's passport. "You landed in Aviano just seven hours ago."

Alan was unsure whether to react with anger or to continue to respond politely. He'd tried both for two hours, and he didn't seem to be getting anywhere. He started again.

"I tackled the man I had noticed in front of me as soon as he drew a gun. . . ."

Suburban Washington.

Shreed had been to the toilet and had splashed cold water on his face. He hated that face, most of all now—a whipped look, hangdog, drained from the effort of telling her. "Janey." She gave no response. Maybe it was his own forgiveness he wanted, as much as hers. "So, Janey, there was this guy Chen. In Jakarta."

No response.

"Jakarta. So we worked out a comm plan, all that old Cold War junk. Then I came back here for a tour and I got into computers. Bad days here, you remember—the Agency was in the doghouse, everybody pulled in like a flock of turtles. You called me 'Captain COBOL.' Remember?" He smiled, used both hands to pull one leg over the knee of the other.

"In those days, you actually did your own programming. And I was good. Real good. They were making the first stabs at a net; they didn't even call it the Internet then, just 'a net,' and I hacked my way into a big mainframe at Cal Tech and staked out some space for myself in the source code. Once I did that, I knew what was possible, and I waited for the Chinese to get good enough for me to use what I knew. I waited and then piggybacked on a couple of Chinese 'students' who were sending computer stuff back on audiotapes, rode their data, and there I was—I had a way in, into China. The trouble was, computers were too new. So what I was, I was like a mold spore that can exist for twenty years in the desert. I had to wait.

"Chen and I were exchanging stuff the old way, dead-drops and that crap, both moving up. It took ten years—then, finally everybody had a

PC. At last, it was *my* world. So I laid it out for the Ops guys—what we could do to the Chinks with computers, what now we'd call information warfare.

"Would you believe nobody in Ops cared, even then? The fact is they were scared shitless—a lot of fake Brit preppies who would do anything to protect the heritage of God and capitalism, and so let's send in some poor lower-class, preferably foreign asset to do our dying for us, but please, no high technology! HUMINT forever!" He wiped his hand over his bristly hair. "Stupid shitheads," he muttered. After a minute or two, he got up and dragged himself to the window. It was raining hard, and there was only a single figure out there, somebody walking slowly in the downpour. There was something terrible about the loneliness of that figure, he thought. He shook himself as if it had been he standing in the rain.

"So I'm a traitor for a purpose, Janey," he said. There, he'd said it— *traitor.* "I'm a traitor with a cause." He continued to stare into the rain. The walking figure was gone.

"I'd have given them what I had, if they'd listened. I'd have risked even prison, if they'd listened. But they made me go it alone. They *made* me be a traitor."

He looked to her for affirmation then, but she was still.

"So I went it alone. I programmed a poison pill, a worm, to fetch something from Chinese military intel. A kind of virus, but one like— what the hell is it? shingles? the one that sits in your spine for twenty years and then pops out—one that would sit tight until I told it to act. Then every time the Chinks upgraded, they took me with the upgrade. I'd go in and tinker a little, snoop around, see how much better they were getting at firewalls and passwords and encryption, and it got to the point where I knew I was going to have to do something or they'd either catch me or they'd wall me out.

"And then Chen lowered the boom on me. Nineteen ninety-four. Turned out I'd been suckered. Now he was going to get serious, and if I didn't play along, he'd turn me in to the Agency." Shreed sighed, made a sound that was something like a laugh—short, barking gags of sound. "I thought I was playing him and he'd been playing me. We'd been doing a circle jerk for twenty years, and it was all a fake to land me. Now, the Chinks wanted good stuff—hard stuff.

"They had a Web site that flacked pornography. That was the comm link; we encrypted data and reduced it to one pixel and buried it in the middle of a porn image. That was what I was doing that night you caught me. I was sending them the data on a classified project called Peacemaker, and when you came in, I got rattled and I sent the last batch in clear. You scared me, baby. I felt like a kid caught jacking off." Shreed massaged the bridge of his nose, sighed again. "Not your fault. Mine. But—" He gave the laughing sound again.

"Chen's really been bleeding me. Chen's an insatiable prick: I'm going to have to—I've got to end it. I've got to wind up my Chinese connection. You see? Janey?"

He put his hand on hers again, felt the skin cooler but not cold.

"Oh, baby, the things I've had to do! And the things I have to do yet!"

He got up, grabbed his canes, swung himself around the room; the movements were restless, angry, the prowlings of something in a cage. Still, his voice was tender when he said, "Maybe it's better you won't be here."

He pulled himself to the window again, then away to her side, across to a corner, back.

"This is how it goes. The Chinks' military intel is the banker for the Party and for the bigwigs who are skimming the cream and sending the money offshore for themselves. Intel also has most of its own secret money offshore; it's what they use all over the world for spying, subversion—you know. It's a lot of money. A lot of money. So what I'm going to do is, on a given day, and it has to be soon, I'm going to activate my virus, and it's going to send little gobblers—like Pac-Mans—and they're going to gobble up all the offshore accounts and all the data about the accounts, every scrap, and put it somewhere else. And the Chinks won't know where. And there they'll be, sitting with their thumb up their ass, with no money for ops, and no Party money, and no money for the bigwigs who will want to know how and why, and who will be trying to take revenge on anybody who stands in the way of their cash, and it's going to be a bloodbath!"

He grinned. "For about twelve hours, and that's all I need. Because the Chinks are going to be between a rock and a hard place during those twelve hours, and they won't know whether to shit or go blind. India is going to be hollering at them from one side, and we're going to be hollering from another, and Pakistan is going to be begging them to send help, and they won't be able to do a thing! They'll be paralyzed.

"And then they'll try to recover the only way they know, which is by strutting around the world, pretending to be a superpower instead of the world's shoemaker. And they'll push some military provocation to make somebody else—India, let's say—back down, *and it'll all be bullshit*! Because China *is* a paper tiger—a hundred goddam nukes, and so far not a missile that they could lob a wad of toilet paper three thousand miles with! An army of goddam peasants, and technology they've had to steal! You know who says the Chinese are a superpower? The same assholes who said that Russia was a superpower!

"Well, I'm going to show what they really are. Their money is going to go down a rathole, and they're going to panic, and then they're going to the brink—and they're going to find that they're eyeball-to-eyeball with us, and they're going to back down, *because they don't have the muscle*!

"So—I had a reason, do you see, Janey? I always had a reason. You're the moralist in the family; you're the one who used to argue the difference between ends and means, so you judge what I've done. Judge me. And then forgive me."

He came to rest at the foot of the bed, his posture appealing to her, begging her. And for a moment, he thought what he saw in return was an illusion—a living woman, eyes open, the faintest of smiles—and then he knew it was not. It was quite real, even to the smears of pale color on her cheeks.

"Janey—!"

She might have said something; her lips parted. But it was her eyes that spoke, sliding aside to look at the CD player. Then back at him. The eyes of a girl, hip and wise.

He got it. *Der Rosenkavalier*. He pushed the Repeat button. A few notes, and Schwarzkopf's voice climbed out of the box and filled the room. It was loud, too loud for him to talk. Seeing her eyes, he couldn't turn the volume down. He could only sit with her, listening.

He sat beside her, and her eyes closed. The music, lush as cream, swirled.

He touched her hand. It was wax. The music spiraled up, the duet, the two sopranos, glory. Then silence.

"Janey?" Now he felt his own desire again, his own urgency. "*Forgive me!*"

But the bird had flown.

OUTSIDE THE HOSPICE, Suter leaned his back against a tree. Music he didn't know played its tinny noise in his earphone, but he was oblivious to it. *A lot of money.* Suter tried to light a cigarette, but his hands were trembling and he had to give it up.

A lot of money. What was a lot of money? A billion? Even two billion?

A lot of money, and Tony knows about it. What would he do with Tony? The man could say that discretion was his stock in trade, but Suter knew that discretion, integrity, all that was bullshit when big money came around.

It frightened him and at the same time dazzled him. What could he do with a billion dollars? What could he *not* do?

He had come out here to get something on his boss. To get a little leverage. Now, Shreed hardly mattered. Now there was *money*. He tried again with the lighter, and it gave a flame and he was able to hold the cigarette in it just long enough to get it alight. He drew in a gulp of smoke, coughed, and, bent over, began to hyperventilate.

He knew that the only way he could deal with Tony was if Tony was dead.

3

Trieste.

BY THE TIME THAT THE JAG OFFICER FROM THE BOAT
appeared, it was close to three in the morning and he had been moved
from the cell where he had been questioned to a comfortable office belonging to one of the detectives, and he was being given strong coffee
and biscotti. One of the cops even made small talk.

The JAG was a lieutenant-commander, middle-aged and short, and
he weighed as much as he was allowed, but he was professional.

"Commander? You all right? I'm John Maggiulli."

"Al Craik."

"You okay? They don't have you as a suspect anymore. Wish I could
say that was my doing, but it was over before I walked in." He lowered
his voice. "Admiral Kessler is kind of freaked. Word we had was that
there had been a terrorist attack. Why didn't you tell them to call the
boat, mister?"

"I did."

"Not their story. They say that you wanted the boat kept out of it and
cooperated willingly in their investigation. What were you doing there,
anyway? Was it terrorists?"

Alan looked outside the office and saw the razor-thin man in the
good suit watching him.

"Not here, John."

"Al, I'd like an answer. This is serious."

"I know it's fucking serious, John! I just shot a guy, excuse me, it's kind of wrecked my day! The Italians thought I might have been sent here to whack the terrorists, or some such crap. I started requesting legal counsel from the boat four hours ago, as soon as I discovered that we were moving beyond routine."

John Maggiulli looked at him. Glared, in fact.

"Shore Patrol says you got a message from your wife. You withholding this message purporting to be from your wife from the Italian police?"

"Roger that. John, I'll make it clear when I'm not sitting in a foreign police station, okay?"

Shaking his head, Maggiulli took his arm; there was a suggestion of taking him into custody. "I got a car, and we're ducking reporters." Alan limped beside him.

The thin man watched them leave.

ADMIRAL KESSLER was in pajamas and a flannel robe, a rather small man who was not at his best at four-thirty A.M. He sat a little slumped, one hand shielding his eyes as if the glare from Alan's story was too much for him. Still, he let him tell the whole thing, leaving out only the woman's saying "Bonner" and the fact that she had asked to meet him in Naples.

"I don't like my officers getting into trouble, Mister Craik. Especially big trouble." He looked at Maggiulli, whom he had commanded to stay. "What I really want to know is why you lied to the Italian cops. Well?"

"Sir, it's, um, a matter of national security that touches on an existing counterintelligence investigation. I'm not in a position to say more until I can talk to NCIS."

Kessler lowered his hand and turned a pair of very bright, very hard eyes on Alan. "Admirals don't like to be kept in the dark by subordinates—you follow me?"

Alan, standing stiffly, bit back the angry sense of unfairness that came up like bile. "I'm eager to tell you, sir, as soon as I've cleared the matter with NCIS."

Maggiulli cleared his throat and said, in the tone of a man trying to coax a bull into a chute, "Uh, Craik has a point, sir—if this is really a sensitive matter—"

"I know the goddam code, John!" He leaned still farther back. "What the hell do you have to do with 'an existing CI investigation'? Your dad died years ago."

Alan winced. Everybody in the Navy knew about his father's death; many people held it against him, credited his promotions to it—son of a hero, the man who had caught his father's killer. He would rather not have raised the subject at all. "It was that case, anyway."

Kessler was unsympathetic. "All right. You get to NCIS pronto, and I want to talk to your contact when you're done. Get it to me by 0800."

"Aye, aye, sir."

Alan headed straight down to CVIC and tried to call Mike Dukas, an NCIS special agent who was still in charge of the old case and who was a close friend, at his office in Bosnia, dialing the eighteen digits with great care. First, the line was busy; then he got a native German speaker who had difficulty understanding him. Could he call back after eight? Alan slammed the telephone down, thinking that eight A.M. in Sarajevo was the time he was supposed to report on his progress to the admiral.

Balked of contact with Dukas, Alan filled out a foreign-national contact report with the NCIS officer on the boat and put himself in his rack, where he fumed and stewed and waited for the dawn.

Utica.

Rose had sat up with her father, drinking too much wine and letting him try to soothe her. Then she lay awake for an hour, then another hour, hearing dogs, the bells of clocks, the freights rolling along the old New York Central tracks. A car went by, its boom box thumping hip-hop bass. Somebody laughed and shouted. Her talk with the detailer went around and around in her head, and she tracked it, around and around, looking for the explanation, the solution, a rat running around and around, looking for a way out—

Rose woke to see by the pale orange digitals of the bedside clock that it was a little after two. Her head really ached now, and the wine rose as a sour nausea in her throat. She would feel really lousy tomorrow. Today.

She went to the old bathroom along the hall, the only one in the house, drank two glasses of water, looked at her bloated face in the mirrored door of the medicine chest. *Some looker you are!* she thought. Well, her face matched her thoughts, anyway. She drank another glass of water and knew she had to do something, anything—go for a walk, go for a drive. Scream. Instead, she went and checked her children and then went downstairs, the dog padding beside her, and by the time she reached the bottom tread, she knew what she was going to do.

She was going to scream for help.

She took the dog out into the cool night and again leaning against the rear of her car, got on her cellphone. She called a duty number of a war crimes unit in Sarajevo, where Mike Dukas, who loved her and was her husband's friend and was an NCIS agent on loan to the International War Crimes Tribunal, was officer-in-charge. What she got was a gravel-voiced Frenchman named Pigoreau who wanted to flirt with her and who finally told her that Mike was in a *grande luxe* hotel in Holland, The Hague, "being kicked up the stairs." He gave her a phone number.

His flirtatiousness made her numb. *Some other time*— She punched the numbers into the phone and pulled her robe tighter around her. The cool air felt good on the hangover, but parts of her were a little too cool.

Pigoreau had been right. The hotel was very *grande luxe.* It was so grand she thought she was never going to get past reception, but finally a somewhat too elegant female put her through, and she heard one ring and then Mike Dukas's growl, and, before she could think, she cried, "Oh, Mike, thank God!"

"Hey! Rose? Rose?"

"Oh, Mike, goddamit, I'm so happy to talk to you! Mike—I need help."

"What the hell. Help?"

So she told him. Two sentences, bam, bam.

"What, you got bounced from the program and sent to some nowheresville, and the orders came out of CNO?"

"You got it."

"Where's Al?"

"Somewhere between Aviano and the boat." She told him about the change to Alan's orders. "First him, now me."

"Which I don't think is a funny coincidence, babe. You with me? You know the Navy—they get on one of you, you both go down. You need somebody to find out what the hell's going on. I don't think it's us—NCIS, I mean. Could be Navy intel, but they don't work like that; they'd come to you and do stuff—investigation, interviews, maybe polygraph."

"But why?"

"Because either you or Al is a security problem, is why. That's all it can be."

"My dad thinks I have an enemy."

"Your dad may not be so far wrong. But maybe Al has an enemy and you're getting the backlash. But this has a kind of stink. Like, it sounds very quick and very from the top down, not by the book. And not the Nav, you know? But I'll check. Listen, give me an hour or two, shit, what time is it there—? I'll check to see if the Navy's involved, other than issuing the orders. But what you gotta have is information. What you do, call Abe Peretz and tell him to find out what's up."

"It's two A.M."

"What are friends for? He's FBI, he'll have an answer by the time you're eating breakfast. Then call me back and we'll talk about what happens next. Okay?"

"I hate to wake people up."

"Oh, do you? Your life is shit, your career is ruined, and you hate to wake people up. Come on, babe, get with the program. This is war."

"You're the best, Mike."

"No, I'm a mediocre Navy cop, but I'm crazy about you, so you bring out the best in me. Now go call Abe and let me get some breakfast."

"You sound grumpy."

"Wait until you hear Abe."

Abe Peretz was a former naval officer who had joined the FBI. Like Dukas, he was an old friend, a kind of mentor to her husband and a counselor to her. He was only a little pissed at being waked up; once he understood the problem, he gave her some hard advice: come to Washington, where the action is.

Half an hour later, she was on the road.

USS *Thomas Jefferson.*

His first official act on the carrier was supposed to have been a brief to the admiral on the purpose of his detachment. The briefing was out the window, however, because of the Trieste mess, and when he showed up on the flag deck at 0800, he was met, not by Admiral Kessler, but by Maggiulli and the flag captain.

"Have you reached your NCIS guy yet?" Maggiulli said. He looked as wasted by lack of sleep as Alan, but he was certainly more nervous.

"I filed a contact report at the NCIS shack on the boat. I keep missing my guy when I call—I got the runaround in Bosnia, where he's detached to a war crimes unit, and I just found out ten minutes ago that he's in The Hague. I've got a call in to him there." He turned to the flag captain. "Am I briefing on the MARI project this morning, sir?"

"The admiral would prefer that you straighten this other matter out first. Commander, it still appears that you're withholding evidence from the Italian police. You haven't offered us any reasonable explanation. People were *killed*, Commander."

"This is a change from two hours ago."

"It is *not* a change!" Maggiulli looked at the flag captain, thus proving that this was a change.

"John, I will continue to make contact with the special agent in charge of the investigation my first priority. He's at a hotel in The Hague, and I expect to talk to him as soon as I leave this meeting."

"Admiral Kessler wants somebody with some authority at NCIS to explain this matter to him, as you don't seem prepared to do it yourself. It looks like you're jerking us around, Craik."

His anger almost exploded, and his face went white. Clenching his fists, Alan said in a dead, rigidly controlled voice, "It looks like *you're* jerking *me* around, John. Two hours ago, you seemed to accept my explanation and told me to call my guy; now you don't accept my explanation! Listen to me—and you, too, sir—because I'm in the right on this and I know the code, too! I am doing my goddam level best to satisfy you and the Italian police *and* my responsibility to a classified investigation! If you want to take me to the mat on it, you do it! Call me on it!"

With a gesture, the flag captain silenced Maggiulli. To Alan's surprise, he spoke quite gently, as if, all along, he had simply been hearing how it would play. "I'll forget the tone of voice you just used, Mister Craik, but you gotta remember the seriousness of this from our point of view. We got a capital ship here in a foreign port where we're not deeply loved to start with. So you just do nothing but work at getting on the blower to your man and make it right, okay?"

"Sir, I also have a detachment to run, and I haven't even met all my officers yet."

The flag captain nodded. "I think that can wait for twenty-four hours."

The man seemed to be saying that his whole detachment could sit on their thumbs until he got hold of Mike Dukas. And then he got it, through the fog of fatigue and anger: if he *didn't* get Mike Dukas and satisfy the admiral, there wouldn't be any detachment—at least not for him. That's why Maggiulli was the attack dog—to give legal cover if Kessler decided to kick his ass off the *Jefferson.* That really would end his naval career. And Kessler knew that, too.

"Sir, with all respect, I request permission to continue with my detachment while trying to locate Mister Dukas." He rushed on almost boyishly. "There's no point in me sitting on a phone if he's at breakfast and doesn't have a telephone handy."

The flag captain thought about that and actually smiled. He picked up his hat, a signal that the meeting was about over. Again, his voice was almost soft. "I appreciate your position. You please try to appreciate ours." He put his cover on and came close, as if he wanted to shut Maggiulli out. "You better satisfy the admiral today, or you're toast."

FIFTEEN MINUTES LATER, Alan was in his stateroom, looking at the black heel-mark on a bulkhead where he had just thrown a dress shoe. Mike Dukas had *not* been at the hotel in The Hague—he had just checked out.

He had tried Dukas's office in Sarajevo again, and, although he had got an English speaker this time, she hadn't known anything, either.

Mike Dukas was in transit.

Now, shaking with anger, Alan tried to talk himself down. He was about halfway there when a knock sounded on his door and he whirled, ready to explode on anybody suggesting that the admiral wanted him to hurry. Flinging open the door, he saw first the captain's eagles on the collar, only belatedly the face above it.

"Hey, Al!" A big hand descended on his shoulder. "Hey, man, I like for my officers to check in with me when they come aboard, what gives?"

Alan's anger deflated like a leaky balloon. It was "Rafe" Rafehausen, friend from his first squadron, onetime nemesis, now the CAG—commander of the *Jefferson's* air wing.

"You going to ask me in, or do I have to push?"

"Oh, jeez—Rafe, am I glad to see you—Christ, man, I haven't had time to report; see, last night—"

Rafe waved a hand. "I know all about it. *Everybody* knows all about it—James Bond Meets Rambo. You don't do things by halves, do you, Craik?" He pushed a duffel bag off the only chair and threw himself down. "Don't let me interrupt, if you were doing something important. You look like shit, by the way, anybody told you that?"

"I *shot* a guy yesterday. How you think that makes me feel?"

"I don't know how it makes you feel, but it makes you look like shit. Come on, what's up—trouble?"

"Kessler." Alan raced through a summary of his meeting with the admiral and then Maggiulli and the flag captain. To his surprise, Rafe laughed. "Hey, Kessler's got a bug up his ass about good relations with foreigners and the media; you come in and shoot up a liberty port, what d'you think he's going to do, kiss you? So call your friend at NCIS, for Christ's sake!"

"*I can't get hold of him!*" Alan started to rant, and Rafe cut him off.

"Get a grip. First things first—the reason I came here besides wanting to welcome you aboard, was to get you to grab hold of this fucking detachment you're supposed to command. Your detachment sucks—clear?"

"Rafe, I only met the guys two days ago; Jesus Christ, give me a break."

"I can't give you a break. And I wouldn't if I could; I need your aircraft in the air and I need them today. Between you, me, and the shitter, Kosovo's going to go ballistic and holy hell is blowing up in the Indian Ocean, and the CAG doesn't have time for one of his commanders to dance around the telephone. You get with your det, buddy, and you start to kick ass; they're a mess."

"Kessler's captain gave me an ultimatum."

Rafe blew out a breath in exasperation. "I'll handle it. Kessler listens to me; he's not an aviator, so he needs me. I'll tell him you're God's gift to the US Navy; I trust you like a brother; if you say it's national security, it's national security. Give me the name of the guy you're trying to reach on the fucking phone and I'll have him found by the time you've done an honest day's work with the det. Deal?"

"The flag captain's word was 'toast.' "

"Yeah, yeah, his bark is worse than his bite. Friel's a pussycat. Come on, gimme the data and get your ass out of here and go to work. That's an order, Craik!"

Alan stared at him and then began to laugh. He reached for his flight suit.

Rafe put a hand again on Alan's shoulder.

"One more thing. There's talk, so watch your step."

"Talk? What—last night—?"

"That, and—you know the boat, everybody cooped up. There's just talk about you taking over the det on such short notice. They say you got bounced from another assignment."

Alan's face went rigid. "I did. And no reason given."

Rafe patted his shoulder. "Guys talk. Just let 'em."

Langley, Virginia.

George Shreed was leaning on his metal canes by his office window, watching a hot wind blow fast-food wrappers through the CIA parking lot. He wasn't seeing them; he was only turning his eyes on them, occupying his vision, while his mind, numb, could not shift his focus from his wife's death. He thought of himself as a hard-ass, but he wasn't hard all the way through; somewhere in there, he bled. He had prepared for the death, had used the word, had said it would happen, must happen, was unavoidable—and now he was as devastated as if it had come as a surprise.

His door thumped under somebody's knuckles.

"Yes."

Ray Suter came in, first his head, then a shoulder, then half his body. "You want to be by yourself?"

"Come in, come in."

"I wanted to say how bad I feel. All of us feel."

"Thank you."

Shreed hadn't turned around. He could see Suter's reflection in the window, beyond it, the trees bowing in the hot wind of a June day. Tonight there would be thunderstorms, a cold front, a change. Even in his grief, he found himself thinking that Suter looked different today.

"Can we *do* anything?"

It was the kind of question that Shreed usually pounced on: *What did you have in mind, resurrection? Did you want to hold a seance in the canteen?* But the acid had gone out of him for a little while. Instead, Shreed said, "Maybe somebody could plant a tree someplace. No flowers."

"Right, right. I heard that. The Cancer Society, right. There's a collection—the girls are taking it up—"

Shreed's back moved, straightened. Was he going to make some comment about the futility of collections as an answer to death? He exhaled slowly. "Thank them for me."

"Sure. Absolutely. Can I do anything for you? You sleep ng?"

Shreed turned, made his way to his desk and leaned the bright canes against a spot he had used so long that the varnish was worn from the wood. "Pick up the slack on the five-year report, if you will; I've dragged my feet there. Yeah, I'm sleeping okay." He never slept much, anyway. "There's a memorial service Thursday. You might let people know."

"Right. Right, absolutely." Suter stood there, well into the room now but still somehow not of it—keeping himself separate. "I feel so helpless." Yet he didn't look helpless to Shreed: he looked—*gleeful?*

Shreed shot him a look. Suter's eyes looked funny—was he perhaps hungover? They were too bright, too—excited. For an instant, a bizarre thought flashed across Shreed's mind: *He knows.* Then it was gone, the idea that Suter could know about his spying too ridiculous to consider.

"I've got a task for you," he said when he had sat down. "One that won't make you feel helpless. Something you'll enjoy, in fact—screwing an old friend." He grinned. "Alan Craik."

"No friend of mine!" Suter cried.

"Old enemy, then. What's the difference? Craik's wife is under investigation. Security violation on the Peacemaker project."

Suter scowled. He had been on the Peacemaker project, too, and had in fact tried without success to get Rose Siciliano into bed.

"I want you to make sure the word gets out that they're security risks. Both of them—where there's smoke there's fire, that sort of thing. If she's in it, so is he. Get it?"

"This is official?"

Shreed started to answer him with acid, then stopped. Suter usually didn't question his orders.

"She's proven herself an enemy of the Agency," Shreed said. "Is that official enough for you?"

And Suter became Uriah Heep, all but wringing his hands, saying, "Right, right—oh, right—"

And Shreed thought, *Not right,* but then he remembered Janey's death, and Suter became unimportant.

Washington.

"It's you, Rose. Not Al. And it's the CIA, not the Navy."

Abe Peretz looked like a casting director's idea of a Jewish professor, with a balding head, unfashionable glasses, and eyes that were mostly dreamy but now and then as hard as diamonds. He was deaf in one ear, the result of a mugging two years before, and so he normally talked now with his head slightly turned so that his good right ear was toward other people.

"What the hell's the CIA got to do with me?"

"And not just the Agency—the Agency's *Internal Investigations Directorate.*" The innocent eyes became hard. "They're hard-nosed and they're ugly—leftovers from Angleton and Kill-a-Commie-for-Christ—and they'd send their own mothers up if she was dicking the Agency. So how come they're on your case? There can be only one reason—you've spun off from an internal investigation."

"I'm not even in their chain of command!"

"Think of it as walking by when somebody pissed out the window. There's a rumor floating around they've got another mole. You don't understand the relief they'd feel if they got a positive on somebody who *isn't* Agency. It means they can say to each other, 'We dodged the bullet.' And it means that they can go public, at least within the intelligence community, and say, 'See, it isn't us—it's the Navy.' And so they went back-channel, probably through the NSC, and sandbagged you."

"Abe, what the hell do I do?"

"You fight." He pushed a piece of paper across his desk. "You've got an appointment at three at Barnard, Kootz, Bingham." She looked her question with a frown, and he said, "Law firm. Heavy hitters—sixty partners, big-bucks political donors to both parties, lots of media savvy. The woman I'm sending you to is the best they got." He grinned. "She just beat us in court. That's how I know how good she is. Unhh—this ain't pro bono work they do over there, Rose. Justice is blind, but she ain't cheap. Bea and I'll help if we can."

She had a quick temper, at best; now it gushed out, pushed by the fatigue and a hangover and the hurt, and she cursed; she said they could shove it; she said she didn't want to be part of a Navy that could treat her like this. And she cursed some more.

He grinned again. "Stay mad. You're going to need it."

4

USS *Thomas Jefferson.*

USS *THOMAS JEFFERSON* WAS AN OLD FRIEND, AND ALAN
walked through the passageways with the familiarity of a man visiting a
childhood home. The ship was preparing to get under way, and the noise
was oddly calming to his own tension. Maybe, as Rafe seemed to believe,
it really would all work out once they were at sea.

His detachment had its own ready room, the lack of an A-6 squadron
in the air wing having left one vacant. Ready Room Nine, all the way aft
and almost under the stern, was the noisiest one; landing aircraft hit the
deck just a few feet overhead, and, during flight operations, conversation
was all but impossible. Heavy iron cruise boxes filled the front of the
room below the chalk board, but at least, he thought, it was *theirs*.

He wanted to speak to his division chiefs and the officers acting as department heads, but the ready room was nearly empty. He also wanted
to find Stevens, the former acting det commander, who probably believed he should have been given the command, even though it was so
screwed up that the CAG had made a special point of it. Getting Stevens
on his side was an important priority, if it could be done.

The det also had a long list of maintenance problems that Alan
thought had been gun-decked too long, but, stepping in late and starting
behind, he had to trust the chiefs to get the planes in the air until he

could find what was really wrong and fix it. As it was, his unit had one aircraft scheduled to launch in four hours, and he wanted to prove himself to Rafe by making sure it was airborne on time.

Alan put his own name on the flight sked for that first event, scratching a jg named Soleck, whom he hadn't even met.

"Where's Mister Soleck?" he said to a chief who was overseeing the unpacking of the maintenance gear.

"Who's that, sir? He our missing officer?"

"*Missing?*"

"Last I heard, there was one hadn't reported aboard, sir.' The chief was very businesslike; if he had heard the talk that Rafe had referred to, or if he had ideas about the new CO who had got involved in a shooting onshore, he said nothing.

But an officer who hadn't reported aboard? And where the hell was he? Alan reached for the only solid ground he could in the uncertainty of the det: a senior chief he knew and trusted. "Where's Senior Chief Craw?"

"Senior's gone down to VS-53 admin, sir."

Alan ducked out of the ready room and swung down the steel ladder to the S-3 squadron's admin section, his bad foot giving him a hippity-hop rhythm. Craw was sitting at a computer terminal with another officer hovering by him, but Alan pushed past.

"Senior Chief?"

"Commander! I thought I'd wait till we had some privacy, but, damn! it's good to see you, Mister Craik."

Alan tried to smile. "It's great to see you, Martin." The use of the senior chief's first name caused them both to look at the other officer, by some ingrained reflex of training and custom that said that officers should not call enlisted, however senior and however close, by their first names. "Lieutenant-Commander Craik, this is LTjg Campbell. His part of the translant ran like a top."

Campbell stammered a greeting and looked embarrassed. They shook hands; Alan had missed meeting him at Pax River. He turned back to Craw. "How bad was the move?"

"Nothing we couldn't handle. The planes were flying off empty and we were leaving half of our spare parts on the beach, but I sort of fixed that first." Martin Craw's sentences implied volumes. *Sort of fixed that first* suggested an argument won.

"What else?" Alan and Craw exchanged a look that meant *Tell it like it is.*

"The inventory was crap and the acting CO released the fly-off officers at 1500. Plus a new guy from flight school wasn't informed that we had an immediate movement and went on leave straight from Pensacola."

"Is that LTjg Soleck, by any chance, who's on the flight schedule in four hours?"

Craw sighed. "Roger that, skipper. I'm trying to reach him. See, nobody ever sent him an info packet or a schedule or anything, so he has no idea we're looking for him, either."

"Do we still have land lines tied in?"

Craw glanced at his watch. "About ten minutes longer."

"Give me a phone. Then I've got to start meeting people."

He called the listed number in Pennsylvania twice. It rang through, but no one answered and there was no machine. Then he called the duty desk at NAS Pensacola and asked for a contact number for LTjg Evan Soleck. The petty officer at the other end shuffled papers for a few minutes and asked to call back. Alan hung up, feeling defeated by telephones in his every attempt, and started helping check the maintenance inventory with Craw and Campbell.

"Why isn't somebody from maintenance doing this?" Alan was looking at lists of parts and numbers that meant nothing to him.

"Not my place to say, sir."

"Fuck that."

"The acting maintenance officer is in his rack getting his crew rest." Alan winced. Rafe had been right: this detachment was a mess.

The phone rang. The petty officer in Pensacola said that he had Soleck's leave papers in his hand and read off the Buffalo phone number listed for contact. Alan thanked him to a degree that clearly surprised him and called the new number, looking at his battered Casio. Past four A.M. in New York.

"Hello?" The voice was thick with sleep.

"May I speak to LTjg Evan Soleck?"

"Yeah?"

"Mister Soleck, this is Lieutenant-Commander Alan Craik, your detachment officer-in-charge. I need you to report for duty immediately."

"Hey, Corky, fuck off, okay? You might have woken my parents."

"Mister Soleck, I'm Alan Craik and this is not a prank."

Long pause.

"Uh, sir? Is this for real?"

"Welcome aboard, Mister Soleck. We flew off from Norfolk thirty-six hours ago and right now we're about to weigh anchor from port Trieste. Do you know how to get travel orders?"

"Uhh—"

"Get your ass down to Pax River today and tell the travel section to get you here ASAP."

"Uh, sir? I have these tickets for a concert in Buffalo? And a date?"

Despite himself, Alan smiled. "Tell her to wait, Mister Soleck. You'll be at sea."

Then he walked down to the hangar deck, getting the feel for his men. No women in the det. Old habit made him start to think, *Just as well,* and then he remembered what Rose would have said. And that made him think of her, and he felt a pang of absence. All this telephoning and he hadn't even tried to reach her, but that had been their arrangement: she would be on the road to Houston, and they would talk when he got to Naples. He glanced at his watch again. Past four in Utica, too, where in another hour she would be waking, saying goodbye, getting the car and heading west. Without a care in the world.

Down on the hangar deck, he was surprised to find aircraft number 902, due to fly in the first event, with her port engine dismounted and a swarm of maintenance personnel covering her. Several men looked his way; they looked at each other, and then they got very busy. Alan smiled at one he knew.

"Hey, Mendez! What're you doing, still in the Nav?"

Mendez, Gloucester-born, Portuguese sailors in his genes, smiled a little reservedly and climbed down from the wing. He wiped his hand several times on his coveralls before presenting it to be shaken. Alan had served with Mendez during the Gulf War; Mendez had introduced him to the methods of loading the chaff and flare cartridges in the S-3's underbelly. Looking at Mendez, Alan felt younger. "You made first class," he said.

"Up for chief this year, sir." Alan nodded and pumped his hand. "Still married?"

"Yessir, with two kids."

"Introduce me, will you?" Alan walked around the plane, and Mendez, always a popular sailor, introduced him to the men working there. Now they weren't a swarm; now they looked at him with interest rather than—what had it been? Suspicion? Alan could feel their questions, the ones Rafe had warned him about—*Why had he lost a posting and got this? What was this guy doing here?* Even Mendez seemed wary, but Alan pressed on. "Remind me when your chief's board is coming up, will you, Mendez?" He looked around. "Okay, help me out, guys—what's the story here?"

In spurts, from various men, he was made to understand that 902 had a bad engine, that "everybody" knew that a new engine had been ordered so that this one could be sent in for rehab. Mendez dug out the sheets and showed him that this engine was two hundred hours overdue for rehab. Alan started to ask why and realized that he could only put Mendez on the spot with such a question, even if he knew the answer. Then he saw Stevens, a short, thick officer in a flight suit, come in with a chief, and he thanked Mendez and the others and moved toward the new pair.

Stevens turned his head, saw Alan, and went right back to his conversation. Alan smiled, an angry tic that never moved his lower lip. They had met for two minutes at Pax River; now, Stevens chose to be a horse's ass.

"Lieutenant-Commander Stevens?"

"Hey, Craik."

Alan excused himself to the chief, who moved a few feet off. "You in charge of this?" he said to Stevens. Alan raised one hand. He did not say "this mess," but the motion accused.

"If you're the new boss man, I guess *you're* in charge."

"Well, the new boss man would like to see the launch plan. And a flight sked that doesn't include officers who haven't reported aboard yet."

"I didn't write either one of them." Stevens hitched at an imaginary belt, as if he was pulling up his guns.

Alan sighed. "Mister Stevens, why don't you call me 'Alan'? Or you can call me 'sir.' " He looked around. "Who's running maintenance?"

Stevens jerked his head at the chief he had come in with, a short, intense man in khakis.

"Senior Chief Frazer runs maintenance, with Mister Cohen as department head," the chief said. "He's up topside. I'm Navarro, sir. Intel chief."

"Linguist?" Alan looked for a handle to remember the man.

"Farsi and Hindi." Alan let part of his mind chew over the implications of those two languages.

"You following the traffic on India and Pakistan?"

"Yes, sir."

"Is this the same crap they do every time?"

"Sir, this is from the hip, but I'd say it looks fucking serious."

"More serious than Kosovo?"

Stevens cut in.

"You done with me? I'm on the flight sked later today."

"So am I." Alan looked him in the eye, enjoying Stevens's surprise. "Just walk with me a minute." He shook hands with Navarro and said he'd see him later, then walked Stevens a dozen paces away and turned on him. "You're the senior pilot in this outfit, right?"

"Yep."

"Got a problem?"

Stevens hitched up the imaginary belt again. He talked to the air just off Alan's right shoulder. "This divided command shit. You don't like my ops plan? Tough. It shouldn't be two guys, one in the air, one on the ground. I'm just being straight with you."

"There won't be any divided command. I'm in charge. I expect the cooperation of my officers. I'm just being straight with *you.*"

Stevens kept his voice low, but the tone was bitter. "*Your* officers! Some of us have been working on this project for a year. You walk in like we're all dicked up and you're gonna save us. Or is it that maybe you didn't want this job in the first place? Maybe you were going someplace better?"

Alan set his jaw, controlled his hands, his temper. Rafe had been right—there certainly had been talk. "Mister Stevens, I'm your commanding officer—"

"Craik, everybody's heard of your father. He was a pilot. He might have belonged here. You don't!"

Alan didn't blink, and his eyes didn't move. Stevens couldn't hold that look for more than two seconds. Alan became very cold and very formal. "Mister Stevens, I don't have time right now for you to have a tantrum. It looks to me as if we're way behind and we have to get a plane off the deck in less than four hours. That's my priority. I haven't got time to dick around with you." He leaned a fraction of an inch closer, his eyes still fixed. "If you can't serve under me, get out. Stay or go, I don't care; just say which!"

"You know they'll cream me if I go!"

"You have three minutes to decide whether you're my senior pilot or a man looking for a new job. If you want to leave, you leave today. I'll square it with the detailer."

Stevens, red-faced, tried again to stare him down and lost. "I'll stay, goddamit—I've always wanted to work for a fucking ground-pounding spy!"

Heads turned throughout the hangar bay. *Spy* came out loaded with connotation, and Alan was briefly back in his first days at the squadron, dealing with the aviators as an outsider, an enemy, where intel guys, "spies," were second-class citizens. He hadn't been there in years.

Stevens started to move away under the wing of 902. He followed and grabbed Stevens's arm.

"Start getting this unfucked. You and I are flying together in four hours."

It all certainly took his mind off Mike Dukas and the admiral.

Washington.

The lawyer's name was Emma Pasternak, and she looked like an underdeveloped photograph of herself. The dress-for-success clothes did nothing to hide her essential anonymity; she wore no makeup, no jewelry, and her hair was cut so short and so awkwardly that Rose suspected the woman cut it herself.

"We're expensive," she said. "We're worth it—but can you pay?"

Rose hesitated. "How much?"

"A lot."

"We're naval officers, for Christ's sake!"

"So mortgage the house."

"It is mortgaged! And I've never lived in it; it's in goddam Houston, and I've got to find a place in fucking West Virginia; my kids are with my parents; my husband's at sea—!"

A long stare. Then: "Can you pay for it? Five years' worth of legal bills?"

"If it's even a year, my career is finished."

"That's what compensatory damages are for." Her hand went to the telephone. "Can you pay?"

Rose thought of her salary, Alan's; of the empty house in Houston; of the house Alan had inherited from his father in Jacksonville, a little dump, but in a good market. They had some savings, a few thousand they'd put into tech stocks for the thrill of it— And two kids, and her with no career if it failed. And some friends.

"Yes."

Emma Pasternak straightened and put the phone to her ear. "Let's kick ass," she said. She started to punch in a number.

"What are you going to do?"

"Scare the shit out of the CIA." She inhaled and drew herself up even straighter. Rose still had the feeling that the woman was an imposter, perhaps a daughter sitting in her mother's chair for the day. She was simply too improbably wispy—until she opened her mouth.

"Let me speak to Carl Menzes, please—Internal Investigations." Pause. Rather icily: "This is Emma Pasternak at Barnard, Kootz, Bingham." She wrote something on a notepad. *Billing me for the call,* Rose thought. *Jesus, I'll be timing everything that happens to me now.*

Suddenly, she heard Emma's voice in a new key, fingernails on a blackboard. "What meeting is he in, may I ask?" Pause "If you don't know, how do you know he's in a meeting?" Pause. "Is he in the building?" Pause. "Well, when you see him, you tell him that I am about to sue the Central Intelligence Agency and him personally in civil court for damages compensatory and punitive, and I think it only fair to chat with him before I file. Have you got that? Oh, and tell him that we met at the Liu trial, will you do that? Oh, *thank* you.' She covered the phone and said to Rose, "The Liu trial, I was on the defense team, we reamed the

Agency's ass." She held up a finger, and her thin lips gave what might, on a nicer face, have been a sort of smile. She nodded at Rose, indicated another telephone, which Rose picked up to hear a male voice saying, "—remember the Liu trial, but not very pleasantly. What can I do for you?" It was a pretty nice voice, she thought—a lot nicer than Emma Pasternak's.

"Did you get my message?"

"Yeah, and I don't believe you're going to sue me, okay? Now, what's this about?"

"This is about a Lieutenant-Commander Rose Siciliano, whom your office has railroaded, unjustly and illegally, and about whom you're withholding information."

"Is that the party on the other phone?"

"What other phone?"

"For Christ's sake, cut the games."

Emma got a little paler. She leaned forward, seeming to talk to a shelf of books on the opposite wall. "No, you cut the games. We're not having it, okay? Get real."

"Or what?"

"Or I go public, right now. I can have a column on the op-ed page of the *Post*, Wednesday's edition, with a pickup in the *Wall Street Journal*. Okay? I can write the head for you, quote, 'CIA Badgers Woman Officer in New Agency Scandal Colon Where the Power Is.' Paragraph. 'Going beyond its mandate and its congressionally authorized powers, the Central Intelligence Agency has destroyed the career of a woman officer with quote the finest record in and out of combat in the US military unquote. Reliable sources within the intelligence community say that the Agency's Internal Investigations Directorate can have got this fine officer transferred out of the prestigious astronaut program and into a dead-end, career-finishing job in Dog's Ass, West Virginia, only by working the levers of the National Security Council.' Paragraph. 'Agency spokespersons could not account for—' "

"Okay, okay, you do a swell improv. You've got nothing."

"Wrong. I've got the balls of two columnists on the op-ed page. How do you want to see yourself—'the last gasp of Cold-War hysteria,' or 'witch-hunter extraordinaire for the New World Order'?"

"I think we ought to meet to discuss this."

"I think you ought to apologize and get the officer's orders changed back the way they were."

He laughed—nice laugh, but not convincing. "You really think you're something, don't you?" he said.

"Get stuffed, Menzes."

"Goddamit, I'm being nice, but I'm not going to let some high-priced legal tart push me and the Agency around."

" 'High-priced legal tart,' I like that. Did you know that's actionable? I may sue you myself, Mister Menzes." She actually seemed to be enjoying herself. "Okay, let's get serious here. I want everything you have on my client, and I want it tomorrow in your office, ten o'clock."

"*You* get stuffed."

"If I don't have access, the piece will run in the *Post* and I'll be talking to the chair of the Senate Intelligence Committee personally before lunch."

"This is a highly classified—"

"Now listen to me, Menzes! You're not listening! I'm making you an offer, and it's one you dare not refuse, you hear me? Get the fucking wax out of your ears! You give me access and you clear this officer's record, or by Christ your agency is going to be in deep shit, and I know for a fact they don't want to be in deep shit because recruitment is down and you stink because of your record in Bosnia and Kosovo, and you're all running scared because the word around town is you've got a mole and you can't find him! Get me?"

The silence on the other end, in Rose's altered perceptions, seemed to go on for minutes.

"I'll get back to you," Menzes said.

"Ten tomorrow morning, your office—access!"

Another silence on his end, and then, almost meekly, 'I may not be able to make that determination."

"When?"

The wind had gone out of him, Rose knew.

"I'll have an answer for you by six." He hung up.

Rose looked at Emma. "Wow," she said.

Emma ran a hand through her hair, making it look even worse. "They haven't got anything, that's why he caved."

"How do you know?"

"I'm guessing. I think we're going to close out Phase One tomorrow, that's the feeling I get, but, just in case, I'm going to hire an investigator." She gave Rose that long, flat stare again. "They aren't cheap, either."

"I already had that figured out." She didn't want some hired investigator; she wanted her friend, Mike Dukas. But he was in Holland. "Whatever," she said. The word seemed to sum up her feeling of helplessness.

USS *Thomas Jefferson.*

At the moment, it looked as if the maintenance was so screwed up that 902 wouldn't make its launch, *and* he hadn't heard one word from Rafe about finding Mike Dukas. Trying to distract himself with a different problem, he worked at analyzing the det's officers, most of whom he had now met for the second time. Aside from Stevens, there were only five. LT Mark Cohen, a pilot, was a difficult, pale man whose resentment and suspicion had seemed palpable, not least because he was the maintenance officer. LT George Reilley, the second pilot, red-headed and always laughing, seemed popular with the men; Campbell, an NFO, was in his first tour, had no reputation of any kind, but had a graduate degree in aeronautical engineering and seemed to have Craw's confidence because of it; LTjg Derek Lang, also a backseater, had hardly registered on him but for that reason seemed unfriendly. The fifth officer was—or would be when he got there—LTjg Soleck. Soleck looked like a disaster, except that he had finished first in his class at Pensacola.

But he needed Soleck. Because Alan had the liberty of putting senior enlisted men in one or both seats in the back end to fly the special equipment, he could theoretically make four crews, once Soleck was aboard. The Navy had intended that the det have only two crews for its two planes, but four would give them flexibility. If they ever got the planes to fly.

Chief Navarro came and sat next to him, his glance asking for attention but not demanding it. Alan finished a message, signed off two equipment requests, and turned to face him.

"You wanted to see me, sir?"

"Did you get the simulator CD from Lockheed?"

"Yes, sir."

"Chief, as of now, you're the MARI training officer. Find a laptop, or better yet, a desktop, and put it in the back of the ready room near the coffeemaker. Strip everything off it except the simulator, okay? So we don't have Duke Nukem running in the ready room?"

"Got you in one, sir."

"Good. Then talk to all the flight crews. Everybody uses the sim, even pilots. But concentrate on the NFOs and the AWs."

A seaman he didn't recognize handed him a message. Alan held him with a wave and read his name tag. Cooley.

"Where do you work, Seaman Cooley?"

"Maintenance, sir."

"Cooley, please locate Mister Cohen and tell him I want to see him. He was on the hangar deck the last I saw."

"Uh, no, sir, he just, uh, left."

"Find him."

Alan knew he was condemning a brand-new man to a long hunt for staterooms. He consoled himself that Cooley would know the ship better when he was done.

The message was from NAS Norfolk. LTjg Soleck had been scheduled on a flight and did O-in-C Det have any other instructions? Alan sighed. *Maybe to send me a guy who can get places on time?*

BY THREE O'CLOCK, he was drinking his seventh cup of coffee, and his mood was as foul as the acrid, thin stuff in his cup. His first flight was an hour away, and he didn't think 902 was going to make it. He grabbed Senior Chief Frazer, the maintenance chief, because Cohen hadn't yet been found.

"Frazer, 902 is due to launch in one hour."

"We're on it, sir."

"Is 901 in better shape?"

"No, sir."

"Frazer, what the fuck, over?"

"901 is down for hydraulics."

"Is this the wrong time to ask why 902 didn't get a rehab for her port engine back at Pax River?"

Frazer looked trapped. Alan realized he was boxing the man into a position where he either had to inform on a shipmate—or his department head—or take blame for something he didn't do. Alan shook his head at his own error. "Never mind. Senior, will I have a bird for the first event or won't I?"

"I'm trying. Yes!"

Alan walked back to the ready room to find Stevens, Craw, and Reilley waiting to brief for the flight that so far had no aircraft. Reilley switched on the closed-circuit TV, and they watched the weather brief and then a quick description of the flight area. The other aircraft in the event were simple carrier quals.

Stevens briefed the emergency procedures in a singsong voice and looked at a map. "We're going about forty miles south, taking a look at the *Willett,* and then flying home. Short event. Any questions?"

Reilley held up a kneeboard card with the NATO and UN communications data. "All this up-to-date?"

Alan reached for it and Reilley handed it over with a minute hesitation. *Am I making this up, or did he not want to show me his kneeboard card?* Alan looked at the card and noted that many of the call signs were unchanged since his last tour here, almost two years ago.

He had imagined giving a little speech about their first operational flight, something to mark the occasion, but when he faced them he saw veiled hostility from Stevens and Reilley and concern from Craw. He searched for brilliant words that would make everything right, and he was about to open his mouth and say something about the det's mission and the need for solidarity when Senior Chief Frazer came in.

"I'm sorry, sir. I need two more hours. I can get both them planes up for the third event."

Stevens smiled without humor. He was relishing the failure, Alan realized, and for a moment he hated the man. He walked from the ready room almost blind, clearing the area before he could say something he would regret.

He wasn't used to failure, and it stung. The feeling that he was personally responsible for a major problem compounded the feeling of alienation that had clung to him since his orders had been changed. He was used to stress, and to danger, but he had begun to feel in this situation as if he was an observer of events, not a participant.

He hadn't got control.

Telling Rafe that he didn't have a bird for the launch was one of the hardest things he had ever done. He had watched the maintenance crisis slide out of his control all day, first the downing of 902, then the problems with 902's port engine that "everybody knew" except Alan, then scrambles to get work done, and condescension from the VS 53 maintenance shop and the slide to failure. And now it was certain, and he walked into Air Ops ahead of Stevens and canked his unit's first operational flight.

Rafe met him going out.

"Problems?" he asked with a smile.

"Yes, sir."

"Sir? Better walk with me, Alan."

Rafe walked down the passageway, slapping the occasional back, looking coldly at a jg running for his brief. Then he pulled Alan into the flag briefing room, empty at this hour.

"I can count the number of times you've called me 'sir' on one hand, Spy. So how bad is it?"

"This is the wrong fucking time to call me spy, Rafe." Alan realized that the storm was still there, and grabbed hold again. "Sorry, Rafe, let me start that again. I just had to cancel my first event. Both my birds are down and I don't have all the parts to fix them because I apparently left some stuff on the beach. That's the worst—the rest is just other crap."

"How'd you end up here with two down birds?"

"I don't know yet."

"Better find out. Kick some ass."

"Right."

"Hey—I know you ain't the bad guy. But you *are* responsible."

"I know!"

"Make it work for you. Sometimes it helps to get mad; you get the assholes' attention that way. Oh, hey—I forgot. We found your NCIS guy."

"You forgot!"

"Yeah, I forgot. I'm the CAG; I have other duties than carrying messages. In fact, I was just gonna give it to you in Air Ops when we got sidetracked with your other problem." He pulled a piece of paper from a shirt pocket. "I've already run this past the flag captain. Here's the deal: your guy is arriving at a hotel in DC about five their time—that's, um,

2300 here—and we've left messages there that he's to call the NCIS office on the ship ASAP. That's direct from Admiral Kessler, so he knows we're serious. We also left messages at NCIS HQ in case he goes there. When he calls, you get your ass to the NCIS office and get on their STU and you tell him whatever the big secret is; when you're done, Maggiulli, the JAG guy, gets on the STU *at once* and hears from your guy that you're a patriotic American who did it all to save the world for democracy. You with me?"

"What the hell is Dukas doing in Washington?"

Rafe rolled his eyes. "Jesus H. Christ, who gives a shit? Did you get all that or didn't you?"

Alan grinned. "I got it. Can I kiss you now?"

5

MIKE DUKAS GOT THE MESSAGE TO CALL THE *JEF-ferson* in the office of his boss's boss at the Naval Criminal Investigative Service at the Navy yard. But, because his boss's boss was flattering him and almost begging him to stay at NCIS and not transfer permanently to the War Crimes Tribunal at The Hague, and because Dukas was trying to parlay that request into a temporary position where he could help Rose, he didn't make the telephone call right away. In fact, it was another hour before he called the *Jefferson*, and only then, when he was talking to the NCIS agent on board the carrier, did he understand that he was really calling Alan Craik. It was damned confusing: three days before, he had been in Sarajevo, this morning in Holland, and why was he calling the husband of the woman he had come to Washington to help?

"Hey—" he started to say.

"Mike, Al Craik. Jesus, you're hard to find! I've got to talk to you—"

"And I gotta talk to you! Have you heard—?"

"Mike, I had to file a—"

"—about Rose?"

"—contact report— What about Rose?"

"What contact report?"

They shouted at each other for several seconds and then both shut up at the same time, and it was Dukas, wide awake now, who took charge and said, "Rose first," and told Alan Craik about his wife's loss of her astronaut's place. Then he told him about the suspicions that were flooding through the Navy about both of them, and about Peretz's discovery that CIA Internal Investigations was behind Rose's fall.

"That doesn't make any sense!" Alan shouted.

"Tell me about it. Don't bother sputtering, Al; we've all said the same thing, and it's a waste of breath. Get hold of yourself—Rose is in deep shit and so are you, by association."

"Jesus, poor Rose! And I've been feeling sorry for myself—"

"This is serious shit, Al. Now what's this contact report?"

Alan had to say "Poor Rose" again, and only then did he get to the contact report and the woman in Trieste who had said "Bonner." He ran through it all quickly—the Serbo-Croat, the shootings, the police, the JAG officer—almost mumbling, as if it had suddenly become almost unimportant.

But it was not unimportant to Dukas. "And you're sure she said 'Bonner'?"

"Absolutely. Otherwise, I'd have—"

"Jesus, old investigations never die! Holy shit, Bonner. Bonner works for Efremov out of Iran; we bust him and send him to prison; now some babe has people shooting at her and she says, 'Bonner,' and you're supposed to snap to, right?"

"She wants me to meet her in Naples—next liberty port."

Dukas could think fast when he had to. He had heard a rumor two days before that Efremov, the Russian/Iranian mercenary, was dead. After only a moment's silence, he said, "Do it."

"Mike, I'm in trouble with my admiral and the JAG guy as it is!"

"I'll give you NCIS cover and clear it with both of them; for now, you tell them it's classified and all will be revealed in the Lord's good time. Then you go to Naples as my agent; I'm your control. You *capisce*?"

"I'm not trained for that stuff."

"Yeah, well, you weren't trained for half the shit I know you've got yourself into, and you came out smelling like a rose. Look, Al, I want you to do it: if she's got real dope on Bonner, I want it!"

"She didn't *say* she had stuff on Bonner; she just said his name."

"Oh, as a way of passing the time? Come on—she sets up a meeting with you by posing as your wife, then she says a notorious spy's name, and we're supposed to think she's just, what? making a pass? Selling Mary Kay cosmetics the European way? Get real—she's got something to sell."

Dukas heard Alan sigh. He sympathized. But, as he had told Rose, life wasn't fair. "You gotta do it, Al."

"Okay. But put it in writing, for God's sake!"

Dukas explained to him that there would be a case number and a file and a classified memo naming Alan Craik as an agent of the NCIS.

"Can you talk to the JAG guy here as soon as I'm done? They think I'm a spy or something, Mike—the shooting stuff has really freaked them—"

"Yeah, yeah, I'll talk to the guy. Jesus, how do you get into these things? She really pretended to be Rose so she could say 'Bonner' to you? Weird, man. Yeah, we gotta go for it."

"Mike, I'm up to my ass with this detachment thing. I don't want to be your agent!"

"One meeting, Al. I promise you. Meet with her once, find out what she's got, that's it."

Dukas heard the hissing silence of the STU as Al Craik thought it over. Finally, he said, "Where's Rose now?"

"Somewhere here in DC. I'm supposed to hear from Abe Peretz in an hour or so."

"Okay—you give me Rose's phone number in an hour, I'll be your agent *once*."

Dukas smiled into the telephone. "That's my boy. Put on your JAG guy. And stop worrying!"

Dukas stroked the JAG officer and, after he hung up, sat staring at an unfamiliar wall, concerned now that he had two cases, not one. Just when he had meant for his life to get simpler, it had got all twisted.

College Park, Maryland.

Rose came to rest in a motel in College Park, recommended by Peretz because it was cheap and it was handy to the District. The hangover still rumbled; the feeling of helplessness kept her in a rage.

The telephone rang. She had to search for it, knocked it off its cradle, fumbled, stammered, "Siciliano!"

"Hey, babe, you sober?" It was Mike Dukas, whom she had last talked to from Utica.

"Mike! How'd you find me?"

"Peretz. I'm in Washington."

"Your guy in Sarajevo said you were in Holland."

"Yeah, well—" He sounded embarrassed. "The deal is I'm coming back to NCIS for six months to a year, then I'll see."

He had been excited about taking over the War Crimes Tribunal's investigative side, she knew. And now he was coming back to NCIS? "Mike, are you doing this for me?"

"Nobody else would get me back to this place, babe."

"Oh, Mike—" She started to cry.

"I love to hear women cry. It really cheers me up. How about saying 'thank you' and we'll get on with it. Look, babe, here's the deal—come on, turn off the hydrant, I need you to listen up—I been here a couple hours, *nobody* here has a case file on you, but there are these goddam rumors going around!" He was talking too fast to get her out of her crying jag. "Anyway, I am now the official investigator for the matter, which is now a case, with a computer-generated case name and number—I saw to that—but it's not a case about security, it's a case about abuse of CIA powers and outside interference, which gives me a very nice bit of leverage. You following me, or you still raining on the carpet there?"

"I follow." She grabbed a Kleenex.

"I talked to Al," he said. "He's got his own problems, which I can't go into on an open phone. You just hang on there, and he'll call when he can get a phone on the *Jeff*. Your turn: what's happening? Peretz says you're seeing a lawyer."

She told him about Emma Pasternak and the calls to the CIA. "I think she'll be okay, Mike, but she's real strange. Maybe—you know, maybe a lesbian, shit, I don't know—"

"That gross you out?"

"Oh, God, no, what d'you think? No, she just isn't—sympathetic."

Dukas grunted. He took a moment, then said, "I gotta make this meeting she set up at the CIA."

"You're not invited."

"What's the CIA Internals guy like?"

"He sounded nice. Nicer than her. I felt sorry for him."

"Yeah, well, don't feel too sorry. This is the asshole gave you the shaft. Okay, so I gotta check around, get a line on him. Then I need to talk to your lawyer and tell her I'm tagging along."

"She won't like it."

"Jeez, I'm terrified. Give me her number."

She read off the number from her book. "Do I go to this meeting, Mike?"

"God, no. You wait for Al to call, get a lot of sleep, call home, talk to your kids, then go to a movie. We'll call you when it's over."

"We?"

"Me and the Bride of Frankenstein. She'll be eating out of my hand."

Right.

ROSE WAS GOING OUT TO EAT, but she couldn't miss Alan's call, and she lay down just for a minute, and then she was waking to hear the telephone and find her hand already on the instrument. Groping it to her, she mumbled something and heard her husband's voice saying her name and then, "How are you? How are you?"

She felt a rush of joy.

Suburban Washington.

Tony Moscowic was wearing a sport coat and a white shirt and an actual goddam tie, because he wanted to look legitimate, and he didn't want anybody at the hospice to remember him from the last time, when he wore an orange jumpsuit. The last time, he had planted the bug that had allowed Suter to listen in on George Shreed's confession to his wife; this time, he was going to remove it. He had his legit clothes and a visitor's badge, and he went right to the room that had been Mrs. Shreed's and jingled his picks in his pocket, ready to pop the lock in four seconds, max, and was surprised and maybe disappointed that the door was unlocked.

Bad omen, he thought. *Too easy is a bad omen.* He closed the door behind him, turned on the light, and he was heading for the wall switch by the bed when a male voice said, "Who the hell are you?"

The fucking bug was behind the wall plate. He could have had the plate off and the bug in his pocket in one minute. Less. Now here was some guy, asking him who the hell he was. Good question, Homer!

"Who are *you*, if I might ask, sir? You're in my aunt's room!" That was his story—sort of. The story, if he got caught with the wall plate actually off and in plain sight, was he was checking out the structural integrity of the building before he moved his aunt there. Weak, but it would work for a practical nurse. Above that level, he got more inventive.

"You have the wrong room," the guy said. He was sitting in an armchair where he'd fallen asleep, Tony guessed. No energy. He was thin, blond, wearing a cashmere sweater that was almost purple, and Tony thought he was a fag, meaning he was here to die of AIDS. Swell.

"Jeez, I guess I do. Seventeen?"

"Nineteen," the guy said. He sounded okay, no longer surprised, maybe kind of amused. He was smiling at Tony. "I just moved in." He smiled some more. "I won't be moving out."

Tony could see now that there were changes in the room. It even smelled different. He was losing his touch; jeez, he could have really put his foot in it here. "You have my greatest sympathy," he said, moving toward the door.

"Yeah. Mine, too." The guy smiled. "See you."

That blew getting the bug. Now he'd have to wait until the guy actually checked out or at least went comatose, and holy shit, the room would probably be filled with grieving fairies holding candlelight vigils and he'd never get that fucking wall plate off. It was really, really unfair. What were they running here, a revolving door, the lady dies one night, the next they've got a new guy dying in her room? Fucking Heartbreak Hotel, for Christ's sake.

He shucked off the sport coat as soon as he was outside the hospice and walked up the street, loosening the tie and tossing the coat over his shoulder. Suter's car was waiting at the end of the block, and Tony took a moment to get his story straight and then walked right to it and got in.

"Did you get it?"

"Piece a cake. Drive."

"Let me see it."

"You nuts or something? It's gone. Wipe it down, smash it good with your foot, throw it in the nearest dumpster. That's my routine. Bugs are like guns—use them once, get rid of them. Drive." So, he'd hung a story on Suter, so what? The important thing was he'd wiped the bug down when he put it in; nobody would ever find it; and if they did, couple years, ten years from now, so what? "You know that doggie is still sick?" he said. "I think it was the pizza. I didn't feel too good next day, either. My neighbor's pissed." Suter said nothing, and Moscowic said, "Some story your boss told! Huh? Huh?" He tapped one palm on his knee. "Treason, you know—jeez, that's worse than child-molesting."

"We have to get into Shreed's house." Moscowic missed the emotions that flashed across Suter's face—fear, then hatred.

"You nuts? What for?"

"Computers. There's a memorial service for the wife on Thursday. You can do it then."

"Djou hear what I just said? You're nuts! You think I'm breaking into some CIA guy's house, you're nuts. And another thing, he'll have a security system, which is no big deal if you don't care who finds out after, but bypass it and try to make it look like it never happens, trust me, you're nuts."

"I want you to go into that house."

"Not Thursday, I'm not. Why?"

"I need a hacker. You know any hackers?"

"Do I look like Bill Gates or something? No, I don't know any hackers." Tony stared out the window at a strip mall. "Vietnamese, they're all Vietnamese," he said, meaning the strip mall and not the hackers. "But I can find you one." Meaning a hacker, not a Vietnamese.

"He's got to be good."

"Oh, that should make it easy. What I think, some kid's been busted and isn't allowed near a computer for two years or something, somebody like that. Itchy, you know? And not a stranger to fucking with the law, because that's what he's already done. Am I right?"

"Then we have to get him into Shreed's house. Only once."

"So what's this Thursday shit? You think I'm going to find the magical mystical hacker by Thursday?"

"Time is of the essence."

"Oh, yeah? Well, caution is of the essence, my friend, so I'm not going in anyplace till I've scoped it out but good, plus finding your perfect hacker is going to take more than five minutes. Let me out at the Iwo Jima Memorial; I'm meeting somebody."

Suter drove without saying anything for several minutes. Then, as they approached Arlington, he said, "You keep your mouth shut about this."

"What'd I say to you the first time we met? You don't fucking listen to me. Leave me off on the other side of the circle."

"If you talk about this, you're dead."

Tony laughed. And laughed. He got out of the car, looked around, leaned back in and said, "Don't try it," still laughing. He watched Suter's car roll away and, because he wasn't really meeting anybody, he walked.

Suter, in the car, was trying to digest what Moscowic had said about treason. It wasn't treason that was proving indigestible; it was the man's talking about it. Moscowic, Suter saw, would have to be dealt with.

6

USS *Thomas Jefferson.*

BY 1000 NEXT MORNING, THE DETACHMENT WAS SHOW-
ing signs of life. The relief Alan felt at having the admiral off his back
had spread to his men: Senior Chief Frazer had located an entire pallet
of missing stuff stored forward in the hangar bay; Reilley, Campbell, and
Lang were in the back of the ready room, getting a lesson in the MARI
simulator from Chief Navarro; and Stevens and Cohen were briefing for
a check flight on 902's hydraulics.

Alan had twenty minutes before his flight with Stevens. He headed
toward the dirty-shirt wardroom, cut into line, grabbed a burger, and
wolfed it down while hustling back, getting there just in time to see the
television change from a movie to the closed-circuit brief. He watched
the young female jg intel officer with professional interest; her brief was
neither brilliant nor boring. Alan scribbled frequencies as fast as he
could.

"No backseaters?" he asked, eyeing the empty chairs behind him.

"We've been changed to a tanker." Stevens still sounded belligerent,
but perhaps he always sounded that way. "In S-3s, mostly we pass gas."
Ordinary S-3s do, you mean, Alan thought. He wondered why Rafe had
put his det aircraft in the tanker pool. The det wasn't supposed to handle
air-wing crap.

"Is 902 going up for a check flight this event?" Alan tried to make professional small talk.

"Yeah. If the hydraulics check, we can take her out tomorrow."

"Need parts from the beach?"

"On the way?" This was the closest to civilized discourse Alan had got with Stevens.

"Roger. I sent a message to Aviano to put the parts and the missing Mister Soleck on the same COD."

"So we'll get a new aircrew and our spare parts? I'd rather have the parts." Stevens didn't look at him. "Sure you aren't too important to ride along on a tanker, Commander?" And there was that damned tone again, a stubborn refusal to come around.

"How about you lighten up, Stevens? It's going to be a long cruise, and you're stuck with me. And, yeah, I've done one or two tanker flights before. Let's walk." He planned to spend the flight talking to Stevens about the det.

He had planned a reorganization, starting with putting Campbell in Maintenance in place of Cohen, because he had an engineering degree and seemed to have his minor responsibilities organized. Cohen got the liaison slot, a dangerous move—Alan had already seen how prickly Cohen could be. In the long run, the success of the project depended on their ability to exchange information with the F-18 squadrons. Cohen was an LSO with a full qualification in F-18s; he had been to school with some of the nugget F-18 pilots. He hoped Stevens bought it. There was more to come, when he had a chance to breathe.

Alan picked up his father's helmet and his thermos and headed for the flight deck, a different man from the one he had been yesterday.

CIA Headquarters.

Emma Pasternak railed at Mike Dukas over the telephone and said *No goddamit he wasn't horning in on her meeting*, but he was already on Menzes's agenda because he was investigating the Agency's interference in Navy procedures, and Menzes must have known it was better to have him. So Dukas got to go to the meeting at the CIA, which actually happened late in the afternoon and not at ten A.M. By the time he shook

Menzes's hand and looked him in the eye, he was prepared for exactly what he got: an ethical hardnose. Well, it took one to recognize one. Menzes was thin, dark, fortyish, one of those people who worked out a lot; he must have been thought a hunk when he was younger, Dukas thought. Now, he looked tired.

Emma Pasternak was late. She was doing the Agency one better than it did other people: typically, it was the Agency who kept the rest waiting. Dukas jumped at the opportunity her lateness offered. "Let's deal," he said. Menzes looked surprised but led Dukas out of the conference room and down the corridor to the big third-floor lobby, where the gold-and-black memorial to the late William Casey dominated one wall. Some people called it The Shrine; cynics called it the SOB—Shrine of Bill. Menzes led him across the echoing marble floor to a spot below Casey's left shoulder. Dukas looked at him, then at Casey (real gold), and then he rested his back against the wall and folded his arms. "Let's deal," he said again.

Menzes looked skeptical. "With what?"

"What have you guys got on Rose Siciliano?"

"I can't tell you. What's your interest, anyway?"

"Straight for straight, okay? She's a friend. But she's also Navy, and you guys have fucked the Navy. What's up?"

"That wasn't my doing."

"Upstairs? Okay, I wouldn't tell some outsider, either. The way I see it, the lawyer lady has you guys by the balls in the PR department, am I right? It's the way her law firm works—lots of fireworks, lots of media. Unless you've got a great case, it's better to give it up, am I right?"

"I'd buy that."

"Have you got a great case?"

He waited until Menzes said, "We overreacted. That's off the record."

"Understood. Okay, what I'm going to do is get together with your Inter-Agency people and work out what happened. That's not your bailiwick, correct me if I'm wrong. Right? Sooner or later, though, you gotta share what you got with us. You see what I'm saying? Our position at NCIS is, will be, you should have come to us with it first."

Menzes gave away nothing. Not a flicker. Dukas tried again. "Give me the outline. Give it to me in one sentence."

"What do we get in return?"

Dukas shook his head. "It's you guys did the wrong here. Am I right?" Not a flicker.

"Give it to me in one sentence *and* get Siciliano's orders changed back, and I'll pull the lawyer lady off you."

"How?"

"Through the client. Never mind how. Come on, Menzes—one fucking sentence, you can't compromise security in one sentence!"

Menzes chewed one side of his lower lip and leaned back against the wall, arms crossed. He was wearing a short-sleeved shirt and a pastel tie, and his arms looked wiry and muscular and hairy. "We got an intercept. Siciliano was implicated. That's two sentences."

"Implicated in what?"

"That wasn't the deal."

"I'd like something to work on. You understand how the Navy works, how easy it is to destroy a career? This is one very, very dedicated officer, a real pile-driver; she's had two kids by planning them for her shore tours, flying a chopper on her sea tours— Let me tell you something. Africa. 1994. War in southern Sudan—you got the picture? She flies a chopper into a hot zone, puts down, and lifts me and another guy out. Menzes, whatever else is involved, I *owe* this woman!"

The two men looked each other in the eye. Dukas knew how hard this was for the other man, who had to evaluate a stranger, measure his own trust, decide how much he had been used himself by the system and how much he owed to his own idea of right behavior and of decency.

"Something called Peacemaker," Menzes said at last. "That's my final word, and if you quote me, I'll deny it." He looked at Dukas's face again. "That means something to you," he said.

"It sure does." Rose had worked on Project Peacemaker two years before. "Okay, we got a deal. Haven't we—haven't we got a deal? You're gonna withdraw whatever you did and get the orders rescinded, send her back to astronaut training?"

"She's on our books as a security risk. This is a very grave situation, Dukas."

"I know that. But you know what the proper procedure is—you tell us and you tell Navy intel, and we do an evaluation and an investigation. It's our call if we bring in the Bureau. Right?"

"Right, but if she's a spy, now she knows we're onto her and she'l—"

"What the fuck, she didn't know the moment she got the change of orders? What are you talking? It's a goddam given of my profession, you're investigating somebody, you don't make waves until you're ready to!"

Menzes shrugged. "That wasn't my call."

"Have we got a deal?"

"Only the change of orders, and what I told you. That's it. We don't budge on access or on anything else."

"Deal." They shook hands. Menzes had a real grip.

A woman's heels sounded on the marble floor like gunshots, and both heads turned to watch her march diagonally across. She was pale, scowling, swinging an attaché case like a weapon she was just waiting to use.

"That's Pasternak," Menzes said.

"What do we do about her?"

"The twelve-hour rule."

"Meaning?"

"We let her scream for an hour, then we say we'll consider it, and twelve hours later I agree to what you and I have already agreed to. Only we don't tell her that." He made a face. "The hard part will be listening to her."

They crossed the lobby and went into the conference room, which looked like a party that wasn't working out: all the Agency people were down at one end, and Emma Pasternak was sitting alone at a long table. Dukas went right to her, stuck out his hand, and said, "I'm Mike Dukas."

She ignored the hand and started shouting. She went on shouting for most of an hour—Menzes's timing was pretty good—and she used every trash-mouth word in the book to batter Menzes. CIA Security, lack of access, injustice, bureaucratic stupidity, and perhaps even (Dukas had stopped listening) rabies. Then Menzes begged her to give them twelve hours.

And, eventually, Emma Pasternak accepted.

Because she knew this is the way it would be! Dukas thought. *Holy shit, she knows about the twelve-hour rule, too.*

"That's—six-thirty tomorrow morning," she was snarling. "You can leave a message on my voice mail. Full access, and my client gets her orders changed back to Houston. Yes?"

Menzes lifted his shoulders. "I'll meet with my people and get back to you in twelve hours."

"You're goddam right you will."

She stood and began to fling stuff into her attaché case. The Agency people withdrew from her as if she had a disease, leaving Dukas alone with her. "Nice job," he said. She shot him a look, went back to stuffing papers. Dukas leaned in, thinking paradoxically that there was something sexually interesting about her despite her noisiness. Maybe *because* of the noisiness. All that energy.

"Menzes has gone out on a limb for you. Trust me."

"Trust you! I don't even know you! You come barging in here, *my* meeting—"

"Ms. Pasternak, look—" Dukas found himself looking down her tailored dress, thinking that there were quite nice breasts down there; Jesus H. Christ, what was going on? And then saying, "This really is an important security matter. Menzes is a stand-up guy who's trying to do his job and defend his agency *and* be fair."

She was breathing hard and her pale face was flushed. He suspected that she wanted to hit him. Lawyers' egos were very big. "You've won," he whispered.

"Get fucked!"

Well, there was an idea. But she annoyed him, too, because she really didn't understand how hard it was for a man like Menzes to have come even this far. "And you get real," he growled. "If he calls your bluff, you've got nothing but some bullshit in the *Washington Post,* and Rose will get creamed!"

Then he thought she was going to lose it, but she surprised him by looking at her watch and then at the CIA people at the far end of the room, who were looking at their watches because it was past the end of their workday, and she said, "I haven't got time to dick around with a Navy cop."

Then there was a lot of talking all at once, and several handshakes, and the Agency people scurried away, and only Dukas and Emma Pasternak were left. She was still trying to jam papers and a binder of vetted documents that Menzes had given her into her attaché. Dukas lingered by the door. Now that it was over, the optimism he had felt after meeting with Menzes left him; never an easy man with other people, he felt awkward. "Nice to have met you, Ms. Pasternak," he said.

"Nice to have met you," she said. She didn't mean that it had been nice to meet him, at all. She meant *Get out of here*. Then she swore because she couldn't get the document binder into the attaché.

"Uh—yeah." He took the binder from her, took the pages out of the cover, and handed the pages back. "You ever, uh, eat Italian food?"

"What the hell does that mean? Of course I've eaten Italian food."

"I'm a, uh, pretty good Italian cook. I'm Greek, but I cook Italian a lot."

She found that the unbound pages would now fit. They looked at each other. "What kind of Italian?"

"Gnocchi." To his ears, it sounded like *nooky*, and he reddened. "Made with butternut squash. A very delicate flavor." He cleared his throat. With Menzes, he had been on a roll, in charge, and now he was a stumbling jerk. The story of his life. "I, uh, thought you might, uh—like some."

She stared at him. "You're asking *me* to dinner?"

"Uh, yeah, I guess—if you put it like that—and we could call Lieutenant-Commander Siciliano and give her the news—"

"At *your* place?"

"Uh, no, belongs to a friend of mine—out of town—"

"It's the same thing! Let me get this straight—are you asking me to dinner, when we've just met and haven't exactly blended, and at your place?"

"Okay, okay, bad idea—I just thought—" He shrugged.

"What?"

"You sort of—interest me." He tried to smile, and the effort made him feel like a dog who's trying to make up for eating somebody's sandwich. He grabbed the door and held it for her. "Sorry. I didn't mean anything."

"Everything means something, Mister Dukas." She swept past him into the corridor. "Well, okay."

"What's okay?"

"Okay, I'll come to dinner. I'd like to see somebody make gnocchi, because when I tried all I got was dough all over the fork."

"You pushed too hard. On the fork." He didn't say, *Probably you always push too hard.* "You're really gonna come to my place for dinner?"

"Why not? We can call Siciliano. But *please* don't try to make any moves, okay? The best I ever hope for from other people is that we don't sue each other."

She turned away. He saw her buttocks move in the tailored skirt.

Life is full of surprises.

E-mail, Rose to Alan.

Subject: IT'S OVER!
I can't believe it but it's over/mike called me just now, just hung up and it's over!!!! they cut a deal with the agency and i'm to go back to astro soonest, waiting to cut orders, i want to go right back and see the kids and head for houston but mike says no, stay until orders/he's so cautious! i still have to fight whatever allegation was made but this will be a couple of years he thinks sorting it out but i'll be in orbit by then and fuck em/ i love you, thinking of you kept me sane, a hell of an ordeal but i felt better thinking of you and the kids but helpless, helpless, my god how do people stand it being caught up in suspicion and all that? Kisses, love, moans/ Rose

Alan sat back and smiled, his whole face transformed. Safe. Rose was safe. Yeah, they'd have to listen to snide remarks for a while. Some semi-friends might drop off. Alan knew that a deal at the Agency wouldn't help him here on the ship, but if it put Rose back on the space shuttle, they were a long way toward home. He laughed aloud, startling a chaplain's clerk near him, leaped up, and headed toward his ready room with a new feeling of purpose.

Everything looked better to him. Even the tanker flight with Stevens, which had been a torment of bad performance by the MARI system—dropped links, bad plane-to-plane communication—and stubborn hostility from Stevens, faded.

In the ready room, he munched a second doughnut and drank his coffee while he fanned through the detachment's bulging message board. There was a NATO Air Tasking Order for Bosnia that didn't include them; that had to be addressed. There were messages for the technical representatives; he skimmed them. Intelligence messages about the frequencies of Serbian radars; Alan made a note that all flight personnel were required to read and initial. A message on decline in manpower retention that he was required to read and initial. He did so, finishing the doughnut in two bites and dusting the powdered sugar off the front of his flight suit.

Some change in the noise level at the back of the ready room alerted him, and he turned in his seat to see Senior Chief Craw coming up the center aisle with a figure in pressed shipboard khakis, a sea bag over his shoulder and his hands full of luggage. Craw had an anticipatory smile on his face.

"Look what I found on the flight deck, Skipper." He pushed the slim figure in khakis forward. A Tomcat went to full power overhead.

"How do you guys hear yourselves think?" asked the figure with what appeared to be genuine concern. A face came into focus—incredibly young, rather pink, eyes as blue and innocent as a newborn's. Alan got to his feet.

"Is this by any chance the missing Mister Soleck?" Alan looked past the new man to Craw. Craw merely shook his head a little, as if to disclaim any responsibility.

A hand appeared out of the pile of luggage.

"Sorry, sir. I'm LTjg Evan Soleck, reporting aboard." He was a little bowed by his load, giving him a slightly gnomelike appearance below the wonderfully fresh face.

"Glad to see you brought a tennis racket, Mister Soleck."

"Oh, that's not a tennis racket, sir. That's a squash racket." Now Craw was laughing openly. Behind him in the back, a small crowd had gathered. Alan smiled inwardly and reminded himself that this young man had been first in his class at Pensacola.

"Did you get in any *squash* in the last few days?"

"Yes, sir! They had a court at the hotel. It was great! And they had really fast Internet connections, too. Europe isn't as primitive as people say." Soleck looked perfectly capable of babbling on (*had he really just said that Europe wasn't primitive?)* but Alan cut him off with a gesture.

"Mister Soleck, you're two days late meeting the boat." They had traced him from Norfolk to Aviano, and found that he was waiting there in a first-class hotel for further orders because he hadn't had the common sense to grab a COD to the boat.

"Yes, sir."

"Care to enlighten me?"

"I missed my assigned flight, sir." Soleck stood a little straighter and looked Alan in the eye. "No excuse."

"And then?"

"And then I made a couple of mistakes flailing around. Then I got another message and got on the COD."

He kept the eye contact. The wide-eyed wetness seemed to drop from him for a moment. He was just Alan's height, thinner but with obvious neck muscle, and he continued to hold his luggage without apparent effort. His demeanor seemed to say, *I screwed up but I'm here. Let's get on with the job.* And Alan was thinking, *Was I ever this young? Am I really this old?*

"What were you doing on the Internet, Mister Soleck?"

"Working on a wargame."

"You played a wargame all day?"

"No, sir. Writing one. And only *after* I had tried to reach the boat and failed."

Alan sighed, careful not to meet Craw's eye. "Okay, Mister Soleck. Get rid of all that stuff, stow your squash racket, and report in flight gear. You're on the schedule in two hours."

"Cool!"

Alan shut his eyes. "Soleck, was 'cool' on the list of acceptable responses at Pensacola?"

"Wow, yeah. Sorry. Aye, aye, sir."

Alan eyed the pile of luggage. "You seem to anticipate a long cruise, Mister Soleck."

"Oh, well, sir, a lot of it's books. Books. Use the time, you know—spare time—" He looked to Alan for help.

Alan pointed at the row of det pubs. Five of them covered the MARI system that was their primary reason for being. "Our library, Mister Soleck. Please have mastered the five MARI pubs by tomorrow."

Soleck looked at the shelf of stand-alones. "Cool," he cried. "Sir."

Alan handed him the message board. "That's after you read and initial these. Carry on, Mister Soleck."

7

Suburban Virginia.

THURSDAY MORNING, GEORGE SHREED MADE BREAK-
fast at the butcher-block island in their big kitchen, her great love, and
he ate his breakfast standing there. He didn't have to move a lot that way,
the coffeemaker to hand in front of him, fruit in the basket where she
had always kept it to his left, breads in a drawer where his pelvis pressed
against the wood. The bread was stale; how long since he'd replaced it?
Could she have bought it? No; she'd been gone for a month before she
died, now dead two days. He felt as if hands pushed down on his shoulders, the weight of her absence.

The cleaning woman would come in today. He wrote her a note. "Buy
bread. Get good stuff, no white paste—you know." He looked around
the kitchen. What else did he need? He wrote, *rice.* He could live on rice.
Chicken breasts. She had been a superb cook. He was not. *Frozen dinners, a dozen or so.* He put some money on the note, wrote the check for
her, as Jane must have done, once a week, years and years. Had he ever
seen the cleaning woman? Must have. An image of a too-thin white
woman swam into his consciousness, swam away. Something about
ADD or OCD or one of those goddam disorders everybody had now.

The telephone rang. He hobbled to the extension on the kitchen wall,
expecting it to be the cleaning woman saying she couldn't come that

day—also part of her image, a certain unreliability that had plagued Janey, something about her kids and her disorders.

"Shreed."

"George, Stan." Rat-a-tat machine gun of a voice, instantly recognizable—a friend (of sorts) in Internal Investigations. "George, they're calling off the Siciliano investigation. Just thought you'd like to know."

Fear surged, and he could feel himself flush. He controlled his voice, however, and said, "How come?"

"She made a lot of noise, got a lawyer. More trouble than it's worth, was the call."

"Bad call. Okay, thanks."

He thought about it as he flossed his teeth. He saw an angry man in his mirror, composed his face better, shrugged into his suit jacket while watching himself and decided that he looked okay. Grieving, enraged, worried, but okay. The suit was for the memorial service, which he would endure because that was what you did, because memorial services were for the survivors, who needed to believe that when they died somebody would also remember and sing hymns and give eulogies. For his own part, no memorial was needed, and memory itself was enough, but grief was now turning one of its corners toward anger and the change was dangerous. He knew his own anger and knew to fear it.

Bad times a-comin', he thought.

His people had missed the woman in Venice and Trieste. He thought he'd neutralized her by tossing Siciliano to Internals. Now the Siciliano thing was falling apart. Bad, bad.

Shreed was no fool about his situation. Talk of a mole had rumbled around the Agency for years; anybody who put scraps of evidence and suppositions together would have had a look at him, if only because he had a finger in a lot of pies and he had been there a long time. But they wouldn't do anything, not actually *do* anything (polygraphs, bugs, taps, interviews), not until somebody like this woman who wanted money gave them cause. Having the Siciliano woman to entertain themselves with would have kept them occupied for a couple of years—all the time he needed—and now they were washing that out and he couldn't afford it.

The Siciliano woman would have to stay a suspect.

It was still too early to go to the office, and he vented his anger by stumping through the house on his canes, trying to erase the signs of Janey. He didn't need mementos—how could he ever forget her?—and the house itself, its smell, its decor, was all hers, anyway. But things of hers that were now useless, from her toothbrush in the bathroom to a pair of old slippers near the back door, had to go.

He stormed through the house. He jammed things into plastic trash bags. He threw things.

When he got to the bedroom where she had hoped to die but where death had come too slowly, he almost refused to open the door. *This one can stay a few days,* he thought, and then, hating his own cowardice, he flung the door open so that it banged back against the wall, and he leaned in the doorway, glowering on his canes, taking in the futility of all fights against death. Magazines she had tried to read, a television he had bought for her, an IV rack, a godawful bedpan thing. He began to throw things into the corridor.

It was when he got to the drawer in the bedside table that he found the things that caused him to decide that it was time for him to wind it all up.

A lot of junk lay in there, lipsticks and pencils and sickroom crap, but there were thirteen ampoules of morphine and two syringes, and they were what did it. He put out his hand to gather them up and throw them away, and he was aware of his hand there, hovering over the drawer, *not* gathering them up, as if the hand knew better than he did. And he looked at the morphine. It was as if a voice whispered to him: *Morphine. You could walk like anybody else with morphine.* It wasn't the vanity of wanting to seem normal that affected him, however; no, it was the idea of *looking* normal.

As if the voice had whispered, *If you could walk like other people, your most identifiable characteristic would be gone, and you'd be invisible.* Which was a way of saying, *You could vanish.*

Then his hand moved and gathered the ampoules and the syringes and, more carefully than he had handled anything else, put them into a plastic sack that he carried downstairs and put into the freezer. By the time he was down there, he saw the implications, was already planning it, gauging the risks, the gains: without his canes, with an injection of morphine and a false passport, he could be out of the country before the wolves got the scent. He'd have to do something else to throw them off—fake a suicide, an accident, or—? He'd work that out.

But he'd have to set up the Chinese disaster first. Set it up and get it running and then vanish. Leaving nothing behind except this house. No lost love, no regrets. She was dead; why wait?

But an escape plan took time, and to gain him time, the Siciliano woman would have to remain a suspect.

Shreed leaned back against the refrigerator and began to think it all out. He looked down at his hands and saw that they were trembling, and for the first time he realized, to his astonishment, that he was scared.

AT LANGLEY, Sally Baranowski was waiting, like everybody else, for Shreed. They didn't think of it just like that, for they all had other concerns, but the memorial service sat in the middle of the day like a pillar in a highway, it and Shreed unavoidable. Plus they were all waiting to see how he would take it.

For Sally Baranowski, waiting to see how Shreed would take something was an old routine. She had once been his assistant (that year's Ray Suter, as she now said to friends, although Suter had lasted several years longer than she), then had briefly followed Shreed in his old job when he had been promoted. That she had failed in that job was partly his doing, she believed—retribution for having once (once) been disloyal to him. He had taken retribution in the best of all possible managerial ways: he had given her so much rope that she had hanged herself. Now she was in a liaison job that wasn't going to go anywhere except toward an honorable retirement thirteen years down the pike.

Still, when she saw Shreed she was shocked. She saw him seldom now, usually thought he was his old, bitter, amusing self, but this morning he looked merely grim. *Is it grief?* she wondered. Hard to imagine Shreed feeling grief, although they said he had adored his wife. No, it was more than grief, something hard and ugly, she thought. *Look out, people.* She was representing her new boss on a committee where everybody else knew each other, and, as the new kid on the block, she found it best simply to listen and watch. And the one she watched was Shreed.

The memorial service was at eleven. She had debated not going but had decided that her own bitterness was better hidden, so she would go and be solemn. Now, the committee chair, Clyde Partlow, kept looking at his watch to make sure he wound things up in time to get there, too. They all had copies of the agenda, which he forced with the brutality of a cowhand pushing cattle through a chute. Shreed said almost nothing.

Then they got to "Security in the 21st Century," and Shreed went through the ceiling. His face flushed a dark, ugly red, and his eyes got bigger and his lips pulled back to show his teeth.

"How dare we discuss security when our own Internal Investigations can't stand the heat being turned up by one goddam accused spy!" he shouted. The meeting had been very low key, and his voice made people jump.

It wasn't like Shreed to shout. *What the hell,* she thought. Had grief deranged him?

"Afraid I don't follow you, George," Partlow said, checking his watch and making sure that the proper note of respect for the bereaved rang in his voice.

"Peacemaker! Two years ago! It tanked because somebody tipped the French and the Libyans, and now our goddam Internal Investigations doesn't give enough of a shit to pursue it!"

Other people thought this was odd behavior, too. She could hear it in the silence, in the changed breathing.

"Uh, well, George, that's certainly a serious matter. Maybe you ought to share your concerns with—"

"I'm sharing my goddam concerns with you, Clyde! You've got Security in the 21st Century on your agenda, or is that just a Partlow nod to trendiness? Goddamit, Peacemaker was my project and you know it, and I've never had the support I'm entitled to!"

He's trading on his wife's death, she thought, and then, *For Christ's sake, give him the benefit of the doubt; the man's so upset he's lost it.* But if he wanted to behave badly and be forgiven, he had the perfect opportunity, she thought. Partlow was more or less Shreed's superior, but, like everybody, he was afraid of Shreed, plus Partlow was a placater and a fence-mender. She knew Shreed's tactics, and, damn it, what he was doing was using his bereavement to force Partlow to action.

Plus, she thought, Shreed really was angry. Enraged, in fact.

"What would you have us do?" Partlow said. He glanced around at the other members of the committee, who were trying to escape by not looking at him.

"I'd have *us* goddam well tell Internal Investigations they can't dump a spy charge just because some smartass inside-the-Beltway lawyer holds a flame to their assholes! Look!" He began to tap the table with a long finger. "You approved Peacemaker! This committee approved Peacemaker! It failed! Why? Because word leaked out and the international community of peace-loving, no-balls, third-world nations bitched to the White House! Now we're on the track of finding out who and why, and Internal says to their suspect, 'Oh, we didn't really mean it, sorry, we'll just back off and you can go betray some other project.' Eh? Well?"

Partlow checked his watch. "If you have a recommendation, George—"

"Yeah, I recommend we shove a poker up our ass so we have some backbone."

"Oh, George—"

"All right, I recommend we vigorously protest to Internal their canceling of this investigation, *and* we go on record with the Director that they continue or show cause why not, which won't sit well because they're already in the Director's shit book because of past failures. Okay?"

"Is that a motion, George?"

"You bet."

A tall man from Ops seconded it with a louder voice than seemed called for. Sally wanted to say that she didn't understand the motion because she didn't know what or whom Internal was investigating, but either everybody else knew or they were so snowed by Shreed's grief that they didn't dare ask. The motion passed on a voice vote.

What the hell is he up to? she asked herself.

When the meeting was adjourned, she lingered. Shreed had gone right to Partlow and was hammering at him about the thing. Even though he'd won, he wanted more. "Now, Clyde, do it now! I don't give a good goddam if you're late for Janey's memorial service, what d'you think I do, take attendance at the door? You want to show some sympathy, get on the line to the head of Internal, he's a buddy of yours, tell him we're not taking no for an answer, either he reinstates the Siciliano investigation or he's dead. Dead, d-e-a-d, as in one too many failures! Do it!"

Siciliano, she thought. *That's the name of Alan Craik's wife. What the hell?* Sally had been there when the rift between Shreed and Craik had opened, something about an event in Africa years ago. Was Shreed still angry, was that what all this was about? Was he trying some petty revenge on Alan Craik through the man's wife?

"Goddamit, just do it!" she heard Shreed shout.

The man's ballistic. But why?

NCIS HQ, Washington.

Mike Dukas was sitting at a borrowed desk in an office already being used by somebody else. The desk wasn't really a desk, only an old typing table from the days of IBM Selectrics, and the chair was a mismatched typing chair that already hurt his back.

"You Dukas?" a voice said. He looked across the room. A black male agent was holding up a telephone.

"Yeah."

"Phone call." He held out the telephone. "Make it quick, will you? I live on that thing."

Dukas took the call standing by the guy's desk. "Dukas."

"Dukas, it's Menzes. CIA Internal Investigations."

"Yeah, yeah, I remember."

"The deal's off."

"Hey—"

"We had a go, then we had no-go. From the top: no deal, definitely pursue, by the book. Your lawyer lady wants to go public, that's her prerogative; it won't change a thing."

Dukas was thinking hard. He couldn't see what had changed the dynamics, but he was a realist; if Menzes said the deal was dead, it was dead. "You kicking it to us?" he said.

"Exactly. 'By the book,' that's what I was told, and the book says it's the Navy's to pursue."

"We oughta talk."

"Nothing'll change, man. This isn't my doing. But, yeah, there may be things to talk about. This case—"

"What?"

"I don't want to talk on an open phone."

"Jesus, Menzes, this is gonna hit the woman hard."

"It hit *me* hard; I don't like to be second-guessed." Menzes was angry. He was a stand-up guy, a hardnose, and somebody above him had jerked his chain.

"We're talking everything here? No change of orders? She goes to Big Turd, West Virginia? No Houston?"

"Back to square one. Only it's NCIS's baby now."

"Yeah, but we wouldn't—" Dukas gave up; there was no point in going over it again. But he wanted to talk to Menzes, so he arranged to meet him next day at someplace called the Old Commonwealth Tavern, aka "the Agency Annex." When Dukas hung up the black agent said, "Oh, thank *you*," in a prissy voice. "I thought I was going to have to charge rent."

Dukas wasn't sure he could tell Rose. He walked along the corridor, looking into offices until he found an empty one, and he went in and used the phone there. First he called Peretz and told him the bad news, and Peretz said they had to have a council of war, the sooner the better. Dukas said he'd think about it, and he called Emma Pasternak, but she was out somewhere.

Then he called Rose.

She was happy. It was in her voice, that husky female sound that made his knees shaky. Before he could say anything, she burbled, "Guess who's in town! He's taking me to dinner!"

"Al?"

"No, asshole, Al's on the boat! Harry!"

Harry. *O'Neill.* Another of the friends who circled the wagons for her when she was in trouble. Of course. Could he get O'Neill to tell her? No, of course not. "Hey, Rose—"

"Harry wants to see you, Mike. I told him my problem is over, that's why he's in DC, was to help me, but he wants to see all you guys, anyway."

"It isn't over."

"I know, there's the investigation part, but—"

"The deal's off, babe. The Agency backed out." He heard her breathing as she put it together. "We're back where we were on Monday," he said. "I'm sorry as hell."

"You mean—everything?" *Everything* meant only one thing—the astronaut program.

"Everything," he said. "I tried to call your lawyer, she's out. I talked to Abe—"

"GODDAMIT TO HELL!" she shouted. "They fucking can't!"

"Abe thinks we should have a skull session. It's not a bad idea, especially with Harry here; he understands this stuff. What d'you say?"

"Oh, Mike. Oh, shit!"

"Yeah. But we can't just sit still for it, babe. We gotta move."

"Whatever." The happiness had gone out of her voice.

"I'll get Emma," he said. *I shouldn't have said "Emma,"* he thought. He hoped Rose wouldn't notice.

Dukas went back to his borrowed typing table. Last night, he had thought he might really wind this up and be back in The Hague in a few days. Now, he knew, he was in for the long haul.

E-mail, Rose to Alan.

it isn't over after all. Mike just told me. deal fell through. Oh shit, i love you so much and i miss you so much and i want to kill somebody for this. I keep saying why me why me but it doesn't do any good. I'm so sorry i've dragged you down with me but don't despair we'll come through we always have. I love you and that's a lot. But goddamit i keep saying to myself who is doing this to us who who who?

8

Rose's motel.

HARRY O'NEILL WAS PUTTING BEER BOTTLES INTO plastic tubs of ice. He was a big, handsome black man who came from money and behaved with the confidence of a Harvard education and a family of big-time lawyers. He had been a CIA case officer, now had his own security company, and had flown in from Dubai to help her.

"We're going to get you out of this," he said, as if he had all the confidence in the world. He held out a bottle. "Have a beer." They were in Rose's motel room, waiting to have the skull session with Dukas and Peretz and Emma Pasternak.

She shook her head.

"Come on, Rose! It isn't the end of the world!"

She started to snap at him but caught herself. Harry really knew about the end of the world: he had lost an eye to torture two years before in Africa. She gave him an apologetic grin, accepted a sweaty bottle.

He winked at her, as if to say: *See? You can fall in the shit and come up holding a diamond.* He was wearing a linen blazer and an electric-blue T-shirt that Rose suspected was real silk, and he was handsome and breezy and rich-looking.

"Sorry," she said. Her smile was halfhearted.

Then Abe Peretz arrived, and Dukas and Emma Pasternak came in right behind him. After a lot of shouted introductions and greetings, people shoved chairs around and grabbed beer and sat down, all but Dukas, who took up the space between the beds and announced loudly, "I'm taking charge of this meeting." Emma started to protest but he waved her down. "I'm the NCIS investigator and it's a Navy case, so I'm in charge." He pointed a finger, the thumb cocked like a hammer, at Emma. "You're here by my permission."

"She's my client, and she remains my client wherever we are! She says *nothing* unless I okay it. She—"

Dukas put his hands on the arms of her chair and leaned his face down very close to hers and said in a tone like a dog's growl, "Shut up or get out."

Before either of them could do something terrible, Rose grabbed Emma's arm and said, "Emma, please! Mike's my friend!"

Emma glanced at her, then locked eyes with Dukas again. Something passed between them. At last, she mumbled, "But no taping. Nothing she says can be used in court. Okay?"

Dukas grinned, patted her arm. He straightened. "So here's what I want to do tonight. I want to chew on it and come up with a way to *attack.* I mean, we're all clear that Rose is being smeared and her husband's getting screwed by association, are we all agreed on that? Okay, so what we want to find is how and why. Rose, I want everything you have on Peacemaker, because this whole thing seems to start there. The word is you gave Peacemaker secrets to—well, we don't know who to. You got reports, printouts—disks—?"

Emma started to say, "What's Peacemaker?" but Rose jumped in ahead of her. "Mike, Peacemaker was more than two years ago! I haven't got anything!"

"Sure, you have. People always keep stuff. It's in a box in a closet or the cellar—bullshit awards they gave you, photos from the Christmas party—"

"Oh, that sort of shit."

"Yeah, and I want it. All."

Angered again by her own lack of control, Rose growled, "It's all on its way to Houston, remember? I don't have a cellar or a closet!"

Harry O'Neill uncrossed his long legs and said, "Computer." He looked at Dukas. "What d'you think?"

"I never used my home computer for Peacemaker," Rose cried. "Everything was classified."

Dukas bored in. "You *never* brought anything home and worked it on your computer? Tell me another, Alphonse!"

Emma half-rose from her chair. "I object—!"

"You stay out of it!"

"This is typical cop bullshit; you're tricking her into making statements to incriminate her."

Dukas stared at her. He stuck his lower jaw out, his tongue running over his upper teeth. "Do you want me to take her into an interrogation room with a tape recorder and a witness? Would that be better? Goddamit, we're here to help her!"

Again, Rose put her hand on Emma's arm. "I'll answer, Emma."

"I don't want you to!"

"Well, deal with it." Rose looked up at Mike. "What was the question? Did I put Peacemaker stuff on my home computer? No, I didn't. I'm a good little naval officer, Mike; I follow the rules."

"Rosie, we got a former Director of National Intelligence who put stuff on his home computer. Everybody does it! I want your computer."

"It's on the way to Houston! And it's clean. *Clean.*"

"Okay." He talked it as he wrote. "Find—truck—en route—Houston—"

The telephone rang.

"Oh, shit—" She sprang up, reaching for it, knocking over her beer. "Goddamit—!" O'Neill and Peretz were both there, mopping at the carpet, and she stepped over them. "Hello!" She sounded enraged, and she hoped, therefore, that it wasn't Alan.

And it wasn't. It was a woman.

"You don't know me," the female voice said. Rose's first thought was that it was some sort of telemarketer, an idea that was gone as fast as it came; telemarketers didn't do motel rooms. Did they?

"Who is this?"

"I want to help you."

The voice was soft, as if she didn't want somebody on her end to overhear. A little tense. Guarded. Around Rose, the room had fallen silent, and the men were watching her.

"Who is this, please?"

"George Shreed is behind what's being done to you."

Rose heard the click as the woman hung up. Even so, she spoke into the phone again. And got nothing.

When she turned back to the room, they were all looking at her.

"A woman I don't know said that George Shreed is behind what's happening."

Abe Peretz exploded. "Sonofabitch—!"

Emma was saying, "Who's George Shreed?" to Dukas, and O'Neill was frowning at Rose in a way that meant he knew exactly who Shreed was, and what was the connection? Suddenly the room was electric where before it had been sullen.

Rose sat down. "I don't get it. Why would somebody—?"

"Agency," Harry said. "She'd have to be Agency to know anything about Shreed. Or she's an old girlfriend with a grudge. Which isn't his style."

"Yes, yes, but—" Peretz was so excited that he was waving one hand like a kid trying to be called on in class. "It's exactly what I was going to say! Shreed was deep, *deep* in Peacemaker."

"Wait!" Emma was on her feet. She had a real bellow when she needed it. "What the hell are you all talking about?"

So, while O'Neill and Peretz murmured together, Rose and Dukas sketched it in for Emma Pasternak: Peretz, who had started a routine, two-week Naval Reserve stint at Peacemaker two years before, had got suspicious of the sort of data he was seeing and had begun nosing around, tracking things back to Shreed and the Agency, a search that had been ended by the mugging that had cost him the hearing in one ear.

"Shreed got him beaten up?" Emma said.

"Oh, no," Rose cried, "I never believed—" Then she looked at Dukas.

"They never followed up that idea," he said. He made a note.

"Well, I would have!" Emma shouted.

"Yeah, you would have." Dukas whacked O'Neill on the knee. "Harry, you think Telephone Girl's Agency?"

"Likely."

"You got any way to find her?"

"Put a tap on Rose's phone."

Emma was screaming, "No way!" Dukas turned back to O'Neill. "Poke around, will you?"

"I have to be in Nairobi on Saturday, Mike." He turned to Rose and started mumbling something about tape-recording telephone calls.

Dukas was making notes. "Abe, I want everything you got on Peacemaker."

"Hey, how about polygraphing Shreed?" Peretz said.

"Not yet." He made a note. "The Agency wouldn't let me polygraph its people without a hell of a fight, and I'm not ready for a fight. Yet." He looked at his notes. "Rosie, does it make sense that George Shreed would go after you because he has an old rhubarb with Al?"

She shrugged. "I don't know, does it?"

Peretz shook his head. "He's a high-powered guy, but he's very personal—he fought the Cold War that way, his personal enemies. A big thinker in terms of geopolitics, but he personalizes everything. Can be very petty."

"Could he be petty enough to go after Rose to settle with Alan?"

"Why should he go after Alan?" Emma said.

Dukas sighed. "A *very* old story. Al and I were in Mombasa in ninety—or was it ninety-one? Al had a contact with a, well, call him a foreign asset, and he didn't know what to do, so he calls Shreed, who's an old family friend. Bang! Al and I get pulled out of country so fast we think we're being deported, and two CIA types come in, and next thing we know, the foreign contact is dead."

"Shreed had him killed?"

"No, no!" Dukas shook his head as if the question was the dumbest one he'd ever heard. "Suicide. Alan had a fight with Shreed about it when we got back to the US, and they've been on the outs ever since. But is that reason enough to lay a serious frame-up on Rose now? I don't buy it." He turned back to Harry. "But just to be on the safe side, as long as you're going to be in Nairobi, how about checking into that death while you're there?"

"Nairobi isn't Mombasa."

"Well, same country, what the hell. Come on, Harry—for Rose, okay?"

Peretz shook his head. "A man like Shreed doesn't wait eight or nine years and then do something like this out of spite. Although, maybe if somebody *else* fingered Rose, Shreed might take advantage of it."

They all started offering theories about Shreed then, and the skull session quickly degenerated into chaos. Dukas pounded on the bedside table with a beer bottle until they all shut up. "Hey! *Hey!*" He hiked his pants up and glared at them, then grinned. "Look, folks, we've allowed ourselves to narrow our focus too soon, you all understand that, right? I think the Shreed thing is . . ." He rocked his free hand back and forth. "At this point it's nothing but a line for us to follow, and all we got is Telephone Girl's voice telling us to." He sighed. "What I think is, George Shreed is a sonofabitch who has nothing to do with Rose's case, but I'm going to follow up, because that's my job. Let's have some other ideas, could we?"

They sat for another hour, repeating some of it, trying to cheer Rose, offering new theories. Did Rose have enemies? Peretz mentioned Ray Suter, who had been at Peacemaker and was now at the CIA and who had tried and failed to get Rose in the sack. Did that make him an enemy? Other names were mentioned—squadron squabbles, professional rivalries. Dukas made notes. Then they began to drift away, first Peretz, then Emma and Dukas, O'Neill last.

It was only when they were gone and she had put the television on to keep her from thinking that Rose remembered that Dukas and Emma had arrived and left together and that something was going on.

LATER, Dukas lay on his back in the dark. Emma was lying half on him, her head on his chest, and he could feel her hair on his bare skin. He thought she was asleep and he was sliding off into sleep himself when she said, "I was married once."

"No kidding."

"It only lasted two years." He felt her raise her head and shake her hair back; her head was dimly silhouetted against a window. "Doomed to failure. Two lawyers."

He thought about that. He thought about it so long he thought she might have fallen asleep, but he said, "What's doomed if you loved each other?" and he heard her laugh, a kind of wheezing, ratchety sound that didn't seem as if she made it often, and she said, "Love? Christ almighty, Mike. Grow up."

She was different in the dark. Her voice was lower, quieter, and she wasn't on the attack. She had that laugh, and of course sex. *Great* sex. He suspected that this separation of light and dark might have had a lot to do with the failure of a marriage, as if perhaps both of them had been like that, and if both weren't in the dark at the same time, there it went. "I never been married," he said.

"Lucky you." She raised her head against the window again, then pulled herself up until she was looking down at where his eyes must have been for her, perhaps even seeing some glint of reflection from the window in them. "You're in love with Siciliano, aren't you?" she said.

He thought about it. There was no good answer, given the situation. "I guess so," he said. "But it's meaningless."

Again, she laughed. "Love? I thought you believed in love. Now it's meaningless?"

"She loves her husband. And he's my friend. What I fee——nothing can come of it, you see?"

She lowered her head on his shoulder. "So, her husband dies somewhere, you wouldn't go to her like a shot?"

In fact, he'd thought about that question. It came down to sex, he thought, and he didn't see Rose and him like this. Once, he had. Now, something different had happened between them. Not that they had passed beyond sex, but he thought of her now seriously, as his friend's wife, as the mother of two kids. Would he go like a shot to father her children? To take Al's place in her life, in her bed? No, he wouldn't, because he'd seen her as a woman who loved one man, and he knew he would never be the man.

He started to tell Emma that, but this time she was asleep.

In the morning, she was grouchy and he was quiet; neither of them morning people, they avoided crashing into each other in the small apartment, drank coffee in silence, listened to NPR as they dressed. As she was rushing for the door, he said, "One thing, Emma."

"I'm in a hurry."

"Forget what was said about George Shreed. You never heard of George Shreed. Okay?"

She sighed too loud and too long, the sigh a child makes when given housework.

Dukas put a hand on her shoulder. "It's too early to go sniffing around Shreed. If you do, you could screw everything—okay? Leave it for a while."

She gave him a crooked grin. " 'Trust me'?"

"Yeah, trust me."

She shrugged. "Okay."

"*Promise?*"

She swung toward the door. "Oh, *puh-leeze!*"

BY EIGHT, Emma Pasternak already looked frazzled, even seedy, but her day was only starting. She threw her suit jacket on a couch, ran her hand through her already messy hair, and collapsed into her desk chair. Bashing a laptop into submission, she began to make phone calls from the list in her scheduler. The first one was to the investigator she had hired for Rose's case.

"Hey," she said. She didn't wait for a response. "This is Pasternak. I got something for you; I want it followed up priority. Yeah, yeah, I know you got other work; push it back in the queue. What I got is a name, I want everything on it, I mean everything—go back to birth records, schools, the whole nine yards. Okay? Name: George Shreed. He's now at CIA, pretty high up. What we're gonna do is get all the shit that's fit to print and hit him with it—scare him to a near-death experience. If he caves, I think we're golden. Okay? Go for it."

USS *Thomas Jefferson.*

When Rafe sent the word that the brief for the admiral was finally a go, Alan threw his notes into a presentable briefing in a rush. He dragged the new officer, Soleck, into his preparations, because it was obvious that Soleck could find his way around a computer, and he was still so new that he didn't have the sense to stay out of Alan's way.

Most of the squadron commanders and a sizable portion of the flag staff were at the brief. The admiral glanced at him several times while other officers delivered readiness reports, his face unreadable. When his time came, Alan went to the front, squared his shoulders, and went for it.

"Good evening, Admiral. I'm going to cover the capabilities of the MARI system and how it can act as a force multiplier for the BG."

"Go ahead, Commander Craik."

"Inverse Synthetic Aperture Radar was fitted on all of the S-3bs in the late 1980s. That allowed us to do long-distance recognition of targets and greatly aided over-the-horizon targeting. MARI, or Multiple Axis Radar Imaging, uses the latest developments in computer-image modeling to allow several ISAR systems to link and provide a sharper, 3-D image. With multiple-axis imaging and a lot of new software, we can get a synthetic-aperture picture of a stable object, like a surface-to-air missile site, a hangar, or a tank."

"How fine is the resolution?" the flag captain said. He didn't sound hostile, at least.

"The contractors say one meter, but I don't think it's there yet, sir. Just before we left Pax River, we got an across-the-board software upgrade that ought to improve both processing time and resolution. I'll be able to tell you more when we've implemented it."

"Have you flown it?"

"Once, sir."

"What's your reaction?"

"It still drops link too often to be considered reliable. I'm not a computer expert, but I think the volume of data exceeds the bandwidth available." Alan glanced at Soleck, who nodded. Soleck had the confidence of a puppy—a newbie who hadn't even flown with the system yet.

Admiral Kessler nodded at him but didn't smile. "I appreciate the straight talk. However, I'm not ready to let your aircraft go over Bosnia. Seems like a high risk in terms of aircrew while you're not sure of the technical side." The admiral looked around at Rafe for his opinion.

"Sorry, Al, but I've got to concur." Rafe looked apologetic. He knew as well as Alan that what the det needed was real-world action.

Alan tried to be persuasive. "Sir, when it works, it's a powerful tool. We'd be able to detect SAM sites, even when they were in passive mode. With the ESM suite, we can catch a radar when it's on and then track it even when it's off."

That got the attention of the F-18 skippers.

"And pass targeting?" one of them said.

"Down to the meter."

But the admiral wouldn't have it. "Then I suggest you get the link fully functional and find your bandwidth."

"Yes, sir."

"Give it your full attention, Craik. Do you understand me?"

It wasn't said with hostility, but the tone carried some nuance. Behind the admiral, Maggiulli gave a slight nod. Meaning, *Cut the NCIS crap and spike the rumors about you and your wife and get with the program!*

"Any other business? Okay, folks, have a good evening." The admiral rose and slipped away, and the rest of the officers stood at attention until he was gone and then moved around Alan and out into the passageway. Alan left the computer to Soleck and followed Rafe, who stopped in the p'way and gave him a slight smile.

"That the late Mister Soleck?"

"He knows computers."

"But not calendars, apparently."

"Rafe, I got a whole detachment of guys here to fly real-world. Everybody else will be racking up air medals while we drill holes in the water. We can *help*."

"Get the link fixed, Al." Rafe gave a small shrug. "Maybe we can have coffee after."

"I've got a flight."

Alan stepped through the bulkhead at frame 81 and turned toward the ready room, to find Soleck jabbering at the female intelligence officer from the EA-6B squadron. When he saw Alan, he waved at the woman, picked up the laptop that had held the brief, and followed.

"That Mary Rennig sure is cute," he said, bright as a new dime.

"Soleck, do you always say every word that comes into your head? Ensign Rennig is an officer in the US Navy."

"Oh—right, sir! Sorry. Anyway, she got me all these great recognition cards!" Soleck held out a complete set of ship and aircraft recognition cards as they ducked through the ready room door, Soleck still talking. "So I'm going to correlate all the recognition cards with the simulator. Chief Navarro says the recognition library on the simulator is 'sparse' and I'm going to input a bunch of new ships."

"Mister Soleck, are you telling me that you are going to add data to a simulator?"

"Well, yes, sir. I mean, all the stuff on how to do it's in the manual."

"How do you know what the radar returns from a ship will look like?"

"Well—jeez, sir, it's—"

Alan remembered a phrase from high school geometry—*intuitively obvious.* Could Soleck possibly be so good that blue-skying radar images was intuitively obvious?

"Better show me before you put them up." Alan felt like patting him on the head.

Washington.

While Alan Craik was dealing with Soleck and Emma Pasternak was talking to her investigator, Mike Dukas was having an outdoor meeting with Harry O'Neill at the Metro Center subway entrance. Without shaking hands, he said, "Sorry to interrupt your day, Harry." He hadn't explained anything on the telephone.

"Make it quick, m'man, I got a meeting with some rich Arabs."

"This isn't about Rose. Something else has come up. I want you to cover for Al Craik on a meeting with a contact."

O'Neill smiled. "I only do that stuff for money now, Mike."

Dukas dug out a crumpled dollar bill and held it out. "I need somebody to cover your best friend."

"Mike, you've got an entire organization behind you!"

"And no budget, and, more to the point, no faith that I can keep it just between some stranger and me and not have it wander off to ONI or, God help us, the Agency." He hunched his shoulders. "Why do you think we're meeting out here like a couple of spooks, for Christ's sake?" He sketched out what had happened to Alan in Trieste, then said that the woman wanted a second meeting in Naples. "Naples NCIS is strung out to begin with, and with his carrier in port, they'll be running around like jumping beans. You know how to do it. You're available."

"Mike, I'm a CEO."

"Nobody's perfect. Come on, he saved your life!"

O'Neill looked at the dollar bill, still in Dukas's hand. "The pay isn't very good."

"It isn't pay; it's an honorarium."

O'Neill laughed. He curled Dukas's fingers back around the bill. "My contribution to the NCIS coffee fund. What do you want me to do?"

Dukas laid it out—finding a route in Naples, arranging the meeting, looking for countersurveillance and bad guys.

O'Neill glanced at his watch. "But make it clear I'm a contract employee, right? Fax me a contract in Nairobi; I want cover if it goes bad." He held out his hand. "Only for Alan and Rose, man." He strode away.

Langley.

George Shreed was sitting in the office of Clyde Partlow. His grief was now taking the form of a kind of psychological sadism, turned against anybody he happened to be with—at the moment, Partlow. On some organizational charts, Partlow was his boss and on others his equal. Right now, Shreed was having sadistic fun making Partlow sweat.

The subject was China. They had just come from a briefing on the deteriorating situation along the Kashmir border and Shreed had murmured to Partlow that they needed to talk "because of the China thing." References like that always scared Partlow—"the China thing" sounded like dragons, or maybe Doctor Fu Manchu's exploding mushrooms.

"The Chinks won't say boo!" Partlow was saying now. He waved an empty pipe. A tall man going a little to fat, he favored suspenders and bright shirts and a boyish haircut—what Shreed called his *Stover at Yale* look. "The buildup is just saber-rattling."

Shreed didn't at all care what Partlow believed; what he was trying to do was set up his own Chinese operation. The India–Pakistan confrontation was looking more and more like an opportunity for him, but he had to make sure that the Chinese were really into it and that they would go over the edge into a confrontation with the United States if they were pushed hard enough. And the way to push was to goose the White House into sweating about China while goosing the Chinese to sweat about the US. "I think we should be prepared for a Chinese insertion into the India–Pakistan thing, and I think—only a suggestion— that we should float an operation past the National Security Council to see where they stand."

Partlow winced. "Where they stand is they don't want to get sucked into anything!"

"I think the Agency could gain back a lot of ground by being right about China this time, Clyde. If we float an idea now, at least they'll remember afterward that we said the Chinks would go all the way on this one."

"They *won't* go all the way!" Partlow had a nasal voice that often sounded like a whine, less often like a whinny. "Will they?"

"Well, we probably ought to point out that the Taiwanese will think it's a fine time to do something really stupid. If the Chinese are involved in the west, maybe ready to use nukes—"

"Oh, my God—!"

"The least we can do is suggest that an American battle group off Taiwan would remind Taipei to withdraw their head from their ass."

"George, an American battle group off Taiwan would *provoke* the Chinese!"

"Not if they're involved with India and Pakistan."

They went round and round, but, as he knew he would, Shreed succeeded in planting in Partlow's head the idea that he had better cover his ass by floating some possibilities at the White House. The whole business so upset Partlow that he excused himself and went off to the men's room.

During his absence, Shreed, who had a better bladder, stood up and looked over Partlow's desk, searching for useful items. He found what he was looking for next to the photo of Partlow's wife: a trophy memo pad from the Director of National Security. It wasn't to use, but only to show off—special paper, embossed seal, eyes-only classification. Shreed had always refused one as slightly tacky, but now he had a use for exactly that thing.

He reached across the desk and tore off two sheets, surprised again to find that he was trembling. *Losing my nerve,* he thought. It was a kind of inward joke to hide from himself the fact that he was frightened all the time now.

When Partlow came back, Shreed was sitting again in the visitor's chair. Partlow looked scrubbed and pink. "I don't like this, George," he said.

"It's a golden opportunity. Should we or should we not cook up an

ops plan to penetrate the highest echelons of the Chinese Communist
Party and the People's Army to find out if they'll shoot when a US ship is
in their sights?"

"Oh, George!" Partlow said. This time he was whining.

NCIS HQ.

Dukas, back from the meeting with O'Neill and trying to pull together the ideas that had been aired in Rose's motel room, came down
the corridor of NCIS headquarters from an office where he'd borrowed
a telephone. He'd made a lot of calls and set a lot of things in motion,
but he didn't feel that he knew a thing. Now, rounding the doorway into
the small office where his typing table stood, he went to the prissy black
guy's desk.

"Phone is not available," the guy said. He put his hand on the telephone to show it was his.

"You Triffler?" Dukas said.

"Yeah."

"You're my new assistant." Dukas smiled. "You're sitting at my new
desk. Please take your hand off my new telephone." He jerked his head
toward the typing table. "Move."

"My effing A!"

"Yeah, life is hard." Dukas dropped a folder in front of the man. "Your
first job—a lieutenant-commander named Rose Siciliano. Do the
paperwork—make a budget, read my report, do a tentative walk-the-
cat-back for a September fifteen Overview Assessment. Get on it, because it needs to be done today."

"I don't take orders from you!"

"You do now. Go see your former boss, third office on the left. He'll
explain to you what the Director of NCIS just explained to him. Now,
please—I need the telephone." He grinned. The guy bolted from the
room, and Dukas sat at his new desk. He took a folder from under his
arm and threw it down on the desk, where it fell open to reveal a Navy
officer's personnel folder. The cover said "Crystal Insight." The personnel
folder said "Rose Siciliano."

USS *Thomas Jefferson.*

Trying to bring the MARI system up to speed. Alan had got Reilley to find them a dedicated frequency, and it made a difference. Stevens had flown the tech reps from the manufacturer twice, and they swore they could have a patch in a week, which was six days too long for Alan. Several of them were huddled around their own equipment in the back of the ready room at all hours, talking about code and parameters. They didn't make much sense to Alan, but he noticed that both Campbell and Soleck understood them, and he got one or the other to give him plain-language reports on their progress.

Whenever Alan looked up, Soleck was there with a question. After one day, Soleck seemed to love everything about the boat, and his puppy-dog curiosity and enthusiasm would have been infectious if Alan had not had so much on his mind. Alan found himself snapping at Soleck because he made such a ready target, but another sleepless night in his stateroom chewing over the problems that surrounded him—his career, Rose, his detachment—suggested to him that Soleck was not the proper target. In fact, Soleck, despite his terrible youthfulness, was something like a genius. By his second flight, he had mastered the multifunction keys that older and wiser men avoided. He could get the constantly dropped link back in seconds. He even knew something about bandwidth and antennas, and the crews were jury-rigging bigger antennas on both planes to meet some new specs that Campbell, Soleck, and the reps had designed.

Prepping for a flight of his own, Alan was on his way to meteorology, Soleck padding behind, explaining the new idea. Alan bumped into somebody.

"Buddy, you lost?" Rafe was standing in front of him, holding a kneeboard.

"You take up a lot of p'way," said Alan, trying to make a joke of it.

"You seem pretty far away, Al. That puppy one of yours?"

"LTjg Soleck, this is Captain Rafehausen, the CAG."

"Wow, have I heard of you, sir!"

"Soleck, I feel like I already know you. Have a nice flight out from Norfolk?"

"It was great! We had a layover in—"

Soleck was not getting the message. "I think the CAG is looking for an apology for missing movement, Mister Soleck."

"Oh, right, uh, sorry, sir. Yeah, I dicked that up."

"Yes, you did. You following Commander Craik to metro?"

"He said he'd show me where to get the preflight stuff. He said they have a window!"

The window was a standing joke to aviators. Metro had one of the few portholes on the ship, a large Plexiglas window that looked out over the flight deck and the weather. Because most of the rest of the ship was in a perpetual half-dark, this window gave metro an unbeatable advantage in predicting the weather. Most sailors could tell day from night only by their watches.

"Soleck, go up one ladder and take a look out the window. Get the preflight and meet Commander Craik in the ready room, okay?"

"Roger that, sir."

"Alan, with me." Alan followed Rafe back down the flag passageway, down a ladder, and into the familiar country around the ready rooms where the CAG had his office. Rafe led the way in, handed Alan a cup of coffee from a Thermos, and shut the door. Seconds later there was knocking. Rafe shouted "Later!" and sat down facing Alan. "The admiral's cooled down some; the flag captain's more or less on your side. I've kept my mouth shut because I knew you were under a lot of stress, but now I want to know what's going on with you and NCIS and this shit in Trieste. Okay, give."

Alan thought through his responses. "Not mine to give."

"Who was the guy you shot in Trieste?"

"Rafe—"

"Nope, I'm not playing. I know that you and Rose aren't fucking spies, Al. I know it. I'm trying to make sure other people know it. You are *not* helping, walking around with your head in the fucking clouds. Granted, your det begins to look better, although it couldn't have looked worse. I want your *whole* focus on that det, Al."

Alan met Rafe's eye and took the plunge. Rafe was a friend. He was not part of an investigation.

"Okay, I'll do this the best I can, Rafe." He summarized what he knew about Rose's trials. Then he jumped to Trieste. "Some woman walked up to shore patrol, claimed to be Rose, and said she'd wait for me in a café. I followed and walked in on a hit. Four guys shooting the place up. I thought Rose was inside and took action. The woman made the time to make contact with me and took off."

"She was *waitin'* for you?"

"Yeah. She's supposed to meet me in Naples. That's strictly between us. I have NCIS clearance to meet her, okay?"

Rafe slumped a little in his chair, his lanky frame bent at an unnatural angle and one of his legs thrown over the arm.

"And you're all hot to meet her in Naples."

"I am not all hot to—"

"Buddy, listen to me real close. This is your job, right here. This det. Tell NCIS to chase this chick on their own. Dealing with her *is not your job*, hear me?"

"Rafe—" Alan found his throat closing.

"No."

"I have to meet her this time. I'll tell Mike I'm out of it after that."

"And then I'll have one hundred percent of Al Craik?"

"Yes!"

"Come tell me when you've told NCIS to do their own work." He scowled. "Better yet, tell me when this MARI system is up and working and you can join the rest of the Navy."

9

USS *Thomas Jefferson.*

ALAN WAS IN THE BACK END, IN THE TACCO SEAT, where his flying days had started. Stevens was the pilot, with the nugget, Soleck, as copilot. Master Chief Craw was in the SENSO seat, and he and Alan were busy working the MARI gear at every target that offered. Off the port wing about seven miles, 902 was also airborne, her port engine restored.

The image of an Italian cruise liner was clean on their screens, with the central superstructure crisply edged and a small glow of radar haze amidships at the swimming pool. The sharp sweep of the bow was perfectly delineated; the radar mast on the superstructure projected so clearly that each of the ship's surface-search radars could be located. It was the sort of shot that technology firms put in advertisements in *Jane's Defense Weekly.*

"AH 902, come to 180. Keep it slow."

"Roger." Seven miles to the west, the other MARI plane made a slow turn to the south. The aspect of the cruise liner changed slowly, from a beam-on shot to a stern-quarter one.

"Stevens, turn east. Turn easy."

"Roger." The S-3 made a gradual course correction. Stevens added power fractionally to maintain altitude. Alan watched the image. It continued to rotate very slowly.

"AH 902, climb one thousand."

"Roger."

The image changed only fractionally; the cruise ship was so far away that a thousand feet of altitude didn't change the attitude of the image by much. Alan watched it. The image remained steady.

"Stevens, take us through a harder turn to the north."

"Roger." The engine whine increased as the pilot added power, and the g-force of the turn pushed Alan back into his seat. It wasn't the hardest turn the S-3 could make, but it was fast enough. The image disappeared. Alan watched the screen. Seconds after Stevens leveled them off, the link was back, and the image floated there again, as perfect as before.

"Not bad." It was a lot better than not bad. They could hold an image for minutes without losing their link, because they had a dedicated channel and a new antenna mounted on the top of the fuselage to carry the link. They had increased bandwidth.

"The auto-resync works." Soleck had sat with the tech reps while they wrote the patch. He never claimed to have done it himself, but Alan credited him with making the idea a reality. "We only lose the link in tight turns. I wonder if the antenna would be better off on the bottom of the plane—"

"Talk it up with the tech reps when we land. Chief—"

"Fuck!" Stevens bellowed. Alan felt the plane sag.

"Hydraulics!" Alan could see Stevens fighting the yoke.

Alan reached in his helmet bag and opened the emergency procedures manual to "Hydraulics Failure."

Suburban Virginia.

George Shreed slept only a few hours a night, those hours often broken by stints at his computers. He had slept even less since Janey's departure for the hospice. Fear of discovery, which he had never expected in himself, gnawed at him at night, and he wondered at it—why should he be scared, if he didn't care whether he lived or died? Why, if the thing he had most cared about was dead, should he fear being caught? But there it was, as bone-deep as hunger, the animal in him running from the predator.

Lying awake in the hours after two A.M., he planned his Chinese operation and used its details to smother his fear: as he'd told Partlow, India and Pakistan were shooting at each other again in Kashmir, close to the Chinese border, with the Pakistanis moving army units up to support the rebels they'd armed in Kashmir itself. The Indians had beefed up their air presence. In Szhinjiang, the westernmost Chinese province and the one closest to the action, two divisions of the People's Army were coming in by railroad with heavy artillery and armor. Engineers were extending the runway at Yehjeng. Rumors were circulating about nuclear warheads on the missiles in the Taklamakan sites, but there was no confirmation. Shreed was doing what he could to lend credibility to the rumors.

He needed to have the Chinese at a crisis point before he pulled out their bank accounts.

And what he needed for a crisis point was American involvement, so that when he emptied the Chinese bank accounts, they'd know the US was behind it.

To get to that point, however, he had to do more.

Shreed got out of bed and dragged himself to his study. It was almost four. In a locked drawer of his desk were the two sheets of NSC memo paper he had stolen from Partlow's desk. One was still blank, his backup; the other had a word-processed memo from the National Security Advisor—forged by Shreed, of course—that needed only the signature. Shreed had even made sure that the printer he had used was the same kind used at NSC, because he knew the Chinese would check—as they would check the paper and even the ink on the embossed letterhead.

The forged memo was short and simple. It told the Director of National Intelligence that under no circumstances would the United States confront China at this time.

Shreed took a pen from a box in the same locked drawer. He had pens in there from the desk of the President, from the office of DNI, from the Joint Chiefs. And from the NSC. His Chinese masters would check that, too, he knew.

He practiced the Advisor's signature several more times, and then, without hesitation, he scrawled the name at the bottom of the memo. After comparing it with an original, he went to one of his three computers and scanned the forged memo in an added it to an already encrypted message headed "Laundryman—Your Eyes Only."

Laundryman was Chen, the control who had started as his partner and who had turned into his evil genius, demanding more and more and more.

Well, now he would get his fill.

"The enclosed reached me yesterday. It is of the utmost importance. I urge immediate transmission to the highest levels of government. Acknowledge. Top Hook."

He embedded the encrypted message and attachment in a pixel and sent it on its way as part of a pornographic image, as he had been sending his messages for four years.

And then he went back to bed and slept for almost an hour, temporarily purged of his fear by the knowledge that he had started the movement toward the end.

Now Chen would report the memo, but he would give it a low reliability until it had been vetted.

As part of the vetting he would demand to have the original, and he would demand a face-to-face meeting with Shreed, because that was what his masters would demand of him.

And when they met, Shreed, who never forgot a grievance and who hated Chen for the years of exploitation, would kill him.

Det Aircraft AH 901.

By the time the F-14 came under them, they had a good idea of the level of the emergency. The F-14 pilot said that there was a hydraulic fluid leak somewhere in the landing gear strut. Stevens had noted, quite dispassionately, that the controls were sluggish and unresponsive.

"We've got tons of fuel, right?" Alan was leaning forward, already out of his harness.

"Yep." Stevens was wound tight. Not panicked, very professional, but tight.

"Why don't we try and deploy the gear now?"

"Three hundred miles from the ship?"

"And three hundred from Sigonella, Paul. If we can't get the gear locked—" He meant, if they didn't get the gear locked and they landed on the boat, they'd go into the net, at best, and ruin the aircraft. If they went to the US Naval Air Station at Sigonella, Sicily, they might bring her back alive.

"Roger that. You know the drill?"

Alan didn't rise to the jab, if it was a jab. Craw had already stripped out the long handle that could be used to hand-crank the landing gear, given time and sweat. Soleck told the F-14 that they were going to try and deploy the gear. Alan had rotated the infrared camera but couldn't get it to rest on the gear—every time it reached the spot, it rotated past.

"Soleck, is that Chris Donitz in the Tomcat?" Even through the static of encrypted comms, Donitz's voice was distinctive.

"Sorry, sir, I don't know him."

Alan ran his thumb down the comm card, nodded, and clicked through his radio options until he was in the net.

"Northway One, can you see my FLIR camera?"

"Wait one. Roger. Fully deployed, but it has some kind of wire wrapped around it."

"Copy. Doughnuts, is our gear deploying?"

"About halfway down. Belay my last—starboard gear is still deploying. Starboard gear appears to be down and locked. Port gear about half deployed."

Stevens rocked the wings several times, hard.

"Any movement?"

"Negative."

Alan switched his comms to "cockpit." "Paul, I think we should go have a beer in Sigonella, but you're the pilot."

Stevens hesitated, then turned his head.

"If we go to the boat, we'll have to put her in the net. Even if we think the gear is locked. Then we have no det; we can't do this with one plane." He seemed to think Alan hadn't foreseen that.

Alan ignored the comment and said mildly, trying to make a joke of it, "Great minds . . ."

"Whatever. Crank that thing for all you're worth. I'll get the tower at Sigonella."

Rafe came on and supported their decision to go for NAS Sigonella; he sent the F-14 with them, and had a VS-53 S-3 with more gas head straight for Sicily to tank them again over the field. Stevens turned down that idea.

"I want to land as near empty as I can." He sounded tense, almost high. "I got a plan."

They took gas from AH 902, increasing their margin of error en route, and turned for Sicily. Donitz's F-14 was a presence, marginally reassuring, just off their starboard wingtip.

Alan had never experienced such a slow crisis. They had hours to play with the systems, to try every combination they could imagine to deploy the gear; each raised hopes but nothing worked. The air-conditioning and the altitude couldn't rid Alan of the sweat he produced, turning the crank. It wasn't such hard work, but the space was cramped the crank handle tore his hands, and, when he switched off with Craw, the sweat immediately turned cold. After an hour, it took both of them to turn the crank. When Donitz informed them that he hadn't seen the port gear budge since his last call, they took a weary break.

"It's jammed solid," Craw said. "I can't even get the crank to turn. It ought to turn easy—not fast, but easy."

"Done this before?" The ghost of a chuckle. In fact, they'd both done it before, together.

"What's the deal?" called Stevens from the front.

"What you see is what you get. We'll give it another heave, but we think the gear is jammed."

"No hydraulic fluid and jammed, too. Fuck."

"Hey, I'm not worried, the pilot said he had a plan." The amusement in Alan's voice was genuine, but Stevens didn't rise to it.

"I'm going to cut Donitz loose," Stevens said. "He can hit the tanker and head home."

"Keep him for five more minutes, so we can cycle the gear one more time."

"Sorry, I'd rather not."

Alan thought over various replies, but his status as mission commander was not the issue here. Stevens needed his support landing the plane, not a pointless argument. Besides, despite Alan's expertise, Stevens was the pilot.

"Why?"

"What if the starboard gear reads a 'retract'?"

Alan couldn't imagine such a thing, but the S-3 was a cranky beast at the best of times, and with no hydraulic fluid, who knew what mechanical miscues could happen?

"And you think you can land this bird as is."

"I know I can."

"How much damage?"

"I'm doing the best I can!"

Alan looked out the window. It was an emergency where there was too much time to think. What he thought about was this sorry detachment he had been given, and Stevens, the most difficult man in it. He and Stevens were as close to enemies as people who worked together could be. Alan thought about the man, his insecurity, his perpetual scowl. At least nobody had ever said that Stevens couldn't fly.

ALAN WATCHED the sea go past his window, then watched the volcano. Nelson had operated here and chased Emma Hamilton. He watched the first hedgerows of Sicily, saw a vineyard and sheep, and wondered if he would get to see them from the ground. It looked pastoral, safe, and close enough to touch. Then the runway filled the viewscreen and the landing was on them, and, despite a temptation to keep his eyes on the sheep, Alan snapped around to the business of the landing. The plane was at treetop height, moving at one hundred and twenty knots, just above stall speed, and descending so gently as to make the motion imperceptible. He glanced back at the fields, warm and totally separate from the freezing sweat and old electric smell of a damaged plane seconds from touchdown.

"Ejection positions," Stevens said. They all pulled their knees together. Alan and Craw crossed their hands over their chests and nodded their heads forward. Alan glanced one more time around his space—yes, the FLIR was retracted, the landing gear handle stowed, everything as secure as possible. He looked out the window one more time at the other, sunlit world.

Stevens set them down on the starboard gear with the softest possible touch, and it held. By constantly manipulating a combination of power settings and flaps he kept the plane rolling on its one solid strut for hundreds of yards, until the plane was simply too slow to stay up; then it collapsed slowly on the half-deployed starboard wing, like an elephant kneeling. The port gear collapsed then against the remaining pressure of the hydraulic fluid, and the plane's weight came to rest on the buddy store under the port wing. The plane slewed wildy, the drag on the port side exceeding the braking of the starboard gear, then turned hard to port, tipped—

And stopped. Stevens cut the engines; the turbofans wound down, but in the cockpit there was no sound. Then Soleck whooped like a Hollywood Apache. They piled out the crew hatch to the tarmac as fire trucks came screaming up. Alan ran around the plane looking for flames.

"No foam! Don't let them use foam!"

The crash crew was already pulling at hoses. Stevens took his meaning immediately, as did Craw: fire-retardant foam was highly corrosive. The fire crew could yet destroy the aircraft that Stevens had landed so well. The three of them ran toward the trucks, standing between the wounded plane and the crash crew.

"No foam!"

"You sure?" The crew chief. He was trying to hustle them away from the plane.

"My authority!" Alan wasn't sure he had any authority over a crash crew at NAS Sigonella, but they backed away. Crewmen took smaller extinguishers and walked around the plane. In minutes, they reported it safe.

Then he watched with Stevens as the plane was dragged a few feet to clear the runway. Right now, with the fuselage resting on the wreck of the buddy store and the collapsed gear, the plane looked pretty bad, but Alan knew that it was better than it looked.

"Now I see why you wanted to land empty."

"If the buddy store had too much gas, and the friction cracked it, we'd've fireballed." Stevens was shaking a little—now. Now was fine.

"That was beautiful, Paul."

"Yeah?"

"We can have this bird back in the air in twenty-four hours."

"That's all you care about, right? Nice job, Stevens—you saved Craik's ass."

"Paul, it was a great piece of flying!"

Two seconds of silence gave Alan just time to think he had gotten through.

"That means a lot, from a guy with your experience as a pilot."

Alan stopped as if he'd been hit, but Stevens walked away.

And that was the end of his attempt to woo Stevens. He looked at the crippled plane, which leaned on its left wing like an image of the crippled detachment. It had been a great job of flying, but it wasn't enough.

"Mister Stevens!" he shouted. Soleck and Craw jerked their heads around. Stevens slowed, stopped, turned.

Alan crossed the space between them with huge strides. He didn't stop until they were eye-to-eye and he knew his own coffee-soured breath was up Stevens's nose.

"You are a hell of a pilot, but you are a lousy officer and a major cause of trouble in this detachment. Morale is shit, maintenance is lousy, and the system doesn't work right—and those things got that way on your watch! Now." Alan lowered his head a little but didn't take his eyes from Stevens's. "You are going to have this aircraft airworthy and on the deck of the *Jefferson* by 1600 hours tomorrow or you are through with this detachment. *And* you are going to get your ass to the communications office of this air base *right now* and you are going to order the det's maintenance chief and his two best mechanics and a new landing gear to be flown here ASAP by our other aircraft! *And* you are going to inform the maintenance chief and the two mechanics that if this plane isn't on the deck of the *Jefferson* at 1600 hours tomorrow, they *also* are through with this det. Do it!"

Stevens's mouth was tightened up like a twisted rubber glove. His eyes left Alan's, came back, left. Abruptly, he turned on his heel and headed for the terminal building.

"Mister Stevens!"

Stevens stopped but kept his back turned.

"Did you hear and understand my orders?"

"Yeah." He started off again.

"Mister Stevens!"

Stevens whirled. "What the hell?"

"Did you hear and understand what I said?"

"Sure I did."

"Then say 'Aye, aye, sir.' "

Stevens paused for a fraction of a moment, but training beat anger. "Aye aye, sir."

"Carry on, Mister Stevens."

Alan turned back to the aircraft. Craw was being busy under the fuselage, but Soleck was staring at Alan, who strode toward the plane without looking back.

"Soleck!"

Soleck jumped. "Sir?"

Alan stopped. "You *will* make sure you are on the return flight of our aircraft to the *Jefferson* with Senior Chief Craw. You *will* work all night there to finalize the new link and installation of the new antenna with the tech reps, now that we know it works. You understand me?"

Soleck jumped again. "Yes, sir!"

Alan walked to the aircraft as Craw climbed out from underneath. Their eyes met. "This goddam detachment is going to get its shit together or I'm going to put every goddam man in it on report!" Alan said.

Craw smiled. "Now you're talkin', Skipper."

10

Suburban Virginia.

THE OLD COMMONWEALTH TAVERN WAS SET BACK from the highway next to a strip mall. It wasn't much on the outside, an old brick house that had had a new front unwisely glued on, with an extension out the back that was no better. But inside it was cool and dark, with islands of light from small lamps, and hunt prints and a lot of old fly-fishing tackle that suggested vaguely English, vaguely country associations. Deep within was a small room that Menzes had called "the hole."

"Hard spot to find," Dukas said, sitting down opposite Menzes. The room was only about ten by twelve, unoccupied except for them. They were actually behind the old kitchen fireplace.

They talked about old houses, and then Menzes said, "I'm sorry about what happened." He waited until Dukas had ordered a dark beer, and, leaning back in his imitation Windsor chair, murmured, "I did as I was told."

Dukas nodded.

"You running the NCIS investigation?" Menzes said.

Dukas nodded again.

"Not my business, but aren't you a little close to it?"

Dukas, head lowered, looked up at him. "When we investigate our own, we're trying as much to save them as convict them. I just got

myself an assistant who doesn't like me at all, so he'll keep me honest."
Dukas picked at the label of his beer. "You want to tell me about this
case?"

Menzes gave him a half-grin, neither happy nor amused. He didn't
know what he wanted, he meant, or maybe he knew what he wanted but
didn't know how to get to it.

Dukas said, "I need this intercept you told me about."

"You'll get it. By the book."

"That could be a couple months. How about we go back to your office, you let me look at it there?"

Menzes shook his head.

"Jesus Christ, you guys toss us an investigation and then you don't
provide the backup? What the hell, you trying to obstruct?"

"Don't talk like an asshole."

"Don't treat me like a dickhead. I need the evidence, or whatever you
guys call it." He peeled some of the label and decided he was going about
it wrong. Menzes didn't want the Agency attacked, even though he was
mad at the Agency; he wanted to help—maybe—but not for free. So
Dukas jerked his head and smiled, as if to say, *Okay, I made a mistake*,
and he took a drink and said, "Right now, it'd help me if you just *summarized* the intercept. Anything. Like—intercept of what?"

"Wireless digital transmission."

"NSA?"

Menzes made a little head bob: *Of course.*

"To Siciliano by name?"

"Unh-unh. No header; it's only a partial, starts with a sentence
doesn't make sense, then you get from context that it's a commendation. Code name Top Hook. Magnificent performance previous three
years, promotion to rank of Senior Major-Colonel, money, et cetera.
Congratulations on graduating Naval War College after outstanding performance as helicopter pilot and participation in Project Peacemaker.
Data passed to us on Peacemaker crucial to our understanding of US in-
tentions in first decade of twenty-first century. Congratulations, felicita-
tions, applause, applause, applause."

Dukas drank again. "Pretty good fit with Siciliano."

"Funny about that."

"Where's it from?"

"We think China."

Dukas contemplated the beer bottle. " 'Course you know it stinks."

Menzes only looked at him. He was wearing a jacket today, still a white shirt and tie. He looked neat and fit and intelligent, like an educated cop who was going to make at least captain.

"Did this by chance come in clear?" Dukas said.

"Encrypted."

"Which you just by chance were able to bust."

"Repeat of an old code."

"Jeez, that was lucky for you guys, huh! Wow." He drank. "Well, you know it stinks." He drank some more, found the bottle almost empty. He and Menzes exchanged a look; Menzes reached over and pushed a button on the plastered wall; a waitress appeared.

"Let me tell you what I think is going down," Dukas said when the waitress had gone. "Here it is: you guys think you got a spy, a mole, a whatever in your own agency. You haven't flushed him or her, you think you're getting close, and you don't want to spook him. You think a nice, noisy investigation of somebody else may give your mole a little sense of security, maybe a year's peace to let you get close, maybe even get to the point where you put a TV monitor in his or her office and a bug on all his phones and maybe in his house, and shit, then you're only two to five years from an arrest. Am I right?"

The beers arrived. Menzes didn't look at him but growled, "I won't say you're wrong."

"You're making a fucking stalking-horse of a fine naval officer!"

"What's the loss of the best officer in the Navy compared to what a spy within the Agency can do day after day, year after year, for twenty years?"

They both drank, and Dukas and Menzes exchanged glances, still trying to know each other, still not there. Finally, Dukas said, "You got a short list for your mole?"

"No comment."

"Is the name George Shreed on your short list?"

It was a shot in the dark, only because of the Telephone Woman's call, and Menzes didn't answer—except that he didn't answer in a way that was itself an answer. For an instant, his face went rigid; he covered almost at once, but there was the residue of a look almost of panic there, of something as unexpected as a sucker punch. Dukas was set back on his heels; a whole new idea burst open: *Holy shit. George Shreed as a spy?*

It didn't make sense, but it made perfect sense—opportunity, motive: Shreed frames Rose to protect himself. He knows Peacemaker; he has all the data, all the files. He gets a contact in China, maybe his control, to send the phony intercept, which was created only to be intercepted. It made perfect sense—except that Dukas didn't have a shred of evidence that Shreed was a spy.

But Carl Menzes maybe did.

Dukas tried to step very carefully. "This sort of leaves me with the half-empty glass and you with the half-full one. We pour them together, you know, and—"

"The word is, 'No extraordinary help.' Not even if your lady lawyer there goes ballistic. She wants to make her case in the *Post,* that's her call."

"In fact," Dukas said with a grin, "since you guys had this change of heart, you'd prefer she did just that, am I right? More smoke screen to convince your him-or-her that the pressure's off. But that's the end of it?—that's where you come down, 'No extraordinary help,' end of conversation?"

Menzes sighed. "I believe in the Agency, Dukas. With all its faults, and I know what they are, it has a job to do. In a flawed universe, it's the best we got."

Picking up on his tone, Dukas said, "But—?"

"Something's not right. It isn't just the intercept, which I know is cooked, shit, what do you think? It stinks to heaven. Yeah, we got a list, and we've had the same list for three years and we're not cracking it. We can't move: you know what suspicion does in a closed community. You worry about one officer's career; my office could end fifty careers tomorrow with one false accusation, one wrong move—it isn't just the one accused that goes down, it's everybody around. We have to be right or nothing."

Menzes picked at the label of his beer bottle and looked grim.

Dukas tried again. "A woman called and told us that George Shreed is behind the Siciliano mess."

Menzes's face went through that rigid instant again. Not much of a liar, Dukas thought; a credit to his character but not a useful one in his profession. "What woman?" Menzes said.

"That's all she said, but it put the name on the table. I'm not saying it's the right name. But I'm telling you, if Shreed is your guy *and* he's behind this crap about Rose Siciliano and her husband, then he's a lot closer to the end of the line than you think he is. He's got to be scared—whoever it is, he's got to be scared—why else this phony intercept?"

Menzes put his head down and rubbed his forehead. "We never had this conversation," he muttered. He went on rubbing his head. "Jesus, some woman called? Why didn't she call us?"

"Maybe she wants it kept outside the Agency."

"Because she's inside?"

"Time to surveil him?" Dukas said.

Menzes shook his head. "Not a chance. I take this and what I've got to my board, they'd laugh me out of the room. Out of my job, more likely." He pointed a finger at Dukas. "And don't you even *think* of surveilling him! If you guys spook him, I'll have your balls!"

Dukas made a face. "You know what kind of budget I got? I couldn't surveil the Washington Monument."

Menzes leaned forward, his tone warmer. "Look, Dukas, I appreciate that you're concerned about Siciliano. I didn't entirely mean what I said about only one officer. But look at it from my side: you're trying to hurry things along to save her career, and I'm trying to work through a mare's nest that'll take years."

"And meanwhile, your mole is scared and can do God knows what. And that's another thing."

"What?"

"What's he scared of? What's set him going all of a sudden?"

The two of them sat there, looking at each other and thinking about that question, and Menzes's face went through its rigid spasm again. "If I knew that, I'd have him. Or her." He gave Dukas a sick smile.

Beijing.

The careful smile marked Chen as a survivor of the Cultural Revolution, a survivor who had learned not to show too much pleasure at anything. Hunched over his daily message traffic, face hidden from the world, Chen allowed himself the hard little smile of triumph. Years of maneuvering and political work had finally sufficed to move his rival, Lao, to "direct operations on the continent of Africa." Lao was gone, never to trouble him again, and while this did not offer him release from the tension that haunted every minute of his public life, it did mark a triumph.

And the next message in the stack suggested even greater things to come.

Top Hook was invaluable. That came through the message with perfect clarity—if it was genuine. A memorandum from the National Security Advisor saying absolutely that the United States would not confront China militarily—it was wonderful!

But was it genuine?

Colonel Chen had a big office with a lacquered desk that faced the door and two severe chairs with inquisitional formality. When he spoke to his subordinates, he sat straight behind the desk, his face immobile, but when he read agent reports, he tended to turn himself away from the door, his body hunched, his whole demeanor suggesting a furtive search for privacy. Today he was hunched almost into a ball, huddled over flimsy sheets of paper in a corner of his desk, so that his secretary thought for a moment that the office was empty.

"Comrade Colonel?" she murmured, her eyes downcast.

"I'm busy."

"I have the *Lucky Star* reports and estimates you ordered."

He turned toward her, his back straightening like a whip released from tension, and he held out his right hand imperiously even as his left flipped the two sheets on the desk upside down, hiding their contents

"Anything else?"

"Marshal Jiang's staff called and expressed the hope that you would visit this afternoon."

Chen rubbed a hand over his bald head and then down his chin. He thought that he gave off an air of bland imperturbability; those who knew him recognized this gesture as a serious sign of stress.

"Tell the marshal I will be at his service."

Their wives had gone to the same school. *That's how it had all started.* Chen had married above himself, into the ranks of the senior officers and Party officials. He had been an intelligence officer on his first assignment, learning how to coopt ethnic Chinese who were living overseas. She had been an intern at the embassy. She had schemed relentlessly at his promotion, playing the Party game at his back. Now he was bound hand and foot to the Cabal, as he thought of it, a group of senior officers who sought to make a big strike on the world stage and move China into the tiny club of military superpowers. Her uncles, her cousins, her friends. Now his allies.

Lucky Star was a listing of the financial assets that he controlled for the group; billions of dollars invested in Hong Kong and across the west—the secret funds of the armed forces and sectors of the Party, taken by fair means or foul and hidden away against the day when they were needed. On good days, Chen believed that those funds would never buy anything but expensive retirements for the Cabal's senior executives. On bad days like today, he worried that the old men meant business, that they really would provoke war to achieve their aims. His last meeting with the marshal had led to the expenditure of several billion dollars to move materiel to Pakistan—aircraft, missiles, tanks. That was the plan—to use Pakistan and India to humiliate the US while they were busy in Yugoslavia. Next would be naval vessels.

He did not control jet bombers or thousands of soldiers or silent nuclear submarines like the other members, but the report in his hands and the two overturned sheets contained his real power—*Lucky Star* and Top Hook. The money and the information.

Chen's status as the man with secrets depended largely on this one agent, China's highest penetration into the corridors of power in Washington. It had taken a long time, entrapping Top Hook and then putting the screws to him. Now, he produced the best intelligence that had ever come out of the United States.

Top Hook had never seemed frightened before; certainly, when they had known each other in Jakarta, he had been a lion, despite his handicap. Now he seemed scared—the business of posting the fake intercept to implicate some female officer of whom Chen had never heard, for example.

He waved the woman out of his office and hunched over his reports, a pencil tracing characters on a pad, his left hand rubbing the top of his head. He would have to have the original of this memorandum, and the only way to make sure it went directly from Top Hook to the Cabal was to get it himself.

He and Top Hook would have to meet—the first time in years. Chen almost groaned aloud at the idea.

But it was essential, not only to authenticate the document, but also to reappraise Top Hook. Was he really what he seemed?

Oak Grove, West Virginia.

Rose had decided to pull up her socks and face reality. The day after the meeting in her motel room, she reported (early) to the Inter-Service Word Processing Training Center as its new executive officer. She had expected Appalachia and gloom; instead, what she found in West Virginia went into the subject line of her e-mail to Alan:

> Subject: DISNEYLAND, WEST VIRGINIA
> Arrived this pm, everybody so goddam nice i can't stand it. No shit, nice nice nice I may be sick. The tower is nice the scenery is nice the job is nice my boss is nice the eighteen hole champi- onship golf course is nice the town looks like they make movies on it and you expect Opie and Aunt Bea to come around every corner. The kids are going to be ecstatic! I'm in hell but the pun- ishment is being niced to death not the opposite. I'm not sure which is worse. Mike says for me to get to work and forget the case and let him handle it/that's what I'm doing. Oh shi I miss you. Off to get the kids. Your nice wife.

USS *Thomas Jefferson.*

Alan took the catwalk without looking to the right or left and strode down into the ship, looking for Rafe. He found him in CIC. "I need to talk to you," he said.

His face told Rafe everything. He didn't quibble. "My office, ten minutes."

Rafe was waiting for him there on time, and Alan closed the door, still in flight clothes, and stood facing Rafe across his desk. "I want real-world tasking for the MARI system. The thing works and I need to prove it!"

"You heard the admiral."

"The thing didn't work when he talked to me. Now it works—our baby-faced newbie had an inspiration and the goddam thing *works*." He leaned forward, knuckles on the desk. "Rafe—*please*. Give us something to do!"

Rafe shook his head. "He won't buy you guys in a combat situation, Al! He's not gonna let you go snooping for radars and SAM sites."

"Rafe—look. My detachment is a mess; you said it yourself. Morale is shit. I inherited it that way; you told me to make it better. What these guys need to get better is some sense of *doing* something, some sense of belonging on this fucking boat! You know what I heard somebody say yesterday? I was asking for suggestions for a det nickname, and a voice from the p'way says, 'How about the Freeloaders?' How the hell do you think these guys can get better if they hear shit like that? *Give them something to do!*"

Rafe stroked his chin. He looked tired. He gave Alan a quick look of disgust, but he began to burrow in a stack of pubs. "You sure the system really works?"

"It's brilliant! We could see the swimming pool on a cruise ship at thirty miles! I've got a report on my laptop; let me print it out and—"

Rafe waved a hand. "Send it to the admiral; I'll take your word for it." He pulled out a thin document in a NATO binder. "There's one low-priority tasking order." He looked up at Alan. "Cigarette boats smuggling contraband from Italy to the Yugo coast."

"Speedboats?" It was a far cry from SAM sites and EW radars. And he had a plunge into doubt: *Could the MARI system identify something as small as a speedboat?*

Rafe held the publication out. "Haven't read it; haven't had time. You want something real-world, this is real-world. You can access NATO for more data via—you know all that." As Alan took the pub, Rafe withdrew his hand and leaned back. "Best I can do, bud."

"Take it or leave it?"

Rafe nodded.

"I'll take it."

Rafe stood up. "What I like about you, Al, you really take time to think things over. Okay, I'll square it with the flag." He shrugged. "If it doesn't work, you can always go back to cruise ships, right?"

HE WENT STRAIGHT to his stateroom and read the tasking order. It was more interesting than he thought: smugglers were moving significant quantities of arms, ammo, and military gear across the Adriatic in ten-meter boats that could hit eighty knots at the top. Nothing else on the water could touch them, and, in the heavy surface traffic of that sea, they were virtually invisible.

Could the MARI system find them and, equally important, pass the information to somebody down there who could intercept them?

He stopped to grab Chief Navarro and told him to get everything he could beg, borrow, or look up on ten-meter speedsters, and then he went straight to the ready room, took down the ops board, and read through the flight schedule. Stevens was bringing 902 back to the boat in fifteen hours. Good. One check flight and 902 could be off. Alan grabbed Cohen and laid on a two-plane "test fight" for early the next morning. Then he told the duty officer to grab the crews he had assigned and have them in the ready room that evening.

Although Alan had no way of seeing it, for the first time he appeared utterly in charge of his unit.

Langley.

Ray Suter got a message on his beeper to call a number he recognized as Tony Moscowic's. He left the office and drove to a strip mall where there was a public telephone, wondering how many other CIA people over the years had used the same phone for more or less the same purpose. Everybody said the office telephones weren't bugged; everybody went outside to make sensitive calls.

"Yeah, this is Tony," the voice said when he called.

"You called my beeper."

"Yeah, what it is, I think I got a way into the guy's house, costs you five thousand."

"Dream on."

"You want in or don't you? I don't give a shit; the money isn't for me."

"Five thousand for a break-in?"

"Did I say that? Mister Suter, I'm not a moron just because I look like one, okay? You're taking me for granted, you know that?"

"Okay, I'm sorry. I'm tense."

"Here's the deal. The cleaning woman comes on Wednesdays to do Shreed's house. I saw her. She got a key. I followed her; I id'd her. I got a cop will pick up her kid for possessing a rock of crack, *which* he will plant on said kid; *that's* what the five is for. Mother gets a choice: she lets us in the house, keeps her mouth shut, or her kid does hard time."

Suter pictured it. He saw a black woman, a black teenager, mean streets. None of that bothered him. "It's bringing other people in. I don't like it."

"What'd I just say? You think this woman is going to let her kid do time? She'd kill first. She'll do it; she'll keep her mouth shut. Once I get a hacker, we go in, we do whatever the hacker has to do, it's over. Yes or no."

Suter didn't like it. He didn't like having other people know; he didn't like having things spiral out this way. But he had no choice, and he liked having no choice least of all. No, least of all did he like having Tony Moscowic know so much about Shreed and what Suter was trying to do with him. A mental image of Moscowic dead floated across his brain. "Okay, I guess," he said.

"What you do, put five thou in bills in an envelope, meet me six P.M. on the dot tomorrow, the Safeway on Glebe Road. Push a cart; I'm pushing a cart; you shop a little, pass me, drop the envelope in my cart. I'll call you in a couple days."

A week before, Suter wouldn't have laid out five thousand for anything. Now, he thought of the billion or more waiting for Shreed to release it—could it be two, three?—and five thousand in bills seemed petty.

He hung up and walked to his car. He didn't like any of it, not at all—all this cloak-and-dagger stuff. Letting Moscowic tell him what to do. Having Moscowic know so much. The idea of Moscowic dead, therefore, became more and more attractive, but he had never killed anybody and he didn't know how you did that sort of thing.

11

THE BRIEF HE GAVE AFTER CHOW AT 2000 WAS SUC-
cinct. He didn't promise the sky. But he held out the possibility of real-
world support to the war in Bosnia, something that the aviators took
seriously. Alan appointed Campbell mission commander and ticked off
a list of preflight responsibilities for him.

The back of the ready room was crowded. Alan had made it plain that
any member of the det was welcome to the brief. Maintenance guys are
not usually invited to share operational details, but Alan had found his
platform to effect change. He wanted the message to get out. And it
wasn't only chiefs standing in the murk behind the projector; there were
sailors of all ranks. Perhaps some came out of curiosity; certainly more
than a few were there because Senior Chief Craw had dragged them.

"Folks, we came out here to test our planes, but NATO is pasting the
Serbs every day. We aren't bombers, and the Air Force has plenty of gas,
so we've been testing our systems and cutting holes in the sky while the
other squadrons support the air war.

"Time to change that. This first slide shows the coast of the former
Yugoslavia." As Alan read the slide, he noted that his intel chief had used

the local spellings of all of the towns. Still, it was a good slide, informative and simple.

Alan hit a switch and the slide acquired an overlay. "This shows the principal smuggling corridors between the Serbs and various Italians who provide them with stuff." Alan had entered the location of the *Jefferson*. "We're sitting between the two principal corridors and we'll continue to do so for two more days before we head for Naples."

"These guys are taking war materials—weapons, ammunition, information, spare parts, you name it, it's moving out of Italy and into Yugoslavia. The Italians are trying to stop it. Up till now, there hasn't been a lot of interest in using NATO assets on the problem, because the chance of a plane detecting one of these little bastards at night is like trying to find a guy on the mess decks after lights out." He looked straight at a maintenance tech's face at the back. "This detachment has the tool to change that."

He had them. Even the guys in back, the guys who knew nothing about the MARI system, were interested. He was offering them something tangible—a chance to play in a bigger game than training and testing.

"I've talked to Air Ops and got a spot on the air tasking order, so this will count as operational flight time. Our two planes are call sign Jaeger One and Two. Captain Rafehausen has given it the thumbs-up. The first flight will go at 0300. All missions will be two planes. Flexing the MARI will be the first priority every flight, but once you have it up in the link and going, your next priority is to look for eastbound fast movers. Soleck?"

"Sir!"

"You were anxious to modify the simulator parameters. Here are some predictions from Rota on what twin-engined cigarette boats might look like on P-3 ISAR. Get with Navarro and give us a guess what they might look like on MARI. Then put them in the system."

"Yes, sir!"

"In time for aircrew to get a look before we walk to the planes. Any questions?"

There was a happy buzz at the back when he was done, and as he shut down the projector and unhooked his laptop, he saw Rafe wink at him.

Washington.

Dukas was by nature messy. He was also active, a fleshy man whose short arms jabbed and swung in constant gestures. A desk was not enough for him, and in the day he had been in the Washington office he had installed a bookcase, buried a chair in files, and piled four plastic crates in a tottering stack within arm's reach.

Triffler, the prissy agent who was now his assistant, was at the decryption center at Fort Holabird, waiting for the geeks to finish with Rose Siciliano's home computer, which had been seized as it was unloaded from the moving van at her newly rented house in West Virginia. The computer analysis would come up blank, he knew—he was waiting for Triffler to call him with that non-news—and then there wasn't much to wait for. O'Neill had given Rose a recorder and told her how to get the Telephone Woman on tape—if she ever called again—but Dukas wasn't optimistic.

He was doing the plod-work of investigation: paperwork and more paperwork. Making notes. Making lists. Making a budget. Checking e-mail. A tiny moment of relief: an e-mail from O'Neill, who was already in Nairobi, about his attempts to find out something about the incident that had got Alan crosswise of George Shreed. Dukas had forgotten all about asking Harry to check it when he was in Kenya; now, reviewing his notes from the skull session at Rose's motel, he remembered. Harry hadn't found much, as it turned out—only that, contrary to the CIA reports, the foreign national whom Alan had contacted in Mombasa had been shot to death, not a suicide. Nine years ago. Did it mean anything? A naive young naval officer; a murdered Iranian asset; George Shreed taking the thing away from Alan; Alan blowing up at Shreed—what the hell? What could Shreed have had to do with a murder in Mombasa, Kenya?

He opened a computer file on Shreed, George; saved the e-mail to it, went back to work. *Better call the Inter-Agency woman at CIA, start to show some muscle—*

His phone rang. Dukas located the ring under a pile of papers, pushed the papers aside and hit the stack of crates and grabbed the third one up as it started to go. The top one did go, falling over backward like somebody hammered in the front of the head, while Dukas was scrambling amid the papers with his left hand to grab the phone. The crate hit with a crash; files spilled; Dukas yanked the phone cord, and the bottom half of the instrument, restrained by paper but pulled by the cord, flew from the desk and hit him in the chest.

"Dukas, NCIS," he said. The crate he had been holding stopped teetering and he let go of it and it, too, went over backward.

"This is Triffler."

"Hey, how you doing."

"What's all that noise?"

"Moving some stuff around."

"My phone sounds funny."

"*My* phone. Sounds fine," In fact, the phone hadn't sounded quite right all day—ever since, as he remembered, he'd eaten a jelly doughnut and some of the jelly had squirted on it. "What's up?"

Triffler went into his iron-assed official voice. "I got the report on the Siciliano home computer."

"Nothing, right?"

"It's *loaded* with classified material."

It was as if Triffler had come through the phone and whacked him. "Can't be!" Dukas cried.

"Loaded." Was Triffler pleased? Maybe he was simply pleased to have something positive to report. "Geeks say there's 'residue in the Temp files,' whatever that means, plus 'sectors on the hard drives adulterated with highly classified materials not effectively deleted from Recycle Bin.' Later on they say something about—let's see—it's about how she tried to delete stuff—yeah, here: 'Attempts to delete show usual lack of understanding of computer technology by naive user.'"

It was the one moment when Dukas, for all his love of her, doubted Rose. He had been jerked around by a lot of women, lied to a lot, conned a lot; it would hardly have been a new experience. But Rose? He felt that gut-sunk nausea that he got when somebody lied to him, then the familiar wave of loathing.

For *Rose?* Jesus, what could he be thinking!

But he had been a Navy cop too long to say such a thing couldn't happen.

"You're sure it's her computer."

"Cast-iron evidence trail. She even identified it for the agent—hassled him, in fact. I got that somewhere—"

"Leave it, leave it. Okay. Listen, Triffler, keep this to yourself, you hear me? I want the whole report on my desk soonest, so get your ass back here today. Tell the geeks to put that computer on ice—nobody else touches it. If they fuck the evidence trail, tell them I'll have their balls in court."

Dukas hung up and sat in the creaking desk chair. The floor was littered with files and fallen crates. He stared at them without seeing them, his heart breaking but his mind racing as he saw the possibilities, the likelihoods, the ways the investigation could go now.

When Triffler came in that afternoon, he shook his head in disgust at the mess. Dukas had cleared enough space with one arm to write long-hand notes and swing around to his computer; otherwise, except for some new Chinese-food cartons, the chaos was as it had been.

"This is a disgrace," Triffler said. He sounded like somebody's mother.

"Where's the report?"

"In my hand. I don't dare put the fucking thing down; it'll disappear."

"Gimme." Dukas held out a hand and took the folder. "If it's any consolation to you, Triffler, I'm not where I'd like to be, either; if I had my druthers, I'd be sitting in a brand-new office in The Hague, with a big-assed receptionist and two gung-ho French cops to assist me, and I'd be running a whiz-bang new program at twice my current salary. But I'm here, and you're here, and I'm busy, so get on with the Siciliano case."

"The fucking day's almost over."

"That's what happens when you waste time arguing. Go, go—I'm too busy to dick around!"

Dukas read the report twice. He was still reading it long after most other people had gone home. The long summer twilight deepened outside and he switched on the overhead lights, then walked from desk to desk, reading, leaning against the windowsills, reading, cutting through the computerese and the e-jargon and adding it all up.

At eight, he called Rose in West Virginia. He didn't mince words. "Rose, you're in deep shit. Your computer's full of illegal classified data."

She went through the same stages he had: it couldn't be; there was some mistake; she just hadn't done that stuff.

"You done? Okay, Rosie, moment of truth. Tell me now, babe, for all time, yes or no: did you *ever* put classified material on this computer? Rosie, before you answer, I'm going to Miranda you—yeah, go ahead, gasp; this is Mike, your old friend, your old admirer, yes, I love you, Rosie, but I can't stand this and I've got to do it right: I'm taping this call. You may remain silent. Anything you say may be used against you. You have a right to a lawyer. Now: Rose: yes or no, did you *ever* put classified material on that computer?"

"No, goddam you. No! No, you sonofabitch!"

"Did you ever put any Peacemaker material on that computer or use that computer for any purpose connected with Peacemaker?"

"No! How many times do I have to say it?"

"You never came home, tired, remembered some notes you meant to make at the office, made them on your home computer and—"

"NO!"

"You had your laptop with classified material on it; you were behind, you had to get done; you downloaded Peacemaker stuff and did the work and deleted it from your home computer—right?"

"NO, NO, NO!"

Dukas sighed. He'd have to polygraph her, for all the good it would do. He turned off the tape. "Okay, babe, this is not on the record. Look, this is hell time—I've got a report, there's no question the computer's loaded with stuff. They infer a conscious effort to delete the stuff and hide the fact it was ever there, by somebody who didn't know computers very well. Come on, give me some help, babe; I need to know it wasn't you. I need some help here."

"I thought you trusted me. Jesus, you of all people."

"I guess—push comes to shove, I don't trust anybody." He sighed again. It was a discovery he made about himself every few investigations or every love affair, and not a discovery he liked. "Help me, Rose."

She was crying. She cried for some seconds. Then she said, "Valdez."

He didn't get it right away, then remembered the Latino kid who had been her pet computer geek on the Peacemaker project. "What about Valdez? He put stuff on your computer?"

"Valdez would know if I put whatever is there on my computer."

"You saying he did it?" It was the oldest escape there was, blaming somebody else.

"No, for Christ's sake! Valdez is a straight-arrow. No, I mean he would know if it was me. He said everybody had a signature. He said he could always tell my stuff because I was a computer illiterate and it was like a signature, and he fixed my programs to make things easier for me."

"Did he fix your home computer?"

"Sure."

Dukas felt drained. Probably she did, too. Would they recover, he was wondering—would the friendship recover? He tried to focus. "Where's Valdez stationed now?"

She sobbed again. He was supposed to apologize, he knew, but he couldn't do it yet. Everything was awful. "He got out of the Navy," she said. "Mike, how could you do this to me?"

"Any idea where he is?"

Silence. He could picture her, squeezing her eyes to stop the tears, swallowing hard, putting her head back with a hard jerk as if she meant to strike it against something. "He took a job in computers." She had an address and a first name for him: Enrique.

Then neither of them spoke. At last, she said, "This is going to take a while to get over, Mike," and she hung up on him.

Dukas went back to the borrowed apartment and grabbed a bottle. He hadn't noticed before how *brown* the apartment was—like chocolate. Walls, rugs, furniture. Deeply depressing. He sat there in all that brown, drinking bourbon from the first glass that came to hand, hating the taste of what he'd done to Rose.

But she could be lying.

He sighed. He put out a hand for the telephone. He could put in a call to The Hague—what the hell time was it in Holland? well, he could put in a call in a few hours—and tomorrow he could fly away and have precisely the office he'd described to Triffler, and the big-assed woman and the two French cops, and he could leave the investigation to somebody who didn't know Rose and didn't give a shit and would probably do a better job.

Instead, he dialed O'Neill's hotel in Nairobi. It was a little after seven A.M. there, what the hell?

"*Jambo!*" The voice was O'Neill's, alert and full of juice.

"I wake you up?"

"Hell, no, I been out for my run before the muggers get up. What's doing?"

"I just Miranda'd Rose."

"Oh, shit, Mike—!"

"Her computer's full of bad stuff."

"Yeah, but Mike—Rose! Hey, man, you can't believe she—? Hey, you sober?"

"Not particularly."

O'Neill led him through it with several questions, got to Valdez and what Rose had said about him, went over that part again, and then O'Neill said, "Leave this Valdez to me."

"To do what?"

"To have him look over that goddam computer. You get it down there where he can take it apart if he has to, Mike—I'll provide this Valdez."

"Shit, why?"

"Because Rose thinks he can save her and I think he can save you. Okay? Now put the bottle away and go to bed, and I'll talk to you tomorrow."

Dukas thought that over. The telephone was still in his hand, the dial tone buzzing because O'Neill had hung up. After thirty seconds, he decided that O'Neill's judgment was probably better than his own just then, so he put the bottle away and went to bed.

IN NAIROBI, O'Neill e-mailed his Dubai office and told them to contact a former US Navy computer specialist named Enrique Valdez, now in the computer world in America. "Hire him and have him meet me for breakfast Monday morning, Willard Hotel, Washington, and don't take no for an answer! Harry."

12

STEVENS HAD BROUGHT 902 BACK FROM SIGONELLA and made no public comment about the "operational" mission he was missing, but Alan sensed that he had said something elsewhere, because some of the sense of purpose seemed to slip away from the aircrew. Late in the day, Cohen came to him in the ready room and said, "How come Stevens isn't on the sked for this?"

Alan was very bland. "Mister Cohen, please tell Mister Stevens that when he has a question, he should ask it himself." He smiled. "Meanwhile, you have enough to do with your own responsibilities."

Stevens showed up thirty minutes later. His sullenness had become outright anger. "All right, how come I'm not on the sked?" he shouted. People at the back of the room were working the sim; they looked around, then began to move out.

"You don't need to shout; I'm right here." Alan looked at him. "You know why."

"I'm the best pilot in this goddam det—maybe on this boat!"

"Maybe you are. You did a hell of a job in Sigonella, and I told you so. But I didn't get your attention with that, and now I'm trying to get your attention with the flight sked—it's the two-by-four with which I'm hitting the jackass." He looked at his watch. "I have a brief, but you and I need to talk. When we've talked, you'll fly."

"I got nothing to say to you!"

"Think of something."

ALAN HAD put himself in a crew with Campbell, Soleck, and Craw for the first anti-fast-mover flight. He wanted to make the operation work, and he wanted his best people. Deep down, he realized that he had also chosen a crew of men who liked and respected him, and that 902 had Cohen and Reilley, who didn't, in the front seats. He told himself that he couldn't hide from them forever without starting to play favorites— knowing from experience where that command path could lead. But this time, the first time, he wanted no distractions from the mission, no comments, no edge. *No Stevens*, he admitted to himself.

The preflight brief went well. The aircrews were a little sleepy, but, even though Cohen and Reilley kept their distance, they seemed up and even eager. They got their televised brief and then Soleck got up and gave them a quick peek at some expected "smugglers," based on photos from Rota and some imagination. Alan had stood over his shoulder while he drafted them. Soleck could be a pain in the ass, but he was smart, and he understood computers and computer graphics better than any pilot Alan had ever met.

They were launching with the first event, so there were no planes launching or landing before them. The flight deck was quiet. Dawn was three hours away, and quiet ghosts in flight deck jerseys moved around the deck, pulling hoses, spotting planes, moving ordnance. Alan checked his seat and watched Soleck check the outside of the plane and discuss the chaff and flare load and react with surprise to the port wing's rocket pod, which Alan had ordered in case they had to show teeth to a fast mover. Rules of engagement forbade him to fire at a suspected smuggler, but he wanted the pods in case—in case he had to fire at a suspected smuggler. He also wanted them for the effect on the aircrew. No one in ordnance questioned the load.

Soleck got the mandatory lecture from Craw on chaff and flare load- ing and got into the plane, while Campbell stuck his whole arm into the engine intakes and checked the fan blades with a flashlight, like a man buying a horse and checking its teeth. Alan approved. He also saw Cohen run a finger over the struts on 902's landing gear, checking for a recurrence of the hydraulics leak. They were thorough, and his spirits rose. Maybe this was going to work.

If they could locate one fast mover and pass it to the Italian coast guard, the effect on morale would be incredible. All they needed was some cooperation from the smugglers.

Nine thousand feet over the Adriatic, Alan felt a sag in his energy as he saw the volume of traffic down on the water. Even with both MARI systems up and running, even with datalink support from all of NATO to deconflict white contacts (merchant ships), he was looking at hundreds of unknowns in a huge expanse of water.

Soleck had put in the smugglers' corridor parameters as an overlay on the screen, but the corridors were hypothetical at best. The system lacked the ability to ignore selected contact parameters, so the aircrew couldn't direct it to ignore, for example, all westbound contacts. They could only watch the patterns, sip coffee, limit their search areas, sip more coffee, and wait.

Sunrise crept closer. The coffee got bitter, then vanished.

Each plane found likely contacts every few minutes, but by the time the possible smugglers gunned their engines and turned into the west coast of Dalmatia, it was too late to give a vector to any of the Italian coast guard ships. The experience was maddening, and Alan began to fear that they would not only fail, but that the frustration would exacerbate the squadron's troubles.

MARI worked like a trooper, however. Cohen kept his plane well off Campbell's axis on every sweep, and, with fiddling, the two crews had almost constant link. They were able to add several distinct images of speedboats to their onboard libraries for future comparison. Soleck seemed obsessed with finding a way to identify individual boats with the MARI system, convinced that he could see slight differences in hull pattern even with one-meter resolution. Alan wasn't so sure. The system had been designed to locate and accurately identify warships, not bass boats.

By 0600, interest was flagging in both planes, except for Soleck, who was focused on small-boat antenna arrays. The eastern sky was pale, and they were almost against the Yugoslavian coast. Away to the west, the link showed Canadian F-18s returning from a sortie over Kosovo.

"Jaeger Two, this is Jaeger One, over." One more sweep and time to head for home, Alan thought.

"Roger, this is Jaeger Two."

"Jaeger Two, let's turn to 270 and sweep west one more time."

"Roger, Jaeger One. Turning to 270." Reilley's voice sounded bored even through the encrypted comms. In front, Campbell turned slowly to the west.

Alan raised the Italians in clear and told them where he was turning. He had spoken with them several times, and knew that they had little faith in his ability to find their needles in the Adriatic haystack. Communication with them was limited, too. They didn't have the encryption to keep comms secure, and Alan had to be vague as a result. As well, their English wasn't much, and he was the only Italian speaker in the aircraft.

They bored holes in the water for ten minutes. Suddenly, Craw said, "Got one," his first words in an hour.

Thirty miles away, the pale light of the eastern sky had worried someone else. Well off the coast, a twelve-meter arrowhead with two distinct returns from powerful engines suddenly jumped from ten knots to nearly forty and headed due east. Alan marked it and imaged it. An identity code appeared next to the image—PG-221.

Craw called it to AW1 Denton in Jaeger Two. Alan located the nearest coast guard ship, almost fifteen miles away to the south and probably too far behind to intercept. They still seemed unimpressed, but they turned toward the contact. According to *Jane's*, the Italian vessel could make thirty-two knots. If their contact was a cigarette boat, it could put on bursts of nearly eighty.

"Jaeger Two, descend to angels 15 and turn to 180. I want you to set up for a bow-on intercept, but stand off until I give the word."

Alan leaned forward into the cockpit. "That bastard is going to outrun the Italians without even knowing they're there." He held on to the frame as Campbell turned toward the contact. Once, he had been nervous about unstrapping in flight. Long time ago.

"I hear you, Skipper." Campbell was dead calm, the archetypal pilot.

"I'm going to put 902 ahead of them and have you come in from abeam, from the north."

"No problem."

"Then we order them to stop and be boarded."

"No problem, unless they don't stop."

Soleck whooped. "Then we shoot 'em!"

Alan whacked Soleck's helmet. "We don't shoot anybody. We call in 902 to buzz them real, real low, right down the throat. Okay? Brian, you're the mission commander."

"Sure, Skipper. Strap in, here we go."

Alan scrambled for the familiar straps while the plane nosed down and powered for the deck, her turbofans suddenly changed from distant vacuum cleaners to avenging furies. Craw had his head pressed almost to the glass of his screen despite the acceleration, intent on his target. Alan got the second clip into his harness and called an update of the contact's position to the Italians. They took a second to respond. Their comms officer reported that they were too far away to intercept. Alan wanted to scream at him but paused, counted to three, and explained that the Jaeger patrol would stop the contact.

Suddenly, the aircraft rolled sharply to starboard and Alan could see waves, close waves, off the starboard wing.

"*Va bene,*" said the Italian, as though making an enormous concession.

"Soleck, get me Jaeger Two."

Craw looked up. "Should be visual any second."

"Got him!" yelled Soleck from in front.

"Don't close yet. Soleck?"

"Oh, yeah." He punched the comms console. Alan switched his comms.

"Jaeger Two, this is Jaeger One, we have visual on the contact, over."

"Roger, copy. In position."

"Jaeger Two, hold your position."

"Roger, copy."

Alan's hands were tight, his adrenaline running. He slammed the comms switch to bring up the guard frequency and said in Italian, "Twin-engined boat with blue hull, this is AH 901, over." Alan cycled through three Italian guard frequencies and got no response.

"Buzz him."

Again, the furies screamed. AH 902 turned her aging bulk on a dime and seemed to ride the tops of the waves. Alan leaned forward to peer out of the windscreen and saw the contact, a low, powerful boat that was leaping along the waves. Campbell took them just astern of it.

"He's up to sixty knots," Craw said.

"Stern reads Sierra Oscar Papa Hotel India Alpha!" Soleck said. Soleck seemed to be having the time of his life. "Sophia—it's named the *Sophia*."

"*Sophia*, this is AH 901, over. Cut your engines and stand by to be boarded."

Sophia continued to race for the Yugoslav coast, now only twenty miles away. The Italian ship was still nine miles to the south.

"Make the next pass up his stern. Jaeger Two, engage!"

"Roger." Cohen had a little color in his voice. Good.

"Right down his throat."

"Watch for 901, we're on the opposing radial."

"I copy, Jaeger One."

And there they were. As Campbell lined 901 up on the wake of the *Sophia*, they saw Jaeger Two fall from the skies ahead of the contact and all but disappear.

"Fuck," muttered Soleck, in front. "Fuck, he's low."

Alan couldn't see Jaeger Two over the console from his seat in back.

"Contact's turning," said Craw.

The *Sophia*, apparently terrified by the sudden appearance of the big gray plane, turned sharply south, her turn giving them a view of the boat's cockpit as she banked hard. There were four men aboard.

"Circle to port and get in behind them again!" said Alan, willing himself to sound as calm as the pilots. "Nice pass, Jaeger Two!"

"Saw a yellow puddle, there, Jaeger One. Want me to do it again?"

"Negative, Jaeger Two. We want him to stay south. Get back east."

"Roger."

"He's turning. Oh, shit. We've dropped link."

"Too many fast turns. Screw it. Soleck, have you got him?"

Soleck's head whipped back and forth.

"Yeah, two o'clock. Headed east. He's got rooster tails! Man, is he moving."

"Got him on ISAR." Craw had withdrawn to an early technology, one that didn't require two aircraft to work. "Seventy knots."

Alan looked at the positions. The Italians were on the southern horizon, six miles away. Not close enough. Jaeger Two was circling north and east to get ahead. Too far away.

"Campbell, how good are you with rockets?"

"I thought you said we couldn't shoot him?" Soleck was beside himself.

"I want to scare him. If we hit him, we've broken the law." *Even if we don't hit him, we're probably breaking the law. The admiral will have my head.*

"Oh, I think I'm good enough to hit the *water*," said Campbell, in the best traditions of naval aviation. "I was afraid you wanted me to hit the *boat*."

"Do it." Campbell lined up the plane with the new course of the *Sophia* and throttled down, riding well above the waves and moving slowly up from behind.

"Jaeger Two, this is Jaeger One, over."

"Roger?"

"Jaeger Two, Jaeger One is firing a rocket over contact's bow. Stand clear."

"Ballsy move, Jaeger One."

"Break, break. Small boat *Sophia,* this is AH 901. Heave to or we will be forced to fire. You have five seconds. Four, three, two, one—"

"Shoot!"

"One away." The contrail appeared to curve, describing a lazy swirl to the right before hitting the water hundreds of meters in front of the contact. The *Sophia,* still well ahead of them, turned south again, heading for a low fog bank.

"Italians on two, Skipper."

Alan looked at the link. The coast guard patrol was close now. He told them of the contact's position and left out the part about the rockets. They didn't sound so skeptical now, but they still didn't have visual contact. Alan thought they were on the other side of the fog bank. And now *Sophia* was turning back to the east.

"We have to turn him south again. Jaeger Two, push him again."

"Roger, Jaeger One." Alan switched back to guard, decided not to worry that the Italians were going to hear all this.

"*Sophia,* heave to or be sunk. This is your last warning."

Campbell lined up and pressed in closer. 902 pounced again, appearing out of a dirty cloudbank right in front of the contact, who turned hard to starboard. For a moment, both of Alan's planes were on a collision course, with the target fleeing off south, visible to both, and in that moment, the white Italian patrol ship emerged like a specter from the fog bank to the east. Her deck gun stirred, just visible to the aircrew, and a tiny white puff appeared.

"Put the rockets away, Brian. I think the good guys won." Alan saw Campbell's finger come off the pickle switch, but any comments were drowned with whoops from both aircraft.

The Italians confirmed the illegal nature of the cargo before the two planes were in the stack over the *Jefferson*. They didn't mention that any rockets had been fired. Alan was writing his report in his mind when 902 called.

"Jaeger One, this is Jaeger Two, over."

"Go ahead, Jaeger Two."

"Hey, have you figured out how you lost that rocket?" Sounds of laughter. A change for the better.

On the flight deck, Alan waited for the other crew and welcomed them with handshakes. Walking to the lock, he fell in with Cohen. "I'm putting myself down for your plane next launch," he said.

Cohen took a moment to digest that, then said, "Whatever," and opened the hatch. At least he held it for his commanding officer to go through.

OF COURSE, Alan came clean to Rafe. He told the whole story in a rush, his helmet under his arm, suddenly a young man again. Rafe shook his head at the story and the change in his friend, shut the door, and went back to the stack of fitreps on his desk.

"Wish I'd been there," he murmured, and turned a page

13

GEORGE SHREED WAS LOOKING AT A SHEAF OF DAILIES that mostly contained trivia but now and then yielded a nugget. Mostly, the dailies were case-officer-level stuff, the material you grooved on if you were down there in the trenches but found less and less interesting as you moved up the echelons of deskwork. For Shreed, however, things like agent reports were a contact with real intelligence. "They remind me of why I'm here," he liked to tell people like Partlow.

Now, his eyes scanned the pages, flicking past this and that detail of contacts and failures and recruitments and information of questionable reliability. He yawned; it was that time after lunch when the body wanted to lie under a tree and digest. "Our animal past," he said aloud and flicked a page.

A phrase halfway down caught his eye. He hadn't really even looked at it, but it jumped at him: *firefight, Trieste.*

It was a simple contact report. From NCIS.

"Naval officer on shore liberty reported contact with foreigner, possibly asset. Lieutenant-commander off USS *Jefferson* was caught in firefight, Trieste, Italy, later questioned by Italian police and released. (See NCIS Case File DL7/27/94-0734.) Under investigation/NCIS control."

Shreed felt his heart stop, then a flush of warmth spread to his face and down his legs. Trieste—where his Serbs had bungled the second attempt on the woman who said she had a file on him. There could be no question it was the same woman; there can't have been two firefights there on the same day.

And the naval officer? Why would a naval officer have got involved? Coincidence?

There are no accidents.

His mind made a leap, *naval officer—Alan Craik,* and he felt it in his heart like adrenaline, but then he thought how unlikely it was that Alan Craik could have been the officer in Trieste, and he dismissed the idea. *It's only because I've sucker-punched the little shit's wife.* Still, he started to make a note for Ray Suter to check on the ID of the officer, but he stopped himself. He didn't dare show too much interest, or he might tip Internals to his connection with the woman. Nor could he trust Suter anymore.

Leave it.

Or had the woman who was blackmailing him made contact with somebody in the Navy? Or NCIS? But she wouldn't do such a thing—the Navy wouldn't have any special interest in what she had for sale. What was she up to?

He chewed on that all the way home, and he ate that question instead of dinner. It made him sick. Was there a connection there he had missed? Had Navy intelligence got involved somehow? Was the woman in Trieste somehow their agent?

Or—?

It was certainly a new factor in his relationship with the woman who called herself Anna. Maybe it was time to change tactics with her.

He sent her a message via the chat room where she had reached him before: "*I like your style. Time we met, don't you think? Maybe we can make beautiful music together.*" And he signed it with the abbreviation she had asked he use: TH, for Top Hook.

Next day, he had an answer.

"*TH, I'm not an idiot. Money talks.*"

He replied, "*Thinking of the future and what we might do as a team—money that would really talk. Will meet your place, your conditions. Hoping to see you soon. TH.*"

NCIS HQ.

Enrique Valdez had put on weight since he had been Rose Siciliano's EM computer whiz. Short, broad-shouldered, he now had the genesis of a midriff bulge from the good life in Seattle. He had picked up the casual clothes of that culture, too, and O'Neill had already had a word with him over breakfast about what he expected of his employees in the way of dress.

The NCIS interrogation room that Dukas had borrowed for the examination of Rose's computer had the bleak look of an institutional dead end—abandon hope, all ye who have the bad luck to get busted here—with a single table with a dead-gray, rubberized top, on which the computer sat like something washed up on a beach.

"Mister Valdez and I are lending our expertise to the Naval Criminal Investigative Service in this instance," Harry O'Neill said. He seemed to be speaking to two geeks from Fort Holabird but was in fact speaking for the tape he knew was turning. "Ethos Security is helping because of Mister Valdez's special knowledge of the particular computer in question."

"Okay, lemme look," Valdez said. He started forward, but one geek put out a hand and the other stepped in front of the computer as if he was trying to hide something indelicate.

"Hey—" Valdez said.

"Nobody touches the computer but them." Dukas made a face. "Evidence trail. Anyway, I got to ID you." Dukas asked some canned questions about Valdez's name and job and how well he knew LCDR Rose Siciliano and what work he had done for her.

"Would you say you would know her computer from the time when you served under her?"

"What, the outside—the case? No."

"The inside?"

"Unless somebody's dicked with it, sure."

"You programmed her home computer?"

"Sure I did."

"Tell me briefly what you did."

Valdez knew he was being taped, too. Still, he rolled his eyes, shrugged, sighed. "She bought it off the shelf with all that Windows shit on it, and I cut the redundancies and added some Linux-based stuff to make it coherent." Valdez looked at the two geeks. "These guys will understand when I say that everything I did on her computer I used a zip drive and put on disk. I mean, you keep your architecture. It's ego, right, guys?"

The geeks nodded.

Valdez grinned. "So, I got disks of what her computer looked like every time I worked on it. If this machine looks different, it isn't hers. Okay?" He was impatient. "Can we boot it up now?"

Valdez seemed inattentive until gray letters began to scroll down the black screen; then he leaned forward. When the Windows logo came up in color, he waved a hand and said, "Shut it down and boot it again, Alphonse." The geek looked at Dukas, who growled. "Do it," and he shut it down and then back on, and Valdez watched the whole thing again, told the geek again to shut it down, and then twisted in his chair to look up at Dukas.

"This isn't hers," he said.

Dukas felt hope bang on his chest, but he fought it with cop skepticism. "How the hell can you tell?"

"How can I *tell*? Jesus— Hey, you—" He punched the geek on the shoulder. "You can tell, right?"

"My name is Patrick," the geek said.

"Yeah, well, Patrick, you could tell after what I said I did on her computer, this isn't Commander Siciliano's, am I right?"

"Uh, well—" Patrick got very pink when spoken to, and he looked uncertain. "Well, this one's all standard Windows and no Linux, I could see that." The other geek said that his name was Josh, and he could *easily* see that.

Dukas, trying not to hope and thinking of the tape, thinking of a Navy court, said slowly, "Explain to me how you know that."

So Patrick booted the computer again, and then both he and Valdez pointed out, as the programs scrolled by, how they could tell this computer had not been streamlined by somebody with a dislike for redundancy and a passion for open-source code. Several times, Dukas would say aloud, "Now, Valdez is pointing at—" and he would read the string of letters that was fast vanishing into the tabletop. By the time they were done, Patrick and Valdez were almost buddies, and Josh was leaning in to do his part, too.

"What d'you think?" Dukas said to Triffler and O'Neill, not giving any sign of his own giddiness. "I need stuff that'll hold up in court."

"You got three guys there will testify."

Triffler, it turned out then, was no fool. "I'd accept what's put in front of you, Dukas, and ask the obvious question: how did the computer get to be different from the way this guy left it?"

Patrick muttered, "Cherchez le hard drive."

"Do what?"

Valdez was nodding. "Absolutely. You check and see did somebody switch hard drives. Huh, guys?" He looked at the two geeks, who nodded and began to speak at the same time.

"How long to switch drives?" Triffler said. He was sounding more like a cop with every minute.

"Two hours? Hour, if you were really good and maybe had some help—?"

Dukas waved at Triffler. "Then, Dick, what we gotta have is the record of where the computer was from the moment it left her house. Call Siciliano, get the date and time she last saw the computer—when she saw it boxed, if she did. Then I want to know every place that computer was, every second of every day in that time period. Use my phone."

"How come *you* don't call her, *Mike*?" They hadn't used first names before. "You know her."

"Not such a good idea just now. Get on it, will you, um, Dick?"

Later Dukas, alone now, leaned against the wall, his shoulders quivering with relief and guilt, convinced now that Rose was innocent, hating himself for having suspected she was not.

LATE THAT AFTERNOON, O'Neill blew into Dukas's office. "Rose has had another call from the Mystery Woman."

Dukas winced. Normally, he would have been the first one to hear this from her.

"This time, she got part of the call on tape. She was so excited, she drove up to meet me halfway to DC. Good thing she did, too." He leaned forward, his good eye sparkling. "I know the Mystery Woman, Mike. I know the voice."

"You're kidding!" Dukas's heart jumped: good news.

"From the Agency. She was Shreed's assistant when Alan first got crosswise of him. *Nice* woman. Alan knows her, too."

Dukas waited, because he knew there was more.

"She's had a bad patch lately—marriage gone bad; career in the Agency gone nowhere—thanks to Shreed, would be my guess. So maybe she's cracked up; maybe she's bitter; maybe she's—you know."

Maybe she's bullshitting us, he meant. "So what'd she say?"

"Nothing new. Kind of rambled—Shreed is a badass; he's after Rose; he's acting odd all of a sudden. The lady had had a few, I think—a little loose, you know?"

"Gimme a name."

"Sally Baranowski."

Dukas thought about it. "Good catch," he said. "Leave it to me, okay?"

O'Neill grinned. "Just trying to earn my dollar, Mister Dukas."

THAT EVENING, after Dukas had introduced Carl Menzes to Dick Triffler at the Old Commonwealth Tavern, and they had all sat down and ordered beers, Dukas said to Menzes without any warning, "Sally Baranowski on your short list, Carl?"

Again, he thought that Menzes was a terrible liar, but this time it was because Menzes couldn't keep his face from looking blank. He might as well have handed out cards saying that nobody named Sally Baranowski was suspected of anything.

"You're a stand-up guy, Carl," Dukas said. "Don't ever take up poker for a living."

Menzes waved the comment away. "Who is Sally Baranowski?"

"Agency employee. I want Triffler to interview her."

"She have anything to do with inter-agency abuse of power—*your* focus, am I right?"

"She used to work for George Shreed."

Menzes stared at him. "Negative. Negative on Baranowski. She's your Mystery Woman, right?"

"No comment."

"Bull! I thought we were going to be straight with each other, Dukas. Yes?"

Dukas leaned into him across the little table. "How about letting us interview Shreed?"

"Negative that. Absolute negative." They were still eye to eye. "You know why."

"You think we'll spook him." He saw Menzes's eyes flick to Triffler, and he said, "Dick knows."

Menzes grimaced. "Nobody interviews him, nobody goes near him. Period."

"How about a guy named Ray Suter? Shreed's assistant." Dukas sat back. Peretz had fingered Suter as a good one to ask about Peacemaker, because he'd worked on the project but had CIA connections. "He worked on Peacemaker, so he's part of the Siciliano case, which *is* at the center of my investigation of inter-agency abuse of power." He leaned in again. "Let me put it this way—for him, I can go through channels. I'd rather not. Can we interview him?"

"Tell me what your interest in Baranowski is."

Dukas looked at him, eyes slitted, looked aside at Triffler and said, "Okay, she's our Deep Throat. But she doesn't know we know."

Menzes digested that while he picked at the label of his beer. His hairy, muscular forearms worked, tight bands moving like rods. Despite the white shirt and tie, he seemed more like some sort of competitor—boxer, wrestler—than a desk jockey. "How do you know she isn't feeding you lies?"

"How about we interview Suter?"

Menzes now shifted his look to Triffler. "By the book. No surprises. Somebody from my office present at all times. Put the request in writing, parameters of the investigation clearly stated."

"You're a prince, Carl." Dukas produced a folded sheet of paper from an inner pocket and laid it next to Menzes's glass. "By the book. We'd like to do the interview as soon as possible."

Menzes started to laugh. He wiped moisture from one eye. "Hey, Dukas, no shit—you're good!"

Even Triffler smiled.

Washington.

O'Neill was off to Naples again to back up Alan Craik, but he had left Valdez in Washington to honcho a new computer-security wing for his company. The company offices were in the glitzy part of town near L and Connecticut, but Valdez found himself in a converted rathole in the old red-light district farther east.

"Don't matter," he had said to O'Neill before he left for the airport, "you pay the electric bill, we're in business." He had installed four Dells and networked three of them himself, then two geeks had got them going on anti-hacking regimens.

O'Neill was serious about developing a computer-security capability, but what he really wanted from Valdez was for him to hack into George Shreed's home computer. He was doing that on his own without telling Dukas, convinced that Dukas would wave him off because he was so sensitive to the Agency's desires; on the other hand, if Harry O'Neill's Ethos Security got caught hacking into Shreed's computer on its own, that was O'Neill's problem and he'd deal with it.

"Hack in how?" Valdez had said.

O'Neill was computer-literate but not a geek. "However you do it," he had said.

"Oh, thanks. Just like that, huh? You ever hack into a desktop sitting in somebody's house, Harry?"

"Uh—no."

"Well, it ain't magic, you know—it's science. We don't got X-ray vision and we don't walk through walls. We need a way in, man, some data, a tap on a phone line—dig?"

"That's your area of expertise."

"Oh, thanks. Can you do a break-in of his house?"

"Jesus, no! My God—get that idea out of your head! Dukas would kill me."

Valdez had nodded gloomily. "Okay. What you mean is, you flew me here first class, you payin' me all this money, now I should get to work—right?"

Harry had grinned. "Right." He gave Valdez his cellphone number. "If anything breaks, call me *at once*. Any time. Anywhere in the world. Don't let me get behind the curve on this, okay?" He had said it lightly, but Valdez had known what Harry meant: if Valdez let him get behind the curve, Valdez was toast.

So Valdez and his geeks had begun to exercise talents that were not strictly legal but that were part of their specialty, and in a long day of hacking they got two of George Shreed's three IPs, with Shreed's account numbers and the phone numbers from which he called. The third provider was a cable operator, and they were having some trouble with that. But they'd get it—they'd get it.

By the next morning, they knew that Shreed worked at his computers in the evening and then at random times during the night. The program also followed Shreed to a couple of chat rooms, and Valdez wondered what he was doing there. He shared his curiosity with O'Neill.

He also learned that Shreed had remarkable firewalls around his computers. Remembering Harry's cautions, Valdez didn't try to break in.

Suburban Virginia.

Ray Suter had had to drive on another of Moscowic's wild-ass anti-surveillance routes, up and down and around and about, using cunning sharp corners and winding lanes, all of which annoyed Suter and made him wish even harder for the day Moscowic would be out of his life. Suter didn't understand what he called "spy stuff," never having been a case officer or even an agent, and he thought Moscowic was jerking him around for the fun of it. *I keep seeing you lying face-down in the river someplace, Tony,* Suter thought with angry satisfaction. The idea perked him up a little. "Does this ever end?" he said.

"Now there's a nice kind of what they call your chicane coming up— see there, where the road got a kinda hula-hoop in it? What I want you should do—"

"Why the fuck don't you do your own driving?" Suter snarled.

"Hey, hey—temper, temper! This is all professional. You don't like it, Mister S., we can break off our business relationship, wha'dyou say to that?"

"I think you're playing games. How the fuck much farther have we got to go?"

"Wha'd I just say? This is *professional*. You get what you pay for, am I right? We're almost there."

And so they were. In a ratty Korean restaurant, a kid who looked sixteen was eating some sort of beef dish and not looking up at them, even when Tony introduced Suter as The Man. The kid was the hacker who was going to get into Shreed's computer. He was actually eighteen and had just got out of two years in a juvenile facility for stealing via electronic means, and he wasn't supposed to touch a computer for five years or he'd go to adult prison for another three. Suter had been told all that.

"Call him Nickie," Moscowic said.

Suter took the kid's greasy plate between thumb and finger and pulled it away toward him, forcing the kid to look up. He had raspberry-dyed hair and enough pimples for an entire graduating class, and eyes like old dishwater. "Do I have your attention?" Suter said.

"You gonna have my fist up your asshole if you ever touch anything of mine again. Give it back."

"I want your attention, shithead."

The dishwater eyes were not quite looking into Suter's but were fixed somewhere over his right shoulder. Like a dog, the kid didn't like eye contact. "Money and a computer," he said. "Then you got my attention."

Suter held on to the plate. "Can you do this job?"

The kid snorted. "Can you?" He snorted again, some substitute for laughter, and an unattractive quantity of mucus descended from his right nostril. "Shit, man. Come on! But I gotta get inside the house, download the files, and connect."

Moscowic detached Suter's fingers and pushed the plate back under the kid's nose, and the head went down and he began to eat again. "He wants an apartment and two computers and five thousand bucks. He can *do* it, Mister S."

Suter wiped his fingers on a napkin. "He better." He walked out, thinking that now he would like to see two bodies face-down in the river someplace.

USS *Thomas Jefferson.*

Things got better. The MARI system stayed up, and, as the aircrews got more data on the parameters of the fast movers, they began to spot them more quickly and more often. The problem remained the Italian surface ships, which weren't fast enough, but the effort counted and at least the det was in the game.

Alan had his talk with Stevens and put him back on the flight schedule. Stevens's part of the talk was bluster and resentment, Alan's part reason and firmness. They struck a deal: they would be Mister Stevens and Mister Craik, and Stevens would keep his private grudges to himself, or he'd be going home early.

Then the *Jefferson* made its turn away from the Yugoslav coast, and they were only a day out of Naples and the meeting with the woman named Anna. Calling from a STU in the intel spaces, Alan got a Special Agent Triffler at NCIS, and Triffler handed Mike over immediately.

"Mike! My God, I got you first try!"

"Al! Hey, jeez, at last." Dukas sounded harried. "When you going ashore in *bella Nap*'?"

"The very thing I'm calling about. What the hell do I do?"

"The very thing I'm about to tell you, what do you think? Your buddy O'Neill is backing you up, but when you see him, you don't know him, you never saw him before, he's just another Italian, right? A dark Italian. Anyway, he's scoped out a route and made the schedule, so you do as I tell you and everything will go like down like a hot slider, get me?"

"Ha-ha."

"Okay. One, don't go ashore until noon local. You know Naples, right? Okay. You hit fleet landing, walk down the pier all the way, and walk up to the old castle on the left."

Alan scribbled on his kneeboard. "What if she's waiting for me at fleet landing?"

"Walk the route I'm describing. *Don't get inspirations.*"

"Mike, after this I'm out of this thing. It's in the way of my job."

"Now, from the castle, walk up the boulevard, past the roundabout, toward AVSOUTH, to the train station. You with me?"

"Pier, castle, train. Did you hear what I said about being out after this one?"

"If she hasn't met you, sit in the station and drink coffee for a while, then head back to the boat on the same route."

"And if she does?"

"Then get on the train with her and go to Pompeii. When you get there, go straight into the ruins and keep moving around while you talk."

"What if she doesn't want to go to Pompeii?"

Mike was silent. Static and STU-III noises on the line. Then "Make it up, Al. But keep moving and keep away from fleet landing. Just in case."

"Have you talked to the NCIS guys on the boat?"

"No need to know."

"Damn it, Mike, I need them to know! I whacked a guy in Trieste and the admiral still seems to think I'm a risk!"

"Okay, okay! I'll call them and say something."

"And after this I'm out."

"One step at a time. First, you set another meeting—tell her where and when. Like in two days, at the train station in Herculaneum. Tell her she might be meeting somebody else, but don't give a description."

"Two days, at the train station in Herculaneum."

"Right. See what she has to say, but don't give anything away. Do I need to repeat that?"

"What is this, Spying 101? No, you don't have to repeat it. Christ."

There was talk in the background, a different kind of static. Dukas said, "If Harry walks past you, real close, with a newspaper, then follow him. It means he wants to talk."

"Oh, God. If he's real close, why doesn't he say 'Follow me?'"

"Now repeat it all, from the top."

Alan looked at the kneeboard in front of him.

"Go ashore at noon. Go up the pier to the castle, then past the round-about to the station by AVSOUTH. If I've met her, take the train to Pompeii. If not, wait and drink coffee. Keep moving. Don't look at Harry. If Harry walks past with a newspaper, follow him. If I talk to her, don't give anything away, get a second meeting, make it for Herculaneum in two days."

"You write all that down?"

"Yes."

"Dumb. Shred it right now. I wanta hear the shredder. Okay, a word of wisdom: don't get heroic. Just do the routine."

"And you'll call the NCIS office on the boat."

"Be careful, Al—she could be trouble."

"That's occurred to me, Mike."

"Good. And, yeah, I'll make up something for the NCIS guys."

Alan's throat tightened. "How's Rose?"

Even over the STU, Dukas sounded troubled. "Oh, she's—okay—I don't see much of her—"

LATER, Dukas called the STU number for the NCIS office on the boat three times but didn't connect. Triffler dug up a cellphone number for one of the agents, and he got the man on the second try and asked him to call Dukas on the STU.

"This's Mike Dukas."

"Yeah, Mike, this is Marty Stein on board the *Jefferson.*" The STU whistled and burped.

"Marty, I got a case here that's very sensitive. You know Al Craik? He's on your boat with a detachment of S-3s."

Subdued rustling, as if leaves were blowing together at the other end of the STU.

"Yeah. Security risk, that's why it's sensitive?"

"Jesus, no! Where do you get this shit? I'm using Craik as a dangle in Naples, and I don't want anybody dicking it up, okay?"

"You don't have to shout. Christ. This the same guy who popped a Serb in Trieste?"

"And it's the same business, okay?"

"Mike, we've, uh, heard that this guy and his wife are, uh, *bad.*" "Bad" came across loaded with meaning.

Dukas thought it was funny that in the most complex business in the world, there was this tendency to want to simplify. Good and bad. Black and white.

"Well, they aren't. Got that?"

"We just keep getting these rumors. Plus the JAG says the admiral's leery of the guy. You sure you want to use him as a dangle?"

Dukas swallowed an angry retort. Instead, he said evenly, "Buddy, if Craik is a security risk, you and I are aliens from outer space. You do everything you can to spike those rumors, and for God's sake don't let my guy's operation get dicked!"

14

Naples.

HARRY O'NEILL SAW ANNA BEFORE AL CRAIK HAD cleared the fleet landing. She was well back from the pier, almost to the castle, sitting outside in a trattoria. First, he had noticed men watching her, and then he had seen her. He had continued to look around, but she had to be the target.

Now Harry watched Alan emerge from the shadow of the gate to the pier and start toward the castle, too, and he saw her leave a coin on her table, watch Alan for a moment, and then move toward the castle. They were on converging courses and Harry could watch them both from his Citroën. He had been there for two hours, going through the usual panics of surveillance: *The target went past and I missed her; the target isn't here; the whole thing is canceled.* Now he felt relief.

She was standing beside the metal railing that surrounded the bastion as Alan approached, her silhouette crisp against the sun-dazzled stone. There were a few men around, more interested in her than in the fortress, but their interest was so obvious that he knew they weren't her enemies or her anti-surveillance. Alan walked right up to her, and his shock was visible when she put her arms around his neck. She said something. Harry cursed not having wired Alan.

She took his hand and he led her up the hill toward the station.

They walked for several minutes, and it was clear that Alan didn't want to hold her hand. She kept looking at him and smiling—dazzling, sexy smiles meant to melt hearts. Harry could see that Alan was not melted; in fact, he seemed to be getting angry. Harry laughed a little and got out of his car to go up the steps to the station. Rose should see this, he thought. Picture of a loyal husband.

Harry beat them into the station by a clear minute and had his tickets in hand when they came to the kiosk. It was the first time he could hear them. Her voice was deep and foreign, a kind of dream voice that went with the rest of her.

"Where are we going?"

"Pompeii. I thought it would give us time to talk."

She laughed. "I have never been to Pompeii. It is very sweet of you to turn this into an outing. A picnic, perhaps?"

Harry boarded two cars ahead of them. He didn't think that either of them had even looked at him yet. She seemed entirely focused on Alan. In fact, to Harry, she didn't seem like an agent at all. He watched them, two cars distant but visible through the doors. She touched him several times and made him laugh, finally. Good.

Loosen up, Al.

The station at Pompeii was the danger point. It had an open platform, and when he had looked it over yesterday at this time there had been no traffic at all. They might be the only three people getting off the train, and it sucked to be black in Italy.

She was laughing now, her head thrown back and her torso arched slightly, one perfect foot stretched across the aisle at Alan. Harry thought of Monty Python. *Let me try and resist the temptation* Brave Sir Robin.

As he had feared, the station was empty. Harry knew that the train would stop for almost a minute; he counted to forty and walked off, going directly to the phone kiosk at the far end of the platform. He called no one, chatted for a minute to no one, and hung up. They were moving far ahead on the dusty road to the ruins, and he was clear.

Harry's principal role was making sure she hadn't brought any friends, and so far she seemed clean. She had moved through four groups of people so far, and no one had crossed from group to group. Harry picked his backpack off the urine-smelling floor of the kiosk and headed toward the amphitheater at the far end of the ruins.

He almost walked into them. Alan must have taken his instruction to keep moving a little too seriously—that, or the mildly pornographic casts at the lower end of the ruins didn't suit his mood. Either way, Harry had just started to climb the levels of the amphitheater for a view when he heard their voices below him. He looked back and saw them edging around an archaeological dig toward the shade at the south end, and he was trapped in the open, along the top.

"This is perfect," she said. The word "perfect" had a purr to it— *purr-fect*. She sat at the edge of the sun on the lowest stone bench. Alan looked behind him and moved on without pausing, and Harry thought that, all things considered, Alan deserved a pat on the back because they'd made eye contact and now Harry knew Alan had seen him.

Alan sat down next to her.

"What is it like, living in that metal monster in the bay?" she said.

"What do you know about Bonner?"

"I like to talk, to know you a little. It has taken me a long time to get to this place. Those men in Trieste, they were there to kill me, yes?"

She kept her eyes on his, a directness that was both feminine and cold. Harry felt that Alan was dealing with two people—a beautiful woman who wanted to be admired, and a cunning animal of no sex whatsoever. The breeze carried the next sentences away, but they both looked serious. Harry could hear only the tone. Then Alan's voice was distinct again. "How did you find me?"

"Do you know the name Efremov?"

Harry knew that one. Bonner's boss. A name from the past.

"Yes."

"I was his—companion. In Iran."

"What do you know about Bonner?"

"You are very brisk, Commander Bond. I had a small speech to make, and you have spoiled it."

"Ma'am, I covered for you with the police, God knows why. Now I'm talking to you. I don't know you, but I know you got me to a café where some guys shot at me. As far as I can see, no one shot at you. Pout all you want, but please answer my questions."

Harry winced. Alan Craik all over. Mister Goal-oriented.

"Are all Americans so rude?"

"Can we talk about Bonner, ma'am?"

"Would you care to ask my name? 'Ma'am' makes me feel quite old?"

She was playing with Alan. All Harry's life, women had played this game with him, and he knew that Alan didn't know how to respond. Other men did it with ease. She wanted something—some recognition of her presence, her magnetism, and Alan was not giving her anything.

"Please call me Anna."

"Anna, I shot a man in Trieste. Men may be hunting you. I don't have much time."

She watched him through her lashes, a feral cat in a fancy collar, and he almost flinched away.

"There is a mole in the CIA," she said. "He is at a very high level."

"A mole, in the CIA. Who, Aldrich Ames? Tell me another."

"I can prove what I say. Names, dates, transfers of material."

A cold hand seized Alan's heart and squeezed.

"Efremov knew this? I'm supposed to trust him? Efremov ran the bastard?"

"Efremov was a professional intelligence officer. No, this was not one of ours—just something he stumbled over."

Efremov stumbled over a high-level mole in the CIA.

"Where is Efremov now, Anna?"

"He is dead." She gave off genuine emotion, and Harry, high above them, felt the surprise that showed on Alan's face. *Efremov had a lover who missed him?*

"Who are you working for?" he asked.

"Myself!" She said it with bitter emphasis. "Only myself. I want one million American dollars for my files on the mole. I have other items as well. They will be sold separately."

"We'll have to meet again."

"Ah, the gallantry! Do you even see me as human, Commander?"

"Okay, Anna, call me Alan. Is that better?"

"Oh, the progress I'm making! We have exchanged names! Does your wife tell you how handsome you are?"

Alan looked at her and smiled his second smile of the afternoon. "Mostly she tells me I'm a gomer."

"Gomer?"

"She tells me I'm foolish for, well, various little things like leaving ice cream in the refrigerator instead of the freezer."

Anna laughed a different laugh, and Harry added a third person to her selves—the courtesan, the spy, and the woman with the real laugh. Harry thought he might like to know the last one.

"Gomer. Yes, men are like that. Blind. Alan, I have information that will prove there is a high-level spy in the CIA. I will provide it to the first buyer with one million dollars in a bank account in Switzerland with an automatic teller card and a letter from the bank."

"I can't get that kind of money." Alan sounded as if he was repeating lines—as he was. Inside, he just kept imagining a high-level mole in the CIA.

"Find someone who can."

"Can you meet me again in two days? Or meet somebody else?"

"I want to meet you." She smiled at him. "You at least saved my life."

"In two days, at the ticket kiosk outside Herculaneum."

"Who wrote this script for you? It might be nice if we walked away from today with a little warmth, don't you think? Or am I like a police informer? Just a piece of trash you wouldn't associate with?"

The breeze came up again. Harry could hear only the intense murmur of their exchange.

Then she laughed out loud, the second peal of totally unaffected laughter she had made. Whatever Alan had said, his recoil suggested that laughter had not been the answer he expected.

"You were on one of Efremov's lists, therefore I thought you were a case officer. That's why I chose you—because I could find you through the Navy, you would know the business, you would know how to deal with me. Now I find that you are a military man who dislikes attractive women. You are no case officer, Commander."

"No, I'm not. I take it you've already offered this information elsewhere?"

"Perhaps. Tell me, what woman *do* you like? Or are you homosexual?"

"My wife."

That did it. Harry sighed. He'd never have given such an answer.

Harry knew she was going to take the second meeting: she wanted the money. Alan had all but promised it, in spy talk—the wrong move, but he had done okay otherwise. Harry didn't relish dropping twenty feet from the top of the small amphitheater, but, short of walking past them, there was nothing else for it. He let himself over the edge carefully, looked down, made a face, and dropped.

ALAN LOOKED AT HER, her face, her lightly tanned skin, the Italian linen dress that fit like a four-digit price tag. Her physical perfection was so total that it was almost alien. She lacked Rose's warm sexuality; she had her own, but there was no warmth to it. He didn't trust her and he didn't like her.

"Somebody will meet you at the kiosk."

"If it isn't you, how will I know whom to meet?"

Alan's brain went into high gear, trying items of clothing, newspapers, umbrellas, all the things he'd read of in le Carré and Len Deighton. Nothing came to mind.

"Carry flowers," she said and smiled, but all Alan saw was her teeth.

A telephone, Naples.

"Hey, babe." Alan's voice was tight with fatigue and excitement.

"You!" Rose laughed and gasped and sounded angry all in the same syllable.

"I haven't forgotten you, babe. I should have called earlier."

"You've got Mike worried sick! Is it over? The thing, I mean—this woman—" Dukas had told her something about Anna, he supposed. *Bad move, Mike.*

"It's over for today, yeah."

"You didn't bother to tell me that you had shot a guy in Trieste, either!"

"I couldn't."

"You bastard!"

"I love you."

"I know you do." Repenting a little. "And it sounds nice to hear it." She laughed her throaty laugh. "Who is this woman? No one will tell me."

"I can't, either."

"Is she beautiful?"

Alan had a guilty twinge from nowhere. *He hadn't done anything.* "She's, uh, quite something to look at, yup."

"Well, the two-TACAN rule does not apply in the Craik-Siciliano household, you hear me?"

"I miss you so much, Rose—"

"That's better." A *whuff* of released air from her end. A good sound. "I'd talk dirty to you, but Mikey's here."

"Somebody wants the phone. I really miss you. When this is over—"

"No, stay on the phone! Just a little while. Say it again—'When this is over.' I want to believe it's going to be over. Soon!"

"We're trying. God knows we're trying." He cleared his throat, found himself husky-voiced. "I love you. We'll be together when this is over."

He headed for the boat and a STU to call Dukas.

"DUKAS."

"Mike, it's Alan."

"How'd it go?"

"It's not about Bonner, Mike. That was a throwaway to get me to meet."

"What the fuck? What's she want, then?"

Alan looked at the little screen on the phone to make sure it was secure.

"She says she can finger a high-level mole in the CIA. She wants—"

"What? Say that again."

"She says she has computer files to prove that there's a high-level mole in the CIA."

Crackling and spitting noises from the secure line. "Anybody could say that."

"She's not anybody, Mike. She says she was Efremov's companion."

"Companion?"

"Mistress. Honey. Whatever. Mike, listen to me. A high-level mole in the CIA!"

"Holy shit." Pause. "Yeah, I heard Efremov croaked. You believe her?"

Alan thought about Anna, with her looks and her feral arrogance. "I guess so, yeah."

"What does she want?"

"One million dollars in a Swiss bank with an automatic teller card to access it."

"Wow, that's original. Al, any crank can come up with the CIA mole thing."

"Mike, I can't get over two things—that the accusations against Rose might be connected to the mole, and that this woman came to me. How would she know who I was, and the Bonner thing, if she didn't have some access to Efremov?"

"Bonner was in the papers. So were you."

"Was Efremov?"

"Fair enough. Yeah, we never mentioned him in our case. Okay. When are you meeting her again?"

"I'm *not* meeting her again."

"You can't *not* meet her! You just said there might be a link between the mole and the case of the woman who happens to be your wife!"

"I know, I know—but— Look, I promised the CAG I was out of this. I got a stack of fitreps to smooth, I've got to ride my maintenance guys, and I'm meeting the tech reps in an hour. Anybody could make this second meeting."

"When?"

"Two days, just like you told me."

"Who do you expect me to send to a meeting in Naples in forty-eight hours?"

"How about an NCIS agent?"

"Nobody with the training. They're in Bosnia."

"I don't have any training, for Christ's sake."

"Yeah, but I *know* you. Come on, it might help Rose. I don't have anybody else."

"Harry."

"No. He's doing too much as it is. Al—for *Rose.*"

Alan leaned his forehead on his free hand. He could argue to Rafe that they were in port, anyway, and he was entitled to some liberty—what if he had a meeting with a woman? So did half the guys on the ship. And it might help Rose: if Anna could really reveal the mole, and it was the mole who had framed Rose, then wouldn't she be exonerated? He made the decision, realigned priorities. He'd have to work harder tomorrow to buy the time. "Okay."

"Good. Meet Harry first. I'll set that up from here. Just look for him."

"How about he just waits for me on the pier?"

"That's not how we do this, Al."

"Meeting's at two P.M. at Herculaneum."

"Half-hour by train from Nap to Herc. Huh. I want you to come down the pier at 1230 local, okay? Look for Harry once you clear the pier. Once you see him, just follow him until he stops and let him initiate contact, got it?"

"Yes."

"Okay. If I have anything else, I'll call Marty Stein, NCIS on the boat, and have him pass it, okay?"

"Roger. I gotta go, Mike."

"You think I'm sitting here for my health? So get moving."

"Love you too, Mike."

Alan hung up the phone and went to his bank of safes in the intel area. This would have been the preserve of the intel officer, if his det had been large enough to rate one. Alan had to be his own intel officer. He spun through the combination to the big safe and extracted a set of files—system parameters on the MARI datalink, with yellow stickies and comments in his handwriting, plus a sheaf of briefing reports from his aircrew.

NCIS Headquarters.

Dukas had got Triffler a real desk and his own telephone, partly by bootlegging a line and partly by moonlight-requisitioning a phone and a STU from a warehouse at the Navy Yard. Triffler had then walled himself off from Dukas's mess with a dozen new white plastic crates arranged into a kind of room divider—irregular, stair-step construction, spaces between crates filled with golf trophies, plants, a piece of ersatz sculpture from a museum shop, and an oversized plastic apple

"Who's your decorator?" Dukas had growled when he saw it. He had yet to pick up the crate that had fallen from his own desk, or its files. Still, he tried to be friendly. "Want a jelly doughnut?"

Then Triffler was gone, researching the history of Rose's computer in the days it had been out of her sight. When he came back, Dukas was

so eager for good news—any good news—that he greeted Triffler like
an old friend, dragging his chair over to Triffler's side of the crates
and pouring himself a cup of Triffler's coffee. Triffler was just telling
him that Rose's hard drive had been switched in an Arkansas transit
warehouse—two fake NCIS agents had appeared there and waved a
forged letter from a nonexistent Mister Tremont in NCIS Security—
when Dukas's phone rang. Dukas groaned and tried to reach through a
plastic crate to get it, knocked over a golf trophy, spilled his coffee, and
groaned again. Triffler already had a roll of paper towels and was mopping the coffee as Dukas jumped past him and at last got to the phone. It
was an encrypted call, so he had to hit the STU, and that really pissed
him off. "Dukas!" he shouted. "I'm busy!"

"Jesus, Mike, take it easy."

"Harry! Where the hell—? Listen, I'm in a meeting—"

"Mike, somebody just turned on George Shreed's home computers.
What I want you to do is—"

Dukas exploded. "How the fuck do you know what's happening in
Shreed's house?"

"Don't ask. The important thing is—"

"You're hacking! You stupid sonofabitch! You could get us both in
deep shit!"

"Mike, *somebody has turned on George Shreed's home computers.* He's
at his office—Valdez already checked. Think!"

Dukas thought. "Menzes?" he said. "Menzes is surveilling him and not
telling me?"

"Possible. Think again."

"Somebody else is in Shreed's house playing with his computers. So?"

"If it isn't us, and it isn't Menzes— Think wild card, Mike."

Dukas hesitated only an instant. "I'm thinking. Bye!"

He grabbed Triffler by the arm and yanked him toward the door.
"We're outa here!"

"Hey—! My suit—!"

"You got a car? Mine's got a bad muffler, makes a hell of a noise—"
Dukas was trotting, pulling Triffler along. "People remember it, right?—
notice it—your car is better. I bet your car is better. Right? What d'you
drive, Dick?"

"Where the hell are we going—?"

Dukas made Triffler drive. As he expected, Triffler's Honda was less than a year old, unblemished. Dukas rode with a suburban Virginia map book spread on his lap.

"*Where are we going?*" Triffler demanded again.

"Shreed's, I thought I told you that."

"You didn't!"

"Well, listen up when I talk to you!" He urged Triffler to more speed, and Triffler, who was a deft but cautious driver, pushed the car to within one mph of the posted speed limit. "We're gonna do a drive-by of Shreed's house and see is anybody there."

"Why?"

"Somebody's using his computers."

"How do you know that?"

"A friend told me."

Shreed's street was tree-shaded and quiet. A few cars were parked along the curbs, but most of the residents were working. A young black man was walking two dogs; two white women pushed baby carriages; a lawn sprinkler threw dotted lines of water toward the pavement.

"It's the white house," Dukas said. "Go slow."

"The Colonial?"

"Whatever—the *white* one."

"They're all white."

"They're all brick, for Christ's sake; the *white* one! Yeah, that one—the one with the hatchback in the driveway. Oh, shit." He said the last words because, as they came close, a thin white woman carrying a vacuum cleaner came out of Shreed's house and began to remove the machine's dust bag. She glanced up and then went back to her work. "Oh, shit, a cleaning lady!"

"A white cleaning lady, at that!" Triffler said.

"Read me the license number."

"Of what?"

"The goddam car in the driveway. What d'you think, the fucking vacuum cleaner?"

Triffler read off the numbers as they cruised past. "Don't look at her," Dukas hissed. "Don't look at her!"

Triffler chuckled. "What do you think, she's going to call the cops?"

"You know what the Agency would say if they knew we were surveilling Shreed's house? They'd crucify us!" Dukas was looking up the street, where four more cars were parked in a line along the curb. "Go slow," he muttered, "like we're a real estate agent and a client, maybe."

"I must be the agent," Triffler said. "I'm the guy with the tie on."

Dukas growled again. "It's bad enough we gotta worry about the local cops here—they know Shreed's Agency; they keep an eye on any Agency guy's house. Hey—"

He had seen a man's head in one of the cars in the line. Something, perhaps the angle of the head, suggested that the man was watching in his driver's-side mirror. Years of stakeouts and surveillance caused a little warning to sound in Dukas's head; his first thought was *local cop*, and then he realized how unlikely such a thing was. "Don't slow—don't look at this guy—" Dukas was trying to see the license plate, but the car was backed tight against the car behind it and it was only as they came almost parallel that he was able to see the first three characters of a Virginia plate. *G7B*. He said it over to himself, writing it on the pad without looking and hoping it would be legible later, because his eyes were swinging to look at the man in the car for one instant and then moving on, face registering nothing, trying to be as blank as a stranger looking over the neighborhood.

And that was how he came to see, for one instant, the face of Tony Moscowic.

LATER, back at the NCIS building, he wondered what the hell he was doing. What he had said to Triffler was true—if the Agency found he'd been near Shreed's house, they'd hang him. And hacking into Shreed's computers—! Even NCIS would hang him. *Rose, Rose,* he thought, *only for you!*

"Bingo," Triffler said in his ear.

Dukas jumped. "Don't do that, for Christ's sake. Clear your throat or something!"

"We got a hit on the license number of the car in Shreed's driveway. Heather Crouthammer. Local cops have a memo on her—she'll be parked in his driveway every Wednesday."

"Cleaning lady," Dukas said. *Shit.*

"You got it."

"*She* didn't turn the goddam computers on, Dick."

"How do you know? Maybe she goes online. Plays games. Gambles, maybe."

"On two computers at once? Come on!" Dukas hunched forward. "She goes there to clean; the computers go on. Funny coincidence. Find out what you can about her. What about the other car?"

"The partial? They're working on it. Not too hopeful."

Dukas thought of the face he had seen in the car. Sallow, cynical, tricky. *The guy was watching the street,* he thought. *I know he was.* He could see the way it was done: somebody went into the house with the cleaning woman, went into the computers while she worked; this guy sat in his car and watched the street, ready to warn the other one if anything suspicious came along.

"Somebody else is after Shreed," he said. "It could be CIA Internal, but I don't believe it. I think Menzes is too straight to lie to me." Or at least he hoped so.

"So," Triffler said, "who else could it be?"

Dukas wouldn't say it out loud, but he was thinking, *A woman I'm sleeping with named Emma Pasternak.*

Suburban Maryland.

Suter had rented an apartment for Nickie the Hacker in a building in suburban Maryland where an international and polyglot clientele from the University of Maryland rubbed elbows with one of the more discreet drug markets in the area. It suited the hacker because nobody asked questions and the pizza deliveries were fast.

"It was a piece a cake," Moscowic was saying. "He went in with the cleaning lady, she does her routine, he don't make a sound in case there's bugs someplace, and he does his thing." He looked at Nickie, gave an encouraging jerk to his hips. "Isn't that true, Nickie?"

"I downloaded everything. He's got some software, man!"

Suter was still looking at Moscowic. "Nobody saw you?"

"Who'd see me? You think I'm some amateur?"

"The local police would have that house on a watch list. Local cops have *my* place on a watch list. Because of my employer."

"Big deal, I'm really impressed. Nobody saw me." Moscowic remembered very well the man who had seen him, but he wasn't going to tell Suter. *Let sleeping dogs lie,* he thought. Just some middle-aged guy in a Honda with a black dude—meaningless. But he could still see that face. Suspicious, intelligent, cynical. A cop's face but not a cop.

"Nickie got away clean?" Suter said.

"Wha'd I just say? He did the job, no problem. No problemo! He carries out some of the trash and shit, puts it in her car like he belongs there, and they drive away." He snapped his fingers. "Just like that."

Suter swung around to Nickie and spoke to him for the first time. "You looked at the files yet?"

Nickie, whose face was down over a pizza, shook his head.

"When are you going to do it?"

The thin shoulders went up and down in a shrug.

"Look, you little shit—!" Suter grabbed the raspberry hair at the back, and the face came up, and with it a knife that gleamed in Nickie's right hand. Cheese and tomato sauce were stuck along the cutting edge.

"Hey, hey—!" Moscowic shouted.

Suter let go of the purple-red hair. Nickie curled his upper lip. Moscowic made quieting gestures with his hands.

"Let's behave like gentlemen here, can we do that?" Moscowic said. The other two looked at him as if he was nuts.

USS *Thomas Jefferson.*

When Alan knocked at the open door, Rafe said "enter" without looking up, took another sheet off the pile of paperwork under his left elbow, skimmed it, and scrawled a signature at the bottom.

"Rafe?"

"Sorry, Al. Wait one." The next item was three pages long. Rafe hummed and muttered as he read it, slapped a yellow sticky on top, wrote a note, and threw it in another pile.

"Dickhead. Not you, Al. What's on your mind?"

"It's the NCIS thing, Rafe. I, um, need to meet the woman again, day after tomorrow."

Rafe scowled, started to say something, then swung to: "What's all that under your arm? That better not be for me."

"Nope. It's my battle plan for the tech reps."

"What are you doing to them?"

"Making them work. They haven't been talking to the aircrew very much. I made the debriefers run down these sheets with the TACCOs after every flight to get data on little stuff: link behavior, range, keyboard usage, function keys."

"Bet they loved that."

"Point is, I now have about two hundred queries and suggested fixes. We're in port; tech reps don't get liberty. So now's the day and now's the hour. And since 'Squash' Soleck got a free vacation in Aviano, he can ride shotgun on it."

"Sounds good." Rafe leaned back. "You're doing a good job now, you know that? No, really. I know what all that paper means, man. And the det shows it—your guys are looking better; hell, even your landing scores are up since you cleaned the clock on that cigarette boat." He glanced at his watch, put his hands back behind his head. "Okay, the NCIS thing. You said one meeting. Now you say another meeting. Well, we're in port." He nodded at Alan's papers. "But you're not going to get much liberty. If you want to spend it running errands for NCIS— Is this the *last* NCIS thing, Al?"

"Uh—jeez, I hope so—"

"I appreciate your honesty, so I'll just rephrase. This *is* the last NCIS thing. Period. Okay?" Their eyes met. Rafe nodded. "Have a ball."

Rafe turned back to his paperwork. Alan had twenty minutes to prep for the tech reps, who weren't going to like the workload he was about to dump.

"*Inshallah*," he breathed.

15

Langley.

SUTER WAS IN SHREED'S OFFICE.

"I got interviewed by somebody from NCIS this morning," Suter said. "About Peacemaker. The Siciliano thing. I told you about it, remember? I just thought you'd like to know." He was trying to sound casual and he sounded like hell.

Shreed made himself calm. "Why would I care?"

Suter flushed. "I just thought you'd want to know." He stared at Shreed.

" 'The Siciliano thing.' The woman you spent an unsuccessful year trying to get in the pants of?"

"She's under investigation for security violations. Remember, you wanted me to try to spread, um, rumors about her and her husband?"

"Did I?"

"But I didn't say anything about that. You don't need to worry."

You don't need to worry. As if Suter knew something. Shreed had got so used to living two lives and being confident of the wall that separated them that he almost automatically dismissed the idea that Suter could know anything about his Chinese-agent self—and yet there was a *tone* in that nervous voice. It occurred to Shreed that maybe Suter was going ga-ga. The Agency could do that to people. He was certainly behaving oddly. Saying odd things. He gave Suter a long look now, trying both to figure him out and to warn him. At last he said, "I don't worry."

"That's good. They asked about my connection with both Peacemaker and the Agency, but they never asked about you. So I didn't bring your name up."

Shreed did a lightning review of his own connection with Peacemaker and saw nothing to trouble him. He had had a semi-secret role, lobbying for the project before Congress, channeling money from some secret funds. And, of course, he had betrayed it to the Chinese. But he couldn't see anything that should worry him about it.

"What did you tell them?" he said.

"I told them that Siciliano asked a lot of questions about highly classified material that wasn't her business. And I told them that she had a very close relationship with an enlisted guy named Valdez." Suter looked pleased with himself. "A computer geek." His shoulders jerked. "I mean, the guy asked me if I knew anything about bad-mouthing Siciliano and her husband, the holy Alan Craik. I didn't tell him you'd told me to do the bad-mouthing. Instead, I talked about her Tex-Mex geek, Valdez. I said that they were *very* close." As Shreed stared at him and the moment got longer and longer, Suter gave a kind of snort that became a giggle, and he began to make semaphoric signals with his eyebrows that were probably meant, Shreed thought, to suggest heavy sexual content. A thought flashed: *He's cracking up.*

But then Shreed was thinking more about the implication of what Suter had said than about Suter's mental state. He signaled that their meeting was over. "Have my notes on all this crap transcribed and on my desk by four," Shreed said. He wanted to think.

Suter got up and gathered the papers and put them into a neat stack with almost obsessive care. He hugged the papers to his chest. "I'm very good at things like the interview," he said. "I didn't tell them *anything.*" He backed away from Shreed toward the door. "Anyway, they're not very bright. NCIS doesn't get very bright people."

"They might surprise you."

Suter made a movement with his whole body, something like a bow, or perhaps the jerk of a condemned man as he reaches the bottom of his fall and is stopped by the noose, and he backed out, staring at Shreed the whole time, his right eye being the last thing to disappear as he closed the door.

"Nutcase," Shreed said aloud. However, he was thinking about the NCIS investigator's questions about what Suter had called bad-mouthing: Did NCIS have some reason to believe that the gossip had started inside the Agency? Had they interrogated Suter because they didn't yet dare to interrogate Shreed himself? He knew how such things were done: he knew that there was talk of a mole—knew it? By God, he had taken part in it! So that when the NCIS interrogator came to ask permission to examine people at the Agency, Internals would say Yes to this one, No to that. And the Nos would be reserved for anybody on their list of possibles, because they wouldn't want to scare the mole.

So let's see how it would go, Shreed thought. *NCIS are investigating the Siciliano case. If Internals allowed them to see the "intercept" that Chen concocted to implicate Siciliano, then they realized pretty quickly that it was cock and bull. Internals knows it, too, of course. But Internals and NCIS are in a sense on opposite sides, because Internals wants to protect the Agency and NCIS wants to exonerate Siciliano. So then there's the matter of her computer— No. No, next there's the Agency almost dropping the investigation because Siciliano's lawyer made so much noise, and then there's the Agency resuming the investigation because, well, because I made such a stink at that meeting the day of Janey's memorial service.*

That was when I went public—public with a very small and select population of the Agency—with my need to implicate Siciliano, although they wouldn't have seen it that way; they would have seen cranky, grieving George Shreed playing the patriotic card. But if there was somebody at the meeting with the right set of eyes—

He thought about the meeting and who had been there. *Partlow. Jeffreys. Breedlove. Goering—* He went around the big table, seeing nobody who might have suggested to NCIS that he, George Shreed, had more interest in the Siciliano case than seemed reasonable.

Nobody.

He went around the table in his mind again. That committee met weekly, always the same. Everybody—

Not always the same. Something had been different, some face at the corner of the table. That's where Handman of Technical Research always sat. *But he wasn't there. Somebody in his place, sitting not at the table but back a little against the wall—*

Sally Baranowski.

My God, how could I have missed it?

Sally Baranowski, who had seen his performance that day and who had every reason to want to hurt him. *Bad move,* he thought. He hadn't taken her seriously.

He reached for his telephone, not for a moment trusting the e-mail system to be discreet.

"Breedlove," a voice said at the other end.

"Mark, George Shreed. I'm wondering how your contact in Internals is. I need a favor. Somebody named Baranowski—"

NCIS HQ.

Triffler had just finished reporting on his interview with Ray Suter. The only thing that stuck out for Dukas was Suter's having implied some bullshit about sex between Rose and the computer guy, Valdez. It didn't make sense. Had Shreed coached Suter to lie about her and Valdez? If he could *prove* that Shreed was behind Suter's answers in the interview—

"Have we got anything new on Shreed?" he called to Triffler.

"If we did, it would be marked in green as an update on the chart."

Triffler had made a chart that tried to track what they knew about Shreed. It was on the back of the door, so anybody coming in didn't see it, but Dukas could stare at it from his desk and try to figure out if it meant anything. But all that the chart gave him to date was Shreed's public biography, which was virtuous and admirable—naval air service, Agency postings in Jakarta and Washington, promotions. In recent months, it got more detailed—"Wife, Angel of Mercy Hospice. Death of wife. Memorial service of wife." And then, "T. and D. surveil cleaning woman—" Triffler's way of saying they had been wasting their time.

So, nothing new. Dukas sighed. He made a note on a sticky and put it on Triffler's report of the interview: "Follow-up interview recommended." But not just now, he knew, because he didn't have the people and he didn't have the budget.

Naples.

Preparing for his second meeting in Naples with Anna, Alan had first to meet Harry. Not seeing him at fleet landing, he paused to watch the spectacle of fleet landing, a last bastion of America and one from which some sailors never quite dared to stray. Dozens of others stopped here to have a burger and a Coke before entering foreign territory (which, of course, offered its own burgers and Cokes a couple of blocks away). Dozens more, having already sampled Naples, waited for a ride back to the ship, gulping down fries and sodas in feeble attempts to cover the taste of mixed beer, pizza, wine, brandy, and "I dare you" exotics like Fernet Branca. Rap and country boomed from radios, each asserting its own version of America to Italy, whose first inhabitants were just visible down the pier where panhandlers in sincere castoffs and hookers in bright clothes forced the sailors to run a gantlet of sympathy and sex.

Alan pushed through the Navy crowd to the shore-patrol post and walked the gantlet without a glance, smiling at the Neapolitan comments he was not supposed to understand. He continued to look for Harry, following a route he had been given by Dukas, past the hookers to the vendors, past the vendors to the first small trattorias, off the pier and left toward San Marco.

Harry was sitting in a big café on the other side of the boulevard, reading a paper with his back to Alan, who spotted him from a block away and crossed the street in the first lull of the traffic. When Alan saw him again, Harry did not appear to have seen him, but, as he walked closer, Harry stood up without hurry, tossed a coin on the table, and walked away from the docks with the newspaper pressed under his arm. Alan followed him, now only a block behind. They walked uphill for two streets, took a right, and then entered a web of smaller streets that Alan vaguely remembered from his childhood as the medieval part of the city. Harry appeared unhurried, but every turn he made caused Alan to accelerate for fear that Harry would disappear in the crowded streets.

Most of Naples seemed to be buying coffee and fish and anything else that was out on tables. Several times Harry stopped and looked, and once he bought something, each stop causing Alan to stop behind him and do the same.

It was a moment's inattention while trying to make one of these forced stops inconspicuous that caused Alan to lose Harry altogether. He looked up from a display of seafood on ice to find that Harry had vanished from a similar stall a street ahead, and he moved toward his last sighting, unable to believe that a tall black man could be so hard to find in an Italian crowd.

Alan walked to where he had last seen him and looked around. He bit the inside of his cheek in annoyance and decided that Harry was headed either back toward the bay or up toward the Vomero and turned right, moving quickly. And there, seated at a tiny café just around the corner, was Harry, who smacked him with the newspaper as he was about to walk by.

"We've got to stop meeting like this, shweetheart."

Alan's annoyance evaporated in the pleasure of meeting his friend.

"Almost lost you, there."

"Nah, you were fine." Harry smiled broadly. "Good to see you, old chap." The fake Brit accent took Alan back to the boat. They had been junior officers together. They had survived in Africa together. The new Harry, the one with only one good eye, was calmer, a little more reserved. Still Harry. They tried to crush each other's hand.

"How's Rose?" Alan said. "I mean, I've talked to her, but you've seen her."

"Mad as hell. She misses you. I've got a note and some packages for you later."

Alan smiled ruefully. "First we work?"

"Yeah. You ready to meet the dragon lady again?"

"I don't like her, Harry."

"No shit. Can you pretend to like her?"

"She gives me the creeps."

"It shows. First, stop acting like she has leprosy. I'm not saying get her in the sack—"

"Fuck, no!" Alan rocked back in his chair.

"Although all things considered, that would probably be best."

"Harry, *old boy,* that is not on, *capisce?*" Alan's fake Brit accent was not up to Harry's standard.

Harry sighed, sipped his coffee, glanced around. Alan waved to the bored waiter and asked for an espresso.

"A little quieter, okay? Look, the dragon lady may have something really good; there were a few prize bits in her conversation. I want to give you a few pointers on dealing with her, and I'd like you to sit quietly and listen."

"I don't plan to get her in the sack."

"Little on-the-spot psych profile. She's a people pleaser. She understands relationships best when they involve sex. That's common with people who got sexually abused as kids. Her self-image is largely based on her looks and the power that gives her. Okay, that's all way too simple, but you have to understand her. I watched you. You don't react to her looks, you don't respond to her allure. In effect, you are dissing her. And she likes you, or at least she did at the start."

"So I fucked the whole thing up."

"Nope. You did all the basic stuff right—you arranged another meeting; you didn't promise her the moon; you kept her going. When she forced you, you started to sound human. *But you need to do better.* Today, you two are going to start real negotiations. Mike wants you to get some sort of peek at the goods, something we can use to check her out. That's going to take some level of interaction. You can't just order her to give you a look at her files, Al."

"Harry, I have a detachment to command, a bunch of guys who think I'm a spy. I can't make a second career of dealing with this woman."

"Man, you were on the way to the Ranch when your orders got changed. What did you think you'd be learning to do there—deal nicely with nice people?" Harry met Alan's eyes. He didn't relent. "Al, this is probably pretty important. Only Mike knows the full score, but it may help Rose, and I think this could be bigger than your detachment. Bear down. Play nice. If it helps, pretend to be somebody else."

Alan retreated to a glazed look that meant he was now staring inward. After some seconds, he said, "Okay, Harry, but this is the last time. Then I want you or Mike to get another guy. Rafe's on my tail about this and he's right. Yeah, I was headed toward the Ranch, but that didn't happen. Now I have another set of responsibilities. I ought to be writing lieutenants' fitreps right now. *That's* my job."

"Tell me your plan for the meeting."

"Three objectives: get a next meeting; get a taste of what she has to offer; get her to lower the price. In that order."

"Right on."

"I can't do James Bond. I haven't got the attitude. But I can do naval aviator. 'Boy, honey, you look great!' That kind of stuff."

"Exactly. Admire her. If she gets too close, hold up your wife. She can understand that."

"I have to carry flowers. That's good, anyway. Flowers to say I'm sorry."

Harry looked at him in mock amazement. Underneath was some real amazement. "Good!"

"No, if I'm going to do this, I better do it right. Rueful about the last meeting. Apologetic. *Sheepish.*"

Harry nodded. "She's probably pretty desperate. She kinda suggested she tried to shop this to someone else, right? And she admitted that these goons tried to kill her. So she's a little strung out. She's looking for a shoulder to cry on. Try a little compassion. Use it as a hook. Then reel her in."

"My dad used to say that when they're crying on your shoulder they're pretty close to getting in the bed."

"Yeah, well, your dad knew a thing or two."

"Not my style, Harry."

"But you'll do us all a lot of good if it seems that it might be, okay? A little comfort is not immoral. She's on the run, she's alone, she needs help. Keep that in mind."

"So I can manipulate her."

"Give the boy in the leather jacket a cigar."

Alan went back to the glazed look. He was thinking about Harry, before and after the Ranch. About things he had said about an agent he loved, who had been killed. Had Harry manipulated her while loving her? Ugly thought. His eyes lost their unfocused look, rested hard on Harry. "It feels dirty."

Harry swallowed the last of his coffee, and his look when his eyes rose from the cup was just as hard as Alan's. "It's an ugly business, Al. I didn't stay with it, if you recall. But this matters. It's bigger than our little likes and dislikes. A mole in the CIA? How many people has he killed? I don't mean to come down on you, but it's bigger than your chivalry."

Alan thought about the woman. She could have the key to men who had plotted to kill his father. After nine years, that really wasn't enough to get him to do this. But she claimed to know that there was a traitor in the CIA. That was big. That was people's lives. "Okay. Once more. That's it."

"*At least* once more. Let me recap: comfort has to come first. Be clumsy, but be sorry, then wonder how she's surviving. Can you offer to keep her on the boat? For her own protection?"

"The admiral would have a cow. He already thinks I'm a loose cannon, maybe a spy."

"She wouldn't accept—it would put her totally in our power. But it's the kind of offer you ought to make."

Alan bit down on a reply. Either he was going to do this right, or he wasn't going to do it. He'd never done a half-assed job in his life.

"Whatever. I use the compassion hook. Offer her bullshit assistance. Suggest that I could fall for her. Then get the date."

Harry smiled.

"I thought Alan Craik was in there somewhere. Finish your coffee. You need to be in Herculaneum in an hour."

SHE WAS STANDING by the ticket kiosk next to the bakery just as he had asked. She looked different, however. Her poise seemed less perfect; there were faint lines on her forehead. Looking at her through Harry's eyes, even at a distance, he saw the trapped animal, not the statue of Venus.

As he approached her, a bunch of red roses under his arm, he felt an impulse to flee or tell her the truth or simply hand her the flowers and walk away. He reached for his dislike for her, but it was harder to dislike the vulnerable woman in front of him. *For Rose, then,* he thought.

"Are those for me?" She reached for the flowers as if they were her due.

"I thought I'd try for a new start. Never met a woman who didn't like flowers." This was the new tone. Act like Rafe, or as he imagined Rafe would act.

She smiled and moved toward him. He turned, and they fell into step walking down the steep street toward the sea.

"This road has been here for two thousand years." That sounded contrived, even to Alan. "I think about them. Were they different? Were they worried? Did they think about the volcano?" She didn't respond. "Probably the way we think about nuclear war. It could happen, but it's best to pretend it won't."

"Do you worry about nuclear war?" The probe was so gentle that Alan didn't even feel it.

"I worry about war all the time."

"Are you afraid?"

"I joined the Navy to prevent it. Just in time for the wall to come down."

"So you are—sorry?" The change in her voice keyed him that this was not small talk. She was probing him for something.

"No, I'm not sorry. The world is still plenty threatening without the Soviet Union."

"And you work to protect the United States?"

She's looking for a handle on me. Looking for common ground, or something she can make appear common. She's looking for the buttons to press.

Sauce for the goose.

"Did you grow up with the threat of war?" he said.

She laughed, a real laugh, a little hoarse. "I grew up in a village. We were always at war. I never thought about nuclear war; only about surviving the next few days. It is a luxury, you see? To worry about the end of the world. A luxury for those who are not fighting their neighbors."

"Where? Who were you fighting?"

"What you would call the 'Stans.' Who did we fight? The next village. The Moslems. Other tribes."

"But you got out." Alan thought of Rwanda and Bosnia.

"Oh, yes. I got out." *There was the hunted animal, right there in her eyes.*

They had passed through the ruins and the reconstruction, and were down to the edge of the sea. The Bay of Naples was a rich, perfect blue under a sky piled with bright clouds. Fishing boats were visible between the mainland and Capri, away in the haze to the left. So was the *Jefferson,* its hull a menacing shape to the right, hard over toward Naples.

"Do you ever go back?"

"I do not wish to speak of this."

Okay, Harry, she's on the verge of tears and pissed. Is that good? "Sorry. Really. I just want to know you better."

"Are you going to buy what I have to sell?"

"Last time, you wanted to talk. Now it's just business?"

"Please. A bad subject. I am embarrassed. I don't like to be—soft, do you say?"

He stepped forward and put a hand on her shoulder.

"I didn't really think about how hard this must be on you. Guys trying to kill you. All I saw was a fashion model looking to make a few bucks." *Okay, that's the compassion hook, Harry. And it wasn't too smooth.*

She rotated under his hand and laid her head on his shoulder. He hugged her hard, as if protecting her, the way he would hug his son. There was no romance in it, but it had some sincerity.

She didn't cry. She put her arms around him for a moment, lightly, and then stepped away.

Nervous and wrong-footed, Alan stepped back, almost stumbled against a bench, and sat down.

She looked out over the bay and then leaned over him, one hand hesitantly laid on the back of his bench. When he looked at her, her eyes were too bright, but the face was bland. She was close to the edge. She needed something. *Refuge?*

"I could protect you on the boat."

"That's very kind of you. But I think it would not be long before I was in 'protective custody,' yes?" She sat down on the bench, her poise a little less studied than in Pompeii.

"They'll keep trying to kill you."

"Perhaps not. I may have found a way to make peace. *Are* you going to buy?"

Make peace. So whoever was hunting her had either offered her a deal, or been offered one.

"Can you give me something, Anna? Some kind of *bona fides* that will convince my people to release the money?"

"More than the name Efremov?"

"And more than the name Bonner."

"Efremov is not exactly a widely known name, you will agree."

"Anna." He took her hand. It had been lying there between them, as if she expected him to take it. Perhaps she did. "I want this over with. It's not my money; I'd just as soon you got it. But you have to give me something to get this moving. So that I can arrive at the next meeting with the money, and you can get free."

"Why do you care that I get 'free'? This is a change, I think?"

The only thing worse than manipulating her is to be seen to do it. Shit.

"Your parents. Are they alive?"

Cheap shot. But it scored: her face twisted.

She's doing it, too.

"They were killed."

"And you escaped?"

"Oh, yes. At least, in the television version." Suddenly, her mouth was trembling, and there was a tremor at the base of her neck that made the veins move. The concentration of her attempt at control was scary.

"I'm sorry. No, Anna, I'm sorry I even brought it up. You're right. I can't play this. Let's get it over with. I'll stop trying to tie you up, and you stop too, and we'll do business and get out of here, okay?"

The too-bright eyes were gazing somewhere over his shoulder. He still had her hand. She was stroking it absently, repetitively, her thumb sliding over his palm.

"Do you know what you are when you are a raped woman in my village? A whore. They sold me in Saudi Arabia for my blond hair. Never a wife, never a child. Just a whore."

He couldn't do it. This was too real.

"Anna—Anna—"

"Efremov saved me. He showed me how not to be a whore. How not to be a tool. *I will not be a tool.*"

She was still rubbing his hand. Her near-perfect English had slipped a little. She looked fierce. Her head flashed around and suddenly she fixed him with her eyes. She seemed to be considering something inside him.

She leaned back with one elbow on the corner of the bench, and now her gaze was frank and appraising.

"Perhaps it is better that we know each other a little better. Yes, I will give you something, and then you will go. But I do not want to meet you in Italy again. I want to meet somewhere I know."

"In the east?" Alan couldn't see how he would make a meeting in the east. *Good. I'm out.*

"Perhaps the Middle East."

"Israel?"

"Don't make me laugh."

"Saudi?"

"I will never go there again, except perhaps to kill."

"Dubai?"

"Perhaps. Or Bahrain? There is US Navy in Bahrain, I know."

Alan looked for a trap but couldn't see one. Bahrain was friendly territory. There was an NCIS office there. The headquarters of Fifth Fleet. A vibrant city and thousands of Americans.

"Good. Bahrain. You know it well?"

"Oh, yes."

"There is a restaurant with a funny name. Up a Tree, Cup of Tea. Say it."

"I don't have to, I know it."

"We'll meet there." He thought that sounded safe. Brits went there, but not a lot of Americans.

"Not to talk. Get a room. I have always wanted to visit the Gulf Hotel as a guest."

"You've been there?"

"As a dancer, yes."

Alan thought of evenings at the Gulf Hotel watching Polish and Lithuanian girls strip for the rich Saudis in the front row. It had been a squadron favorite right after the war.

"I'll see what I can do," he said.

"One week from today. At eight in the evening, local time. With my million dollars."

She smiled at him, back in control, sure of herself. She had stopped stroking his hand and she placed it on her shoulder, leaning into him as if to kiss him. He was startled again and his indecision became paralysis as she leaned in gracefully, but she didn't kiss him. She put her mouth against his ear.

"The mole is called Top Hook. That is what the Chinese call him. *Two* tidbits, my heart."

She slid out of his unintended embrace. He thought he felt the brush of her lips on his cheek, but he was never sure because his mind was stunned by the familiar expression she had used: *top hook.*

She turned like a dancer just a few feet away from the walkway to the ocean.

"Tell your black friend he should introduce himself." Then she was gone.

"YOU'RE BEAUTIFUL, shweetheart, beautiful."

"She made you, Harry."

"So I heard. Hard for her not to, with me sitting twenty feet above you at Pompeii. You in love yet?"

"Oh, for Christ's sake—"

"I am. Christ, she's good. The whole soiled flower thing—"

"Harry, for God's sake. She was crying!"

"Hey, bud, I'm not saying it wasn't true. I'm just saying it was well done. She got to you a little?"

"I'm not cut out for this."

Harry cut him off with a chop of the hand. They were walking up the Via Angevini, almost alone in the early evening, surrounded by eighteenth-century façades now black with soot and car exhaust. The ancient castle towered above them, a malevolent gray-orange in the dying light.

"I wasn't kidding, Al. You were great. I'm sure that you were genuinely fed up with manipulating the woman, but the change, when you went from trying to pull her strings to self-disgust? It was perfect. It was recognition for her. If only for a second, she had converted you. It made her day."

"That wasn't some tactic I dreamed up!"

"That's why it worked. Because it was *so* real. So lighten up. Did you get the goods?"

"I didn't lower her price."

"Yeah, you missed a couple of agenda items. That's okay. She's as tough as anyone I've ever worked, and you're keeping up. Behind on points, I'd say, but still in the game."

"I am not taking leave to go to Bahrain."

"I hear you, but that's going to depend on other factors. Don't keep me waiting, buddy. What did she whisper in your ear?"

"She told me that the mole is run by the Chinese."

"That's good. That's really, really good."

"And that they call him Top Hook."

Harry stopped walking. He didn't look at Alan for a moment. He put his hands behind him and looked out to sea, where the long, boxy shape of the carrier dominated the harbor entrance.

"Well, well." Harry seemed to be talking to himself.

"Come on, Harry. Don't tell me I don't have the need to know."

"Not for me to say—I leave that to Dukas. But I'd say that your soiled flower has the goods. And that's going to rock Mike's world."

" 'Top Hook' is a Navy expression, Harry. Best landing score on a carrier. Best pilot."

"I was in the Navy, too, old boy."

Alan shook his head. "It's not Chinese."

"Give that man a kewpie doll."

Alan was about to say that he had been overwhelmed when he had heard it from Anna because of the implication that a naval aviator's term had given a code name to a spy, but they were suddenly interrupted by a voice calling to them from above.

"Hey, are you guys Navy?"

"Who wants to know?" Alan looked up to the terrace above them. He sounded angry.

"Shore Patrol. Got your ID?"

Alan reached in his breast pocket and took out his battered ID, still covered with stickers from former ships.

"Sorry, sir. You really ought to get a new ID, sir."

"I'll see to it when I get back to the boat. Is that all?"

"Is your friend Navy, sir?"

"No. What's this about, sailor?"

"Recall, sir. We're informing all liberty personnel that liberty is closed at 2000 local. Last boat leaves fleet landing in a little over an hour, sir."

"How come?"

"All liberty canceled, sir."

"Why?"

"I'm sure they'll tell you on the boat, sir."

"Time for a cappuccino, Alan?" Harry waved to the tables on the black-and-white marble of the terrace.

"Here? Sure."

"Sir, uh, shouldn't you be—"

"Petty Officer Lannes." Alan was reading the man's nameplate. "I'm pretty sure I can drink a cup of coffee with my friend and still catch the boat, okay?"

"Yes, sir."

The cup of cappuccino was purely an act of defiance. The café was crowded, and they didn't return to the subject of Top Hook, except that Harry told Alan to call Mike Dukas as soon as he was on the boat. Otherwise, they talked about nothing. It was a good nothing, and it defied the creep of time. They were old friends who rarely got to see one another, and all their contact in Naples had been professional, or at least conspiratorial. In twenty hurried minutes they tried to make that up, swapping stories and tidbits. After, Harry walked Alan all the way down to the landing and hugged him, then handed him an envelope and a package from Rose.

"See you in Bahrain."

"Fuck off, Harry. I'm not going to Bahrain."

"We'll see, sweetheart. It's my home ground, these days. Stay safe."

"You too. Kiss Rose for me, if you see her."

They shook hands once more, and Alan hurried through the crowd toward the boat.

The ferries were packed with unhappy sailors. Many had barely got ashore. Some had missed liberty altogether. Alan looked for somebody to give him news, but those he knew were as ignorant as he, and the liberty-boat officers were mostly air-wing guys with little knowledge but a lot of speculation. Veterans could remember the same things happening in Naples in 1990, when the *Eisenhower* sprinted to the Red Sea to threaten Saddam Hussein.

"Iraq's attacked Kuwait again."

"It's Israel."

"China's shutting the Taiwan Straits."

"Russia's declared for Serbia and we're at war."

Alan thought it had to be Pakistan and India, but the Balkans loomed, too. *Twice in a century?*

As he ran up the ladder from the ferry buoy to the carrier's stern, he heard a sailor shout it down.

"Pakistan's fighting India!"

His thoughts returned to the det.

NCIS HQ.

"Seventy-three positives on the partial," Triffler said.

The words meant nothing to Dukas.

"The license plate. The car near Shreed's house? You and me driving by, guy in a car—?"

"Yeah, yeah. Seventy-three! Holy shit."

"I tried what I remembered about make and color; that knocked it down to forty-some." Triffler looked up. "Camry, I thought. Blue."

"It was gray."

"It was blue!"

"Gray."

"Williamsburg blue, kind of a grayed-down blue—"

"Dick, for Christ's sake! Gray, blue, what the hell! You didn't get the make or the year?"

"I was driving. I pay attention to what I'm doing."

"Seventy-three hits, Christ!" Dukas rubbed his head. "Okay, put the whole list out, local PDs and state cops. Any hit on anybody on the list, we wanta know. Mark it priority, national security, direct to you or me." He looked at Triffler. "You got a problem with that?"

"I think it's a misuse of tax money."

"Oh, good."

"I feel very strongly about taxes."

"So do I. They pay your salary, and if you don't do your job, you won't be earning one. *Capisce?*"

Triffler's face was set in a kind of mask of tragedy. Muscles worked in his cheeks. After several seconds, he said, "Your management style leaves something to be desired."

"Yeah, I missed that meeting on total quality management."

"A good manager values the input of his subordinates."

Dukas laughed. "Dick, you're as good as a bumper sticker! Look—" He rubbed his head again. "*Please* put that out as a priority request— okay? I do value your input. I just don't agree with it. Okay?"

"I don't like working for you," Triffler said.

"Neither do I."

USS *Thomas Jefferson*.

Alan had been back aboard for an hour and he hadn't called Mike Dukas—too much to do. He walked down through the enforced calm of the air-wing spaces and entered the controlled chaos of the intel spaces and waited for an hour to use one of the secure telephones. Then he called Mike at home and got no answer. He looked at his watch and tried Mike's work number.

"Dukas."

"Is my watch wrong, or should you be home?"

"Al. What happened? I expected to hear from you hours ago. I'm waiting for you, okay?"

"Mike, we're a little busy here." A young jg pushed her head and shoulders into Alan's phone cube and asked him if he would be long. He waved her away. "Can we go secure?"

"You push." They waited while the seconds whirled by. The jg was still hovering. A rush of white noise told Alan that they had a link.

"What happened, cowboy?"

"Harry hasn't called?"

"Plan was, you were going to call. I've been sitting here picturing both of you gunned down by Serbs. *What happened?*"

"She showed. The meeting was hard. She's pretty tightly wound—"

"Alan, did she provide any hard data? Did she say anything useful? Give!"

"Fine. Whatever, Mike. I'll leave out everything that happened and cut to the end. She made Harry. And she said that the mole is run by the Chinese—"

"She said that? Right out? Not coached?"

"—and that they call him *Top Hook*."

Secure phones cover most human sounds. The white noise now masked Dukas's reaction. Alan, unable to wait, finally said, "I set a meeting for a week from today in Bahrain. You'll have to send somebody."

"Why?" Dukas sounded grim.

"Mike, watch CNN. I'm on an aircraft carrier headed for the Indian Ocean, okay?"

"Oh, yeah, the India thing." Alan had experienced this disconnection from carrier reality to home reality all too often. On the *Jefferson*, India, Pakistan, and China had just become the focus of life. At home people were still worried about other things like mortgages and report cards and spies.

"So I'm out." The jg was all but dancing behind him.

"No, you're not. Rose is fine, thanks for asking."

Alan snapped his chair around and glared at the jg. "Give me a second, okay? This isn't a personal call, Lieutenant." She vanished. "I can't do another meeting."

"She just became my number-one priority."

"Your number-one priority is clearing my wife!" *And me*, he thought.

"Al—" He could hear something odd in Dukas's voice. "Look, I've got to ask you to trust me, okay? I'm not going to tell you why, but I think that meeting this woman is *part* of clearing your wife."

"I don't get it."

"I know you don't. That's what 'trust me' means."

"But Mike, that means the cases are connected. How the hell—?"

"Don't—"

"This is new! Is it something I just said?" He was thinking, *Anna? Chinese? Top Hook?*

"*Don't ask!* Okay? Jesus! Don't you know what 'trust me' means? Just meet the woman again, will you? I swear to you, I think it may help Rose."

Alan thought he had a right to demand an explanation. But then, Dukas had a right—an obligation, in fact—to keep things compartmentalized. *Trust me.* "It's a good thing we're friends," he said. "Okay. But I need help—I've promised this is the last one."

"I'll go to the wall for you on this."

"Suspicion is making my job tough, and it also makes asking favors of the admiral a major pain in the ass, you understand?"

"I hear you."

"Okay. See what you can do. Where do we go from here?"

"You keep your head down and find a way to Bahrain. I start trying to find the lady a million dollars."

Suburban Virginia.

George Shreed had a vial of his own blood in his freezer. It had been remarkably easy to get. He had complained to his urologist's office about prostate pain, and they had ordered a PSA test, and after the aide had taken the blood and propped the vial in the rack, he had simply switched it with somebody else's and walked out. He supposed that the results of the test might be peculiar—perhaps the switched blood was a woman's—but that would hardly concern him.

Of more interest was his Chinese control, Chen. The forged NSC memo had clearly excited him, and, as Shreed had expected, he had demanded to see the original. No dead drop would do for such a transfer, as Shreed had known; Chen thought both himself and the memo far too important to trust to an intermediary. So Chen had sent Shreed a contact plan complete with communications and fallback and escape, and the only fault in it so far as Shreed was concerned was that the plan called for the meeting to take place in Belgrade. Belgrade might once have been a fine place for such a meeting, but now NATO was bombing Serbia, and going there would be far more difficult than a dozen years before. Probably, he thought, that was why Chen had picked Belgrade, to keep his American spy in his place.

And maybe Chen knew that Shreed would like to kill him, and Belgrade would be a tough place to pull off a killing.

"You sonofabitch," Shreed muttered to himself.

"But—not bad," he thought as he studied the passport that Chen had sent. It was Canadian (maybe a sop to his agent's worry about being American?) and used an old photo of Shreed that he had left with the Chinese a decade before. He had worn a fake mustache for it. "Stupid," Shreed muttered now. Disguises were idiotic, he thought, and he had told Chen so at the time, but the Chinese had liked putting Shreed into this partial falseface. "Jerking me around," Shreed growled.

He was still talking to himself. He had started doing it a week or so after Janey had gone into the hospice, as if he had had to fill the silence. "Losing my marbles," he said now.

Still, the forged passport was a good one. He'd have to cook up some sort of fake mustache if he used it. It gave him a total of three passports: this one, a real one, and an old Agency one from his last days in

Operations. He was supposed to have turned that one in, but he hadn't, and eventually the bean counters had forgotten about it. He kept it in a safe-deposit box in a bank, with an unregistered pistol and ten thousand dollars. Just in case. For years, he'd paid the rental on the box and never gone near it. Just in case.

"And now it's almost the case," he murmured. "Push is coming to shove."

He put the Chinese forgery into his freezer with the ampoules and the vial of blood, and he began to plan how he would kill Chen when he got to Belgrade. "Not easy," he said to himself as he heated his dinner in the microwave. "But things that are fun are never easy." After three minutes, the microwave pinged and he took out the plastic dish and began to eat, leaning forward against the kitchen counter.

"Yum, yum," he said aloud. "Dogshit simmered in bat piss and served on a bed of pigeon droppings."

The terrible food made him think of Janey, who had been a splendid cook. His shoulders drooped. He tried to replace thoughts of her with his Chinese plan.

16

USS *Thomas Jefferson.*

THE *JEFFERSON* RACED EAST, EVERY INCH OF HER
thousand-foot length vibrating to her propeller shafts and her twin nuclear reactors. Despite noise dampening and earplugs, the ship *roared* at
thirty-eight knots. *Jefferson,* packed with six thousand sailors and a hundred aircraft, ran faster than a greyhound, faster than most small boats
and a great deal faster than any other vessel of her size; and behind her,
the speculation of the world boiled like the water in her wake.

Other carriers would have to keep the watch in the Mediterranean.
Other carriers would handle Bosnia and the Serbs. As Alan scrambled to
read the message traffic he had missed in Naples, the *Jefferson* rushed to
avert, by her presence, a catastrophe born of malfeasance and inattention in equal parts. China, said the experts, was looking for an opportunity to flex her power and show her determination. China wanted the
US to lose face. The reports did not say that China had been deluded
into this stance by George Shreed, because the men who wrote them
thought the Chinese inscrutable and alien (thus capable of anything)
rather than human, fallible, and gullible.

Alan reviewed the incidents in the first hour he was back aboard: a
terrorist attack in Kashmir, a bomb in a market in Lahore, a border incident in the high country on the Northwest frontier. These incidents
were commonplace; their like could be seen in every decade since the

partition of the Raj in 1947. The step from cold war to saber-rattling was so common between India and Pakistan that it seldom raised any interest in the intelligence community or the press.

Four days ago, however, when Indian Air Force pilots bombed a "terrorist training facility" in the Northwest Frontier Province of Pakistan, Pakistani pilots in brand-new Chinese-built Mig-29s had struck back, downing three Indian aircraft and destroying a strategic forward airfield. Pakistan, always the underdog in the match-up, had rarely responded so promptly. Aerial skirmishes and artillery duels had followed all along the border. Pakistan had unleashed a barrage of hidden long-range SAMs and punished the Indian Air Force. India had delivered an ultimatum.

To Alan's reading, that much of the story was familiar. That Pakistan had a surprising inventory of equipment was a new wrinkle, but the rest of the tale read like a sequel to their other border incidents.

The menacing difference came next. The Indian ultimatum was answered not by Pakistan, but by China—a counter-ultimatum that made extortionate demands of India in territory and political concession. To Alan's eye, they were demands calculated to force rejection. India could no more face China than, realistically, Pakistan could face India.

China's ultimatum was due at 0600 GMT on Tuesday. Alan looked at it; it was an odd time, as it gave days for tensions to drag on. It was of a piece with China's dangerous stance, making demands far beyond China's real power. He made these points to a series of visitors, leaving them dissatisfied and anxious. Then he looked at the date on his watch and did a calculation. China was threatening a world war in five days.

Alan went to see Rafe.

The *Jefferson* raced east against the rumor of war.

Suter's apartment.

Suter owned a handgun. It was only a tiny Beretta .22 he'd bought for his ex-wife when she was still his wife and thought that drug-crazed black kids were going to mug her on a daily basis. When she had left him, she had thrown it at him, not having enough courage to shoot him.

Suter had downloaded from the Internet a recipe for making a silencer from a toilet-paper tube. "Sounds crazy but it works!!!!" the Web site had boasted. It did sound crazy, but Suter was one of those smart people who don't know how much they don't know, and it made sense to him because he didn't really know guns. He'd read in one of the late George Higgins's novels about putting a .22 behind somebody's ear and killing him with one shot.

Suter had never killed anybody before.

And, although he didn't know it, he was out of his depth: like somebody vain about his swimming abilities who ignores warnings about a tide, he was being swept out into the deep blue—although the tide, in this case, was his own greed.

He had cobbled up three of the makeshift silencers and tested two of them in a park near Fort Hunt. The little gun looked ridiculous with the toilet-paper tube duct-taped to its two-inch barrel, more as if the tube were wearing the gun than the other way around, but the usual sharp crack of the small cartridge was muted. Not silenced, but muted. Of course, he couldn't aim the gun. The toilet-paper tube blocked the sight. But he was intending to put the barrel, or at least the toilet-paper tube, right against Tony Moscowic's mastoid, so aiming was not really a consideration.

What Suter was waiting for now was rain. He intended to shove Tony's body into a branch of the Anacostia River, but he would have to have a good, heavy rain beforehand so the channel was full and would carry the body away to the Potomac. It would turn up eventually, but so much the worse for wear, nobody would connect it with Suter.

Most of Tony Moscowic's records were in the Moscowic head, and if a .22 slug was in there, too, what then of the records? The only item that might give trouble was a notebook that Moscowic always carried. He would have to lift the notebook from Moscowic's body before he dumped him into the North Branch.

No problem.

Washington.

"Like hell!" Emma Pasternak hissed. She was loud enough so that other people in the restaurant looked toward their table. "Fuck you!"

"I asked you, Emma—have you got somebody looking at George Shreed?"

"You suspicious sonofabitch," she said.

Dukas couldn't figure if she was overdoing anger because she was innocent or because she was guilty. "You promised me you'd lay off him until I gave the word," he said.

"I didn't promise you zip." She sipped her wine. "I don't owe you anything, Mike."

He almost lunged toward her; the silverware jingled. "Have you got somebody surveilling George Shreed?"

She too leaned forward. She licked her lips, pursed them. "N-O. Get out of my face."

Dukas sighed in disgust. "Even if I believed you, I wouldn't believe you."

She laughed at him. He looked angry. Later, they went to his chocolate apartment.

USS *Thomas Jefferson.*

Alan was having no success in trying to explain to Rafe why he was supposed to be in Bahrain in four days.

"No. That's final."

"Rafe, this isn't some sort of personal—"

"Don't bullshit me, Alan. That's exactly what it is. Personal."

"—favor, it's a mission, for God's sake. It's important! Lives could be at stake!"

"Whose? More lives than the men and women on this carrier? Maybe this is why we don't put intel guys in charge of things."

"Rafe, it's one day. In and out. If we're flying around the clock, of course I don't go. But Jesus, you know as well as I do that we may just bore holes in the water and wait."

"You told me you'd be out of it. You said 'one last meeting.' That was you, right?"

"Yeah, that was me. I also said I'd get my det moving, and I have."

"Half of them hate your guts."

"Fuck, is this my CAG throwing that shit at me? Why do they hate my guts? 'Cause they think I'm a fucking spy. How can I fix that? I can help catch the spy." Alan was shouting.

"Sounds pretty personal to me, mister."

They were chest to chest, and their tempers were long lost. Rafe was the larger man, but Alan's anger outburned his friend's. Out in the blue-tiled passageway, several sailors had stopped to listen. At some level, despite the roar of engines and the omnipresent vibration of the main shafts, both of them caught the change in movement beyond the door. It reminded them that there was no privacy at sea, that arguments between superiors got around. Alan realized that he was bellowing tidbits about a matter too secret even to be whispered. So he glared. Then he turned on his heel and slammed the door behind him.

Langley.

George Shreed had decided that he would have somebody kill Chen with a gun—one of the Serbians he had hired to eliminate the woman in Venice, in fact. They had failed him there, but they could hardly miss a Chinese sitting on a park bench in downtown Belgrade. Could they?

It would have to look like a routine crime in a city where crime was nothing if not routine. The bombing and the isolation of "Yugoslavia" (he couldn't think of it anymore without the quotation marks) had made times hard, and hard times breed hard crime. So there they would be, Shreed and Chen, sitting on a bench chatting about treason and betrayal and their own kind of crime, and two men who looked like petty thieves would come up and shoot Chen dead and steal Shreed's money. (It would be a cosmic joke, he thought, if by mistake they shot Shreed and took Chen's money. Well, God likes to laugh, too.)

But, ruling out the intervention of divine practical jokes, Chen would be killed as part of a Belgrade crime wave.

"Not very original," he said aloud. He and Suter were sitting in Shreed's office, going over the day's burden of paperwork. Shreed usually found he could more or less read it and think about other things at the same time. Today, he was thinking about murder, but he hadn't meant to speak out loud about it.

"What?" Suter jerked as if he'd been goosed. He'd been thinking about shooting Tony Moscowic behind the ear, and he thought Shreed knew.

"Oh—mm—this goddam position paper on Kashmir. Not very original." Why did he sound apologetic, Shreed wondered.

"Kashmir's getting dangerous," Suter said now. He'd put the bullet behind the mastoid, he was thinking, not *in* the mastoid—too much bone for a .22.

"What's that?" Now Shreed sounded irritated. He had been watching Chen get gunned down.

"I *said,* Kashmir's getting *dangerous.*" One shot, *pfft*—no more Tony.

"It isn't Kashmir; it's China," Shreed muttered. They should shoot Chen in the *back* of the head, he thought.

"The Secretary's flying over tomorrow to ask them to stay out. Didn't you read the brief?" Have to aim up a little to put the bullet in the brain.

Suter's tone brought Shreed out of his reverie, which had just put Chen on the pavement, bleeding and dying. Suter was talking too fast; what was the *matter* with him these days?

Shreed thought again how much he really disliked his assistant and that thought gave way to one of replacing him. Dangerous just now, though—Suter knew too much about him. First things first—Chen and his Chinese plan. He began to think about Chen again, and the bullet in the back of the head, and Belgrade, letting his eyes scan the paperwork and his hand almost automatically make notes.

Across the desk from him, Suter was staring out the window at the corpse of Tony Moscowic.

USS *Thomas Jefferson,* off Alexandria, Egypt.

The massive engines were silent. Alan stood on the catwalk on the starboard side, already regretting the impulse that had brought him topside and looking absently into the haze to the south, where Alexandria's port smudged the horizon. Ahead, merchant traffic scurried to clear the area because the carrier needed the whole width of the Suez to move. Their Aegis cruiser, the *Fort Klock,* had just caught up to the halted *Jefferson* and anchored alongside. An Arleigh Burke–class destroyer that had been visiting Piraeus, Greece, was coming fast, just visible on the distorted horizon to the north. The delay while the canal was cleared raised the level of frustration aboard, but it was allowing the battle group to gather.

Somewhere, Rose was waking to a new day. A picture of her, face contorted with anger and hurt, had been with him since he woke. He didn't know where it had come from, but its intensity scared him. He couldn't recall when he had seen that particular look or whether it was a creation of his unconscious mind. Rose was still under threat. He wasn't doing enough to help her. He hadn't called her again from Naples because of his preoccupation with the meetings and his hurried departure.

Alan had been through the Ditch in '90. Rafe had been a hotshot lieutenant then, a tough bastard who thought intel guys were wimps. Perhaps he still did.

Alan's mouth twisted into a wry smile. Rafe was right and wrong about Bahrain. It *was* personal. He'd been an idiot to deny it. But his personal quest happened to have national security overtones, and he'd been too angry to explain. Too conscious of security. And Rafe had a certain air about him of being *right*. It could help with command, but it could also stick in your gut. Too damned *right*.

Alan remembered the first time he had realized that Rafe, then his nemesis, was not always right. Rafe had landed on the wrong carrier during an exercise. Suddenly he had been vulnerable. Later, Alan had seen him lose an okay grade in a landing when he was in the race for the coveted Top Hook slot. Again, vulnerable. Not blaming others, not denying his fault. Simply less armored, less perfect. Less *right*. As if he might have moments of self-doubt like other mortals.

Rafe was showing the same signs as the CAG. Everything was not perfect, and Rafe was showing the strain. The self-doubt. And it surfaced in spats over issues like letting Alan go ashore in Bahrain. *Is Rafe taking a beating from the admiral over his loyalty to me?* That could be behind the anger. *Or does Rafe suspect me a little? Is he a little unsure?*

Alan remembered Rafe, later that first cruise, getting the Top Hook award. By then, Rafe was his friend, and he had been amazed to see Rafe accept the award without arrogance, wearing an uncertain smile, as if surprised that he had won after all.

There were voices above him, where sailors were moving about.

". . . so the CAG accuses him to his face of being a spy. I heard it."

"Fuck that noise. He told the CAG he needed to catch the spy. I was there, too."

"You got shit for brains, you know that?"

"Hey, Coloredo, shove it. I know what I heard. Rathausen's his bud. You know it. Skipper ain't no spy."

"You'll see. They'll arrest his ass and drag him off. None of us will ever see the other side of E-4. Watch."

"You'll never make E-4 anyway, lardass."

Spy. Top Hook. Alan took a deep breath and exhaled slowly, his eyes snake-like in the gloom, focused on a point halfway to the invisible horizon.

And what had been nagging at him for a day, the little fact that wouldn't come and wouldn't go away, came clear: a picture on the mantelpiece of his boyhood home. In his memory, it still sat there. Not his father winning the award. His father handing it to the next guy with a big smile.

Alan bolted through the watertight door and down the passageway on the O-3 level, headed for the secure phones in the intel center. He didn't pause to ask permission, moving an officer out of a phone cubicle with his glare. Then he sat and dialed, waited, dialed. No answer at Mike's office. *What the hell time was it there, anyway?* He dialed Mike's apartment. The moment the phone was picked up, he shouted, "I've got it, Mike! It's been bugging me since she said the words and I've got it. Top Hook!"

A woman's voice said, "Just a minute, okay?" The phone rattled, and he heard her say, her voice muffled, "It's for you."

Washington.

Mike took the telephone from Emma.

"Dukas."

"Mike, it's Alan, Jesus, I'm sorry, but—"

"What's up?" He waved Emma away.

Emma was naked. She flipped herself off the bed and pulled on one of his shirts. Dukas was clearly waiting for her to go before he started talking. Why? Emma knew that information was power. What kind of information was Dukas getting that he didn't want her to know?

She scurried to the bathroom and flushed the toilet, and, as she did so, she shouted, "Mike? What? What did you say?"

As she expected, he couldn't hear her clearly, and he came as far toward the bedroom door as the telephone cord would allow and said, "What?"

By then, she had her hand on the bathroom telephone.

"What?" she shouted.

"I didn't say anything, for Christ's sake!"

She picked up the extension, covered the mouthpiece. "I thought you did!"

"Jesus—"

His phone had been held at arm's length, away from his ear, and he hadn't heard her pick up. As she intended.

Dukas put the telephone back to his ear and said, "What have you got, Al?"

"Top Hook! It *is* George Shreed, Mike. He was Top Hook on the *Midway*, right after Dad." He sounded impatient, as if he wanted some immediate, big-bang response. Alan burst out again, "Don't you get it? Shreed is Top Hook! Top Hook is the code name of the mole inside the Agency! Jesus, Mike—"

"This is an open line, Commander."

Alan was silent. "Oh, shit—"

In the bathroom, Emma was staring at the back of the closed door, the extension phone at her ear. *They really thought George Shreed was a mole?* Now, there was information that was power!

17

The Pentagon.

NEXT MORNING, GEORGE SHREED WAS SITTING IN A briefing about the bombing campaign in "Yugoslavia," and he was so bored with pictures of bridges and electrical-switching stations that he wanted to throw up. It would serve all these jerks right, he thought, if he did: here they were, dicking around with a bunch of third-world Europeans who couldn't even put an aircraft in the air, and the Chinese were moving troops to the Indian border on one frontier and massing missile launchers opposite Taiwan on the other. *It's the Chinese, stupid!* he wanted to shout.

But he didn't. He was being extra-good, keeping a low profile, making no waves. He'd got the information he wanted from his contact in Internals that "a female voice," probably from the Agency, was, indeed, in touch with the NCIS people investigating the Siciliano thing. The woman had to be Sally Baranowski. Whom he would take care of in his own way.

Which was all right as a delaying tactic, but overnight he'd faced the truth that killing Chen in Belgrade wouldn't work. Was, in fact, counter-productive. Not that he couldn't handle the practical details. He had set up a cover story with the Agency, made reservations to Budapest to check some ops-readiness stuff there; from there he'd do an overnight in-and-out to Belgrade, using the passport that Chen had sent him. He'd have to do without his canes (too recognizable) on the Hungarian flight, probably have to use the morphine. Then wait around in Belgrade for a contact, a lot of stupid tradecraft, then sit with Chen and hand over the forged memo so that the Chinese would do something really stupid. But it was all tricky, and he didn't want to do it; he needed to get Chen somewhere else, somewhere more on his own terms.

Half-listening to the briefing, he was thinking about the memo and the fact that of course he couldn't kill Chen in Belgrade, because Chen was the one who would have to carry the memo back to Beijing for authentication. If he killed Chen in Belgrade, the memo would be instantly suspect. No, he'd have to hand it over and smile and let Chen go. Thinking about killing Chen that way was simply happy bullshit—daydreaming.

What he needed was a plan, not a fantasy.

Shreed sighed. He started to plan it all over again.

USS *Thomas Jefferson.*

They were in the Ditch now, moving as fast as safety would allow through the dirty water, with the Sinai on their left and Egypt on the right. The uncertainty of the situation had communicated by some invisible mechanism from the admiral all the way down to the deckplates.

"We don't have a target list. We don't have any tanker support. We don't have any friendly bingo fields. We don't know who we're supposed to fight. We're just supposed to *get there.*" Rafe was bitter. "Nobody seems to have any hard data on the new Pakistani stuff. We don't have a reliable air order-of-battle for either side. My intel folks are reading *Jane's,* for Christ's sake."

"Rafe—"

"We're in the Suez Canal. CNN is having a field day. Our battle group is spread across the Med behind us. What are we supposed to do?"

"We're sending a message, Rafe." Alan had now said this three times. "Air Force is moving units in the Persian Gulf. I'd guess that we're trying to get the Gulf States to allow us to base tankers and what not. What about Diego Garcia?"

"It's a rock in the middle of a war zone. They're flying twenty-four-hour combat air patrol."

"They'll have tankers soon, if not already."

"Al, I can't count on that." Rafe shook his head in disgust. "And Pac Fleet has their hands tied. China has moved fleet units into the Taiwan Straits. *With* Silkworm missiles."

"So I read."

"Why? China can't face us, Al. You've said so yourself."

"Ask the National Security Council."

"You're not helping."

"Rafe, I'm as far behind as you are." *I'm not here as your personal intel advisor, Rafe.* Alan had spent the last four hours explaining the situation, as he understood it, to a legion of aviators. The intel folks were frantic, trying to catch up with events in an area that had been assigned to two junior officers a month ago. They had written and briefed every few days as a contingency. The sudden explosion of the situation had caught them all.

"What can China throw at us?"

"They might, and I stress might, be able to forward-stage some air into Burma-Myanmar. They have a surface-action group transiting the Straits of Malacca, about as far from the scene as we are. Realistically, India has more of a blue-water navy than China. India should be able to wreck the Chinese and fight Pakistan at the same time, at least at sea. In the air and on the ground, it's a different story. But not if we support India. China can't win against the US in the Taiwan Straits, and they can't hope to beat India before we respond."

"Nukes. They can use nukes."

"I'll tell you this, Rafe. It's a guess. Somebody in China has fucked up big. Remember how the Gulf War started? Iraq misread the signals from the US. Thought we would play along if they annexed Kuwait."

"Thought we wouldn't fight, you mean."

"That's all I can see. Somebody in China is under the dangerous delusion that we won't back India. And we're making a very public dash toward the scene of action to demonstrate that we will back India." It didn't sound too bad, put that way.

He looked up at Alan and raised an eyebrow. "China's really that weak? That they couldn't match us conventionally in a stand-up fight?"

"China couldn't win a war with France, and a war might just expose the real roots of dissatisfaction in the country. They lack any real trained troops, their air forces are mostly untrained and totally GCI-harnessed, and their navy has no blue-water potential at all. To be honest, Rafe, I'm not sure we're confident that their nuclear deterrent will work. They are not a superpower in a military sense."

"How did we get here, then?"

"Rhetoric exerts a strange fascination, Rafe. And China is holding some card here that I'm not seeing."

"So when we show them some muscle, they back down?"

"That's how it's supposed to work."

Alan wished he had convinced himself.

The carrier would not deviate from her course to launch or recover aircraft, and the air wing was idle. Maintenance continued, but aircrew sat and played cards or ran on the flight deck or sat and complained. Every unit had dropped weeks of work and preparation. Alan's det had lost their new role of catching smugglers, and every unit had forfeited some role in the NATO air effort. The troops had lost their liberty in Naples. They were sailing toward an unknown ocean and a potentially disastrous war. The younger ones were excited, the veterans pensive. Bickering and griping increased. In the det, factions dampened by action and success acquired renewed life and tempers flared.

Alan sensed it all. He forced his aircrews to the simulator, made Soleck and Navarro spend hours getting Chinese, Pakistani, and Indian data into the system, drilled his crews, and ignored the stares and whispered comments from Stevens's group. He had them at the brink of becoming a cohesive unit and he wasn't backing away now.

And in the back of his mind, he thought that what they all needed was to *do* something. To help send the message. He thought about the unrefueled range of the S-3 and started measuring distances in the Indian Ocean. Because China intended to push them to war. In four days.

NCIS HQ.

Dukas had spent most of the night trying to figure out how Al Craik's flimsy identification of Top Hook with George Shreed could be used.

The trouble was, it was purely inferential. What he wanted was hard evidence. He put his face in his hands and blew an exasperated sigh through pursed lips.

"It can't be that bad," a husky voice said right next to him.

Dukas jumped.

It was Rose.

He scrambled up; the crate of files fell over on the floor again. "Ro-Rosie—" he said.

She came to him, put her arms around him, and leaned her face on his chest. Triffler stared through a gap between the philodendron and a suction-cupped Garfield.

"I can't stay mad at you, damn it," she said.

"Rose, Rose—I'm so sorry—"

"You were doing your job."

"I wanted to kill myself—"

She looked up. "Harry said you got drunk. I hope the hangover was awful."

"Killer."

"You've done your penance; you're forgiven." She kissed him.

"Rose, what are you doing here?"

"Seeing my old pal Mike Dukas."

"What are you doing in DC?"

"Making the rounds. Alan's idea—see every Navy guy we've ever known, scotch the rumors, press the flesh, try to make something happen. Mike, they're saying terrible things about us!"

"Yeah, I know; I hear things." He had his arms around her and didn't want to let go. "Jesus, you feel good."

"You, too. But knock it off, or people'll start talking about us." She pulled away from him. Dukas became at once too buoyant, too active, couldn't help himself. "Hey, Dick," he called, "come on over here, meet the star of our show!"

Rose turned, stricken. "Star!"

"Joke."

"Some joke. It's okay—it's okay—but I get pretty sick of being what you call 'the star,' Mike—"

She shook hands with Triffler, and, in turning, saw the chart on the back of the door. "Wow, you *are* serious about George Shreed."

"Only kind of testing the waters."

"Looks like more than that to me. You got something new?"

"Oh—well, Rose—"

"Alan said something, too. We send a lot of e-mails; he said that something had happened in Naples and now he saw why you guys were suspicious of Shreed."

Dukas and Triffler exchanged a look, and Dukas moved Rose back to his side of the office. "I don't think you should know too much about this, Rose—"

"I'm just the defendant here!"

"No, no, it isn't that. I'm walking this tightrope with the Internals guy at the Agency. If he got even a whiff that we were talking outside the office about Shreed—"

"This isn't outside the office. Emma says you're not very forthcoming with her, either—and by the way, what's going on between you and Emma?"

"Emma? Pasternak, you mean?"

"Mike! Hey—it's me. Are you and Emma—?"

Dukas sighed. He pushed a chair for her next to his desk and called to Triffler for coffee; sitting down, he put his hands on the desk and stared at them and said, "It's just physical."

She gave a peal of husky laughter. "What does *that* mean?"

"Emma and I have a mutually satisfying physical relationship, how's that?"

Rose stared at the coffee cup that appeared next to her. She shook her head. "And I thought she was maybe gay." She smiled up at Triffler. "Great coffee. Starbucks?"

Triffler looked hurt. "I grind my own. A shop on M Street mixes it for me; in fact, they sell it as Triffler's Blend. You get the touch of vanilla?"

"Oh, yeah." She talked coffee for thirty seconds, then decorating and the wall of crates, then clothes and where could she buy her husband a jacket like that one? and in that short time she succeeded in doing what Dukas had not: Triffler became her friend. When they were finished, Triffler looked at Dukas as if to say, *See how it's done?* and walked back to his desk, whistling.

"Nice guy," she murmured. Dukas rolled his eyes, but she missed it. "So," she said, "*is* it Shreed?"

"I really don't know, babe. I just don't know."

She was wearing civilian clothes, a dark dress with a rather full skirt that she pulled up a little to cross her legs. She looked pretty and vulnerable and a little tired. "You going to get me out of this, Mike?"

"You know I am. But—"

"I know. 'But it takes time.' " She put her hands over both of his. "Harry told me who the Telephone Woman is. I want to talk to her."

"No, no—"

"Listen to me, Mike. She wants to help but I think she's scared; maybe if I go to her, give her some support—"

"Menzes would crucify me."

"Maybe if I'm a real person to her, with a face, not just a voice on the phone. Maybe she'll give us more—facts. Something."

"Have you told Emma?"

"No, have you?"

He shook his head. "I have to compartmentalize. I like Emma; I like what we do together. But she's—"

"On the other side?"

"One of the other sides; there are about six. Yeah, I can't be completely honest with her."

"Or with me?"

He winced. "Anyway, I don't want you to scare off our Telephone Lady."

"I won't. Really."

Dukas pursed his lips, thought hard. "Don't tell me about it, then. And don't tell Emma."

"You got a lot of compartments, Mike."

He nodded. "It's a mare's nest of a case."

"What was Alan up to in Naples?"

He shook his head.

"He said he was doing something for you." When Dukas shook his head again, she squeezed his hands. "Hey, I'm the good guy, remember? Or—are you still suspicious of me—?"

"No! I swear it, Rose. But what Al's doing is another thing altogether. Honest."

"He thinks it's Shreed."

Dukas kept his left hand out so that she'd keep hold of it with his right, he rubbed his eyes. "Al talks too goddam much. He got a hit on 'Top Hook.' This is not to get out of this office, okay? I've got to tell Menzes at Internal, but he's the only one who's in on this, so keep your mouth shut. See, 'Top Hook' was supposed to be *your* code name when you leaked the Peacemaker stuff."

"Which I didn't do."

"Which you didn't do; therefore, somebody else did. Therefore, when somebody elsewhere in the world mentions Top Hook, I think there's a connection."

"What's it got to do with Shreed?"

He shook his head. "End of conversation." He patted her hand. "Hey! New thought. Your Navy pal there, Valdez—"

"Yeah, Harry hired him! And he proved my computer had been tampered with. He's the best, just the best!"

Dukas called Triffler over. "Dick, tell Lieutenant-Commander Siciliano what your interviewee told you about her and Valdez."

"Oh—well—this is hearsay, okay? But, um—he said that you and Mister Valdez were, um—'very close.' "

"We were. He saved my life."

Dukas interrupted. "The implication was *very* close."

She stared, then exploded. "That's bullshit! I was his division officer; I couldn't operate without his special skills—I took him with me when I traveled because I fucking *needed* him, but—! Who the fuck said that?"

"I can't tell you," Triffler muttered.

"Tell her," Dukas said.

"Regulations say—"

"Tell her!"

Triffler straightened. "Guy named Ray Suter."

To Dukas's surprise, she threw herself back and laughed. She blew a lock of hair off her forehead. "That slimy sonofabitch! He would have been my first guess. Oh, shit, Suter the Seducer! The only thing nastier than a woman scorned is a man scorned."

"You think that's the only reason he'd say something about you and Valdez—revenge?"

"What other reason is there?"

"Well—he works for Shreed."

"What, you think they're a conspiracy?" She made it a joke.

To Dukas's surprise, it was Triffler who defended the idea. "They don't have to be spies or something to work together to discredit you and your husband. They both got reason to dislike you. Or—" He cocked an eye at the chart on the door. "If Shreed really is behind it, then Suter's a perfect patsy for him if he's trying to lay blame on you. Especially if he knows that Valdez is the one who cleared you on the computer stuff—if he can smear you and Valdez as lovers, then what Valdez did for us is suspect. See?"

Dukas shook his head. "No way either Shreed or Suter could know about that."

"Oh, no? You filed a report with Menzes, right? You don't believe there's a leak out of that office?"

"No, I don't."

Triffler shrugged. "Dream on."

"We've got to believe in something, Dick! We gotta have a place to stand! You can't investigate a case if there's no truth anywhere."

Rose stood. "Hey, hey, guys. Lighten up. You're on the same side, remember?"

Triffler and Dukas looked at each other. Triffler shot his eyebrows up and down, a rather Groucho Marx gesture, and then he said to Rose, "You're not leaving us, I hope."

"I am. I'm having lunch with Admiral Pilchard, at the Army-Navy Club, and then this afternoon I'm doing some congressional offices." She stuck out her hand. "A real pleasure, Dick. We'll be seeing more of each other, I know."

Triffler made pleased sounds. Still seated, Dukas watched them, surprised again by this new side of Triffler. Then Rose kissed Dukas's cheek and said she'd call him really soon. "Don't compartmentalize too much," she said as she bent over him. "It's bad for your emotional health." And then she was gone, leaving a faint ghost of perfume.

"That's some pretty woman," Triffler said.

"She's married."

"So am I. So?"

"I didn't know that!"

Triffler looked down at Dukas. "There's lots you don't know. In fact—Dukas, they tell me that those guys worked for you in Bosnia thought you walked on water, but the way I figure it, you were all from different countries, so nobody spoke the same language and they never got to know you. I do speak your language and I never yet heard you say one positive, personal thing. For your information, my wife is named Germaine and is big-time cute; I have two kids; the boy is a freshman wide receiver at DeMatha and the girl is a super-smart student at St. Anselm's. I have loving sex on a regular basis and I'm a Redskins fan. And what that pretty woman who was just in here sees in you, I don't get!"

Dukas had meant to get around to a little personal stroking just as soon as he got on top of the case. Anyway, he had thought that maybe Triffler was gay and he hadn't wanted to pry.

Maybe, when all this was over, he'd work on his management skills.

Washington.

Because of what she had overheard about George Shreed on Mike Dukas's phone, Emma Pasternak called her investigator. She was in a hurry—she was always in a hurry—but she knew she had to do this one exactly right.

"George Shreed," she said. "You with me? I asked you to— Right, that guy. Okay, I want *everything* you've learned about him, and I want it messengered to me by four today so I can take it home with me—okay?"

The woman on the other end said that that was fine, no problem, but was there a problem, because it sounded like Emma was taking this away from her?

"No, God—! No, I picked up a piece of information from another source, and I need to see exactly where I am. What I'm looking for today is Shreed's Navy record—he was a pilot in Vietnam, a carrier called the *Midway*— You got that in the file? Great!"

Emma dropped her voice. She sounded almost uncertain. "Unh—one thing, hon—don't get me wrong on this, but do you by any chance have any kind of, um, computer surveillance or anything on Shreed's house?" She listened to the angry denials from the other end. The woman there was almost spluttering. "Okay—okay—just asking, hon, just asking! Because somebody asked *me,* as if I'd do such a thing, and I thought—you know, I just thought—maybe—okay, okay—don't get on your high horse—"

18

THE PLANTINGS AROUND SALLY BARANOWSKI'S WERE out of control. They looked as if they hadn't been trimmed since last fall. The grass needed cutting.

Not a happy house, Rose thought. She pulled into the driveway, which was only two ribbons of cracked concrete that led nowhere—no garage, no carport, only a grassless area where a VW Golf seemed to be leaning against the house.

She rang the doorbell and stood back so that Sally Baranowski wouldn't feel threatened. A lot of experience with young pilots and even younger enlisted people made Rose believe that Baranowski's phone calls might have been far more about Baranowski herself than about George Shreed. Maybe simply wanting to make contact. Maybe simply wanting to feel good about having done one positive thing. Or maybe simply wanting to be rescued?

Rose was aware of a darker dark behind a window. No lights, except at the back of the house, but something there behind closed drapes now. Then, a sound at the door. And a wait that seemed to threaten to last until the stars came out.

"What is it?"

The door had opened almost soundlessly, so little that Rose could see nothing through the crack. But the voice had been a woman's, and there was an odor, probably food and—vodka?

"Hi. Mrs. Baranowski?"

"What is it?"

Rose moved in a little and put her right toe against the door. "I'm Rose Siciliano."

The other woman's hesitation gave her time to brace her leg and put a hand on the door near the knob; then Sally Baranowski tried to push the door shut and Rose, reacting against it, put her right hip forward and pushed with her hand.

"I don't want to talk to you!"

"Please—Sally—we've talked—"

"No, we haven't—go away—"

Close to the door now, with the other woman just on the other side, Rose got the smell of vodka more strongly. It disgusted her and threw her off for a moment, but she knew she recognized the woman's voice; she swung her hip hard against the door and it yielded, and Rose slipped inside.

"Please let's talk," she said into the near-darkness.

"Go away!"

"Sally, you tried to help me—you did help me; you helped a lot—let's talk."

"That was a mistake. That never happened. I don't know you."

"You know my husband."

The woman backed away. Rose moved forward until she could see a spill of light from the kitchen and the woman partly silhouetted against it. As if defending some indiscretion, the woman said, "I didn't know your husband at all well. Not at all." If she was drinking, the alcohol wasn't affecting her much.

"Alan talked about you. He said you backed him when George Shreed was against him."

"That was a long time ago."

"Look, I don't want to bust into your house if you don't want me. But I'd like to just talk. Can't we do that?"

"I've been told not to talk to anybody."

"When?"

"Today. My boss told me that I was talking out of turn and I'd better stop."

"But you— He couldn't know."

"He did. You told somebody, didn't you?"

"Only the people who are helping me. None of them would tell!"

Sally Baranowski chuckled. It was a surprisingly rich sound, as if she really enjoyed the joke. "You don't know the Agency. Everything is a secret, and there aren't any secrets." She moved; Rose heard the movement rather than saw it. "Come on into the kitchen."

The tiny kitchen was like the yard, but worse. Dirty dishes had been stacked on the drain board. The window of the microwave was filthy. Fast-food containers jutted from the yellow trash bin, which was too full to close. A vodka bottle stood on the table.

Rose knew that Sally had a child but saw no sign of one. Maybe upstairs? A tough atmosphere for a kid. As if sensing her interest, Sally said, "My daughter's at my mother's. I sent her home because I thought my husband might—" She shrugged. "We're having a real ugly separation." She tried to smile. "He already took my dog."

"I'm sorry."

Unhappiness is like an environment: it alters the body and the face, even the clothes. Sally Baranowski was taller than Rose, and she had been slim but had put on pounds that made her warm-ups bulge at the waist. Depression, not alcohol, made her face older than her years, which Rose guessed at late thirties. Her ginger hair hung slack. "Not your concern. Can I fix you a drink? I'm drinking too much, as I'm sure you've heard. You have heard, right—you've discussed me with all these people who are helping you?"

"Only four people."

"But you *did* discuss me." She lit a cigarette. "How'd you identify me?"

"One of my friends recognized your voice."

Sally's eyebrows went up; her lips pursed, the expression one of mocking acknowledgment. "Some Deep Throat I am." She leaned back against the loaded countertop. "I don't want you to stay. They might see your car."

" 'They'? Isn't that a little paranoid?"

"I don't know what's paranoid. I don't know anything anymore. What do you want to talk to me about?"

Rose sat down. The chair seat was a little sticky; so was the table when she put her fingers on it. "Why do you think George Shreed was behind the accusation that I betrayed classified material?"

She tapped ash into the dirty sink. "I was in a meeting where George pushed your investigation really hard. I think something had happened, like it was going to be called off, and he went ballistic. It wasn't even the right meeting for it." She shrugged. "So, I called you up."

"Do you hate Shreed?"

Sally thought about that. "Yeah, I suppose so. He destroyed my career." She chuckled again. "My marriage, I destroyed by myself." She drank from a glass that had been standing on a windowsill over the sink. "Your husband's a nice guy. I liked him."

"Let me help you."

"No, no, it's me who's helping you. What are you, drunk?" She smiled. "You want to help me, do the dishes?"

Rose stood. "You got a sponge?"

"I'm joking."

"I'm not. I like to do things. Come on—let's clean up a little."

"My place is filthy, right?"

"Right." Rose smiled. "You want to wash or dry?"

"I want to get drunk and pass out. But I'm not that far gone yet, and I have terrible hangovers. Plus I have to go to work every day, and would you believe that I take that very seriously? Even now."

And then she began to talk. She dried and Rose washed, and Sally talked and Rose listened. Later, they sat in the now cleaner kitchen and Rose drank a weak vodka-and-tonic and Sally made coffee. "I don't want to be a drunk," she said. "I really don't. But God! You get tired of yourself. Weepy, whiny, self-pitying you—I mean me." She chuckled again. "I haven't told you anything you came to hear."

"As a matter of fact, you have."

"What, you came to hear my life story?" She knelt suddenly and put her hands on Rose's arm, looking slightly up at her. "Look, I wanted to help you because I saw Shreed blow up over you, and I know what a bastard he is. But now—they *know*, which means that he knows, and that man can do *anything*. I can't help you any more."

"Maybe I can help you."

Sally shook her head. "Stay away from me. I'm poison now. Anyway, there's nothing else I know."

"You don't know what you know, do you? You worked for Shreed; you've watched him; maybe somehow you know why he came after me."

Sally shook her head. "You may just have been standing there. A target of opportunity. George sees the world in only one way—his. He's incapable of seeing somebody else's point of view. He sees the world this way, and he sets out to do something to the world, and if you're standing in the way, too bad for you!"

"What's he trying to do to the world, that I'm standing in the way?"

"No idea. No idea at all."

"He put the blame on me for something about a project called Peacemaker."

"I didn't have anything to do with that. I was running Section 6 then—that's George's old stand, which I got when he was moved up—so I didn't sit in on meetings or anything that involved Peacemaker. Only afterward, we heard that it had been aborted by the White House, and maybe there was a security leak. Are you supposed to be the leak?"

"What's Section 6?"

"I can't really tell you that. All I'm supposed to say is that we vetted certain aspects of operations."

"Peacemaker didn't qualify as an operation?"

Sally hesitated, then grinned. "You're quick—quicker than me and this vodka, anyway. No, I guess it's okay to say—Peacemaker was someplace else."

"But Shreed was in it, I know, because he had this slimy character named Suter planted on the Peacemaker project team. I know, because I was there."

"Holy God, Ray Suter? Mister Makeout?"

Rose's eyebrows went up. "You, too?"

"Sweetie, he tried to come on to me the first time we were alone—*and* I was married then. I still get the eye from him."

Rose stared at her and smiled. "He's George Shreed's assistant."

"Oh, I know that—" Sally straightened. "Ch no—I'm not going to bed with Ray Suter so you can know what George Shreed is up to!"

"You wouldn't have to go to bed with him."

Sally put down the almost empty glass. "You're dangerous, lady. Good at your job, right?" She took out another cigarette. "And I thought George Shreed was ruthless!"

"Sally, I only meant you could talk to him. You might hear something."

"Actually, he can be kind of charming." She blew smoke out of the side of her mouth. "Don't count on anything."

Rose stood. "Don't risk it. I know you're worried about—them."

"Yeah. But I'm soberer now—drunks are paranoid, did you know that? My father was an alcoholic. They lie, they cheat, they steal, they think everybody's against them. Comes with the territory."

They talked a minute or two more. Rose asked no more questions. Sally steered her through the dark house with one hand on an arm. At a front window, she paused and looked out through a narrow gap in the curtain, just as she must have when Rose rang the bell. "Just checking," she said. "So I'm a *little* paranoid."

The sky was dead black—no stars, no moon. "I gotta run; it's going to rain!" Rose said goodnight and walked to her car and turned to wave.

Before she got into the car she found that all four tires had been slashed.

Washington.

It began to rain at ten o'clock. By ten-twenty, the rain was heavy, and the cars slowed and the sidewalks were empty. Crime went down.

The gutters were swept clean, and the rubbish flowed down storm grates into the sewers, where gathering rainwater rushed through black tunnels and splashed into the rivers. By midnight, three underpasses in the city were flooded and cars could not go through. By two in the morning, the North Branch of the Anacostia was running fast and brown. The fish ladder in Riverdale was entirely under water. A supermarket cart that had lain on its side, exposed like the skeleton of some beached sea creature, disappeared in the flood and washed three hundred yards downstream before it caught in a dead tree. The banks, mud and concrete riprap, were cleansed of the trash and glass and condoms that had been piling up for weeks.

Ray Suter woke and heard the rain and decided that today was the day.

NCIS HQ.

Dukas was in his office at seven next morning and on the phone to Abe Peretz at seven-ten.

"Mike, what the hell are you doing awake at this hour?"

"I've been awake since five. I've had two women in my apartment all night."

"That would keep you awake, all right."

"Abe, I was sleeping on the floor, because Rose was in my bedroom and somebody you don't know was on the sofa. Listen up—I need some advice and maybe some help." He told Abe about the slashing of Rose's tires. She had called him from Sally Baranowski's and asked for his advice, and he had told her to call the police, and then he had got AAA and had picked the two women up and taken them back to his place.

"Okay," Abe said. "I got the picture. What d'you want from me?"

"I need a place for this woman to stay a couple days while she gets over being scared to death. You got a big house. How about it?"

Abe hesitated, then sighed. "Bea'll have a cow."

"So, cows give milk. Tell her it's for national security."

"Yeah, fat chance. Anyway, sure, I'll make it okay."

"This woman I'm sending to you, Sally Baranowski, she was giving us information about Shreed. Rose went to see her, and bingo! her car tires are slashed. Funny coincidence."

"So you think—mmm."

"I'm thinking of you getting mugged and beaten up. See, if the way he works is first he sends a warning—like you first getting your orders changed, then getting beaten up—and then he really gets nasty, then Sally really maybe has something to worry about. That's why I want her safe for a while."

"But how did he find out about her?"

"It looks like there's a leak in CIA Internals."

"Oh, Jesus."

"Yeah. And I can't go to my man there, because if he knows I'm talking to Sally, he's going to say I'm violating inter-agency policy and he'll tie me up in official bullshit and I'll be spending all my time trotting around Washington covering my ass. So talk gently to this woman and see if there's anything else you can get out of her—anything like similarities to what happened to you. I'll be honest with you, all of a sudden I think we're dealing with a dangerous man."

"What about Rose?"

"Rose is a rock, you know that. She's okay. Anyway, I don't think he'll hurt her, because he needs her—if I'm right that he implicated her in the first place to cover himself, then he needs her out there for the same reason." He hesitated. "Just to be on the safe side, I told her to carry."

"A *gun?*"

"No, a sandwich. Jesus, Abe. He could be a dangerous guy! You're the one who said that everything is personal for him."

"We keep saying 'he'—you're sure it's Shreed? That's a pretty sensational conclusion, Mike."

"I'm not sure. Nothing's sure. I'm just trying to find a place to stand on, Abe—that's why I'm coming to you."

After he had hung up, he stared at the chart on the door for several minutes. Then he walked over and wrote in the dates and approximate times of the tire-slashing and his having spoken Sally Baranowski's name to Carl Menzes. After a moment, he added Peretz's mugging and, way off by itself, the death of the Iranian agent in Kenya. Then he sat at the desk again and thought about how he would use three agents he had asked for to help in the investigation. While he drafted an outline of assignments for them he was thinking about Sally Baranowski and the CIA Internal Investigations Directorate.

When he had the outline, he went up the hall to talk to his boss, who, instead of giving him the three agents even part time, told him to spend less money, not more.

"I got a budget meeting Monday, Mike; I gotta show some cuts. No, you can't have three agents; you can't have *one* agent, and I'm tempted to jerk Triffler back so I can put his salary someplace else. Forget Siciliano for now; it's a long-term thing. Word from ONI is to concentrate on the inter-agency abuse of power—it's cheaper."

Going down the hall, Dukas thought, *Like hell I will,* and he grabbed his telephone, thinking about Sally Baranowski and the slashed tires, and dialed Carl Menzes's number.

"Carl, Mike Dukas," he said as soon as the call was answered. "You got a leak in your office, and if you don't plug it today, I'm going to interview George Shreed under oath."

THAT WAS THE DAY that Ray Suter got ready to kill Tony Moscowic. For Dukas and Triffler, it was a day of frustration—paperwork, dead ends, more questions. The *Jefferson* made its way through Suez. Sally Baranowski, frightened, stayed in the Peretzes' house all day and shadowed Bea Peretz like a child shadowing its mother. George Shreed waited.

19

Suburban Maryland.

RAY SUTER HAD TO CONCENTRATE ON EVERY DETAIL of driving, every stop, every turn, because he was so excited he felt as if he was on a drug. If he took his hands from the wheel, they shook. His knees felt weak, his thighs liquid. He kept belching.

The little .22 and its cardboard silencer were taped under the dashboard. He was in it now, so high on the idea of killing that he didn't care whether the silencer worked or not. He was just going to do it.

I can do anything.

Moscowic was waiting for him outside a Wendy's on Route 1. *Another of his goddam stupid tricks,* Suter thought. *Countersurveillance routes, secret phone calls, out-of-the-way pickup points—what a shithead!* Moscowic always dictated the wheres and hows, and Suter had let him; it had suckered Moscowic into thinking of Suter as a loudmouthed jerk who paid big money.

And now the loudmouthed jerk was going to kill him.

"Wet," Moscowic said when he got in. A drizzle was sifting down, and he had beads of moisture all over his cheap rain jacket. "What's up, you gotta get me out on a night like this?"

"You said you were going out anyway."

"A manner of speaking."

Whatever the hell that meant.

"You said you wanted to show me something," Moscowic said.

"That's right."

"What, for Christ's sake? I was watching television."

"Then you aren't sacrificing anything, are you."

Moscowic began to tell him all the things that were good about television. Suter let him talk, glad to have him distracted while he drove to Bladensburg and the remains of an old pier that was crumbling into the North Branch.

"Hey, where we going?" Moscowic said, at last aware of the industrial landscape around them. Or maybe he had always been aware; he was sharper, Suter had to remind himself, than he seemed.

"Where I can show you this thing."

"What is it?"

"I have to show you." Suter heard suspicion in Moscowic's voice, so he added, "It's about the kid. The hacker."

"Nickie?"

"That hacker, yes."

"What's he done? I bet he done nothing. He's good—you know the judge that sent him up called him a menace to the new economy? What's he done?"

"I have to show you."

Suter glanced over, saw, in the lights from another car, Moscowic's frown. Moscowic seemed to like Nickie. Or was it simply that Nickie was his discovery?

They passed the darkened Indian Queen Tavern, and Suter made a quick right and left, and Moscowic said, "Hey."

"What now?"

"Where the hell?" Moscowic was turned almost all the way around to look behind them. "We're heading for the fucking river. There's nothing over here."

"There's a place to stand. The only place you can see what I want to show you."

"It's across the river?"

"Exactly."

"How come we aren't across the river?"

Suter gave the sort of sigh he hoped sounded like righteous exasperation. His right leg was vibrating on the gas pedal, and he felt as if he was going to jump right out of his skin, leaving his clothes and his skin sitting there, driving the stupid car with this stupid boob in it. He took deep breaths.

"This is not a good neighborhood," Moscowic said. "Jesus, why didn't you tell me, I'd've brought a weapon. Jesus, Suter."

Suter let the car glide to a stop. A hundred yards farther along, the lights from a marina glowed between the leaves of sodden trees. On their left, a wall of greenery hid the highway, and on their right a twisted hurricane fence guarded what had probably been a junkyard. Beyond it, across the river, the lights of an old working-class town and the high-rises of a project were haloed by drizzle.

"No way you can see Nickie's apartment from here!" Moscowic said.

"I didn't say you could. Come on."

When he got out, Suter thought his legs would give way. He leaned one hand on the car and took another deep breath. "Come *on.*"

"I think you're a wacko," Moscowic said, but he got out.

Suter opened the glove compartment and took out a pair of light-weight binoculars, which Moscowic studied, even leaning back in a little to see what Suter had. *He knows,* Suter thought. *Or he's just always suspicious.*

"Here." He handed the binoculars to Moscowic. "You'll need these."

He had thought the binoculars were a brilliant touch. They gave him cover as he closed Moscowic's door and then grabbed the .22, feeling his hands almost too strengthless to pull it loose from its tape. He held it by his side with his left hand as he locked the car.

"Let's go," he said. He started down the path beside the hurricane fence. He didn't look back, didn't wait; he had planned all of this, every step, but he hadn't factored in his own tension. It was the worst thing he had ever gone through. Not from any horror of killing, not from repugnance at the act, but from the tension.

I can do anything.

"This better be good," Moscowic said behind him.

The path was greasy with mud, and there were puddles right across it in several places. Suter couldn't balance well enough to take the sides; he simply waded through. Moscowic took the sides, chuckling at Suter. "Ruining your shoes," Moscowic said. "This really worth a pair of shoes, Mister S.?" He laughed again.

The path led to the dilapidated dock. Three aluminum rowboats were dark shapes on the riprap. Suter picked his way over chunks of broken concrete and stepped onto the dock's slimy planks.

"Come on."

"That's not safe."

"I walked all the way out when I was here before." His voice was shaking. He had to clear his throat to speak. "We're not going all the way. I just want to show you what I found."

Moscowic edged up beside him. He had picked up a stick to use as a cane, and he poked ahead of himself like a blind man. The water swirled ten inches below their feet.

"You got the binoculars? Look across the river—the second high-rise from the left? It's the fourth window from the top—" He had to make it sound as if there really was something there to look at.

Tony raised the binoculars in a halfhearted way but didn't quite put them to his eyes. Suter transferred the pistol to his right hand behind his back. He found that Moscowic was a little closer than he had intended, almost leaning on him. Suter moved to his own left; one foot slipped, and he started to fall, caught himself.

"You okay?"

Suter was starting to hyperventilate. "Look where I tell you, will you? I want to get out of here!"

"*You* wanta get outa here! Listen to the guy!" Moscowic raised the binoculars to his eyes.

Suter put the cardboard tube against the other man's left mastoid and pulled the trigger.

There was a slightly muffled report and a brilliant flash in the darkness, and shredded paper suddenly appeared on the hair at the back of Moscowic's head, plastered to it by the wet. Suter smelled burning hair and paper.

"Hey!" Moscowic said. He put his left hand to his head and turned. "Hey!"

Suter stared at him. The stupid sonofabitch had moved just as Suter had pulled the trigger—that was all he could think. Moscowic had turned his head, maybe feeling the tube brush his hair, and Suter had fired a shot that hadn't killed him.

"What the *hell*—!" Moscowic was gasping. He took his hand away and looked at the blood, almost as dark as the river in the dimly re-flected light.

Suter felt as if somebody was choking him. He gagged. He fired again, the shot loud this time. Moscowic grunted and clapped his left hand to his chest. His eyes were wide.

Suter fired again.

Moscowic swung his stick and whipped Suter across the face. The pain was shocking. Moscowic seemed to be chanting: "You shit—you stupid dumbfuck shit—"

Suter fired again and then again. Moscowic groaned and sagged to his left. Suter realized he might go over into the river alive, and, sobbing in his terror, he grabbed the front of Moscowic's jacket, pulling him off the dock so that he fell to his knees on the broken concrete.

"I knew, you slimy sonofabitch, I knew. . . ." Moscowic's voice was thin.

Suter was blubbering, vocalizing gasps—"Unnh—uh—unnnn—uh—" He picked up a piece of broken concrete and brought it down on Moscowic's head. Still he didn't go all the way down. He groaned again, a horrible, animal sound, and Suter brought the concrete down again, and this time Moscowic fell at his feet, still alive, still able to roll on his side and try to grab Suter's leg.

Suter screamed at the touch. He smashed the concrete into Mos-cowic's face. And again. And again. Until Moscowic was quiet.

Suter backed away into the cover of the bushes, weeping; then he threw up. He felt a little better, but he was numbed by what had hap-pened. He had had no idea how hard it is to kill another man. *Five shots.* Then, *What the hell had he done with the gun?* Panicked, he felt in his pockets, his hands on fire, torn by the concrete. He turned his burning hands up into the rain, like a man asking for mercy.

Moscowic groaned.

Suter sobbed, and he went down on his knees to look for the gun.

Moscowic moved.

Suter scrabbled around on all fours, going toward Moscowic, away from him, sideways toward the dock, back. He found the .22 in a pocket between two chunks of concrete. The cardboard silencer was gone.

He crawled to Moscowic and put the barrel right against the man's left eye and pulled the trigger. Then Tony Moscowic was dead.

Suter wanted to run, but he made himself sit there. He made himself go through it and think what he was supposed to do next: It didn't matter about the cardboard silencer, so let that go. It didn't matter about the cartridge casings, because he'd handled them with gloves on, so let them go. The rain—maybe—would wash his blood away; nothing he could do about that, anyway.

Book, he thought. Tony's notebook, in which he kept all his cases, incredibly messy, incoherent, but a record that would damn him if anybody could figure out Tony's code. He put a hand on Tony's chest and felt the wet, went through Tony's pockets and found the little spiral book in the upper pocket of the nylon jacket. One of the .22 slugs had gone right through it. He found Tony's keys and threw them into the river; he wanted it to look like robbery, and he knew now he could never go into Tony's house and search it, anyway. He couldn't. He took Tony's wallet.

The rain fell more heavily.

He tried to pull Tony Moscowic to the dock. Just as he had had no understanding of how hard it is to kill a man, so he had had no realization of how heavy and unyielding a corpse would be. Before he had Tony's buttocks on the dock, he was weak from the exertion. Ready to give up. But he had the desperation of the cornered animal, and he pulled and pulled, then pushed the body and rolled it. At last he was far enough out on the rotting dock that he could see the lights of the marina a hundred yards downstream. He felt naked out there with those faint lights silhouetting him. He began to shake.

He looked down at the lights, then across the river.

He crawled back and picked up a piece of broken concrete and put it inside the bullet-riddled nylon jacket, then put another in the other side and zipped the jacket up. His hands were so cold he could hardly grasp the zipper pull.

He toppled Tony Moscowic's body into the brown water. It sank head and torso first, as if Tony were having a look around, snorkel fashion, and the dark water carried it downstream, spinning slowly and sinking away.

Ray Suter watched it go, unable to move.

20

Istanbul, Turkey.

ANNA LOGGED OFF THE YOUNG MEDICAL STUDENT'S computer. Harun had been delighted to find a woman who spoke Persian in the youth hostel, devastated when she wouldn't sleep with him. Women who wore blue jeans and lived in youth hostels were supposed to be loose. Western decadence was the lure that had brought him to study in Turkey, after all.

By not sleeping with him, she had evaded all of his Iranian male contempt. He wanted her. She led him by the prick. They sat in a café and sipped thick coffee and she used his ancient laptop to log in through a Turkish university net.

She thought of Alan Craik. A boy, like the boy beside her. Boys could be led. Shreed was not a boy, but an old, bitter spy. A professional manipulator. He would be dead to most of her wiles, and that made him impossible to manage. On the other hand, he had the knowledge to survive and prosper that she needed. Craik didn't. She couldn't see Craik leaving his life to follow her, but even if she managed it, what sort of partner would he be? Perhaps more biddable than Shreed, but hard?

He pursued Bonner like a thing from beyond the grave. Efremov had said that with respect. Craik was at least handsome, even winning in a quiet way. She could lie down next to Craik without a qualm, perhaps even look forward to it. His eyes were powerful, as Efremov's had been.

There was something in Craik that drew her, and she fought it as she had since she had first seen him shouting for his wife in the café in Trieste. No one on earth would wear that look and shout for her, but he had responded to her when she had let him know a little of the truth of her life. He was a man who felt things. Shreed would use her like a towel. She was tired of old men.

She was tired of boys, too.

She stretched, absently displaying her perfect midriff below her sleeveless top to the boy seated opposite. He pawed her with his eyes. She smiled a little vacantly and typed a series of keys.

"I have to use the washroom, Harun."

He smiled wolfishly at her. An hour later, he found that his laptop had been slicked down to core memory. In the hostel, two young Arab women discovered that their passports had been stolen. None of them ever saw her again.

USS *Thomas Jefferson.*

Alan's solution to inaction was work. He sat in his stateroom, grinding away at a stack of first-class-petty-officer evaluations that were ready for signature, then reviewing his jg fitrep drafts, but his mind was on the map of the Indian Ocean pasted over his desk. Three feet above him, the distorted voice of Céline Dion pounded through the deck. A steel-beach picnic was in full swing on the flight deck, and Alan needed to get some air. He changed into running clothes and headed for the party.

He ran into his own people as soon as he emerged on the blast furnace of the deck. It was a hundred and eight degrees in the shade, and it would get hotter as they entered the Red Sea. He got a burger and the allowed beer from one of the stalls set up at the deck edge and moved to where most of his officers were lounging in deck chairs. Reilley and Cohen were tossing a Nerf football. Stevens was describing a flight to Campbell, his hands flat in the universal aviator symbolism representing aircraft. Soleck was lying back and fondling a female helicopter pilot with his eyes while she played volleyball on a net stretched between two F-18s.

"Hey, Soleck, keep your eyes in your head."

"Oh, yeah, hi, Skipper. She's real cute. Kinda flat-chested, but—"

"Soleck! She's an officer in the US Navy, for Christ's sake."

"Sure is a great Navy!"

He thought he was funny. He was twenty-two years old.

"Soleck, I'm serious as a heart attack. If you can't learn to treat women like fellow professionals—"

"Whoa! Attention on deck, it's the CAG!"

Rafe looked like a poster for the Navy in a clean haze-gray T-shirt and faded USNA shorts.

"I'll just go play volleyball." Soleck grabbed his shirt and vanished.

"He as sharp as he looks?" Rafe said.

"Soleck? Sometimes I think he's hopeless. Sometimes I think he's a genius. I was just starting to give him the 'don't drool on the female cadre' lecture. Same one as had so much effect on you, as I recall."

Rafe put his arm around Alan's shoulder, a gesture that did not pass unremarked on the flight deck. Alan squeezed his arm and turned to face him. "I have an idea I need to turn into a plan."

"Talk to me, Al."

"I want to put recon way ahead into the IO as soon as we get to the bottom of the Red Sea. I'm thinking a big chainsaw right out over the IO."

"And you're thinking that the MARI system might just win its spurs."

"Right."

Alan had the map of the vast reaches of the Indian Ocean in his mind. The Gulf of Aden opened like a mouth into the scene of action, the Arabian Sea. From Socotra Island at the eastern end of the Gulf of Aden, it was less than two thousand miles to Karachi, Pakistan, or to Goa, India, the two antagonists' major naval bases. By the time the *Jefferson* reached Socotra, now fourteen hundred miles away, the Chinese surface-action group could be near Sri Lanka. All the players would be on the board.

If the *Jefferson* and her escorts pressed hard, they could be at Socotra in three days. If they raced and left the escorts, sooner. Rafe looked at him, considering. "It's one hell of a long way."

"Doable, Rafe. With even a modest tanker plan, we could get a good look at the Ceylon Channel. And we'd be south of the action, if they're sparring."

"They're already sparring. An Indian frigate sank a Pakistani missile boat about an hour ago."

"It's a lot like a war, isn't it?"

"Looks like shit, and it tastes like it, too."

"Rafe, getting a scout would serve a lot of purposes. It ought to scare the piss out of the Chinese; they'll have no idea where we came from. If we show our hand, I mean. And it might just help convince them we mean business. But I have to say it: they might shoot."

"Yeah."

"So we can't just have the MARI birds. We'd need at least one or two shooters. That's a lot more gas."

"We plan it both ways. F-18s would go a long way to convince them we were close. On the other hand, they can't have any serious aircover."

"Maybe not. Also, remember that the Indians will be all over them. We can't be the trigger that starts everybody shooting."

"Yeah. Okay, Al. You have ideas, I have ideas. Let's get some pens and start planning. I'll get everybody together when we have a draft. We plan it both ways; a strike package and just the two MARI birds and their gas. I expect it will have to be approved all the way up the chain to CNO."

"Higher than that, Rafe."

"And then, if we haven't started WWIII with China, maybe you can slip off to Bahrain, okay?"

The words marked a change in Rafe—conciliation, or new information?

PART
TWO

Flight

21

Washington.

ALONE IN HER OFFICE IN THE EARLY MORNING, Emma Pasternak reviewed her e-mails and her voice mail and her paper-work, keeping her investigator's file on George Shreed open in front of her. She knew what she was going to do, but it was too early yet. She worked on, glancing at her watch every half-hour. Finally, the watch told her that it was after nine-thirty and time to act.

She reached for the telephone.

Langley.

George Shreed picked up the telephone without looking at it. He was pretending to listen to a former congressman orate on the subject of a missile defense system while, in his own head, he was concentrating on the problem of revenging himself on Chen. Giving an apologetic cock of the head as he touched his telephone, Shreed held up a hand.

"Sir, I'm sorry—" It was his receptionist, who had the fear of being fired in his voice. "The caller said it was urgent. Priority Sta-—"

"Put him on." He gave the ex-congressman a fleeting smile.

"Am I speaking to George Shreed?" It was a woman's voice.

"Speaking."

"Mister Shreed, this is Emma Pasternak of Barnard, Kootz, Bingham. I represent Lieutenant-Commander Rose Siciliano in an ongoing national security case."

Shreed felt the hair at the base of his skull rise. "Yes?"

"Mister Shreed, is it true that you're a Chinese agent who uses the code name Top Hook?"

His mouth went dry and his gut dropped. He stared at the ex-congressman, who was cleaning the fingernails of one hand with a fingernail of the other. "Is this a joke?" he managed to say.

"No joke, no kidding, no bullshit. I'm going to court today to request a subpoena to depose you under oath, hopefully tomorrow, about your role in the scapegoating of my client. Any comment?"

"I think that if you have such an absurd action in mind, the place to go is the Agency Security Office. They pass on requests for interviews. Goodbye."

He tried to hang up, but her voice froze his hand.

"Listen, Shreed, I'll have that subpoena by three and I'm coming after you tomorrow! Under oath! I'll bring a court steno and you by all means have somebody there from your Security office! I'll want two hours, because I've got *lots* of questions about a Chinese agent named Top Hook who uses the Internet to pass US secrets! Get me?"

He lowered the telephone into the cradle. He managed to smile at the former congressman. "Somebody who wants to subpoena me," he said, as if it were a joke. His knees were trembling, but he kept his face pleasant and his hands steady. After a glance at his watch, he said, "I'm sorry to cut you short, Congressman, but the people upstairs have me down for a meeting in ten minutes."

The ex-congressman went right back to his spiel, which really had to do with his allegiance to the defense contractor who now paid his salary. Shreed pretended to listen while his heart pounded and his mind kept snarling at him, *It's over, it's over, it's over—*

HE TOLD his receptionist he was feeling sick and was taking the rest of the day off, and he hobbled down to his car in its privileged parking space and drove himself slowly out of the Agency lot and made the turn toward his home. Checking ahead and behind for surveillance, he detoured to a major artery and drove for ten minutes toward the district, then took the turnoff for Tyson's Corner and its traffic and its upscale high-rises. He had actually visited a doctor out here sometimes, so the route might make some sort of sense.

He found himself having to plan an escape too quickly. He thought he had been planning ever since Janey's death—Jesus, only nine days ago—and, now that the moment had come, he wasn't ready. In fact, he realized, he hadn't believed that the moment would come at all. He hadn't believed he would really have to flee.

He turned down toward the doctor's and watched behind himself for a tail. *The call from that woman could have been a fake to flush me. Maybe they've known for months—a couple of years, that's how long it takes them to get their act together—* Seeing nobody, he pulled into the big parking lot that surrounded the doctor's isolated high-rise on three sides, drove up and down two parking lanes as if looking for a space—there were plenty, but he after all was a man with a handicap—and then coasted through an almost hidden gap that took him into the parking lot of the next building. He turned right and exited immediately, went around the block three-quarters of the way, and headed for home.

What he was supposed to do now was notify Chen and initiate an escape plan. The Chinese would pull him out within six hours, and tomorrow he'd be in Beijing, a hero.

Which was the last thing he wanted.

HE PUT THE CAR in the attached garage rather than leaving it in the driveway. Entering the house through the kitchen, he went at once to the freezer and took out the morphine, the syringes, and the vial of blood, which he fanned on the countertop as if making a display. He was thinking that he would have to go to the bank where he had the safety-deposit box with the old passport and the money. No point in taking the gun. He did, however, add a folding Spyderco police knife with which you could rip open a can or a car seat or a human being.

He would have to call his doctor and make an appointment for late in the day. He would need time to sew the Chinese-furnished passport and his legitimate passport into whatever clothes he wore—blue jeans and a T-shirt and another shirt over it, he was thinking, and a jacket and a baseball cap—and he would need time in an airport toilet to stick on the false mustache. No, better do that at a gas station. He was thinking that he had to ditch his canes and put the blood in the car and—

He went to his computers. He had to do this part exactly right. If he didn't, he'd lose the years of preparation and the triumph he had prepared. His moment. His justification, when they'd all see at last how right he was and what he had achieved.

He began to download files to disk. He'd have preferred making a single CD-ROM, but his laptop didn't have the capability. He should have prepared for that, he thought. *Bad planning. Thought I was planning and I was just dicking around. Now I'm behind the curve.* He checked his watch. He hated the fact that he was sweating and his heart was beating too fast and he felt light-headed. Downloading files from the second computer, he double-checked his mental list and saw nothing that he'd missed. Everything would go on two disks; the rest was dross now. He moved to the third computer and downloaded the algorithmic password file and the ultimate-go file, which would trigger the program in the University of California mainframe and start the money pouring out of the Chinese intelligence and party accounts.

"And that's all I really need," he said aloud.

He began to dismantle the computers. What he wanted was the three hard drives; when each one was out, he reassembled the computer so that it would look quite normal. *Should have had substitutes to put in,* he told himself. *Stupid. Should have had drives full of innocuous shit to smack in there.* But he hadn't. He hadn't really planned it well enough.

Because he hadn't believed.

He straightened with a screwdriver in his hand. It occurred to him that he hadn't believed he'd have to flee because he hadn't thought anybody was smart enough to catch him.

"Jesus, a beginner's mistake," he said. He shook his head. *But how did that bitch know?*

He stopped and booted up the laptop and embedded a message in a pixel and sent it to the porn site. It read: "Laundryman: Cannot make meeting Belgrade. Conflicts here. Will reschedule soonest. Top Hook."

He took the three hard drives to the garage and stacked them on and around a big transformer that they had had in Jakarta and never got rid of. Dusty now, looking more nineteenth-century than twentieth, it had adapted the local electricity to their American appliances. It had ruined several computer disks for him until he had understood what a powerful magnetic field it created. He plugged it in and let it fry the hard drives.

He cut his hair short.

He drove to the bank.

He turned off the transformer and smashed the hard drives with a hammer, then swept every scrap into a trash bag and put it in the car.

He roamed the house. The house must look as if he intended to live there forever. And as if he had come home for the reason he had given, that he had felt sick: he opened the medicine cabinet, got out some Pepto-Bismol and Imodium tablets and put them on the top of the toilet tank.

He put a Patsy Cline CD on and sat in the empty house, listening to it until she sang "Crazy," and then he listened to that again. He couldn't go out to Janey's grave to say goodbye. He thought of the mound of new earth with bitterness, the raw dirt covered with some stupid blanket of green plastic to look like grass. No flowers, no goodbyes. The song ended and he turned the player off.

"Crazy," he said. The song had already been a classic when they had met. He astonished himself by his sentimental attachment to it. Tears were in his eyes.

With distaste, he injected himself with the morphine.

When it had settled in and the first hot glow was over, he went once more through the house and checked again that everything looked normal, so normal that the house could have been used as a setting in a Disney film. *The American Home,* he thought. His legs pained him less, and he was even able to clump downstairs without his canes, holding the rail and teetering on legs no longer used to supporting him.

At the door to the garage, he turned and looked back into the kitchen and to the breakfast room beyond, scenes of seven thousand mornings, kisses, fights, shared lives.

"Crazy," he said.

He didn't pack a suitcase.

He didn't take a raincoat.

He didn't say goodbye.

USS *Thomas Jefferson.*

Mission planning used to be done anywhere that there was a flat space for charts, a handful of pencils, and room for the planners. The computer has changed all that. The interlocking circles of missile ranges, fueled radii, and threat-radar coverage can all be displayed on a screen at the flick of a button. Guesswork as to the possible course and location of enemy units can be done scientifically, with vectors on colored graphics and far-on circles indicating maximum possible movement. The danger for the computer generation is that the graphics look so finished that they threaten to become reality, rather than remaining an assembly of hypothesis and WAGs—wild-ass guesses.

Rafe belonged to the generation that still preferred paper charts. Rafe still hand-copied his own strip-charts for low-level cross-country flights, because the time it took him to calculate the fuel and draw the lines helped him to understand the terrain and the hazards. Alan had reached seniority with the computer, but his professional conscience agreed; a hand-done chart full of SAM sites and missile coverage rings served to teach the maker to know his enemy's air defense intimately. So the first draft of the reconnaissance mission, already code-named Opera (for the famous Beijing Opera) Glass (for looking at things far away), was done on paper charts with grease pencils, the way missions had been planned since the Second World War.

The word spread. The intelligence specialists began to pile pertinent message traffic under Alan's elbow, and somebody else brought them coffee. An hour after they began, Chris Donitz strolled in and began to work fuel figures for the F-14 Tomcats, which they would have to use for long-range aircover. Alan sent for Stevens and Campbell and assigned them to do the same for the MARI planes, and DaSilva from the S-3 squadron came in with two pilots and an NFO and started to work the tanking numbers. Alan and Rafe explained the mission in snatches and let the chart on the table do most of the talking.

Alan slipped comfortably back into the role of intel officer. He read quickly, took cryptic notes, and shot off sentences to clarify intelligence points. Rafe tried to plan both package options, but when he took charge of the large package and put the F-14 skipper in charge of planning the smaller, Alan was pretty sure that Rafe had made his decision.

Alan sharpened a pencil and started to draft a message to Fifth Fleet in Bahrain. Behind him, Brian Ho, the air wing intelligence officer took in as much of both plans as possible and started to craft a brief to go in front of the admiral ASAP, because, without the admiral's approval. there would be no request to Fifth Fleet, much less to the Joint Chiefs.

"Threat," murmured Rafe. "It all comes down to the threat. If they have aircover, we have to have fighters."

Alan tossed a three-page report on the chart and took a slug of coffee.

"Su-27 Flankers at Bussein. They moved there two days ago. They might be sending more right into Pakistan."

"Where the fuck is Bussein?"

One of the hovering ensigns reached over and pointed to a town noted as "Bassein" on the coast of Burma.

Rafe glanced up. "Do you know that, or are you guessing?"

"Um, guessing, sir."

"Glad you have the balls to say so. Find out." He turned to Alan. "Can they refuel in the air?"

"Probably. They were practicing it last year. No point in putting those Flankers there if they can't reach their ships." Alan was immersed in an old FOSIF WestPac report on Chinese tanker training.

"Flankers got some long legs, too," Ho interjected. "Maybe twelve hundred miles? Combat load? Someone look that up."

"Fuck. We don't know much, do we?" Rafe took a swig from his coffee.

"Rafe, I think it's possible, but not probable, that the Chinese have air."

"What are they doing so far out? I mean, let's just think this through. Will they even come around Sri Lanka? Why would they? India has carriers, a real navy. Hell, their submarines are damned good, too. Chinese are taking a *huge* chance if they come this far. What if they plan to stay over in the Bay of Bengal?"

"Last reports show them on track for Sri Lanka. Indians are protesting like mad, but it's international waters, and India is still at peace with China. Hell, aside from the fact that they're shooting at each other, India is still technically at peace with Pakistan. And maybe the Chinese are counting on India to be smart enough not to shoot."

Alan had stopped writing. He leafed back through the reports under his elbow, found the one he wanted, and read it carefully, drinking the last of his cold coffee. Stevens touched him on the shoulder.

"We'd have to tank twice. No way around it."

"Tell Rafe."

"Roger." Interesting. Stevens had pitched into the plan and started working. Stevens was often the nay-sayer in group activities, and Alan had thought that this tendency had probably kept him from promotion. But today he had been one of the first to arrive, and he had started off simply fetching materials until Rafe gave him a job. Alan went back to his report, took a few notes, and looked around. "Sanchez?" He only knew her name from the number of times he'd seen her with Soleck. *Where* was *Soleck, anyway?*

"Sir?"

"I don't know how you'll do this, but I want to know if either of the planned Chinese Jiangwei II frigates ever got delivered to Pakistan. Says here they were completed last March."

"Spell that for me, sir?"

"Here, just take the report. Call Office of Naval Intelligence, get them on it."

Rafe had looked up from his own work. "I miss smoking, sometimes." Others laughed. Rafe bent over to Alan. "Give."

"Just a thought."

"Spill it."

"I'm wondering if the Chinese aren't going round to Pakistan to deliver some ships. Like maybe the whole damn flotilla."

"*What?*"

"It's been done before. The Russians used to do it with submarines. At the opportune moment, the Chinese become advisors, they run up the flag of Pakistan, surprise!"

"Christ!"

"Well, yes and no. A few modern warships would change the balance in the AOR, yeah. But the Indians still have the upper hand in training and material. And they'll be watching that Chinese group like hawks. But if it coincided with something else, hell, it could work. It'd be a coup for both China and Pakistan."

"I buy it."

"Don't buy it yet, Rafe. I've sent Ms. Sanchez out to get some facts. Hey, Campbell! Where's Soleck?"

"Ready room."

"Call him and tell him to start putting together a simulator on Chinese hulls." Alan leafed through a *Jane's*. "So-remenny's already there. Luha class, Luda class, Luhai and Jiangwei, Jianghu FFGs That'll keep him busy. Damn it. Look how many new-design hulls the Chinese have built in the last three years, Rafe. Mister Stevens, what's Soleck doing?"

"Writing a standard mission overlay for the ACR."

"Whatever."

Sanchez was back. She grinned in triumph. "Two Jiangwei I frigates have been paid for but not delivered. They're both missing from imagery at their South Fleet anchorage."

"Nice job, Ms. Sanchez. Thanks." Rafe smiled at her. "Now I *really* buy it."

"We'll know for sure when MARI images their flotilla. Sanchez? Ask DNI if anyone has a composition on that Chinese group. Maybe the Australians? Or the Malaysians? Anyway, Brian"—this to the CAG AI—"put that on the 'intel' slide and in 'objectives,' too."

"Roger." His fingers raced across the laptop in front of him. "Voilà. Ready to brief."

Suburban Virginia.

There was a flight out of Dulles to London at eight-thirty. Shreed made the reservation at a pay phone, using the old Agency passport name. They wouldn't ping on it for days, he knew and all he needed was twenty-four hours. Everything he was doing was designed to give him twenty-four hours—get out of the US, find a protector, then get the memo to Chen—and then if things went right, he'd have disappeared into a black hole. If things didn't go right, well—what would he care?

His neighbors, if they had even noticed, would say that he had left in his car; the Agency would believe that he had left for his doctor's and then disappeared.

Then they would find the car.

He drove west to a strip mall and dropped parts of the destroyed hard drives into a dumpster, then a little north to another and then west again to a third, where the last of the hard drives went into the trash. Detecting no surveillance, he went south to a small park and put on his traveling clothes in a men's room. He made a face at himself in the mirror. In London, he would darken his hair, but he didn't want to leave any possibility here that somebody would remember his buying the retoucher. With the baseball cap and the jacket on, he looked like an engineer on vacation. Or maybe a low-level entrepreneur getting ready to coach the Little League team.

Or a spy getting ready to bolt.

He took the vial of his own blood and poured most of it in a single small puddle into the trunk. The rest went on the rear bumper, where he smeared it with his hand, and—only a drop—on the right rear fender.

In the thickening dusk, he drove north to the Beltway and then around Washington on the west and north and then north again to White Flint Mall, and there he parked the car, locked it, like Everyman going shopping, and walked away.

There is a Metro stop at White Flint. It connects with Metro trains to northern Virginia, from which a bus service connects with Dulles International Airport.

THE *JEFFERSON* and its battle group plowed on into the Red Sea. An ASW screen had been thrown out ahead of it. Sonar tails were in the water, and, in the ASW spaces, AIs and helo pilots boned up on Chinese, Indian, and Pakistani submarines.

In West Virginia, Rose slept. One of her children whimpered in a nightmare and she woke, listened, and put her head down. The dog, hearing a dog far away, put his head up to the window and raised his ears and growled. These early warnings could not be taken seriously, however, and she made the dog lie down, and the child was quiet, and Rose slept.

In Washington, Sally Baranowski lay awake in Abe Peretz's guest room, thinking of Ray Suter and the almost pleasant evening she had spent with him. Something was up, she thought; she had thought it a dozen times during their dinner together. Sometimes she thought it was something about Suter, then something about Shreed. Suter, his hands bandaged, had been tense, although not too tense to propose sex, which she had laughed away as "too soon." But she couldn't escape the thought that something was very wrong with him. And then, being as near depression as she was, she could not escape thinking, *Maybe there's something very wrong with me.*

Mike Dukas slept alone. He hadn't been able to reach Emma. He dreamed about Rose, about a vast hotel, about stairs and doors, all of it somehow a movie in which he was an actor but had no script, and he woke after a scene in which he had walked and walked down a passageway of many doors yet never moved past a single one of them, as if the floor had been a treadmill under his feet. "Going no place," he said as he woke, finding the room cold.

Tony Moscowic, dead, swayed just above the bottom of the Anacostia River. The fat on his decaying body almost balanced the concrete chunks in his jacket, and his corpse, neutrally buoyant, neither quite floated nor quite sank. Down at his right ankle, a rusted pipe had snagged his pant leg, and, as the swollen river dropped and the current lessened, he stayed in that place, a dead man waiting.

22

THE BRIEF TO THE ADMIRAL WAS AN ANTICLIMAX. He took the brief at speed, grabbed the laptop, scrolled through the slides, and asked if they had a message ready for CNO. Alan handed over his draft message to Fifth Fleet. The admiral changed the "To" line to JCS OPS and made Fifth Fleet a "Via." Then they waited as he massaged the message. "Send it. Give me the whole brief tonight. Large package all the way; no point in pissing on them when we can kick them. Okay, make it so. Lieutenant-Commander Craik, stick around a minute."

He waited until they had all filed out except the flag captain and the JAG officer. Then he looked hard at Alan. "Commander, I have a message regarding your support to NCIS on my desk. I'd have liked to have been informed, but I gather this was done on the fly. Some crap has stuck to you because of it and I want that settled, got it?"

"I'd like it settled, too, sir. There are a lot of rumors on the mess decks. It isn't helping me run my det."

"Concur. I'm going to have the NCIS guy say a few words after your brief. Commander, let me just say this. You seem to be involved in some spy crap that's pretty important in Washington. I got a wrong impression about it, and it looks to me like you were a little outside the box. You have a reputation for going outside that box, and you could do yourself a favor by keeping your chain of command informed of all of your activities."

"Ah, yes, sir."

"You going to tell me it's too sensitive?"

"No, sir. We may have discovered a senior mole in the CIA. Working for China. It all started with a connection to my dad's death."

"Well, well. You've about tripled my knowledge of what the hell is going on. Are you still involved?"

"Yes, sir. I'm supposed to meet the, uh, agent, the person who may have the data, in Bahrain in two days." Alan was sweating again, and he still hadn't had time to change his shirt. None of the three men facing him looked friendly, although Maggiulli looked a lot less accusatory than he had lately.

"We'll see. If it's up to me, you're out of it, but I have a feeling it's not up to me. Now go do your job."

"Aye, aye, sir."

Alan walked out of the admiral's briefing room with Tony Maggiulli on his heels.

"Just understand, okay? You made a mess in Trieste and left us to hold the bag. You looked bad, withholding from the Italian cops and from us. Even a one-liner about the level of the operation would have saved you a lot of crap from our end."

"I didn't know what it was about, then. Or that my wife had been accused of espionage. It was all over the boat when I got here. I didn't have a clue what was going on."

"Well, next time, talk to a lawyer, okay?" Maggiulli stuck out his hand, and Alan shook it.

London.

The WAGN line crosses the River Lea a little north of Clapton, a part of metropolitan London that most tourists never see. A path runs along the river, part of the Lea Valley Park system, coming from Limehouse Cut and the Thames on the south and running north to Waltham Abbey and then to Ware. The Lea—the river that Izaak Walton once fished—is not much where Limehouse Cut runs into the Thames, and it remains an urban and industrial waterway for several miles, but then its banks grow greener and the spaces on each side widen, and by the time you reach the railway bridge where the trains cross, it is a pleasant, watery space.

The five-seventeen to Cambridge crosses the river here. Marcus Huckabee rides the five-seventeen every weekday of his life. He always sits in the same seat, the third from the end on the downstream side, just as, on the trip into London in the morning, he sits in the fourth seat, downstream side. Every day, on both trips, he looks aside as the train crosses the Lea and takes a moment to study a row of posts along the western bank of the river by the path.

Marcus Huckabee has seen something on one of the posts only three times in seven years. Each time, he did what he was paid twenty pounds a month to do: he telephoned a number in Fulham and said, "There's a package for Hannah at the shop." That was all. That was the entirety of Marcus Huckabee's part in espionage.

Two of those times, the thing on the post—once a Coke bottle, once a glove—had been left by a walker who had found it on the path. The third time, the thing (a lager can) had been put there by Marcus Huckabee's handler, who was testing him.

Today, lowering his newspaper, Huckabee looked aside and was pleased and, as with the other times, excited to see a red cap on one of the posts. Third from the end, exactly where it should be, although he reported anything on any of the posts. *Red cap, third from the end,* he told himself. It was important to remember the details, because his handler would contact him later and ask.

As soon as he got home, right after kissing his wife, Huckabee called the number in Fulham.

Within two hours, the Mossad office in Tel Aviv knew that a foreign friend, not yet an asset, wanted to make contact.

At ten o'clock London time, George Shreed checked a mark on the wall of the cinema in Brunswick Center and walked to a bench at the far end of the shopping mall, where a middle-aged woman was waiting for him.

He had been gone for twenty-one hours.

NCIS HQ.

"Suter hasn't seen him since yesterday. I think he's worried, but he says he isn't."

Mike Dukas didn't see much in Sally Baranowski's call. Still, you had to encourage your agent, even when the agent was as informal an acquisition as Sally. "But you said he went home sick."

"His receptionist says he went home sick yesterday morning. The DO logged a call from him yesterday afternoon saying he was heading to the doctor's but he was sure he wouldn't be in today."

"Well, there's some bug going around."

"But he didn't call in this morning. We're supposed to call in daily if we're taking sick leave."

"Thanks for keeping on top of it. I really appreciate it. Check on him tomorrow, will you?"

"Mister Dukas, I get really bad vibes about this. George isn't the kind of guy who stays home sick. I used to work for him, remember—you could have terminal flu, he still expected you to be there."

"Well, thanks. You're doing real good. How's life at the Peretzes?"

She laughed, the first time he had heard her laugh. The night that Rose had brought her to his place after the tire-slashings, she had seemed a basket case to him. "It's pretty noisy," she said.

He laughed, too. Bea Peretz and her daughters were high-decibel arguers. "You take care."

He was going to dismiss what she had said, but he remembered the warning he had given Menzes: his rabbit was getting ready to run. Could George Shreed have run? But why? Nothing had changed.

Still, what she had told him nagged.

He called across to Triffler. "Hey, Dick—play telemarketer for me, will you?"

"Oh, shit!"

"Yeah, go on, you told me you moonlighted at it once—I bet you're dynamite." He had been asking Triffler more personal questions. "Just get on the phone and make one call for me, okay?"

"Who to?"

"George Shreed. I just want to know if he's home, okay?"

Triffler walked around the wall of crates to Dukas's desk. He looked disgusted. "Why me?"

"Because I can't do that shit and you can! Will you call him?"

Triffler looked at the wall. His lips moved. He nodded. "I'll do the prescription-drug spiel. His phone listed?"

"One is, one isn't. Listing is G. Shreed." Dukas pushed a paper with the number across the desk.

"Okay, so I can say 'Mister Shreed.' Okay—" He did a quick rehearsal for Dukas's benefit. " 'May I speak to Mister Shreed, please? Mister Shreed, this is Thad Blaine calling from the Vital Health Foundation, how are you this afternoon, sir? Do you realize that the cost of prescription drugs—' Okay!" He picked up Dukas's phone. "My wife may call on my line; the dog was sick—here we go—"

Triffler dialed. He waited. He listened. He hung up. "Answering machine."

"Shit."

"Could mean nothing."

"I know, I know. Anyway, thanks, Dick." He looked at Triffler. "Baranowski thinks he's been out of sight too long—since yesterday sometime."

"Melodramatic. She's unstable."

"I know, I know. Still—" He put his hand on the phone. "If I tell Menzes, he's going to cream me for withholding information. If I don't tell him, Shreed could be in Tehran."

"Wait a day."

Dukas and Triffler stared at each other. Triffler was the cautious one, and Dukas reminded himself of that and that sometimes caution is misplaced. "Unh-unh," he said and started to dial.

"Thanks for your confidence in my judgment."

"I value your input." He waited as the telephone rang. So did Triffler, who, despite his advice, wanted to know what was happening. After five rings, however, somebody else picked up and told Dukas that Menzes was in a meeting. Dukas left his name and number and asked to be called back before the end of the workday.

"What day does that cleaning woman do Shreed's house?"

"Wednesdays."

"Well, that won't work." It was Friday. "Let's see what Valdez has got." He dialed another number.

"*Nada,*" Valdez said. "There was some computer use middle of the day yesterday, then nothing. No traffic last night, which he doesn't usually fail to do, being a night person."

"What about the other hacker who's on him?"

"He's still there, man, just waiting. Just like me."

He hung up.

"I don't like this," he said to Triffler.

USS *Thomas Jefferson.*

The brief ended up in the VS-53 ready room, because it had the most seats, and because Rafe had decided to fly one of the VS-53 birds for Opera Glass. There were sixty aircrew packed into a space meant to seat forty, and the back was crowded with intelligence personnel, alternate crews, and flag staff. The admiral was sitting in the squadron skipper's seat, front row on the aisle, and the embroidered cat symbol on the headrest shone in the reflected light of the projector.

Rafe stood at the front of the ready room, a tall, lanky figure in a rumpled flight suit, and sixty pairs of eyes were glued to him as he slapped the screen with his pointer. The digital image showed the Indian Ocean from the Gulf of Aden to Sri Lanka. West of Socotra Island was a carrier shape. That's where the pointer rested.

"Evening, folks. Okay. Opera Glass is a long-range recon mission with a supporting war-at-sea package and fighter support. Our objectives are to locate and identify the Chinese surface-action group last located off the map in the southern Bay of Bengal. I want this to sink in, folks. We will be carrying war shots, but we're not going to shoot unless we're provoked. More on that in rules of engagement. What we want is to show the flag and convince the Chinese that we can find them and hurt them if we want to. More than that, we want them to know that we're here and we're serious. That's what's going to make it dangerous for us, because the mission is pretty provocative and they may not respond like our old friends the Russians would." He nodded sharply to the sailor running the machine, and the computer-generated slide changed in a blink.

"Okay. Here's the package. Two MARI-equipped S-3s at the tip of the spear, with two VF-162 Tomcats to keep them company. Six VS-53 tankers with gas at these three points. All of the 53 birds carry a buddy store and a harpoon. That's in case we have to go in shooting. Four F-18s with HARM back here covering the gas. The MARI birds go to Green Bay, here, tank, and start the search pattern here, at Dallas. When they locate the target, we either start bringing assets up the chain or we don't, depending."

Rafe took a drink of water and looked out into the dark where the aircrews waited.

"That's the basic mission. Twenty-two planes in the chainsaw, then another six on alert five. At launch plus seven hours, we start rotating the chain. That's the tricky part. For about thirty minutes, during this event," Rafe went to a slide showing the cyclic ops cycle, "we'll have about half the air wing going up the chain and half coming down. It has to be perfect, and we can't practice. But it allows us to sustain the search at the pointy end for about five more hours and keep support packages ready to respond. With a little luck, and some ducting, we ought to be able to cover the whole area from Sri Lanka south to Point Denver, here, and west to Point Dallas. The devil's in the details, though. Listen up and hold your questions till the end. Write 'em down if you have to."

Rafe was followed by the JAG with the rules of engagement. The JAG spoke for almost five minutes, but what he said boiled down to "Don't shoot until shot at, and even then don't shoot." He closed by saying, "Weapons release will be held by the flag throughout," for the third time. Then Brian Ho, with the intel portion: a lot about Chinese radar parameters, a cheat sheet for LantFleet sailors who had never seen a Chinese system, and another on the Pakistani and Indian navies. Kneeboard card after kneeboard card on missile ranges and reaction times.

"They may have air support, in the form of Su-27 Flanker B's out of Myanmar/Burma. Also watch for the Indian stuff listed on kneeboard three. No one out there will be particularly friendly, so ID everything you can. Everyone remember what a Tu-16 Badger looks like?" Grins. The Badger was an ancient Soviet plane still used by the Chinese. "They have some fitted out for sea-strike. They have long legs and they could be out for support. They may even do some ASW."

Aviators got up and talked about fuel loads. LTjg Sanchez briefed the comm plan. Her kneeboard cards were simple and accurate, color-coded by role in the mission package; they represented seven hours of work.

"High Noon is the Strike Lead. Lone Ranger is MARI one and Tonto is MARI two. The tankers are Wagon Train one through six, and the Tomcats are Gunslingers. The F-18s are Riflemen. It's all on the yellow card. Frequencies within your stations are color-coded. Thanks." She ducked out.

The brief rumbled on for more than an hour. When Rafe went back to the front and asked for questions, the briefing team endured another ten minutes of details that surfaced a fuel-consumption error and a lot of questions about the rules of engagement. Rafe announced that there would be a brief recce review of Chinese, Indian, and Pakistani hull types and aircraft in the VF-162 ready room in an hour. Then he looked at all the people in the ready room, running his eyes over them slowly as if measuring them.

"Two days ago, China delivered a war ultimatum to India. It has three days to run. This is real, folks; we have to find 'em and wake them up to the New World Order. Or in three days we'll be playing with fire."

The admiral nodded at Rafe and gave him a thumbs-up. Then he waved at a man in civilian clothes who was hovering in the doorway behind Rafe.

Rafe looked at the man and held up his hands for silence.

"This is Special Agent Stein from NCIS."

"Ahem, yeah. Admiral Kessler has asked me to drop by to say something. Commander Craik is being, ah, instrumental in supporting an ongoing counterintelligence investigation. I have here a letter of commendation from the Director of NCIS that I'd like to present to Commander Craik. Admiral, shall I read it?"

"No, Marty, I think we'll save that for the awards ceremony. But thanks, and well done, Commander. Okay, boys and girls. If this thing gets approved, it launches in twenty-two hours. Get moving."

Alan thought his throat would burst, it had swelled so hard. The effect of the announcement was immediately visible: everybody was making surprised faces at everybody else.

London.

Shreed, wearing an English suit and tie, and with a wooden cane, was sitting in the Palm Court of the Langham Hotel. A businessman in an even more English suit and tie was sitting next to him at right angles, rather red in the face from sun and aggression, one of those Thatcherite go-getters who look as if they mean to eat you raw.

"We have to know what you're bringing," he was saying in a surprisingly quiet voice.

"Myself."

"My people would like something as a *bona fide.*"

"Your people can go fuck themselves. They know me."

The man sipped his coffee. "They'd really like *something.*"

"They'll get something if they're willing to deal."

"They don't want to take a pig in a poke."

"Neither do I. Forget it." Shreed made a movement to get up.

The businessman laid a hand on his arm. "No, don't. Please, don't get angry." He smiled a toothy smile. "They'll just have to vet you that much more thoroughly at the other end, you know." He put his hands up in mock surrender. "You're too much for me. You can leave at seven. I'm terribly sorry, but two security people will go with you; they'll have a passport for you. I'm told to say that we deeply regret any implication that you can't be trusted to make the flight alone."

Shreed ignored the smile. "I'll take the passport and a ticket to Nicosia. No minders, no 'protectors.' A room in a good hotel. If they try to snatch me and stick me in a safe house or fly me to Mossad headquarters, it's over. Tell your people that."

"Please, Mister—Ackroyd—you must accept *some* conditions."

"No, it's Tel Aviv who must accept some conditions. If they don't like it, I'll go home."

"They'll never agree to Nicosia. Nicosia is full of Palestinians."

"Exactly."

The man passed a hand over his face. "Let me consult with my people."

"You better consult fast. I'm not staying in London past midnight."

He had been gone for twenty-six hours.

23

THE *JEFFERSON* AND HER ESCORTS WERE OUT OF the Ditch, and the moment they were clear of the navigational nightmare at the southern end of the canal, the carrier had again leaped forward to her full speed. Jordan dropped away to the east, and Egypt was a dirty yellow smudge to the west. A forty-knot wind generated by the huge ship's passage blew African sand and heat through the p'ways; it was one hundred and twelve in the shade of the tower, and the sunset wind blowing over the deck was red hot.

No one lingered on the flight deck, but men and women came up from below to see Africa and to feel the incredible heat. Flight operations remained at a standstill, and a group of sailors labored in the heat to replace the nonskid that had been worn down to bare metal by aircraft on the deck. Alan stretched his arms over his head and looked off the starboard side at Egypt and Somalia and thought about the past.

It was hard to picture George Shreed, his father's wingman, as a traitor. Yesterday, looking at the photo of the Top Hook ceremony in his mind, the connection had seemed obvious. Today, he considered the man's ambition, his manipulations, and his relentless scheming at the Agency and couldn't see George Shreed betraying his country. Certainly, Alan's dad had said that he had come home from Vietnam a bitter man.

The politics within any large bureaucracy had a corrosive effect that Alan had witnessed first hand.

Alan thought that Shreed was capable of using and discarding individuals. Was it a long step from personal betrayal to treason? He knew enough to know that falsehood was the foundation of espionage. Lies about identity, lies about purpose, lies about sides and roles and information.

When he thought about Naples and Harry and Anna, he no longer regretted missing his own trip to the Ranch. The cold manipulation that Harry had preached as the method to manage Anna struck Alan as being a dark magic that would eventually warp the user. He tried to imagine what a man would be like after decades of seduction and betrayal every day. He couldn't imagine what ends would justify such means, and, although he could imagine the effect on Shreed, he tried not to wonder how the Ranch had changed Harry.

Alan had to face the fact, however, that Harry the professional was a different man. He didn't want to examine that too closely. What he had seen of Harry in Naples had shocked him, rather like finding that a close friend was cheating on his wife. But Harry had cried at a stop on the flight out of Africa, after trying to sell a group of people beside the road on democracy and personal liberty. That was the real Harry. A man who had high ideals and cared deeply for people, both individuals and masses. Not the man who told him that the battle for an agent's soul was often won in small talk. Not that Harry.

Did George Shreed care for anything? Alan stood in the heat, looking over the sea to Africa, and wondered.

Cyberspace.

do i know you, sir?
We haven't met, but friends of mine have tried.
oh you
Many things have changed.
have they??? you suggested we might meet 'm not sure i'm
interested my attempts to meet you have had very exciting
conclusions

I'm thinking of changing jobs
ah that changes things doesnt it
We might make a very powerful team.
we might if i survived the experience
What guarantee can I offer?
i pick the venue :)
I hate the whole smiley face thing. Okay you pick it.
skating rink
Where?
figure it out
When?
24 hours
How will we meet?
you wander i'll find you when i like it
No. I will not be that vulnerable.
too bad you tried for me twice youre not in position to preach
trust
I'll wait ten minutes.
you do as you like i will approach you when i like it
Ten minutes.
see you in dubai who knows perhaps you will see me as well

USS *Thomas Jefferson.*

Stevens was done with the brief, and he came back to the water cooler in the back of the ready room and touched Alan's shoulder.

"How come you're in my plane?"

"Because you're the best pilot."

"Okay. I just wanted to—"

"Alan! You got a minute?" Rafe, in full flight gear, stood with his helmet under his arm.

"I'm with you." Alan turned back to Stevens. "See you at the plane in five."

"Sure. Whatever."

"Read this?"

Alan took a message board from Rafe and looked at the top message.

"Jesus saves."

"Yeah. The Australians have put their fleet units on alert and are sending a task force."

"And ASEAN is falling apart."

"The East Timor thing didn't help. Taiwan is torn. Vietnam still hates China. Australia has muscle."

"Fucking odd time for the Aussies to decide they want to be players."

"China has moved their East Fleet units into the Taiwan Strait. Seventh Fleet is on full alert."

"And Opera Glass is still a go?"

"No one's said boo. We're going."

Alan pulled Rafe out of the passageway into the comparative privacy of the VS-53 maintenance office. Men and women in float coats and deck helmets were moving purposefully around. VS-53 was struggling to get their last plane off the elevator and on the deck.

"Rafe, we're playing for a lot of marbles here, right? We're *fucking* close to World War III in the Indian Ocean."

"I hear you."

"I'm venting, okay? Just bear with me. We have to send the right message. They have to buy that we are here to fight if we have to."

"Without fighting. Yeah, bud, I'm the CAG, okay? I know the mission. You know the joke: Mrs. Luce, I *am* a Catholic?"

Alan shook his head. "I'm tensed up."

"Get over it, Lone Ranger. It's time to play ball."

24

Langley.

WHEN, LATE IN THE DAY, MIKE DUKAS HADN'T HEARD
from Carl Menzes, he drove to the Agency's headquarters and went
looking for him. As it turned out, Menzes was in his office but with
somebody, so Dukas cooled his heels for fifteen minutes before the door
opened and Menzes ushered out two somber men and stood looking
around as if daring anybody else to take up his time.

"We need to talk," Dukas said.

"I've got a case. Been breaking all day. I'm beat." Menzes looked less
well-pressed than usual, it was true. He passed Dukas through the door
and came in behind him. "What's up?"

"I need you to check if George Shreed has split."

"Jesus Christ, you don't kid around, do you? What do you mean, 'split'?"

"Gone missing. Flown the coop. Dropped out."

"Why?"

"I have a source says he hasn't been in his office since yesterday about
ten. He doesn't answer his home phone."

"Goddamit, Dukas, if you've flushed him with your NCIS bullshit—!"
Menzes blew out his cheeks angrily and swung around to a computer
terminal. He punched keys. "Yeah, left the office sick yesterday, called in
sick today. So?"

"Called in sick *last night* for today, is my understanding."

"I haven't got that." Menzes was hitting more keys. "He's due to fly out to Budapest tonight on Agency business; we've got that covered here and in Budapest, perfectly routine stuff. Due back Monday morning."

He swung back to Dukas. "What's your problem?"

"I think something's funny."

"So do I—you! There's stuff you're not telling me."

They stared at each other. Menzes pushed the knot of his tie up even tighter. A muscle twitched in one lean cheek. Dukas said, "He's an obsessive computer user. His computer hasn't been on for more than twenty-four hours."

"You interfering sonofabitch!" Menzes was standing. "You're surveilling him!"

"It's passive, I swear to God—no way he could know—"

"You're breaking a federal law! You don't have a court order, or I'd know! You stupid, interfering goddam sonofabitch!"

Dukas took it. He let Menzes read him out for fair—and Menzes was good at it. Behind that lean facade, Menzes was a passionate man, and he let his passion pour like hot tar over Mike Dukas. When he was done, Menzes stopped, breathed, and said as a closer, "God knows what damage you've done!"

"Now will you check to see if Shreed has flown the coop?"

Menzes locked eyes with him. Then he whirled to the computer, picked up his telephone, and jabbed in a number he got from the screen. After thirty seconds, he pushed down the phone cutoff and dialed another number. And waited. And hung up.

"No answer on either the listed or unlisted telephone. Doesn't mean a thing." He sat down. "Tell me the rest. All of it."

Dukas shook his head. "NCIS case. You gave it to us, remember? 'By the book.' "

"By the book, my ass! You've compromised one of the Agency's most important cases in decades!"

"Oh, really? Now Shreed *is* the mole? A week ago, you'd hardly admit he was on the short list." Dukas sat down, too, as a way of signaling some intention to accommodate. "Carl, if he's bolted, it isn't because of something I did. Yes, I'm ahead of you on the case and I know things you don't, but I haven't set him off. But it scares me when a suspect goes missing for twenty-four hours."

Menzes put his forehead on the fingers of his left hand and massaged the two prominent knobs there. He sighed. "What do you want?"

"We can't let the weekend go without knowing where he is. The Budapest thing—I didn't know about that. You just let him fly off to a foreign place like that?"

"He's a senior official; he can go where he wants, subject to telling us and to us checking on him."

"What time is he supposed to fly out of here?"

Menzes looked at the computer. "Eight."

Dukas checked his watch. "Three hours. Put somebody on it, will you, Carl?"

Menzes looked disgusted. "Just what I needed. Okay, there's somebody out at Dulles anyway, as you very well know. I suppose you want me to stay here until eight."

"You got it."

Menzes shook his head. "You really fucked up, Mike. How the hell could you?"

"I haven't fucked up yet! I'll have fucked up when I have to give up on him. Has it ever occurred to you that it's you guys, with a five-year lead time on an investigation, who fuck up?"

"What have you got on his home computer?"

"Nothing. We know when it's warm, period." He didn't admit that that wasn't quite true, that Valdez had in fact been with Shreed to a chat room, and that there were three computers, not one. "How about you guys?"

Menzes shook his head. Again, they locked eyes, and Dukas didn't flinch. No way he was going to tell Menzes about Valdez and the wild-card hacker. Not today. Maybe, if Shreed was really gone, Monday— "How about having the local cops drive by his house, just to check it out for signs of life?"

Menzes shrugged.

"Come on, Carl."

Menzes picked up his phone; hunched over with it pinned against his left shoulder, he picked at his nails as he talked. "Get the DO's logs on Shreed, George, for the last three days. Check for sick calls and give me the times and the exact wording. Then flag the Dulles office about Exit Permit 99-1374, departing 2000 hours for Budapest; I want confirmation of check-in, baggage, and confirmed boarding." He leaned back and dialed again, this time to ask the police in Shreed's town to check his house for signs of activity.

Dukas was still there at six-twenty when the police reported that everything looked normal.

And he was still there when the Dulles office called at seven-thirty to say that Shreed had not yet checked in.

And at eight-ten when the Dulles office called again.

Menzes listened. His face was blank. He hung up.

"Plane's in line for takeoff. Shreed is not aboard." He threw a pencil. "Oh, Christ."

Dukas was standing by the window. It was starting to rain again. "He made an appointment to see his doctor yesterday. Better check if he kept it."

Menzes stared at him and sighed, then reached again for the telephone.

Dubai, United Arab Emirates.

As the Gulf Air flight rolled to a stop at the terminal, the young woman in 22C got out of her seat and wandered back to the bathroom. Sheila Horne, a female flight attendant, felt sorry for her, as she had all the marks of a new recruit for the Gulf Air staff. Anyone blond and shapely could make a living in the Middle East. Sheila had hoped to talk to her for a moment as she left the plane, but when she looked back toward the bathroom, the girl was nowhere to be seen. Maybe nerves? Sheila hoped she wasn't muling drugs, and by the time she collected her in-flight bag and prepared to deplane, the passenger in 22C had lost all interest for her.

When the sliding door to the bathroom opened, a shapeless woman wearing a veil, a face mask, and a floor-length *abya* emerged. She was not the only woman to change into acceptable local dress before leaving the plane. Although there were no religious police in Dubai, life for a woman could be very hard if she showed too much of herself. Most Arab women who traveled abroad changed when they returned.

Harry's team at the airport waited for a beautiful blonde to emerge. They were mostly Westerners, and they had learned to ignore the BMOs—Black

Moving Objects—that were local women. They knew which flight she was on, and Harry had got the passport name she had used from Istanbul. They watched and waited, and they had to report their failure when Harry arrived on the next flight.

Wrapped in black anonymity, Anna had entered Dubai and vanished.

USS *Thomas Jefferson.*

Alan walked out on the flight deck and was hit, as he hadn't been in years, by the grim majesty of the full weight of the air wing's power. Around him, on every side, dozens of aircraft fired their engines and rolled to their pre-launch positions. As Alan watched, two VS-53 S-3s launched, one from each of the forward catapults, and two VF-162 Tomcats began to roll into the shuttles to take their place. The chainsaw was launching, and the planes and reserves of gas that would make it possible for his two planes to search the ocean twelve hundred miles away were slowly uncoiling from the stack over the carrier and moving over the ocean ahead of the bow. The portside Tomcat dipped her nose as she locked into the shuttle and seemed to quiver with feline anticipation, jet-engine haunches vibrating, head down for the pounce.

Then the jet-blast deflector seemed to grow out of the deck behind the jet and obscured all but the tip of the vertical stabilizers and the canopy. Her pilot put her to full power and there was a crash that was felt throughout the ship as the catapult flung the Tomcat off the bow and into the chainsaw. Two F-18s rolled into the catapults with a different eagerness, more like warhorses scenting the smoke of a distant battle.

Alan was in the last plane to launch. He checked his chaff launchers mechanically and turned to watch the spectacle. His cards were onboard; the computer was cool despite the one-hundred-thirty-degree heat on the deck, and he was in no hurry to get into the oven. He found Stevens and Soleck and Craw all watching with him, as the catapults ground remorselessly through the air wing, flinging plane after plane into the dawn. The roar was deafening, the fire and heat supernatural. Every few seconds, another sharp crash indicated that another plane had launched. Endlessly, the deck crews moved in their intricate dance, moving planes into the launch sequence, spotting new arrivals from the hangar deck, moving the launcher into the shuttles. Regardless of sweat and fatigue, they moved, flashed their lights, locked the shuttles, and knelt to let wings pass over them.

Suddenly his S-3 was fourth to launch, strapping in as Soleck and Stevens exchanged the ritual of the preflight. Alan listened to the Strike Common frequency, deprived of his datalink until the g-force of launch was past and the computers could be engaged. The heat was like nothing any of them had ever experienced, made worse by the layers of flight suits, turtlenecks, and gear they wore against the cold that waited above five thousand feet.

The air-conditioning was losing the struggle with the heat. The plane stank of a full load of JP-5, its own aged electronics and the new-plastic smell of the MARI gear. Four men added a human tang.

Sweat flowed down Alan's back and pooled on his seat. His oxygen mask tasted of sweat and rubber and ancient bile.

It was unbearable. It went past unbearable. Alan watched the temperature pass one hundred and thirty-five degrees and began to wonder what the heat limit for the human frame was. The last planes launching always got the worst; the deck collected heat from every engine that went to full power and cast it back at the next launch.

When the plane ahead of them on cat three went to power, the surge of heat washed past the blast deflector and over their sweltering cockpit and the temperature went up again. Alan had been hot in Africa and in the Caribbean, but he had never known anything like this.

They crept up to the shuttle. The cavalry charge of the launch was gone, and the flight deck was nearly empty. The other det bird, Tonto, launched from the starboard-side forward catapult, and they were the last. Alan felt the increased tension and the faint snap as the shuttle bit home, and he looked out his tiny portal at the empty deck and the exhausted flight-deck crew, and he remembered the last time he had been last to launch, with a bird already lost to sabotage and Rafe's wife a cripple.

"Everybody happy?" Stevens asked. He seemed buoyant and Alan smiled, full of adrenaline and overheated well-being. He was going to do something very hard, and he was going with a unit he had helped to mold. They were going to try to save the world. He flipped a thumbs-up forward to the cockpit, and Stevens gave the crispest salute of his life.

And then they were off.

THE COLD AIR over five thousand feet froze them in glaciers of their own sweat. Everyone was soaked through, and the wet suits and turtlenecks were suddenly a liability against the chill of altitude. Stevens and Soleck pulled down the air-conditioning and began to discuss the possibility of the heater. Alan worked with Craw to get the computer loaded and to begin the sequence that would bring the MARI on line and into synch with the other plane, already more than fifty miles ahead. Alan had the datalink picture on his screen before he turned to the MARI, and his teeth began to chatter.

The chainsaw was more than one-third complete, with the first tanker station established and the first F-18s, the deep reserve, already in place. If the Chinese were really where they were supposed to be, if they were competent and ready, they would now have a possibility of detecting those F-18 radars brushing the sky over their ships. It wasn't likely, but the ducting of the Indian Ocean was famous to radar experts all over the world.

"Hey, Skipper!"

"Soleck?"

"Hey, you know this isn't the first time the Chinese navy's been here."

"Huh?"

"Commander Ho, in the brief, said this deployment was 'unprecedented.' "

"And?"

"In the fifteenth century, they sent a huge fleet this way. They demanded tribute from India and set up some military colonies in Africa."

"Soleck, is this pertinent to anything we're doing?"

Stevens cut in. "Hey, give him a shot. He helps pass the time." It was almost civil, from Stevens.

"Okay, I'll bite. Then what happened?"

"After fifty years of increased trade and contact with the outside world, China folded. The Emperor basically decreed that nothing outside of

China mattered. The fleet was scrapped. If they hadn't, Vasco da Gama might have found a Chinese empire waiting for him when he brought the first western fleet into the Indian Ocean."

"Why do you think they folded?"

"This is the neat part. Because their merchant class was suddenly getting too rich, taking over at home. And foreign stuff was catching on, changing things."

"That sounds familiar."

"That's why I thought you might like to hear it. Besides, like Mister Stevens says, it passes the time."

Point Dallas, 800 miles ESE of Socotra Island, Indian Ocean.

Stevens hit the funnel dangling under the VS-53 S-3 perfectly, slapping their probe in and then turning very slightly to stay in formation with the tanker. The tanker was itself moving east so that they wouldn't lose a minute toward their goal. Soleck watched the gas and called the fuel load aloud. Stevens massaged the controls, making fractional corrections to keep the probe in the funnel.

The chainsaw stretched away behind them. When they left Point Dallas, there would be only four planes left at the front of the operation—the two MARI birds and their front-line air cover, two VF-162 F-14s. The entire massive launch had been intended to get these four planes to this point, eight hundred miles from their carrier. Now they would fly on, a further four hundred miles. Or more. Somewhere to the east were the Chinese ships.

"Okay, we're full."

"Roger. Wagon Train Six, this is Lone Ranger breaking away."

"Roger, I copy breakaway."

Stevens backed off his airspeed just enough to pull his fuel probe gently out of the basket and rolled out from under. He pulled alongside the other S-3 and the crews waved, and then he pressed on, with Tonto beginning to separate to the south. The F-14s stayed between the two MARI birds, a little below them and a few miles behind. The E-2C was too far behind to see an enemy or provide a vector, and the S-3 radar was not designed to find air targets. If it came to an aerial engagement, the F-14s would have to count on their own RIOs and their own radars to find the enemy.

Alan looked over his screen one more time. He had a good link to the other plane. His radar was currently locked off, but warm. It was time to do what they had come all this way to do.

"Paul, I'm going to tell Lead we're going live."

"Roger."

"High Noon, this is Lone Ranger, over."

Alan fiddled with his screen resolution and realized that there was moisture from condensation on his screen. His clothes had begun to dry, and his teeth weren't chattering, but it was still cold as hell. They were high, almost twenty thousand feet. This was not a stealthy approach.

"Lone Ranger, this is High Noon, go ahead."

"Ready to start the music, High Noon."

"Concur. Good hunting."

Alan nodded at Craw, and he activated the first sweeps from the radar in the S-3's nose.

Over the Indian Ocean.

Soleck had surpassed himself in creating a baseline overlay for the area of operations. He had mined unused portions of the MARI system's memory and had input current data from landmasses and borders to SAM sites. He had done most of it by uploading existing databases from the ship, and, because of his work and the datalink, they had a set of grid-box overlays to show their search pattern. It was a small visual aid, but it simplified the whole mission, and, as the first search box was completed with no hit, it suddenly changed color.

"How'd you do that?"

"There's a lot of waste space in that system," said Soleck primly.

FOUR HOURS LATER they had six colored boxes on their screens and no concrete hits. MARI had identified a dozen merchant ships, an

Indian Ghodavari–class frigate, and a dhow riding the last of the monsoon from Somalia. The Ghodavari raised their hopes for a while, as they expected to find Indian ships pacing the Chinese group. But they saw nothing else. The Indian ship seemed to be moving slowly, waiting. Alan used his track ball to draw an imaginary line from Sri Lanka to the Indian picket, and then he slowly ran the radar in surface search mode up his line, calling out directions to Stevens. He began to register small hits toward Sri Lanka—fishing boats. Otherwise, an empty ocean.

They had all feared a chaotic ocean full of neutral hits, merchants and oil tankers going about the world's business, but the merchants were smarter than that and the sea was empty. Twice, Alan reported his status to High Noon. Because of the empty sea, they were well ahead of schedule, more than halfway complete. Now they were on boxes a little east of Sri Lanka, Stevens moving the plane up and down the sky in search of ducts that would get them a peek over their already immense horizon and into the unknown seas beyond. Craw and Alan were both masters at the art of ducting, and they took turns, one resting his eyes while the other stared relentlessly into the unblinking screen, cycling the radar from surface search to image when a contact met certain undeclared parameters and then cycling back.

Twelve hundred miles behind them, the carrier began its second great pulse of activity as the first elements of chainsaw two launched and began to creep up the chain. The tankers and fighter support of the first wave turned for home, grateful to escape from the five hours of torture strapped to their ejection seats. In the two MARI birds, and seven miles behind in their F-14 escorts, there was no hope of relief. They were too far east to be relieved; indeed, the plan had never expected it. In an hour, they would start to run back to the replacement tanker from the second wave, hundreds of miles west of them at Point Dallas.

Alan was getting intermittent peeks into a box east of Sri Lanka and slightly south, well over the radar horizon and almost three hundred miles away. He almost passed over one contact, a lone banana that was degraded by the duct and appeared almost as two small contacts at the very edge of his surface-search capability.

"Possible contact in box eleven. Senior, watch ESM. Going to image mode."

Alan hit the selector switch. No image appeared.

"Lost the duct. Mister Stevens, up a little?"

"Aye, aye." The plane moved sluggishly into a shallow climb. At this altitude, the S-3's turbofans didn't have much air to bite.

"Tonto, I'm trying to image grid C17 in box eleven. Do you copy?"

"Loud and clear, Lone Ranger. We have the contact. We're at angels 26."

Alan recycled the radar to surface search and regained the contact. In the old S-3B, you had to guess at the effect of the duct; there was no reliable method of knowing how far out the reflecting tunnel of weather conditions had carried your signal. The MARI gave a reliable prediction of the effect of the ducts. He found himself looking at a contact almost four hundred miles away, more than twice their radar horizon.

Alan held the contact and got an image. He didn't look up from his screen because the contact was so fragile. He felt for the comms switch with his right hand and toggled it.

"High Noon, this is Lone Ranger, over?" Craw was leaning out of his seat to look at the picture. Then he looked back at his own screen.

"That's an Eye Shield, sir." Eye Shield was a Chinese air search radar. ESM had caught it. A duct transmitted signals both ways.

"Soleck, are you seeing this?"

"Yes, sir. That's a Jianghu."

"Concur. See the returns from the mast aft of the superstructure?"

"Roger. No slope to the bow. I just built one of these on the simulator last night. It's a type two."

"Lone Ranger, this is Wagon Train Four. I'm relaying to High Noon." The voice sounded tinny and distorted through the encrypted link. Alan switched back to transmit.

"Wagon Train Four, this is Lone Ranger. I have a pos contact." He looked away from the screen just long enough to scan the coded kneeboard card taped next to his screen. "I make it a Blackfoot Two. Repeat Blackfoot Two." It not only resembled Soleck's radar prediction, but it also made sense: an old ship placed in the position of maximum vulnerability as an advance radar picket.

"Sir? Either the duct just changed or they just woke up." Alan glanced away from the swimming image on his screen and watched as radar hits began to scroll up the SENSO screen, so many and so fast that they filled it as he watched.

"I think we found them."

"I think they found us, too, Senior."

Langley.

Dukas and Menzes had sat in Menzes's office for an hour without news. There had been lots of activity but no news, and all they knew that was at all pertinent was that Shreed hadn't kept the appointment at his doctor's office.

"Let's fish or cut bait," Dukas mumbled. "Is he gone or isn't he?"

Menzes was doing routine paperwork, filling the time. "We don't know."

"When do we know?"

"When he turns up someplace."

"Bullshit, Carl! Come on! You going to report him as gone or aren't you?"

"I'll report him when I know something solid! I've got a team in his house; all I know is he isn't there and everything looks normal. I am not going to declare somebody as disappeared when I don't know the facts!"

Dukas stood up. "Yeah, well, I got people who maybe can't wait for the facts. I'm going to use your phone." And he called his boss's boss on his private line at home.

Washington.

The Chief of Naval Operations was watching Opera Glass on his own datalink at the Pentagon when an aide appeared at his side. It was late at night, but he was there and his people were there, because he had given his approval to this operation and now he wanted to make sure it went right.

"Telephone," the aide murmured. "Urgent."

The CNO scrambled out of his armchair and hurried out, calling, "Carry on!" over his shoulder; a minute later, he was in his office.

He grabbed the office phone out of the aide's hand as soon as it was presented. The aide whispered, "Walker at NCIS."

"CNO here."

"Sir, this is Chris Walker at NCIS. I'm the Deputy Director for Counterintelligence."

"Sure, Chris. I'm in the middle of an important operation."

"I understand, sir, but, um, so is this. Sir, this is not fully substantiated, but we have reason to believe that a very senior CIA officer may have defected to China."

"Holy crap. What do you know?"

"One of our senior agents has an operation that, well, seemed to involve a senior CIA official. Anyway, our suspect may have just bolted."

"When?"

"We don't know. The Agency is stonewalling, and he may have been gone for as long as twenty-four hours."

"Christ, he could be in China by now!" The CNO realized he was yelling at the wrong man. "Sorry, that was uncalled for. What do we know about him?"

"Name is George Shreed."

"Never heard of him. Why's he important?"

The other man hesitated. "It looks like he's a spy."

The CNO winced. "What was his access?"

"He had about everything, sir. Total code access, for example."

"Jesus. *Jesus!* Access to codes?"

"I'm afraid so."

"And he's been gone twenty-four hours?"

"Max—we think. We don't have confirmation, let me make that clear. The agent on the case called me at home and I'm trying to pin this down, but I thought you needed to know. I have to call the DNI, too."

"Keep me informed. Thanks." The CNO handed the phone back to his aide and moved across the room to his desk. "Get Magnussen in here." Magnussen was a senior intelligence officer. When he hurried in, the CNO was scanning a page of classified data; he looked up, his face harsh in the desk light, and said, "Correct me if I'm wrong—if the classified codes are compromised, we might as well try to communicate in clear."

"If the wrong people got the codes, yessir. As you know, though, codes go missing and nothing—"

"Assume they've gone missing in the hands of somebody who works for another country."

Magnussen shook his head. "It'd be a disaster. We'd have to do a worldwide rekey. Or else."

The CNO nodded and dismissed him with a look.

"Get me the Director of Central Intelligence." Another aide began dialing while the CNO took off his dress blue jacket. "I don't care where he is."

Over the Indian Ocean.

They were fifty miles farther east, farther from their tanker and farther from home. They had intermittent electronic contact with the Chinese, and Alan was reminded of the descriptions of the first sightings of the Japanese carrier force near Midway in World War II, glances from a seaplane through thick clouds. The seaplanes and torpedo bombers were the S-3's ancestors. Even then the location of the enemy over the horizon had been important enough to risk big, slow aircraft that could stay aloft and in the search for hours.

"Lone Ranger, this is High Noon, over." Rafe, at last.

"Copy, High Noon. Loud and clear."

"Lone Ranger, I have the reported location of the main body as zero five north, zero eight zero east."

"Roger. Close enough."

"That's not . . . . . . them, Lone Ranger."

"High Noon, please repeat."

". . . expected . . . . . . Ranger."

"I'm losing you, High Noon. Concur that contact is south of expected location."

". . . Ranger!"

"Wagon Train Four, this is Lone Ranger. I've lost contact with High Noon. Please request he advise. We are five zero minutes from refuel. Break, break. Gunslinger One, do you copy?"

Donitz's drawl came through perfectly.

"Gotcha, Lone Ranger."

"Anything out there?"

"Two guys with real sore asses, Lone Ranger."

The S-3 crews could get up and stretch. The F-14 pilots and RIOs were trapped in tiny cockpits, strapped into their seats for the whole ride.

They tanked the F-14s from their buddy stores as planned, and then they drove east together with their eyes open, and behind them the chainsaw raced to prepare for their return.

Washington.

"He's in bed."

"Tell him that it is a matter of *immediate harm*. Use that phrase." The CNO jotted notes on his doodle pad.

Another aide entered. "Sir, *Jefferson* may have a contact. They're having some comm problems up the chainsaw."

"He's coming to the phone." The CNO picked up the handset, took a deep breath, and sought to sound calm. "Can we go secure? I'll push." Tinny sounds and a warble. The right message on the screen. He flashed on a bad night landing he had done fifteen years ago. It was like that. "Can you confirm that one of your senior officers has run off to the Chinese? I'm sorry, that's not going to cut it. No, I've got half an air wing about to make contact with a potentially hostile Chinese force, and I have the need to know. Confirm it, or deny it absolutely."

The CNO looked up for a moment and snapped his fingers. "DNI, in here *now!*" Then his head went back down to the phone. "So he *is* gone. Oh, he *may* be gone." He looked at his notes from the conversation with Walker at NCIS. "This is somebody named George Shreed, right? What access did this guy have? No, I'm not going to wait. Did he have codes? With all due respect, this is an *immediate-harm* issue. Did he have access to military codes? I take that as a yes. Okay, let me spell this out for you. I'll call the President and check, but until this guy is either caught or he shows up somewhere, we have to assume the Chinese can read our crypto, right? And I have a big mission package in the air." He slowed the rhythm of his words. "I have to call it back."

The DNI entered the room and read the note the CNO had scrawled while talking. He scribbled at the bottom and then picked up a spare phone and started dialing. The CNO glanced at the note: *Pos C-c Jianghu II 200NM SSE Ceylon.*

He went back to his call. "I can't take that risk. I have to recall it. You have to order a worldwide rekey." He didn't sound at that moment as if he was talking to an equal. "I'm well aware what a worldwide rekey means, sir. It means that for up to forty-eight hours our communications are crippled, meaning that the eyes and ears of my fleets are screwed. It means that I don't dare send a ship or an aircraft against a real enemy." He listened and then said in a grim voice, "No, we don't know for sure that this Shreed stole the codes, but we don't know for sure that he *didn't*. So absent positive confirmation, you have to order a rekey!" He listened again and his jaw tightened. "He isn't *our* spy—he's yours. I suggest you catch him and find out for sure that he's not passing crypto codes. Until you do, *order a worldwide rekey*—and pray nobody starts shooting."

He put the handset in its cradle with exaggerated care. "Dick, do you ever get the feeling we don't all work for the same government?"

The DNI smiled grimly. The CNO stopped writing and looked at his executive assistant.

"Tracy, get me the *Jefferson*. And have them get me the strike lead for Opera Glass. If the brief this morning was right, he's called High Noon."

Point Denver, Indian Ocean.

"Sir, that Sovremenny just went to target acquisition on Smerch."

"We're a little out of range."

"Just thought you'd like to know."

"I expect they're sending us a message, Senior. Our MARI signal will look like a target acquisition signal to them until—"

"Slot Back! Two signals!"

Alan glanced uselessly at the ESM screen and keyed his push-to-talk switch. His brain translated the Slot Back call into a pair of Chinese Air Force Su-27s.

"Gunslinger, we have company."

Point Dallas.

Rafe listened to the orders from his carrier incredulously.

"Big Star, this is High Noon. I have intermittent contact at best. We're just executing Opera Glass Bravo, over."

"High Noon, this is Big Star. Pack it in."

"Big Star, I do not concur, over."

"High Noon, that's an order, not a request. Circle the wagons. Repeat, circle the wagons. Do you copy?"

"Roger, I copy, Big Star."

Rafe felt his hands open and close on the yoke, and he looked out over the endless half-circle of sea and thought of Alan, five hundred miles ahead of him. Recalled without explanation. Had the Pentagon got cold feet? What signal were they sending to China now?

Point Denver.

Craw held his finger over the locate switch until he had three cuts on the Slot Back and then he pressed. He exhaled as the computer located the triangulation two hundred miles to the east. Then he put his cursor on the contact and pressed a button to put it in the datalink.

Seven miles behind Craw, Donitz's RIO saw the contact on his screen and placed his own cursor on it.

"I want to put the radar on him."

"Wait one." Donitz flicked a switch to get the Strike Common frequency.

"High Noon, this is Gunslinger One. I have pos contact with two goblins and I want to turn the lights on."

". . . wagons, over!"

"High Noon, I read you broken and do not copy."

"Gunslinger One, circle the wagons, over."

Donitz was struck dumb.

"High Noon, do you copy contact with two repeat two gremlins?"

". . . over?"

Donitz made up his mind. Rafe had just ordered them to turn for home, but he clearly didn't know what was happening up here, and while Wagon Train Four and Six switched off at Dallas, there was no one to relay.

"Turn on the lights!"

Two powerful F-14 radars reached out toward the updated datalink contacts and grabbed them. Both RIOs registered the Slot Backs moments later as their ESM systems caught up. The Su-27s were beyond the useful range of their radars.

"Nose's hot."

"Gunslinger, Lone Ranger turning to 270 and going for the deck."

"Tonto turning to 265 and going for the deck."

"Gunslinger One, this is Lone Ranger. I think they're following me."

Both Su-27s were moving fast now, diving from almost thirty thousand feet.

Donitz knew he was supposed to avoid conflict but if he turned and the Flankers took Craik, he'd never live with himself. He and Craik went back. Donitz called his wingman. "Press, Covey." This sent the F-14s forward toward an engagement.

Alan was trying to raise Rafe when he heard Donitz decide to press the engagement. He was sure that Donitz had the situational awareness to make the call, but he wasn't sure that Donitz had heard the "circle the wagons" code that ordered a general break-off. Donitz was covering their scramble to get down where they could turn and have at least a tiny chance to duck missiles. Stevens had them diving just a little faster than the peacetime airframe rules allowed. They still had a few options, and Alan scanned the chaff and flare counters while he called Rafe.

When he couldn't raise Donitz, he knew that it would be up to him. He wasn't really senior to Donitz; as an intel officer, even as OIC of the det, he didn't really have the right to command in the air. But Donitz was his friend and would probably follow his lead. Why the hell had Rafe ordered them to break off? What did he know?

Seconds ticked by as the aircraft closed. The S-3s dove, big grapes falling as fast as they could. They were dead at this altitude. Alan ticked through the data available to him. The Su-27s were at the extreme limit of their range; they had to be or they would have gone to burner. They couldn't follow the group down to the deck, whereas the two S-3s could gas their F-14 escorts and still make it back up to the tankers at Point Dallas. If Donitz turned away, the Chinese would draw the wrong conclusions. The mission would be a failure, except for the hoard of data they had collected on the Chinese group. Alan would be willing to bet anything that those ships were en route delivery to Pakistan. The radar handling had been hurried, but one of the missing Jiangwei II frigates had been imaged. Not the time to think all that through.

He had to keep Donitz from pressing in. It all came down to trust, and Alan trusted Rafe. He pressed his comms.

"Gunslinger, this is Lone Ranger. Do not engage!"

"Ranger, they're following you down and closing. I want to stay nose hot and lined up."

Suddenly Rafe's voice came through loud and clear.

"Gunslinger, do not engage. Repeat, do not engage!"

"Roger, copy. High Noon, Gunslinger has two gremlins in pursuit Lone Ranger, range one four zero."

FIVE HUNDRED MILES behind the action, Rafe was out of the picture, listening to the distant events, feeling the calls of the pilots in his hips as he unconsciously tried to urge his plane to be there with them.

"Big Star, are you copying this? The Chinese are 140 from my scouts and pressing." And he slammed his fist into the windscreen next to his head.

Washington.

". . . 140 from my scouts and pressing."

The CNO was grabbing the keyboard of the JOTS repeater terminal as if he could fly it. The Su-27 symbols were clearly marked. What he saw could have been coincidence or it could have been a trap. If the F-14s turned away, it was possible that the Flankers might get one of the S-3s.

"Tell High Noon he has to break off regardless of provocation."

It felt like surrender. The Chinese pilots were being aggressive as hell, and he had just ordered his boys to run for home. He had to believe that the Su-27s wouldn't fire at an unarmed S-3. If they did, he'd just sacrificed them to buy the day he'd need to have new crypto. Otherwise, the Chinese might be watching the same plot he was, right now.

Point Denver.

"Gunslinger, break off!"

"High Noon—"

"Now!"

The Su-27s seemed torn between the S-3s and the F-14s. Donitz gritted his teeth.

"Do it, Gunslinger!" That was from Lone Ranger. Alan had a long head. Rafe wasn't a fighter guy, but he must know something.

"Covey, break left and go for the deck."

"Copy." The two F-14s turned away from each other in unison and headed for the water and Point Dallas.

Stevens kept the dive steady through eight thousand feet. Alan kept a hand on the chaff, but his mind was running on overdrive.

"They can't come down with us. They can't have the gas."

"They're at twenty thousand. Somewhere around four zero miles."

With the F-14 radars off the Flankers, they had only the ESM gear to measure the range and rate of closure, an imperfect tool at best. Alan began to feel the change in temperature and humidity as the plane neared five thousand feet, where the S-3 dumped cabin pressure. His ears started to pop. His throat was sore. He shut off the MARI system, like a workman careful of his tools, and set his screen to ESM, getting the same picture as Craw.

Soleck was rocking rapidly back and forth in his seat, watching the sky above them.

A minute passed without an ESM hit. They were below five thousand feet, the turbofans whining away at full throttle. Here, they could at least turn, and looking down at them was the worst aspect for the Chinese radar, no matter how good the technology was. The sun dazzle off the waves could also distract an IR missile like the Flanker's AA-10. So they had a chance, and they were ready to go a lot lower, too. Rafe had once dumped an Iranian fighter in the water because it tried to turn low with him and lost energy.

The second minute passed, and they still had no contact.

"Playing possum or turned for home."

"Turned for home." Alan almost felt it unlucky to say the words, but even with a tanker, those Flankers were an incredible fifteen hundred miles from home. They had to turn. And now that they felt that they had caused the Americans to run at the mere sight of them, they'd be happy to go home. Alan shook his head bitterly and tried to outstare the screen in front of him. If the mission had been to convince the Chinese that the Americans were here to fight if they had to, they had failed badly.

Why the hell had Rafe ordered them home? Alan couldn't believe that two Su-27s on a long fuel tether would have turned even once with the two Gunslingers. Donitz could have kept his nose hot and bored in, sending the message loud and clear. But Alan had heard the order and the tone of Rafe's voice. Rafe had meant business. Discipline held. And now they had turned tail and run.

In all four planes, discomfort piled on anger and multiplied. They had to tank twice, and Stevens slammed the basket both times, his anger coursing through the plane. He was silent except to make the required calls. Even those had the old touch of sarcasm that had been missing on the way out.

Every time Soleck opened his mouth, Stevens told him to shut it.

Alan poured the dregs of his thermos into his cup and felt his gut heave at the bitter, metallic taste of old grounds that mingled with his fatigue and the unaccustomed flavor of defeat.

And China's ultimatum was sixty hours away, and pressing forward.

25

Washington.

LATE AT NIGHT, MIKE DUKAS SHOWED UP AT ABE PERETZ'S house, soaked to the skin and looking as worried as a beagle.

"Shreed's split," he said when Abe opened the door. "The Baranowski woman still here?"

"We have a telephone, Mike."

"Yeah, you ought to hang it up now and then so somebody can call in. You going to ask me through the door, or do I stand out here all night?"

Abe, flustered, drew him in and began to pull wet clothes off him. Dukas hadn't brought a raincoat that morning, and in the end he needed to go upstairs and put on dry clothes that weren't designed for his wide body. As he dressed and sipped whiskey, Abe asked him about Shreed: Why had he gone? Where? When?

Dukas kept giving empty answers. "We're not even sure he's really gone. His car's gone from the garage, we know that—the cops looked in through a window. He didn't keep a doctor's appointment, but the neighbors remember seeing him yesterday. He didn't make a flight to Budapest he was supposed to be on—Agency business." He pulled a purple sweatshirt that said "Dig Mozart" over his gut. "I want to talk to Baranowski to see if she knows anything about where Shreed might go. Anything!" He pushed his feet into a pair of Birkenstocks. "You talk to her?"

Abe shook his head. "Nothing. She doesn't believe he's a spy, Mike. She thinks he's a one hundred percent prick, but she can't conceive of him being a traitor."

Dukas finished the whiskey. "Neither can Carl Menzes. Push comes to shove, he doesn't really believe that George Shreed is his mole. I mean, he wants *not* to believe that Shreed is his mole."

"It is kind of a stretch."

"Not for me. If it was Shreed that hurt Rose, I'll hammer him. First, I got to know he's gone and where he's gone."

"You checked the airlines, the trains—"

"Yeah, yeah, they're doing all that. Those goddam canes, they'd be hard to miss, right?" They were moving downstairs, Abe two steps behind and higher. Dukas half-turned to say, "If he's the mole and something flushed him, he's got an escape plan and they've jerked him out by now. He's in Beijing or someplace." Dukas chewed his lip. At the bottom of the stairs, he turned to face Abe and then, when they were on the same level, lowered his voice to say, "The party line is it's China. I think maybe not. Al's made a contact with a woman—this is absolutely hush-hush, Abe; the Agency doesn't know—that gave us a code name for what she says is the mole inside the Agency. It could fit Shreed. But what's more to the point, she said some stuff to Al about Bonner, the guy we got for setting up his father with the Iranians, right? So I think this woman's got Efremov's stuff. Efremov died last month in Tehran. I figure she got out with something of his—records, files, who knows?—and now she's peddling it. So, suppose she's also peddling it to Shreed? Or suppose she's using it to get Shreed to be the new Efremov in Tehran— huh? Suppose *that's* why he ran—he got an offer he can't refuse?" He lowered his voice still further. "He was on a chat room with somebody who at least came on as female, and he says, 'We should meet.' What's that sound like to you?"

Abe, too, spoke almost in a whisper. "Then it's the Iranians got him out of the country?"

"Nah, they don't do that stuff very well, especially over here. They'd arrange to meet him someplace. If it's the Chinese, then he's long gone, but if it's the Iranians—hell, he might still be hanging around."

"And?"

"And I want you to do me a favor."

Abe made a face. "Let's get another drink." He led the way to the kitchen, where he poured more whiskey. "What d'you want?"

"I want you to get the name of the Iranian asset that got killed when Al and I were in Mombasa in ninety-one. Remember? It was the thing that got Al and Shreed crosswise of each other."

Abe handed him a glass. "Al turned to Shreed for help, and then the two of you got jerked out of the country, and then the guy was dead. I thought Harry was checking on that."

"He did. The guy didn't commit suicide, as the Agency had it. He was murdered. Now I need his name."

"What're you saying, Mike—that Shreed killed the guy?"

"I don't need to say that. All I need is the guy's name, so I can tell some friends that the guy was *maybe* betrayed by one George Shreed, and would they please keep an eye out for him. Get his name, will you? All Al ever called him was Francey."

Abe cleared his throat and pulled his glasses down to make his professorial face. "Franci—F-R-A-N-C-I. It's what the Iranians call a Westerner—a 'Frank.' "

"Whatever." Dukas guzzled whiskey. "I need his real name. FBI must have it in a file someplace—Iranian asset, Mombasa, ninety-one—"

"You know what time it is?"

"You know how important this is?"

"Jeez, first you borrow my clothes, now you're sending me to the Bureau at midnight!"

"Yeah, you better get going. Where's Baranowski?"

Abe shook his head and started to hunt for his car keys. Before going, he had to have an obligatory shouting match with his wife about what he was doing, and Dukas had then to sit still for a shouted scolding from Abe's wife. After that, he was allowed to see Sally Baranowski.

USS *Thomas Jefferson* 0330 GMT (0630L)

Lone Ranger was the last to land, as they had been the last to launch. Rafe watched with bitter pride as his chainsaw collapsed with discipline, each station retreating down the line, taking or giving its gas and then slipping away to join the stack over the carrier as the sun rose in a halo of fire over Africa. Now the monster that had spat them forth full of hope was taking them back. Rafe's landing was a square three-wire and an okay.

Lone Ranger went into the break low, but Stevens corrected and put himself in the groove without a wobble. Alan knew that Stevens was exhausted because he no longer made remarks, sarcastic or otherwise. But he flew them through an unspectacular okay and survived rolling the plane to a precarious spot with their tail dangling over the water by cat three.

Alan began gathering the wreckage of kneeboard cards that he and Senior Chief had created in the back end during the last seven hours. He needed to piss, and he wanted food and sleep.

The sun was rising in a spectacular blaze of pink and orange fire off the starboard side. They were heading north, then. Still running from the Chinese.

"Al, you got any idea what happened there?" Stevens was standing behind him in the hatch. The use of the first name seemed unconscious.

"I don't really want to discuss the decision-making."

"Fuck that. You probably made the right call. Donitz didn't have to listen, either. Why'd we run?"

"I don't know—Paul."

"Well, *find out*. Sir. You want to know something? In the last two weeks, you and Rafehausen almost had me convinced that I might be able to get O-5 out of this cruise. You two are like a force of nature. This op, it was like nothing I've ever been on, right? I mean, I missed the Gulf. I don't have any green ink."

Alan smiled hesitantly, caught on the wrong foot and still expecting a fight. "I want to know as bad as you."

"I doubt that. You're a golden boy, Craik. You aren't overweight, your shit don't stink, stuff that would destroy other careers doesn't even stick to you. I want to know because this fucking op was my ticket. I was going to get my medal and my O-5. And the way I feel right now, if you tell me the President recalled us, I'm going to fly to DC and cut his balls off. You find out and tell me, okay, *sir*?"

"Paul, you were great. It's worth saying, even if the mission went flat."

"Want to know something? I've always been great. This ain't bullshit, Alan. I've always been great, and it just hasn't ever mattered." Stevens turned back to his seat, jerked his comm cord hard, and dropped through the hatch in the bottom of the plane.

Under him, in the bowels of the ship, the great engines turned the giant screws to their maximum rotations. The carrier shook as the rotations increased, and a taste of spray came over the bow to touch Alan's face forty feet above the water. With all her planes safely back aboard, the *Jefferson* was going back to full speed.

Washington.

"Sorry to wake you up," Dukas said.

Sally Baranowski smiled. "I wasn't asleep." She knew he was checking to see how sober she was, and the fact was that she was as sober as he, maybe more so.

Dukas was thinking that she looked a lot better than he remembered— nice smile, nice face despite the lines that anxiety and a sense of failure had scratched there. He led the way to Abe's study and sat her down in a chair where he could see her in the desk light. Bea brought in coffee for both of them and left after telling Mike that he had no consideration for other people and was he planning to spend the night, and if so would he please use the living-room sofa because Sally was in the guest room, and he was welcome to stay but he sure didn't have any consideration.

"Thanks, Bea."

"Huh."

Dukas and Sally Baranowski faced each other. Dukas figured they were thinking the same thing because they came from the same world: he had set it up like an interrogation. It was no surprise when she said, "So what is it you want to know?"

"George Shreed."

"Yeah?"

"You were right—it looks like he's out the door. What I want to know is, where would he go?"

She laughed. "The world's a big place. George is a smart man. Experienced. Where *wouldn't* he go?"

"Yeah, I know. I'm asking you to do me a miracle. Find him for me."

She shook her head. Her smile became rueful, and he thought she must have seen that smile in the mirror a lot in recent years. She was a vulnerable woman, perhaps most vulnerable of all to her own demands on herself. "You worked for him," he said gently. "You must have known a lot about where he went, what he did. Operations he designed. People he met. Just think back—any time he ever did any of those things differently? Any time he ever said anything funny? Any time you thought, this is a little peculiar?"

She looked off into a dark corner. The smile vanished, replaced by a frown. "Binary Conquest," she murmured. She turned back to him and the smile came back. "That was an operation. Actually a type of operation. George was a great believer in doubles, turning agents and guessing they'd be turned back, playing all sorts of mind games. Then he'd try to turn the control who was running the double. It was like Alice in Wonderland. Other people in Ops Plans didn't get it, didn't agree, but George really pursued it."

"That was peculiar?"

"No. It was just George. Being a hardnose."

"What else?"

She rambled, not from any mental laxness but from a deliberate randomness, trying to let her brain relax so the past would talk to her. She gave him a few ideas, but nothing solid. Finally, Dukas said, "China?"

"George hated China. Really hated it. In off moments, when he wasn't being official, you know? he'd say things like, 'We have to have a war with China,' or 'It's the Chinese, stupid!' "

"Would he run to China?"

"God, what a thought!"

"He could just have been a very good actor."

She shook her head. "George was no actor. What he hated, what he loved, was right on the surface. Oh, he'd been a really good case officer, and I suppose he did what we all have to do, trick the agent, lie, manipulate, all that—but when you knew him, you could see what he felt. I got to know his wife a little. Nice woman, the love of his life. She said it, too—'George just hates China.' " She frowned.

"What is it?"

"I just remembered. 'Chinese Checkers.' " She swung her face to him, half in shadow now. "It was a name he gave to one part of Binary

Conquest. I remember thinking it was such a funny name for him to pick."

"Kid's game."

"Yeah, exactly, but 'Chinese'? Just odd, for him. And—"

"What?"

"I'd forgotten it. Chinese Checkers didn't work—maybe that's why he used that name. It was three operations that kind of got buried. You know, swept under the rug? Don't know why, it just did—I suppose George decided they were no good."

"What were they?"

"Oh, just three operations he set up and then didn't run. You know, like you do—comm plans and all that, but we never designated an officer, so they never got implemented."

"What, this was just pie in the sky?"

"No, they were real enough; they just never got implemented. How did that go? George did those himself. . . ." Her voice trailed off. She was looking into the dark again. "Christ," she murmured, "what a perfect way to meet somebody." She looked at Dukas. "He laid out the routes himself; he said he liked to keep his hand in. Jesus, if you were going to meet somebody on the sly, what a great way to do it." Her eyes were open a little wider, excited. "Have I remembered something, or what?"

"You tell me."

"Well, no, I mean—George wouldn't let you into that part of himself; he'd say 'I'm going to retrace my past,' meaning when he was an ops officer in the field. And you'd let him, because it was private and it was kind of touching, this handicapped guy who had been a station chief and all that, reliving the old days." She paused. The frown came back. " 'For a rainy day.' "

"What?"

"What he said about Chinese Checkers when I asked him once. It was after we kind of had a falling-out. I was still working for him, but there was a lot of tension between us because I wouldn't go along with him on something—the Alan Craik business, in fact—and I was questioning some of the things he did, and I know now he'd already decided to fire me. But I asked him one day about Chinese Checkers, which was still in the files and never been implemented, and I was being a smart-ass and I said something like, 'Why are we keeping this dead shit around?' and he goes, 'For a rainy day.' " She stared at Dukas, then shook her head as if to clear it. "It's raining."

Dukas got it. They talked some more, with Dukas trying to find other anomalies in her memories of Shreed, but she kept coming back to the same thing. Finally, she jumped up. "I'm going in to my office."

"It's the middle of the night."

"There's always people there. I've got to know. If I remember it right, and if Chinese Checkers is still alive—well, it's all I can give you. The best I can do."

Dukas told her she didn't have to, and he told her it wasn't wise to go driving around the Peretzes' neighborhood at that hour, but by that time they were moving toward the door and she was putting a coat on. Dukas grabbed a raincoat he hoped was Abe's and put it on over the sweatshirt, and too late he remembered he was wearing sandals that weren't even his.

USS *Thomas Jefferson*
0400 GMT (0700L) Sunday.

Rafe grabbed him in a brief hug as he came off the flight deck and on the catwalk and then led him down through the watertight door and into the passageway that led to the blue-tile spaces, the admiral's kingdom.

"Give me a sec," Alan called over his shoulder, and he bolted into the men's head on the O-3 level just short of the blue tile. Rafe waited until he emerged.

"We got screwed." Rafe was still *on*. He still looked completely in control, and if he was bitter or angry, it didn't show except around the bottom of his mouth when he smiled. He kept flexing his right hand, though, and Alan could guess what that meant.

"What happened?"

"I don't know. I know that our orders came all the way from the CNO. Admiral wants to see us."

"I can't see how that's going to be good."

"Come on, Al. We're seniors, now. We aren't going to get put in hack."

They exchanged a glance.

"I can't imagine anything better right now than a week in hack. Just wake me up when it's over."

Still burdened with flight gear, they passed Rafe's office and the Combat Information Center and went straight to the admiral's briefing room at frame 133.

The flag captain greeted them at the door and ushered them in.

"He'll be with you in a moment. He's using the flag channel to talk to DC. He's pretty pissed, but you guys aren't the target, so keep it calm, okay? We're on the same side here."

Alan, who had never had a pre-meeting apology from a flag captain, began to wonder what the hell was going on. Rafe simply picked up a copy of *Aviation Week* and started leafing through it. A moment later, a steward poked his head around the corner from the passageway and then pushed through the door with a tray of the *Jefferson*'s chocolate chip cookies and coffee.

Alan poured coffee for both of them and smiled a little, thinking of the number of times that he'd done this for Rafe in the air. The cookies were still good, and they wolfed them like kids.

"Let me do the talking, Al," Rafe murmured, dusting crumbs off his chin.

"You're the boss." In the next room, the Flag TAO was bellowing at someone. His intensity was audible but his words were lost in the rumble of the *Jefferson*'s speed.

When the admiral entered the room, they both snapped to their feet. They were surprised by the warmth of his first remark. "As you were. You guys must be beat."

"Yes, sir." Rafe brushed his hand through his hair and then down the front of his flight gear.

"What gets said here doesn't leave this space, got that?"

"Yes, sir."

"We got fucked, gentlemen. The CNO scrubbed the mission because the Navy's plans and codes may be compromised."

Rafe went rigid by Alan's side. He leaned forward a little and spoke very quietly.

"Sir, I could have lost planes out there. We could have talked in the clear and still beat them. They would have turned away. Nobody would have fired."

"Captain Rafehausen, that may be the case, but it wasn't your call, and it wasn't mine. The CNO has another battle group in the Taiwan Straits, and it's within easy strike range of the Chinese coast. He was not willing to risk an engagement that might have been used as a provocation. That's just about a quote."

"How'd our codes get compromised, sir?" Alan could see the strategic implications already.

"That's why you're standing here, Commander. A senior CIA officer has defected to China. There's a chance he hasn't reached there yet, but the CNO didn't know that two hours ago. Familiar to you, Craik?"

"Sir, I'm afraid I don't—"

"The name George Shreed mean anything to you?"

"My God."

"He's bolted. He had unlimited access, and we're starting a worldwide rekey of all our crypto. That will take almost thirty-six hours; almost right up to the Chinese ultimatum, in fact. We have no idea what else he took with him. Don't you have a meeting in Bahrain about this, Commander?"

"Yes, sir." Alan thought for a moment. "But if we know that Shreed's the traitor, I'm not sure what my meeting in Bahrain is about."

"Find out. That just became your number-one priority. In fact, it just became *my* number-one priority. I have a request from NCIS to get you a million dollars in cash. We've just about got that. I'm thinking of sending Captain Rafehausen to fly you there because he's got the weight of rank and he knows what's going on."

Alan spoke. "Rafe's the CAG. If the worst happens, and you have to fight—" What Alan was thinking, however, was that this might be the chance that Stevens had asked for.

Rafe was shaking his head. "I'll go if you tell me to, sir. But this is Craik's game, and he doesn't need a baby-sitter. I don't need to drive his air taxi, either."

"I'm not positive that a baby-sitter isn't exactly what Mister Craik needs, but I'll wait on events. Okay, Mister Craik. You take a det plane and a crew of your choice and a million of my dollars, for which you *will* sign your life away. If you can do *anything* to get this bastard, you do it. Shoot the mother. I'm writing you orders with about fifteen vias, so if you need to go anywhere, then gas the plane and go, or take commercial aviation, or whatever. It's authorized. How soon can you leave?"

"The meeting is in a little less than twelve hours. It's a seven-hour flight."

"Go sleep. By the time you wake up, it will be a six-hour flight. The *Jefferson* is driving you on the first part of the trip. Got to be the most expensive passenger trip of all time."

Langley.

By two that morning, they knew that Chinese Checkers, despite Sally Baranowski's memory of it as a live entity, had been canceled. Dead as a dud sitcom. Gone. All the file said was, "Delisted for causes of nonuse."

Sally was first flustered, then depressed. "I dragged you all the way out here for nothing. God, my memory—!" Her skin looked suddenly sallow and she seemed to sag. "It's a big nothing."

"When was it canceled?"

"Oh—let's see—" She tapped some keys. "Hey! Last week!" She looked up at Dukas, her face suddenly hopeful. "Funny coincidence, huh?"

"Even if it was canceled, could he still use it?"

"He could use the comm plans and even the local contact agent if they hadn't got around to paying him off, or if the local just went on walking the routes out of force of habit. That happens sometimes—you cut an agent loose and they're almost homesick; they go on through the motions out of—nostalgia, I guess. So, yeah, he could use Chinese Checkers still. It'd be like a ready-made setup."

"But he never used it before that you know of?"

"He never *activated* it. But I know he checked it out a couple of times; he even said so. Like he wanted people to know he was doing it." She tapped the keys. "This is his open travel log—approved travel that would include his vacation stuff with Jane, meetings, conferences, like that. We all have one. See, he logged out to Pakistan in ninety-five; that's a

Chinese Checkers country. And he went to Indonesia in ninety-seven; that's another one. The logging means that he had Agency permission and a country clearance; he was probably there for some other purpose, but he could have done a walk-through and contacted the local agent at each one. But the agent wouldn't know if he did anything else; a local agent in an unactivated net is just a pass-through, a gofer. See, what Chinese Checkers was really for was to set up a small network that could go on at very short notice, with the one agent-in-place to do the legwork for an ops officer when he came online." She stared at the screen. "But, Jesus—what a great way to make a meeting!"

"If you were a spy, you mean."

She seemed awed by the implications. "But George Shreed—! He screwed up my life, and I hate his guts, but—Jesus, not George Shreed!" She looked up at him again. Her expression was more fear than anything. Dukas patted her shoulder, feeling the solidity of her body. Letting his hand rest there, he could feel a brassiere strap under her T-shirt, and even, he thought, a slight tremor. "You done good," he said and patted her again. "Is there any way to get the comm plans, even though this scheme's been canceled?"

She shook her head; her hair brushed against his hand. "Gone. It may be somewhere in a computer, but not where I can get at it."

"Goddamit." He said it so softly it was almost a sigh. "If he was using it to meet somebody, then it might be what he'd use now he's running. Dammit! To come so close—"

She logged off the computer and stood up. She was chewing her lip, and she stretched and yawned to cover what he knew was tension, probably the tension of withholding something from him. He watched her, both interested in that solid, slightly beefy body and repelled by the suspicion that she was hiding something. She dropped her arms and finished her yawn and they stood there. Her eyes flicked around the cluttered office; when they met his, they slid away again at once. He let the silence build and build.

But she didn't speak. She took his elbow and turned him toward the door and reached for the lights. "Time to go," she said.

Dukas had thought she would crack, and she hadn't. He was sure there was more, and he had missed the moment to learn it.

But outside in the parking lot, walking the quiet early morning with nobody else in sight, she gave the moment back to him. She said, "There's something I didn't tell you." She looked aside at him. "I'm paranoid; I thought, you know, they might have my office bugged." She laughed, but not with humor. "You work here long enough, you think like that. Anyway—" She fetched a sigh, like a breath hard to draw and exhale. "I've got the Chinese Checkers files."

He hid his surge of excitement. "How come?"

"When George canned me, I went sort of nuts. I thought of doing things—revenge, just plain small-minded meanness, a lawsuit—I didn't know. I took some stuff—downloaded it on disks. Including Chinese Checkers."

"You were suspicious even then?"

"No! I just—hell, maybe I was. Jeez, I never thought of it that way." She shook her head, and her hair swung around her shoulders. "I sure broke a couple of laws."

"Where's the disk?"

"In a bank. Mike, if this gets out, I'm toast."

"You'll be okay."

"No, I mean it—the Agency has no mercy for people who snitch. Trust me: they'd go harder on me for downloading files and giving them to you than they will on George, if they catch him. George at least has something to trade—Christ, a lifetime of spying." She laughed again. "They'll give him a goddam golden parachute to tell them all about it! But me, I ain't got nuthin'. "

"Honesty doesn't pay."

"*Failure* doesn't pay. Anyway, Jesus—take care of me, will you."

He promised her secrecy: nobody would know where the Chinese Checkers file came from but him. He would make no copies. He wouldn't testify about it in court.

But he knew he would, if he got George Shreed.

So did she.

She held his arm for the last steps across the dark parking lot, the asphalt shining with rain puddles under the lights. Dukas felt as he always did when he was compromising somebody—sending an agent into a tough place, offering a deal with a witness—protective and guilty. He squeezed her hand against his side.

"Do you ever eat Italian food?" he said.

296 ☆ Gordon Kent

She was surprised. "I love it."

"I make a pretty good gnocchi. Butternut squash and mozzarella." He cleared his throat. "Thought you might—I never had dinner last night, you know? My place is, um, sort of on the way to Abe's."

She leaned against his car. "It's after three in the morning. We're talking breakfast, I think."

"Well—I got some Shredded Wheat."

She looked at him, perhaps puzzled, perhaps amused. "I think I better take a rain check."

"Oh. Okay."

In the car, she was silent until they were out on the highway, and then she said, "I really meant it about the rain check. Why don't I bring you the disks tomorrow—today, I guess I mean. Then maybe—"

He thought that sounded pretty good. He felt a twinge of guilt about Emma, because he knew exactly what he and Sally Baranowski were planning, but he was realist enough to know that Emma was sliding away from him, although he didn't yet know why.

HE CALLED his old war crimes unit in Bosnia from his apartment. It was after ten in the morning there, and his French friend and second-in-command Pigoreau sounded almost chipper despite his cigarette rasp.

"Mike! When are you coming back, amigo?"

Dukas growled a sarcastic reply. His own voice was hoarse with fatigue. "Pig, I got a favor."

"For you, anything. Well, almost anything. When are you coming back to us?"

"I got a headache here, Pig. Then if I'm lucky, The Hague. Listen, we used to have a couple *mujaheddin* who owed us one."

"You mean, who were terrified of us. Yes?"

"Find one who's married a Bosnian woman, better yet got a couple of kids. Then tell him he wins big points with us for spreading news of a dangerous criminal who's responsible for the murder of an Iranian Moslem who was serving Islam undercover in Africa. Okay?"

Pigoreau laughed. "Mike, what are you cooking?"

Not gnocchi for Sally Baranowski, he thought. "I need to get the word out fast. See, it's like this, Pig—" He tried to tell Pigoreau only enough. "There's a guy's on the run, maybe he's heading for Iran. I think he's going to go through Islamic countries to get there. Maybe somebody'll see him, you know?"

"Mike! A needle in a—I don't know the word—"

"Haystack, we say. Yeah, but I'm desperate."

"This is for the beautiful Rose?"

"How'd you know that?"

"She called me, Mike. To find you, couple of weeks ago. A beautiful voice—"

"Can you do it?"

"Of course, but you know, one man—do you know where he's going, his route—?"

"I know that he walks with two steel canes and is pretty much busted up from the waist down."

"Ah." He heard Pigoreau chuckle. "That is a different business. *Bien sûr*, finding a cripple makes it just possible. Of course, maybe he is in a wheelchair, or a golfing car, or—"

"I'll e-mail you a photo."

"You got a name?"

"George Shreed—S-H-R-E-E-D. Tell the *mujaheddin* he's a dangerous war criminal."

"Is he?"

"I say he is, and I'm still on the roster as the head of the unit."

"Very good."

"Implicated in the death of Ben Ali Houssan, a.k.a. 'Franci,' in Mombasa, Kenya, 1991. Franci supposedly was a suicide, but in fact he was shot twice in the back of the head."

"By this Shreed?"

"Don't put it like that, Pig. Just connect his name with it and say that's why we want him. Reward of ten thousand dollars." *And that will just about clean Mike Dukas out of money,* he thought. "If our guy spreads the word and we get confirmation from at least two other countries that the photo and the wanted posting have got there, he gets a thousand bucks and indemnity in Bosnia." *And that really will clean me out.*

Pigoreau whistled. "It's a good thing I trust you, Mike."

"You got a problem with this, Pig?"

Pigoreau did not. For him as for Dukas, the law was a goddess whom you had sometimes to worship, sometimes take into your hands.

"You're a *copain,* Pig."

Dukas hung up and sat hunched over on his bed. In fact, he hated cutting corners on the law. Those were the wrongs that filled his thoughts when he couldn't sleep. Maybe they were the things that kept him awake in the first place.

He sent the photo and fell into bed and, despite his guilts and regrets, fell instantly asleep.

26

Nicosia, Cyprus.

GEORGE SHREED HAD LIMPED RIGHT THROUGH THE lobby of the first-class hotel where Israeli intelligence had reserved a room for him, leaving his luggage with a porter at the desk and seeming to head for a men's room that was hidden from the public around two corners and down a flight of carpeted steps. At the bottom of the steps, he had turned left instead of right as the discreet sign had directed him, and then he had picked his way to the hotel kitchen and out the back door, and by the time his trackers got there, he was gone. He got himself a room in the old Greek quarter and hired two off-duty Turkish cops to cover his back, and then he set up a meeting with the Israeli intelligence people who were supposed to have been on his tail the whole time.

He met Lieutenant-Colonel Begin of the Mossad in a café. Shreed's bodyguards sat at tables behind and on each side of him; Begin's people sat toward the street. The off-duty cops looked at Shreed; the Israeli muscle looked up and down the street.

"This is quite unnecessary," Lieutenant-Colonel Begin said, waving a hand at the two Turks.

"A matter of point of view." Shreed flashed a grim smile. His legs were aching because his morphine was running low.

"You are making it tough for us to like you," Begin said. "You want to make a deal, and you act like we're thieves."

"I act as if you're Israeli intelligence agents, you mean. I don't want to get snatched off the streets of Nicosia and flown to Tel Aviv in a mailbag. I want to sit here like a civilized defector and make a deal."

"What have you got to deal with?"

Shreed managed a laugh. "You know who I am, Colonel."

Begin was lounging back in his chair, his crotch rather aggressively pointed at Shreed. He had a brute's face and a soccer yob's haircut, and his body was thick and hard. He looked like a man who was not opposed to the idea of violence as a legitimate form of persuasion. He drummed his fingers on the metal table. "Why are you doing this?"

"That's none of your business."

Begin turned to one of the men behind him, exchanged a look with him. He turned back to Shreed. "What do you want?"

"New identity—lifetime. A house. A pension. Protection."

Begin's body heaved once with a laugh. "Why us?"

"Because you love American secrets."

Begin rapped twice on the table and pulled his legs in, coiled his body and stood. "I'll get back to you," he said.

"You have twenty-four hours."

"And then?" Begin gave him a nasty smile.

Shreed shrugged. "Iraq? Iran?" He shrugged again.

Begin looked at him now without smiling. He looked at Shreed's two off-duty cops and gave one contemptuous snort, then signaled his own men and strode out of the café.

Shreed sat on, drinking coffee. He agreed with Begin about the two off-duty cops, and that realization caused a gulf to open: the sense of displacement of the man who has put everything familiar behind him. For the first time since he had fled Washington, he felt the vacuum of isolation and the fear of being forever outside. If he didn't get protection from Israel, where *would* he go? He shuddered and tried to think of where he could buy morphine.

I'm so lonely, baby

I'm so lonely I could die. . . .

Washington.

Dukas was in his office before eight, grainy-eyed and worn-looking but awake. He had brought two of the largest containers of coffee that a fast-food swill-shop could sell him, along with four glazed and fried things that were called doughnuts but looked more like half-collapsed hassocks. He went through his phone messages and found nothing of immediate concern.

Nothing had broken overnight. If Shreed had really fled, he had now been gone for more than twenty-four hours—enough of a lead to place him anywhere in the world. Dukas refused to think about a safe George Shreed, a George Shreed who was smiling somewhere while his Chinese control patted his back and told him how welcome he was in the People's Republic.

"You sonofabitch," he said out loud.

He was munching on the third hassock when Menzes called.

"Where the hell have you been?" he shouted.

"I've been here, Carl. Here and on the way here. Give me a break."

"I won't give you a break! You've blown an investigation that took years, and I'm going to ream your ass!"

"Carl, what the hell—?"

"Your goddam Siciliano's lawyer has fucked me over, and it's your goddam fault!" Menzes was really shouting now. There could be no doubt that the rage was real. Dukas listened to it—the second time he'd let Menzes read him out in twenty-four hours—and waited until it had run down, and then he said, "I don't get it, Carl. What's going on?"

"Like hell you don't get it! You told that bull-dyke lawyer cunt about Shreed and she's blown everything!"

"Wait a minute! Carl, Jesus—what's happened now?"

"Don't come the goddam innocent on me, Dukas! You knew it all along! You were conning me, you sonofabitch! You knew—you knew—!"

"Knew *what?*"

Menzes stopped. Dukas could hear him breathing. In a lower, dangerous voice Menzes said, "That cunt *telephoned* Shreed the day before yesterday and told him she was going to depose him under oath! She said 'Top Hook' to him! And yesterday she filed for a subpoena requiring George Shreed to appear before her to be deposed in the matter of

Siciliano *v.* Central Intelligence Agency. How could you not know, as you're fucking the bitch?"

Then Dukas was angry. He was angry because Menzes knew about him and Emma, and angry about Emma herself and their relationship, because, *yes,* he had compromised something when he let her get close to him, and he was angry because Menzes had made him guilty. But what he said was, "Cut the insults, will you?"

"If I could think of worse ones, I'd use them! If you were here, I'd punch your fucking nuts off."

"Carl, I swear I don't know what the hell you're talking about. Yes, I go to bed with Emma Pasternak; no, I don't tell her about the case and I specifically walled her off from what I know about Shreed. I'm not shitting you: *I don't know what you're talking about!* How do you know Pasternak called Shreed?"

Menzes was silent again, this time to get control of himself. He seemed calmer when he said, "Shreed's receptionist logged the call. I talked to him two hours ago."

"How do you know what she said?"

"We taped him, what d'you fucking think? You think we don't tape CIA employees? Bullshit! Pasternak asked him if he's Top Hook! Pasternak actually used the word 'spy.' "

"Oh, shit," Dukas groaned. "Oh, *shit*! That's why he ran!"

"No kidding." Menzes was sarcastic but less angry. "How could you not know that?"

"I swear, I didn't. Pasternak's a fucking loose cannon. But how did she know? I never mentioned Top Hook to her, honest to God, Carl! I didn't tell her any of it! Nothing!"

"Then the Siciliano woman told her. I don't frankly give a flying fuck; it came from your side, that's all I need to know. You and your people blew my investigation!"

"Your 'investigation' was sitting on its ass and had been for five years! You didn't have zip until we came along!"

"Don't shout at me!"

"Don't you shout at me!"

"Fuck you, I'd like to rip your tonsils out!"

"Fuck you, too!"

Then Dukas became aware that Triffler was standing in the doorway, a raincoat dangling from one arm. How long he had been there was unclear, but he looked startled. Dukas dropped the telephone back into its cradle. "Menzes," he said. His face felt hot and he was breathing hard. He sat.

"I was sure it was somebody you knew." Triffler came closer. "I'm awfully glad I didn't bring my kids in today to see where Daddy works."

Dukas put his head on one hand. "Dick, I'm very, very angry and if you do anything to upset me, I'm going to kill you. Go away and do something for a while."

Then he sat there and thought over what Menzes had told him. He saw the chronology of it: Emma calling Shreed; Shreed panicking; Shreed fleeing. And doing it so quickly that it looked as if he really had initiated an escape plan, simply signaling his local contact that he had to be lifted out and then vanishing.

Meaning that he really was in Beijing now, accepting the congratulations of his Chinese control.

"Oh, shit!" Dukas threw a tray of files against the wall.

He walked it backward from Emma's call to Shreed. How had she learned about Top Hook? The answer lay in *where* she would have used it pretty quickly after getting the information, he knew. So if she called Shreed day before yesterday, then she had known on Wednesday, maybe Tuesday at the earliest.

And Tuesday night she had been with him.

And Alan had called.

And he had said that George Shreed had been Top Hook on the *Midway*.

Jesus, he thought, *she did get it from me. I just didn't know she was getting it.*

And he didn't need to examine the *why* of Emma's call to Shreed, because he knew her well enough now to know that she would do anything for her client, including flushing an important spy to prove her client innocent.

He woke Emma at her apartment, and she sounded cranky and croaky. "What do *you* want?" she said, as if Dukas was the last person who would ever have a reason to talk to her.

"Did you call George Shreed and tell him that you were going to depose him and ask if he was a spy with the code name Top Hook?"

Pause. Then: "What if I did?"

"Did you get that information by eavesdropping while you were at my place?"

"What if I did?"

He exploded. "Jesus Christ, Em, don't you know what you've done?"

"I got my client off the hook, that's what I did."

"You compromised this country's security!"

She laughed at that one. Then: "I thought getting Siciliano off was the most important thing in the world to you, Mike. You *love* her, right? You want her back on her career track, right?"

"But, Jesus—Jesus, Em, to go behind my back— You used me."

She hooted. "Grow up." She was right; he deserved that one.

"You set Shreed off. He's gone."

"That's exactly what I wanted to happen. I've won!"

"*Won?*"

"Won Siciliano's case, asshole. I'm a *lawyer.*"

She had known they were going to have this conversation. Maybe she had even scripted it in her head, because she changed the tone. "Hey," she said more gently, a smile in her voice now, "I didn't hop into bed with you because I thought I'd get the dope on Shreed that way. I *like* you." He was supposed to respond to that, he knew, but he couldn't— not the way she wanted, anyway. He thought that if it had been her nighttime self, he might have made his peace with her, but in the light they were doomed.

By then, she had figured it out, too. Her voice was wry. "Does this mean I won't be sleeping over anymore?" she said.

Dukas hung up.

He sat there for several minutes. When he had collected himself, he walked over and spoke to Triffler through the crates, his voice soft. "Dick, I'm sorry for what I said earlier. I was out of line. I apologize. Would you please get Carl Menzes on the phone and—tell him I need to talk to him." Dukas was afraid that if Menzes heard his voice first, he'd start hurling obscenities again.

But Menzes had partly got over it, too. His voice was controlled— ungiving, angry, but restrained. Dukas told him that he had been right; that it had been he, Dukas, who had inadvertently tipped Emma Pasternak. "It's all my fault," he said.

"Okay. I'm going to initiate a complaint, and NCIS can deal with you however they want. I'm going after Pasternak for violation of national security."

"I'll testify."

"You're goddam right you will."

Nicosia.

The afternoon sky was bright but distant, only a narrow ceiling of hard blue above the brown streets where George Shreed hobbled. He had two wooden canes now, and, because they lacked supports for his forearms, he moved painfully. They were only old-fashioned wooden canes with bent handles, not really made for a man who had to swing most of his weight on them to move himself forward.

The two rent-a-cops dawdled behind. They were bored with him and afraid of the Israelis. They wanted their day to be over; he had had to offer extra money to make them stay. For a little more, one of them had told him where he could buy morphine but had refused to get it for him. They were only a little better than nothing. He glanced back. They were too far behind him, he thought. The Israelis might try to snatch him right off the street, and those two might make sure that they trotted up too late.

Or it could be the Chinese, if they had caught his use of the passport they had sent him. Or the Russians, if the word was out. Or his own agency.

He was running out of time. He had disliked Lieutenant-Colonel Begin on sight, but he couldn't let personal feelings get in the way now. He had to find a safe place.

I'm so lonely, baby. . . .

A child appeared in front of him. He seemed to materialize there, brown face turned up as if seeking the sun, a shock of black hair falling over his forehead. Perhaps he was nine years old, and he had the face of a Turkish angel.

"What you want, guy?" he said. "What you want? Woman?"

Shreed stared down at him. "Morphine," he said.

The child vanished into a crack between two of the buildings. Shreed started forward, but he heard one of the cops behind him grunt and then mutter something that certainly sounded negative—*Don't? Not yet? Not him?*

A man stepped from a doorway several houses along the street. He gestured at Shreed, his palm open and then cupping closed, open and closed, open and closed: *Follow me.*

Shreed swayed forward.

JAMAL KHOURI was a detective sergeant in the Nicosia police and an agent for the PLO. The two jobs rarely conflicted, his duties to the PLO comprising mostly reporting on what he was doing and what was going on inside the Nicosia police. Yet he was a loyal Palestinian and hoped to return to what had been his father's house in Palestine before the State of Israel had come into being. A displaced man, he took his divided life, his divided loyalty, as a given.

When he saw the man with the wooden canes, he was walking a self-created beat to check on drug activity and his own informants along the route. He cared little about petty drug sales; unless they became violent, he ignored them, yet petty drug dealers made good snitches if they were rousted now and then, and so he walked this route once or twice a week, checking, reminding them of his presence, getting tips.

And then he saw the man with the canes. A memory clicked—a very recent memory. Just before he had left home, in fact, an e-mail had flashed on his computer from a comrade in Turkey who had sent it to his entire list of Islamic contacts: an American who had murdered an Iranian agent was wanted. There had been a photo attached. And the telltale clue that the wanted man walked with canes.

Khouri watched the man's painful progress over the rough brown stones until he met with a petty dealer whom Khouri knew as Mustache. The man with the canes was obviously an American; Khouri would have taken note of him even if he hadn't had the canes. He felt a rare excitement, and he moved closer, keeping to the wall of the buildings as the two men huddled in a doorway, just visible to him across the street and beyond the corner of a building that hid one shoulder and leg of the man with the canes.

Khouri moved with his back against the house walls. Mustache spotted him and even gave him a look, as if to say, I'm just doing business here; don't blame me.

The American's back was turned. Khouri wanted to see his face. Then, because of something Mustache did—hurrying the buy or fumbling the money—the American turned, and Khouri saw him.

And he was sure.

"Hey!" he shouted. He began to run, reaching across his navel to draw a Turkish copy of the .32 Mauser from a belly holster. "Hey, police—!" He said it in English, and, as he did so, he held out the gun, the barrel pointing up, the side turned toward the drug deal. "You—American— against the wall—!" He didn't expect a man with two canes to resist.

Then everything happened at once. The man with the canes gave some signal with one of them and shouted in rough Turkish, and Khouri shifted the gun into shooting position, stopping in the middle of the street only ten feet away. Mustache detached himself from the American and backed away, pushing money and God knew what else into a side pocket. Khouri heard shouting to his left and turned, and two men were running at him and one had a gun out, not yet ready to shoot, the gun just coming from a holster behind his fat right hip.

"*Polisi!*" the man shouted.

"Police!" Khouri shouted back. He didn't know the men, and he knew all the cops who came into this part of the city and all the cops who busted drug dealers. These were fakes, he was sure, maybe two tough guys who had been following the American to roll him.

But the other man's gun kept coming out and up, and Khouri shot him, and the astonished man stumbled to a stop and stared at his chest, where blood was spreading over his yellow golf shirt. Then Khouri felt a smash of terrific pain in his right arm and realized too late that the American had come close enough to hit him with a cane his gun jumped to the pavement and clattered and slid to the gutter, and Khouri turned to fend off the crippled man, only to see him already starting away, and he tried to push back the pain in his broken arm and pursue when his legs went out from under him and he lost consciousness, his last thought that he had been shot from behind and that probably the shot had hit his spine.

SHREED FORCED himself almost to a run, his legs screaming with the pain of it but strong enough to carry him to the corner, where he staggered around and out of the line of the gunshots. *"Gonif!"* he shouted. A woman had come out of a house and stared at him. *"Gonif!"* He didn't know the Turkish word for thief, and the Yiddish word was there, somehow, blotting out the other languages in which he knew the word— French, German, an Indonesian dialect. But the woman seemed to understand. She stepped into the cross street and looked down at the carnage and began to bellow in high-pitched Turkish.

Somebody took Shreed's arm. He was going to resist, until he saw it was a little man years older than he with a *yarmulke*. He beckoned and led and talked quickly in a throaty, guttural Yiddish. *"Gonif,"* Shreed said, and let himself be led away. He had ten new vials of morphine in his pocket.

Washington.

Ray Suter was in his apartment, pacing. Suter spent a lot of time now trying to blot out the killing of Tony Moscowic. He hated to admit he had done something badly, and he knew he'd done that one abominably.

Suter thought something was wrong, but he couldn't identify it.

Shreed was in Belgrade, he believed. Suter had been a little worried when Nickie the Hacker had told him that Shreed hadn't used his computers Thursday night—a change of pattern, always troubling—but he'd signed out sick Thursday afternoon, Suter knew. Then, presumably, he'd stayed in bed Friday and flown off to Belgrade.

Suter didn't like Shreed's being off someplace. *With my money!* Maybe that was what was wrong—too much tension carried on too long—

When the telephone rang, Suter twitched as if he'd had an electric shock.

"Suter."

"Mister Suter, this is the duty officer at CIA Seven. Would you report as soon as possible to the third floor, please? Wait in the lobby there. You'll be met."

Suter knew that if he spoke, he'd stammer. *What the hell is on the third floor? Is it about Tony Moscowic?* He licked his lips, breathed. "What's this about?"

"I'm just relaying the message." He gave it all again. Suter started to say that it was Saturday, but the voice said goodbye and was gone.

27

LATE IN THE AFTERNOON, DUKAS WAS CLEANING UP files and handing them to Triffler, who looked stunned. Dukas had decided to bow out of the Siciliano case and take himself back to the War Crimes Tribunal.

"But you didn't do anything!" Triffler protested.

"I blew the investigation."

"You didn't."

"I let somebody get too close to me, and she got information from me and she flushed the suspect. That's culpability, Dick." He handed over another file.

"But, jeez—! I was just getting used to you."

"Think how neat the office'll be without me."

"Yeah, you're a slob, and your management style sucks, but—I like you, Dukas."

Dukas, shocked, looked up at the thin black man. He was so surprised that the ringing of his phone didn't immediately register, although his right hand went to the instrument as if it had ears of its own. Then he picked it up and turned away to cover his confusion.

"Dukas."

"Mike, Mother of God, where you been?" It was Pigoreau. The satellite delay made it seem as if he was calling from the moon. "I called and called!"

"I been at the office all day. Hey, Pig—"

"Mike, shut up! We got a contact. On your guy, the *mutilé* with the canes. You with me?"

Dukas leaned into the desk and pressed the phone tighter to his ear. "Shreed?"

"Some guy thinks he saw him in Cyprus, but it's a big ball of shit, Mike. We're trying to get clarity, but all we know is there was shooting, this guy's in hospital, the cops are running around like dogs with hard-ons. A complete *brouhaha*, but I had to call you, because maybe your guy was there."

"Who's in the hospital? Shreed?" His heart was pounding.

"No, the guy who thinks he saw him. He's a Palestinian, I think, but also a cop—I think we're talking about the same guy. Maybe there were two cops, I can't tell, they're all fucked up. We got the story from the *mujaheddin* because he wants his thousand dollars."

"Holy shit. Gimme a minute here, Pig." He was crouched over the desk; when he glanced up, Triffler was staring at him through the crates. Dukas covered the mouthpiece and lifted his head long enough to growl, "Some guy thinks he's spotted Shreed." Then he lowered his head again and said, "Pig, you there?"

After the satellite delay, Pigoreau said, "Yes, yes."

"Where in Cyprus, Pig?"

"Nicosia, Turkish sector."

"I'm on my way, Pig. Get me some contact data—names, phone numbers. The hospital where this guy is. Don't call me; I'll call you, 'cause I'm gonna be on the run."

Satellite pause. "This may be nothing, Mike."

"Pig, right now I'm settling for nothing. I'll call you back."

He hung up and swung on Triffler, invigorated. "Dick, get NCIS Naples on a STU, tell them I've got a breaking case in Nicosia, Cyprus, and I need local support. Jesus, they're Turks there. I'll need a translator. Plus I want an in with the local Palestinians—NCIS Naples should be able to help on that, because the Nav port-calls in Haifa and God knows where else, and they'll have Palestinians on the payroll. Got it?"

Triffler nodded and reached for his telephone. Dukas reached for his own and began to thumb through a limp-paged old address book for a travel agent.

"You reporting this to Menzes at the Agency?" Triffler called across.

"Negative. If I get a positive confirmation, then—then we'll see."

IT WAS ONLY after five that Dukas remembered that Sally Baranowski was supposed to be coming to his apartment for dinner. And to deliver the Chinese Checkers disk. And, perhaps, other things. Well, that was all down the tube now. He called the Peretzes and cursed their kids for tying up all three of their telephones. (How could two kids use three phones? With a computer, he supposed.) He called four times and never got through.

"Dick!" Dukas was heading out the door. He wanted Sally's computer disk, but he was going to be on an eight o'clock flight out of BWI, no matter what. "Call these numbers every five minutes until you get somebody." He scuttled back in to scribble the Peretz numbers on a file folder. Triffler was horrified to see the clean surface of the file ruined. "Give them this message: Mike has been called away. Will Sally please get the disk to his apartment before seven. Got it?"

Triffler repeated it in the bored voice of somebody who has a crack memory for detail. Then he smiled at Dukas—a rare moment—and said, "I thought you were giving up the investigation?"

"I am—as soon as I catch George Shreed. Look, Dick, I don't know where the hell I'm going from here, so it's your baby now. Okay? You can run with it?"

Triffler held out his hand. "Not as well as you, but I'll do my best."

Dukas was in his apartment by five-forty, but hardly in the door when the telephone was jangling; he ran for it, thinking it would be Pigoreau again. Instead, it was Triffler.

"It never rains but it pours, Mike. The cops found a body in the Anacostia River."

Dukas was fixed on Shreed, and the only body he could picture was the vanished CIA man's. Triffler heard his confusion and said, "Cops, Mike. A body. They ID it as a private investigator named Tony Moscowic. Been in the water two–three days, they think."

"Dick, what the hell are you telling me?"

"The guy you saw in front of Shreed's house, Mike—remember? The day we went to check it out because Shreed's computers were on, and the cleaning woman had her car in the driveway and I was driving and—"

"Yeah, yeah, I remember! So what?"

"You got part of the license plate of a car that had a guy in it. You made me put out a flash on the partial, which the state DMV got seventy-three hits on. So a smart cop in Bladensburg, he did a routine check on their corpse and he got a hit on our list from the license plate. Get this: six .22 slugs in him and his face was bashed in with what they think was a concrete block."

Dukas didn't see how it fit. He didn't see why he should care. That part of the investigation was behind him, back in what seemed another age, before Shreed had split. Yet he felt the responsibility of having turned the investigation over to Triffler, a man who would want to dot every *i* and cross every *t*.

As if he had heard the thought, Triffler said, "You're the one who can ID him, Mike, and I need that to go forward. I was driving—I didn't see him."

"Connect him with Shreed's house, you mean. Yeah. What'd we do about that cleaning woman?"

"Nothing; we been too busy. You think I should move on her?"

Dukas's mind was leaping ahead. "Yeah, because what we have, I think, Dick, is somebody else also on Shreed—the hacker that Valdez is watching, now this guy. Can you run with this, Dick?"

"You bet. But you got to ID the guy—put him at Shreed's that day."

Dukas groaned. "Have the cops fax a photo to airport security at BWI. I'll look at it on my way out. It's the best I can do. Hey, did you get the Peretzes?"

"I'm trying."

"Rotten kids."

He was packed and wondering what he was going to do for money when his telephone rang again. This time it was Abe Peretz, whom Triffler had finally reached. Sally Baranowski was cut.

"Tell her I can't make it tonight. She had something important to give me. But something's come up with the investigation and I'm outa here, Abe. Goddamit."

"You flying? What airport?"

"BWI. British Air to London, eight."

"If she comes in, I'll tell her. Maybe we can do something."

Then he hit an ATM and headed for Maryland, dumped his car in the satellite lot at BWI, and waited through what seemed an endless trip to the terminal. The wait at the counter was even longer, but he got through that with the help of a security man to whom he showed his NCIS badge, pleading the need for speed because he had to look at a police fax in the security office. He had twenty minutes before his flight left when he arrived, panting, at the security office and again presented his badge and his ID. A fax was slapped down in front of him, and he was looking at two photos, one of Tony Moscowic as he had been when he got his driver's license and one as he had ended up on a gurney at the morgue. The desk man who had given it to him averted his eyes.

"You seen this?" Dukas said.

"Once was enough."

"Never know it was the same guy." He called Triffler's number on his cellphone and left the message that, yes, the man in the driver's license photo was the man he had seen near Shreed's house. Then he was pounding along the corridors of the terminal, cursing the line at the security check, running, dodging, thinking, *Tony Moscowic, what did you ever do to George Shreed to deserve this?*

DUKAS WAS AT THE GATE, out of breath, his heart racing, and the airline people were waiting for him, the last passenger to board.

And so was Sally Baranowski.

"I thought you'd want this," she said. She held out an envelope.

"Boarding pass and passport, please," the attendant said.

"You're great," Dukas said. "This is great."

"I knew it was important to you."

"Would you board, please, sir?"

"This isn't exactly gnocchi with butternut squash."

"Well—another rain check—"

"*Please* board the aircraft, sir."

"Now I'm the one asking for a rain check."

"Well—any time—"

"Sir, if you don't board, I'm going to close the aircraft door!"

"Yeah. Well—" Dukas thought of kissing Sally Baranowski, but he thought he hadn't known her long enough, and women didn't like that stuff. He was wrong. She grabbed his arms and kissed him, a big one right on the mouth. "I'm looking forward to it."

Dukas grinned. "You bet." Then he was racing down the carpeted tunnel to the plane.

28

COLONEL CHEN RUBBED THE BALD SPOT ON THE TOP of his head and then rubbed his face with a movement so habitual that he was unaware he had done it. Then he checked his uniform in the mirror for the second time, pulled sharply at the hem of his tunic, and stepped through the swinging door of the officers' lavatory. The corridor was packed with senior officers, messengers, attendants, and civilian functionaries.

He breathed in sharply one last time and exhaled with the control of a devotee of t'ai chi. Then he pushed open the door to the Red Room and entered, walking briskly past the ring of desks. The generals were in the center of the room, sitting or standing in an orderly crowd in positions that delineated rank and merit. The army dominated; the air force held important corners; the Navy was relegated to the fringes, although today a single admiral had made his way to the central group where the Old Man sat majestically in a carved chair.

Chen was the only intelligence officer in the Red Room. The old guard distrusted intelligence officers.

"South Fleet reports that a scout group of US aircraft approached our ships but turned away as soon as our fighter cover engaged," the naval officer in the center read with enthusiasm. He was a southerner, and he gestured with his free hand as if giving a speech. Chen pursed his lips in distaste.

"So the Air Force made good its forecasts and kept the covering force refueled?" asked an Army officer.

"There has not yet come a point where our ships lack the cover of our brave airmen." The Air Force general's comment sounded more sarcastic than pious.

"And the Americans turned away? We are sure that they were not merely short on fuel?"

"They ran like rabbits. And they dove away, all the way down to the ocean. I believe that this indicates that they had plenty of fuel." He looked at Chen. "The unverified memo that Top Hook allegedly stole from the US Security Advisor seems to be authentic."

A little buzz of mutual congratulation filled the Red Room. The Old Man gestured with his cane at a tea girl and looked around him with the imperious gaze of a falcon. He saw Chen near the edge of the army group and beckoned to him.

As Chen bowed, the Old Man nodded and spoke. "One victory does not win a war. I agree that your man's memo is looking authentic in the light of today's events, but I am an old man, Chen, and I hesitate to commit us to an action we might regret."

Chen's heart pounded. They were on the brink, and they held the winning pieces in their hands.

"General, if we hesitate too long—"

The general cut him off with a sharp chop of his right hand.

"Our ultimatum with India expires in forty-eight hours. You have plans to meet with your Top Hook?"

"Yes, General."

"I want you to take him. Bring him and the original of the memo here. When he is in your hands and has no option to retreat, then I will be prepared to commit my forces."

"That requires a delay of almost two days." Chen regretted the nervous breaking of his voice and the anger of his posture instantly, and he could see from the closed faces of the men around him that he was alone in his desire to move quickly.

"The delay will allow us to move aircraft and reposition forces. And I prefer to hold all of my pieces when that ultimatum expires. I do not trust spies." The old eyes studied Chen, who had to admit to himself that he was, after all, a spy. "There is too much at stake. Do not quote to me from the ancients, Colonel Chen."

None of the men in the room knew how tenuous Chen's hold on his agent was. Chen had feared double agents since he had graduated from the academy, and he worried about nuances in every signal from Top Hook, but today's success should have been the vindication of his career. His work could catapult China into the front rank of world powers. The old generals were hesitating on the brink of victory. Who knew what delay might bring in the dangerous realms of diplomacy? Why had they given India so long to decide?

But Chen's real fear was that Top Hook, always a fickle agent, might revolt, and that he would bear the whole responsibility for failure.

"Sir, I still believe that we should strike now." Chen glanced around and found himself isolated, alone against the leadership, his only support some younger men too junior to argue. Nervous enthusiasm had compelled him to make a last effort to change the general's mind. *They're in disarray!* He wanted to scream at them. *Who knows where they will be in two days!*

"I do not agree. You will meet with him and bring him home to his new father. We can learn more from him in an interrogation chamber than in these cryptic notes. Bring him home."

Chen swallowed hard. "Yes, sir."

"Where will you meet him?"

"We have an established contact point in Pakistan."

"Have you a team prepared?"

"It was to have been a clandestine meeting." Chen passed his hand over his head. "Only an intelligence team."

"Insufficient. You will use paratroopers from the Eleventh and a transport from the Air Force. See to that."

Chen hid his anger behind a mask very like the masks that surrounded him. Four years of planning now depended on the vagaries of an agent and the will of an old man. If Top Hook missed the meeting, these men would withdraw their support from the bold gamble and cover their cowardice by blaming him. He could feel their eagerness to withdraw, now that they were at the brink. Chen blinked once and straightened his back. *I didn't want this,* he thought. *You did. And if it fails, you'll blame me.* "I will bring him to you, General."

"Do so."

Dubai, United Arab Emirates
1200 GMT (1500L) Sunday.

When Anna had said to Shreed in the chat room, "the skating rink," she could have meant only one place: the skating rink in Dubai's great shopping mall. Now, she waited there for Shreed.

Below her on the ice, a girl in a skating costume built up speed, legs pushing her forward in pulses, until just short of the barrier she leaped in the air, turned once with juvenile grace, and sank back to the ice in a crouch. Some of the shoppers in the mall who had stopped to watch gave little nods of satisfaction, and one or two hissed or applauded quietly. She wasn't world class, but she had grace and heart.

Anna looked at the girl's expensive skating costume and the servant waiting for her. In Tajikistan, such talent might lead to a sports academy and real training. This spoiled Arab girl would flirt with excellence for a while and then marry, to spend the balance of her existence behind the walls of a house. Perhaps a rich husband would build her a place to skate.

Down on the level of the skating rink, on the far side where there was a tunnel to the convention center on the other side of the boulevard, was a man Anna had seen before. She couldn't place him, but his muscled bulk and large American face had featured in her life sometime recently. He looked like a watcher, and that doubled her caution.

She went into the record shop on her level. It had neck-high racks of CDs, illegal copies made in Singapore or mainland China. Crowds of giggling Arab girls, their black coverings hiked up to reveal flashing, sequined shoes, rifled the racks in search of their favorite Western pop singers. Anna could browse among them and still watch for Shreed through the plate-glass wall and over the second-level concourse.

She checked the clock on the wall behind the Pakistani cashier.

The meeting's window of time would open in two minutes. She moved to the cash register and paid for the three albums she had chosen. Paying, complete with a bit of haggle, ate more than a minute. When she emerged on the concourse, the meeting time had begun; however, she expected Shreed to arrive near the end of it, to show that he was not to be ordered about.

She walked slowly along the top of the concourse. Few Westerners passed, and none met her idea of Shreed, whom she knew only as old and Caucasian. Haste and distrust had placed barriers between them. Perhaps he wouldn't come. Perhaps this was another trap.

She saw the muscled American she recognized from a few minutes before near the bottom of the escalator. Was he a watcher? One of Shreed's? She would have to pass him to get to the vantage point she had selected down by the skating rink. She would have to risk it. She glanced at a mirror in one of the fashion shops, assured herself that no part of her above her ankles showed, and stepped lightly on the escalator.

She was committed.

Halfway down, she realized that the muscled man had been at the airport when she arrived, too. She smiled beneath her veil, pleased to have made the connection. Almost certainly an American. If that was the case, there would be other watchers, and she glanced quickly over the lower floor from her height on the escalator, looking for some hint of movement or stillness that might reveal more. The escalator descended inexorably toward him. Ugly man, with fingers missing from his hand and a face capable of brutality. He had moved to the bottom of the escalator and was alternating watching it and the tunnel.

Anna clung to the assurance that her veil was impenetrable. She stepped past the watcher without a glance, almost brushing his arm where it rested on the partition. She was invisible, and her heart leaped as the pure joy of outwitting her foes hit her with a rush like a drug.

She turned right as she passed him, rounding a partition and nearing him a second time. Her route required it, but now she was confident, and she had to restrain an impulse to commit some silly act. She wanted to pinch him or to laugh aloud. Instead, she continued past to the lower-level shops, watching the elevators from the hotel lobby. She had taken one straight from her room to the concourse, allowing no opportunities for interception, and she believed that Shreed would do the same.

A small Pakistani stood near the elevator. He was out of place here; no Pakistani could afford to shop in this gleaming concourse. He seemed to feel the weight of this social inferiority, avoiding the eyes of passersby. She marked him as another watcher.

She reached the coffee shop at the far end, entered exactly at her planned time, walked carefully to her planned table and took a seat, fussing with her handbag and the plastic bag of CDs like any other Arab woman on a jaunt. She spoke careful English to the waiter, having decided that English would seem less remarkable than her stilted Arabic. The coffee stall was a good watch post, so she had to assume that another of its patrons would be a watcher, too.

And who are the watchers? she wondered. Shreed had said he was changing employers. Perhaps his old employer was watching for him? The idea troubled her; the CIA were formidable, as Efremov had taught her. Or were the watchers another set of killers trying to make up for Trieste and Venice?

She began to doubt the wisdom of remaining for the meeting. Either Shreed had sold her again, or a third party had access to the chat room, something she had feared from the first.

She didn't really want to make an alliance with Shreed, that was her real problem.

What do I want? She had come this far, and she still didn't know.

Five minutes into his window, and he still hadn't showed. She got her coffee, managing her veil and her coffee cup with the ease of long practice. She began to speculate about the patterns and behavior of other patrons, but none of them gave any clear signs of being a watcher. Six minutes.

The Arab skater had finished a short break and began doing long, backward sweeps around the rink. Anna assumed that the young woman had paid for the time alone. Anna thought that her legs were too short for real competition. Seven minutes.

A black man who emerged from the elevator was instantly familiar. She had seen him twice in Naples with Craik. Just for a moment, she wondered if Shreed and Craik were partners, if she was utterly their dupe, trying to play them off while they laughed together offstage. But her Efremov had told her that Shreed hated Craik. The idea was absurd, born of fear.

The black man changed the balance too much. Her arguments for and against the meeting shifted one last notch and she *knew* that she had to move immediately and leave Shreed to fend for himself. She waved at the waiter and reached in her purse for money.

When her head came up, she saw him.

He was neither so old nor so crippled as she had expected. He was leaning over the Plexiglas partition above her and to the right, almost directly in front of the record shop on the second level. She cursed their mutual distrust, their lack of shared signals, and she paused in indecision. *Warn him? Leave him?* Still high on risk and the invisibility, she decided to warn him, if it could be done without too much risk.

The black man and the muscled American passed each other. She watched their hands talk as they focused on each other, and she rose and walked boldly to the elevator. She worried that, having just descended the escalator, her five-minute stop for coffee would be too transparent, but her worries depended on the watchers' being able to sort her black covering from those of other shoppers, and she told herself that she was safe. She reached the elevator, and the doors closed behind her. She pressed the button for the concourse, went up in the humming car, and came out just a few yards behind Shreed.

Another group of Arab girls, or perhaps the same group, still giggling, came out of the record shop and stood a few feet from Shreed, watching the skater, gossiping about her movements, her costume, her status.

Anna walked over to them as if she had known them all her life.

"Look at her show herself! Anyone can see her," said one with adolescent scorn that failed to hide her envy.

Anna leaned her head into the circle.

"I could never do that," she said in English. "*There are so many people watching.*"

They tittered, surprised by her intervention, but she was already moving away, back toward the elevator. The older man turned stiffly from the railing, inclined his head the smallest fraction, and began to move toward the escalator. She reached the elevator, one of a small group, most clutching their hotel-floor keycards like badges. She opened her purse and rifled it for her own, her blood roaring in her ears.

She had warned him. He was in her debt. She hoped he saw it that way.

The doors opened, and the black man was standing directly in front of her.

HARRY COULDN'T pin the feeling down, but suddenly some change in movements told him that the meeting was happening *now*. None of his men had seen anything. Harry was convinced that the woman could pass as Arab; that was the only explanation for her invisibility at the airport. Shreed, on canes or crutches, should have been an easy target. It was possible that Valdez had got the meet wrong, or that *skating rink* had another meaning. But now they were in the window of the meeting time; the woman and Shreed had to be close, and Harry had decided that Ibrahim, stationed by the elevators, wasn't seeing everything on the concourse.

"I'm coming up." He barely had to lean his head to murmur into the mike set in his lapel.

"There's an old white guy—"

"Where?"

"Leaning over . . ." static. The elevator closed and blocked his radio. Damn. *Damn!* Of course Shreed would stay high where he could watch the action. The elevator doors opened on a bevy of Arab women who were clutching their cardkeys and the plunder they had accumulated in the mall.

". . . escalator?"

"What?" Harry was trying to push past the women, his focus down the concourse to the escalator.

On the periphery of his vision, he saw one of the women draw her keycard out of her purse as she entered the elevator. The doors began to close. The manicured hand had been lightly tanned, the fingers tapered, the nail polish clear.

Anna. Screw her. He wanted Shreed. He ran down the concourse, looking for Ibrahim.

"Ib! Where are you?"

"He's in the tunnel. I'm following." Dave Djalik, his other watcher, was running down the edge of the rink, clearly visible. Harry took the escalator two steps at a time, dodging locals and leaving a string of Arabic apologies in his wake. He leaped the partition at the bottom and entered the tunnel a few meters behind Djalik.

"Did you see him, Dave?"

"Negative!"

They ran along the curving corridor. They both smelled the blood before they saw the body. Ibrahim was lying at the foot of the steps to the convention center, his throat cut with a sharp blade, and he was dead. There was blood everywhere, all over the floor, even along the base of the tiles that covered the walls. Shreed had stood just there, behind the upper doors, picked his moment with precision, and risked that no one would see. He was a desperate man. Harry had never hated him before, but Ibrahim had been his first local man, loyal to a fault, ambitious and clever. Now he was a carcass drained of blood.

They ran into the convention center, but Shreed was gone.

"Dave, put out an APB through our friends. Tell them I'll pay ten thousand bucks for information on this guy. He has to try to flee the country."

"Thought you wanted this quiet?"

"The Agency wants it quiet. I want Shreed. Okay, keep it personal, Dave—we won't give them his name on the murder. I'll deal with the cops. You keep the pressure on Shreed."

"And the woman?"

"I think she was there. She's due to meet with Craik tonight in Bahrain—maybe she's headed for the airport. You stay on Shreed."

"Sure, Bwana." Djalik flashed him a smile and trotted off. Harry pulled out his cellphone and called the police. He was already thinking of what he was going to say to Dukas.

ANNA NEVER went back to her room. Forty minutes later, still anonymous, she was in the air.

29

Nicosia.

THE PLANE WAS FULL OF EUROPEAN VACATIONERS headed for the beach. Dukas, who had stayed in his seat until most of them had crowded forward like some herd of ruminants heading for greener pastures, grabbed the seatback in front of him and pulled himself up. His legs were stiff, and, when he stood, weak with fatigue. He needed a shave. Even without a mirror, he knew that his eyes were baggy and the shade of red you got with either too much booze or not enough sleep. He humped his lone bag down the littered aisle and through first class, which looked as if a battle had been fought there. An attendant gave him a more-or-less smile. He operated on automatic going through passport control and blew by the thundering herd that was waiting to recover its enormous loads of baggage, walked out of customs with a wave of the hand and into the arms of a tall man who was waiting with a sign that said, "NCIS."

"Mister Dukas?"

Dukas stuck out his hand. "Thanks for meeting me."

"I am Mister Wahad." He had brilliant teeth and black hair streaked with silver, his manner that of a businessman who worked very hard at selling himself. "We will take a taxi," he said, and grabbed Dukas's bag and headed for a doorway. Over his shoulder, he said, "The event happened in the Turkish sector, so we have to cross the UN line. You should have landed at Ercan, you know."

"I would have had to fly to Istanbul—too much time."

Wahad grinned. "Let's see how much time it takes to cross the line."

Wahad was Lebanese, a kind of permitted alien on both sides of the green line; he spoke Turkish and Greek and English and German as well as Arabic, and he knew his way around both the Turkish and the Greek sectors. He was also recommended by the NCIS office in Athens.

"Do you know the history of Cyprus?" he said. He made a face. "Some of the police on the Turkish side are very nationalistic. You know what I mean if I say 'settler mentality'? You see the same thing in Israel."

They were driving through modern streets with heavy traffic. The sidewalks were crowded and noisy, many of the people clearly tourists—perhaps the same ones he had seen on the plane, or at least different ones wearing the same baseball caps and carrying the same bottles of water.

"I've put you up at the Saray in the Turkish Republic," Wahad was saying. "You'll be comfortable there. Turks like Americans."

"Even Greek Americans?"

Wahad laughed. "Sure, you will be fine. Maybe, with the three cops, not so fine—we'll see."

"I was told there were two."

"Three. A real dustup, Mister Dukas. Two of them apparently shot each other, and there was some sort of drug deal going on with this fourth man—the one you want."

Dukas looked aside at him, not sure how much he knew or how much he was supposed to know; he filed away the "drug deal" as not making any sense. Wahad made a gesture, closing the fingers of one hand into a fist. "I am discreet; it's how I make my living." He grinned again. "All I know of the fourth man is that he exists and you want him."

"Where is he?"

"Nobody knows. For now, I'm taking you to the hospital." He adjusted his necktie. "One of the wounded is Palestinian. He, I think, is willing to talk to you. The other one, a Turk, is—" He raised his eyebrows.

"Not talking?"

"Afraid to talk, I think. We will see. For him, I will translate for you; with the Palestinian, there will be somebody else, also recommended by NCIS. We will see."

Bahrain 1300 GMT (1600L) Sunday.

The Gulf Hotel, where Alan was meeting Anna, has a mixed clientele that includes the wealthy, the powerful, and members of the US armed forces. Flight suits and uniforms cross paths in the marble lobby with thousand-dollar suits and traditional Arab dress. It hadn't changed since the end of the Gulf War, and Alan had a sense, not of coming home, but of returning to a well-loved vacation spot. He got their keys from the desk, Soleck and Stevens just behind.

"Sure does take me back," Stevens said.

"Thought you missed Desert Storm."

"We had a det here in '92," Stevens said, looking up at the ceiling forty feet above his head. "I lived in this place for ninety glorious days, crawing per diem like a P-3 guy. I bought a truck when I got home."

Soleck, whose experience of military hotels was limited to Super 8s and Great Westerns, couldn't seem to look at enough things at once. He devoured the scantily clad starlet rotating her hips as she crossed the lobby; he stared at the dignified older men in traditional dress sharing coffee at a low brass table near the door, and he even spared a glance for the hostess, a beautiful Pakistani woman with perfect English and perfect control of her hotel.

"Don't wander off, okay?"

Soleck was still staring about him like a hick in the big city. Stevens raised an eyebrow.

"Stay in the hotel till I come back. If I need you guys, it's going to be fast. And Soleck, don't let that suitcase out of your sight." The suitcase had a million dollars in Navy cash in it.

"Whatever." Stevens was eyeing the concourse of shops that led down to the first of three bars. "I'll be by the pool."

"Ready to fly." Alan meant sober. As soon as he said the words he knew he was out of line. Stevens simply looked at him and then smiled. "Sure, massa. Whatever you say."

Alan left them in the lobby and headed for his room. He dumped his flight gear on the nightstand, tossed his backpack on the bed and rifled through it. He had the gun he had carried in Africa, and he pushed that back to the bottom of the pack. Nothing the hotel needed to know about. Then he pulled out his PT gear and changed into it, did some quick stretches, and headed back to the lobby.

He ran a little too fast to the souk, just over a mile away down the al Fateh Highway, and paid a little too much for a bag of anonymous pagers. He stopped at a phone kiosk and called each to check them, and then he ran back up the sweltering streets, around the traffic circle, past the most imposing mosque in the world, and back to the Gulf Hotel. He showered, decided against a second shave, and dressed in khaki slacks and a polo shirt. Then he tidied the room a little, placed a small photograph of Rose on the dressing table, and called the front desk. He had a message, and neither Stevens nor Soleck was in his room. He keyed the message.

"Al, Harry. She was here and she tried to meet our other friend. I don't think they made contact. I don't know what game she's playing, but you're on your own tonight. I'm trying to find our other friend, and you can reach me on my cellphone at 971 S E C U R I T Y. Press one when the message starts and it will ring through, okay? Stay safe, bud."

Alan sat on his bed. Why would Anna try to meet Shreed in Dubai after Shreed had tried to kill her? And just before she was to meet with Alan in Bahrain? Was she playing one off against the other? Did she want Shreed as the new Efremov? Or was she simply a sick woman, playing very dangerous games?

He found his crew at the pool. Soleck was lying on a deck chair with a book, the nylon suitcase with the money wedged behind his back for a pillow. Stevens was sitting in the shade with a glass in his hand, watching a chorus line of airline hostesses fling their blond hair around.

Alan pulled up a chair by Stevens and passed him two pagers.

"Give one to Soleck."

"Sure." Stevens clipped one to his shorts. Alan took a hotel pad out of his pocket and began to scribble.

"These are numeric codes. Anything with seven digits is a phone number; call me back ASAP. Otherwise, this number means get your flight gear on and get the plane warm, and this one means we're scrubbed and you can buy one of the Lufthansa girls a drink. Okay?"

Stevens watched him with a beneficent air. "You always work this hard?"

"Good planning gives you more options when everything goes to shit."

"Should I write that down?"

"Paul, back off, will you? I'm going to this meeting and I want to know that you guys are set."

"I could sit here all day. And there ain't nothing in this glass but iced tea, in case you planned to have a sniff."

Stevens was on his high horse again, and Alan could have mounted his quickly enough. It struck him as odd that the better he knew Stevens, the more he found something likable in the man, although he would have been hard-pressed to explain it. But Alan couldn't quite get his foot in the door with Stevens, and he seemed to have a talent for putting his foot in something else.

"Sorry, Paul, I was a dick."

Stevens nodded, but his eyes were back on the women at the bar. "Whatever."

Washington.

Dick Triffler had spent a bad night because of Tony Moscowic. It was bad enough that Dukas felt guilty, worse that Dukas had abruptly left, leaving him holding what more and more looked like a bag with a hole in it. But what worried him most was his realization, actually reached a couple of days before, that everything about that day when they had driven past Shreed's house was tainted.

He had sat up part of the night thinking about it. The television, sound turned low, had blinked and cavorted in front of him, and he had unthinkingly worked the remote and paid not a bit of attention. His mind was on an investigation that could yield only unusable evidence— evidence that any court would throw out because it was based entirely on Valdez's illegal surveillance of Shreed's home computer. It would make no difference that Valdez was Harry O'Neill's employee and not NCIS's. It would make no difference that Shreed was a potential security risk. The CIA could go after him internally, but they could never take him to court on a foundation of an illegal surveillance.

Triffler had made his eyes red and his shoulders stiff thinking about how to deal with it. Dukas, he suspected, would simply have gone around it and planned, perhaps, to fudge when he got to court. But Triffler was not a fudger. He was not even a fibber. He was a tightass, a hand-on-the-Bible, honest-to-God, truthful man. What he had worked out was that he could be no help with the death of Tony Moscowic because he knew of Tony Moscowic only because of an illegal act. And, although he was sure that it was important that some third party was also surveilling George Shreed's home computers, he couldn't tell Menzes or anybody else, because that information had been obtained illegally, too. All that he could do was try to cause other people to rediscover what he knew, and to do so in a way that was itself legal.

Bummer.

So, having put himself back to bed at four, he got up at eight feeling bleary and looking like hell. His wife even said, "Where were *you* while I was sleeping?" He only shook his head and made pancakes as she oversaw the bacon and eggs, and then they sat down with their kids— family-ritual Sunday breakfast: the family that eats together cheats disintegration together.

At nine-thirteen, he got a call from a detective who wanted to know if he had any interest in checking out Tony Moscowic's house.

"I'm going out," he told his wife.

"It's Sunday, for God's sake!"

He made a face.

The detective's name was Moisher, and he looked about eighteen, an impression not helped by the baseball cap or the baggy jeans. He was actually thirty but new to detective status, and an air of gee-whiz clung to him. "This is some case!" he said when he met Triffler outside Moscowic's house, a ratty little frame structure behind Route 1 in Beltsville, yellow police tape across the door.

"Your first?" Triffler said.

Moisher blushed. "I've been a cop for nine years." He shrugged. "First homicide I'm in charge of, yeah. We don't get a lot of homicides 'Well, we do, but not good ones. Difficult ones, I mean. What can you tell me about it?"

Triffler winced internally, thinking of the tainted evidence chain, and decided to play it as the older, wiser one. "Later." It was a relief from being Dukas's stooge.

The house was even rattier inside, and large enough for only a living room with a gas fireplace, one bedroom about the size of a large car, and another room that you might have used to keep a cat in but that Moscowic had used for an office. Tony had been a Redskins fan (banners, beer glasses, team photo) and a porn fan (boxes of magazines), but he hadn't been a cook and he hadn't been much of a housekeeper. He must have watched a lot of television, though, to judge from the copies of *TV Guide* and a big chair and a bigger TV.

"You already been here?" Triffler said as they stood together in the office doorway.

"Unh-unh. Somebody else."

"Lab?"

"Yeah, we use PG County. They did it last night."

Triffler had already seen that there was print dust everywhere. "They done?"

Moisher grunted. He pointed at an ancient copy machine on the desktop. "Every week or so, he made a photocopy of this little book he had, and he sent them to his accountant."

Triffler felt as if he was back with Dukas. "There's something you're not telling me."

Moisher blushed, grinned, and produced a sheaf of paper from his attaché case. "Surprise! It's really why I got you out here." He gave the papers a tap. "Copies of what the deceased sent his accountant. I woke the guy up at seven. Couldn't sleep."

Triffler took the papers. They went back several years and ended a week before. On each one was a copy of two facing pages of a small, spiral-backed notebook. The writing in it was crabbed, sometimes in pencil and sometimes in pen, never very legible "Where's the book?"

"Missing. Not on the deceased, not here. The accountant—his ex-brother-in-law, not a bad guy, just doesn't want to get involved—says he never left home without it. Quote, 'That book *lived* with him. He took better care of it than he did my sister.' Meaning, maybe somebody killed him for the book?"

Triffler was looking at the recent weeks. "Somebody who didn't know he made copies, in that case." He put the last page on the desk and switched on the lamp. The photocopy was pretty dim, a copy of a copy, but he could make it out.

"Interesting, huh?" Moisher said.

"You already been over it, I take it."

"Right!" In fact, what Moisher had wanted this morning was an audience, and that was why Triffler was there. Moisher was pointing at the entries. "Most of them, the brother-in-law got a name and address from the deceased, very straightforward. He bills them, they pay. End of the year, he does the deceased's taxes. But sometimes, like once in a blue moon, he gets a client doesn't want to leave tracks and pays cash. *Then,* see? he puts a dollar sign next to the entry, like this one." He tapped a line of the faint notebook page that said, "$1G Hotshot retainder."

"What the hell's 'retainder'?"

"I think he meant 'retainer.' " Moisher was embarrassed for Moscowic's spelling. "Hotshot's a code name."

"I bet we don't know who it's a code name for."

"Afraid not. I guess he was pretty stand-up about that—very secretive, the accountant said, really protected the client's privacy. Drove the wife nuts, among other things."

Triffler had been looking ahead and not entirely listening. He had found four Hotshot entries with dollar signs, and the amounts were significant. The second, however, had something new, a scribble that looked like a rising sun—an uneven oval with rays coming out of it.

"What the hell's that?"

"Guess." Moisher was bursting to tell him.

Triffler turned on him. "Look, Detective Moisher, I didn't come out here to guess, okay? I don't play guessing games, even with my kids. If you know what it is, tell me."

Moisher blushed. "It's a bug. Get it? An insect, so, a bug."

Triffler looked at it again. "I'd get a turtle, but not a bug. But okay, I suppose the brother-in-law told you it's a bug. So, '3G bug at AMH.'

Three thousand bucks to—what, bug? plant a bug?—on AMH. Who's AMH?"

"It says 'at AMH.' I think it's a place."

"Okay, *what's* AMH?"

"I was hoping you'd know." Moisher looked very young, rather moist.

"Well, I don't." Triffler looked back through other pages, saw nothing that set off any bells and nothing recent enough to be likely. He returned to the last page and read the four entries again. The last one, dated shortly before he and Dukas had driven by Shreed's house, was a corker: "5G entry S's." S's house? Five thousand dollars to get into a house—Shreed's? *Pretty expensive lock-picking.*

"See anything?" Moisher said, as hopeful as a dog who hears his dish rattled.

Triffler took his elbow and led him out of the office. "I have to tell you something. A sad story. Okay?"

Moisher looked puzzled.

Triffler took a breath. "Everything I know about Tony Moscowic is tainted. Even if I knew some things, I wouldn't tell you, because I'd destroy your case if I did. You couldn't take them to court, and you couldn't take anything you learned *because* of them to court. So I'm not even telling you why I wanted Tony Moscowic's name in the first place."

"Because of his car." Moisher all but wagged his tail.

"Forget that! Wipe it out of your mind! It's tainted!"

"But you do know what 'AMH' means!"

Triffler sighed. "No, I don't. But if I did, I couldn't tell you. Get it?"

Moisher looked sad, then brighter. "Nobody'd know but us two. I could say I found it out on my own!"

"In court?"

Moisher looked sideways into a corner for help. "Sure."

"Then you're a fucking idiot." Triffler headed out the door.

"Don't you talk to me like that!" Moisher shouted at him.

"You're talking perjury, Moisher—you think that isn't idiocy?"

Moisher came close and almost whispered, "We have to do it all the time."

"Yeah, well, I don't. Anyway, this is peripheral to my case. It's all peripheral to my case. What NCIS wants is for me to investigate a female officer who's got the shaft, period." *From George Shreed—we think— whose house may have been worth five thousand dollars for Tony Moscowic to effect an entry, but we can't know that and we can't tell you about it.*

"I thought you'd be real excited," Moisher said, downcast.

Triffler stood there, looking for an exit line. Finally, he said, "You got a card? Give me your card. Maybe I'll think of something." And he meant it, except that he meant something legal.

Cyberspace (9,000 feet above the Persian Gulf)
1530 GMT (1830L) Sunday.

someone is lurking here so let's not get too open okay?
They weren't mine.
of course they weren't i know who they were
Do tell.
too complicated
I WANT TO KNOW.
friends of the us navy
I see. Do you still want to meet?
yes
Buy a copy of PGP and install it. Give me an e-mail address.
my first name and my birthday in numbers at hotmail.com i
have pgp
Good. I'll see you in thirty hours.
perhaps

The use of e-mail for espionage communication was in its infancy. The great powers and their cautious spies still distrusted the computer, and she felt the thrill of the pioneer. Anna had fifteen anonymous e-mail accounts and each one had a simple code that she could use to pass it. Some were dates from history, several were telephone numbers, one related to an advertising jingle. All of them were disposable, each maintained through its own web of credit. She was quite proud of the result.

She stretched and watched the island of Bahrain through the aircraft window. Then she accessed the account she had sent to Shreed, downloaded the file there, and closed the account. Anyone who wanted that file could get it, but it would take time. Several Web sites listed the times that big computers would take to break various commercial encryptions. PGP got a rating of forty hours.

In forty hours, she would be someone else, somewhere else, with a lot of money. Or she would be dead. Either way, by then, the watchers would be welcome to the file.

First, she had to meet Alan Craik in Bahrain.

30

Nicosia.

THE HOSPITAL ON THE TURKISH SIDE OF THE GREEN
line was like many Dukas had seen around the world—better than most,
hardly luxurious, a place where he hoped he'd be okay himself if somebody shot him.

"Doctor Irmanli." Wahad introduced the doctor as if he'd invented
him, although Dukas suspected they'd never met before. The doctor
gave a small bow and ignored Dukas's hand. *So much for Greek-Turkish
relations.*

"How are the two policemen who were injured?" Dukas said. Irmanli
looked at Wahad, who translated. Wahad had told him that the doctor
spoke English, but he wasn't going to do so to Dukas. Irmanli rapped
out words.

Wahad translated. "One had a bullet in the right pectoral, did some
bleeding, is doing well. The other—the Palestinian, a detective—was
shot in the lower back and suffered shock to his spine, which temporarily paralyzed him. He is now able to move his limbs, but pieces of
the bullet are in his right kidney and elsewhere. He is stabilized."

"Can I talk to them?"

"The doctor disapproves."

"Tell the doctor I'll risk his disapproval. I need to talk to both of them."

The doctor understood that well enough without the translation, because he spun around and gestured to a bulky man twenty feet away. Dukas had already seen him, registered *cop,* and risked a small smile in his direction. The man lumbered over and, to Dukas's surprise stuck out his right hand.

"Gorzum, Turkish Republic police," he said. "I am six months in Minneapolis."

"Dukas, Naval Criminal Investigative Service. These hurt boys yours?"

Gorzum shrugged. "I am sent to deal with you." He had a thick accent, a voice that sounded phlegmy and muffled, but the tone was not unfriendly. "I am information and liaise. Just now keeping the medias from the door." He grinned and showed a gold tooth.

"The hardest job on the force," Dukas said. "When can I see your boys?"

"Oh, now. Now, if you like. But—no tricks. I am six months with Minneapolis police as intern, I see a lot of tricks. Don't do none."

"Okay, no water torture and no good-cop, bad-cop. That's it?"

Gorzum unfolded a sheet of paper and coughed in its direction. "We get this from your Navy criminal service. They ask cooperation and et cetera like that. What I want to know, what the hell you doing here?" His gold tooth flashed.

"I'm following an American."

"Some important guy, you follow him to here!" Despite the emphasis, it was a question.

"We think he stole Navy secrets." This wasn't strictly true, but it was simple, and anyway Dukas had spent his waking hours on the plane thinking that if this really was George Shreed who had turned up in Cyprus, he could be as dangerous here as he might have been in China, because the million-dollar question was, What might George Shreed have brought with him? So saying "Navy secrets" was merely a convenient way of expressing the fear that George Shreed, with access to a vast amount of American classified data, could be a very dangerous man.

"He was buying morphine," Gorzum said. The word *morphine* hit Dukas, even through his fatigue. Momentarily, it made no sense— Shreed had no record of drug use—and then he saw it. *That's how he got out of the US without attracting notice. The sonofabitch is walking*

"Morphine for his pain," Dukas said. "He's crippled—handicapped—bad legs."

"Buying drugs very bad thing here. Especially tourist. Bad example."

"You want to prosecute him?"

Gorzum nodded.

"First you gotta catch him."

Gorzum nodded some more.

"Can you catch him?"

Gorzum shrugged, then smiled. "Can you?"

Washington.

Alone in his grubby computer center, Valdez analyzed the Shreed-Anna chat room exchange and noted that their next meeting time was to be in thirty hours. *She must be some bitch, man—she's meeting with Al Craik today, getting it on with old Shreed in thirty hours.* Valdez noted the facts in a window and sent the note, encrypted, to O'Neill.

He didn't know her birthday, however, and he didn't have the tools to simultaneously select thousands of numbered Annas at the hub, so he couldn't figure out the account number she had given Shreed in the chat room. He wasn't even sure her first name was Anna, in fact, so he tried watching Shreed's laptop until Shreed sent an encrypted document in fits and starts, as if he had a poor connection. Valdez shook his head. Too many bytes in the encryption key. Beyond his reach. *Finito.*

Bahrain 1600 GMT (1900L) Sunday.

The restaurant where Alan was meeting Anna sat in a lane behind the Gulf Hotel. The street was residential, and the atmosphere warm, friendly, and European, despite the Thai menu. The patrons varied from expat Brits looking for a night out to hungry students with limited budgets. It didn't feature live floor shows or breathtaking waitresses and so was not a favorite with the US military personnel living nearby. Alan stood out a little as he went to his table; too American, not tanned enough to be an expat. An Aussie at the bar gave him a hard stare.

The menu appeared unchanged since Alan had last eaten here in 1993. He ordered an iced tea and watched the door. Scenarios chased each other around his head. *Shreed had offered her more money. Alan had been a sucker from the first and she was somehow allied with Shreed. She had been playing with him since Trieste.*

The time for the meeting came and went. Alan drank his second iced tea, and then a third. He ordered satay, and found that he had devoured the plate without noticing the taste. She wasn't coming. His feelings about that were too complicated to pin down. Relief was there, and some little element of hurt that angered him all the more.

"Planning to eat without me, Alan?"

He was sitting over the wreckage of the appetizer with two sticky hands and a spot on the front of his shirt. She was wearing a crisp linen shirt and blue jeans, her face as perfect without its usual glitter of cosmetics as it had been in Naples. Her lips touched his cheek firmly and he cursed inwardly when his pulse responded. He hadn't expected to be so glad to see her.

"Slow flight from Dubai?" He was wiping his fingers with a napkin. She sat across from him; the waiter held her chair and she held every eye in the room.

"I had trouble getting a cab into Manama."

"Have a nice chat with Mister Shreed?"

Her eyes had a faintly liquid quality that made her a difficult target for his angry stare, as if she were never too far from tears, but her head snapped round like a cat's spotting a bird.

"Your black friend must have told you that there was no meeting. I'm hungry. May we eat?"

"I certainly recommend the satay."

"I really do apologize for being late. It is—unsuitable?"

"Unprofessional?"

"Really, Alan. You sound jealous."

Alan pondered that while the waiter was captivated by her smile and given his marching orders. Alan found that she had ordered for both of them without reference to him at any point. Rose often did the same. The picture of Rose deciding his edible future in an Afghani restaurant in Newport restored his humor. He did *not* want this woman. He wanted her information. And she no longer had much to offer.

"I'm naive, Anna. I hadn't realized that I was in a bidding contest."

"It isn't a contest."

"There's certainly no hurry. I know who your man is, of course; what else do you have to offer?" *Too strident. Win the battle of the small talk.*

"Please, can we speak of something else while we eat?"

"What would you like to discuss? Music?" His intended sarcasm fell flat. She tilted her head slightly, like a curious puppy.

"Music would suit very well, I think. What do you like? What do you listen to, at home?"

Alan tried to remember the last time he had listened to music, at home or anywhere else.

"I used to like folk songs. Rose loves Italian opera." It was as if, by saying her name, he had a talisman against the formidable magic deployed across the table. "My dad loved Wagner."

"Really? No rock? No Madonna?"

He laughed, because of the image Madonna brought to mind.

"On the boat, just before the pilots get briefed for a flight, we used to play cuts from MTV." He looked at her for signs of interest.

"Yes, I know MTV."

"Back during the Gulf War, one of Madonna's songs was top on the list. I don't know if anyone cared about the tune, but every pilot liked to watch her move around, you know? That, and the Kim Basinger dance scene from *9½ Weeks.* Every time I hear those songs, I feel like I'm about to launch."

Anna laughed, the real laugh that didn't cut out when the owner was through with it.

"English is so full of innuendo, isn't it?"

Alan held his ground. "Do you know Italian?"

She shook her head, but laughed.

"What do you listen to?"

"I love music," she said simply. "I can listen to almost anything. I used to listen to Mozart, over and over. I just bought some of what you call 'alternative' in Dubai." She stopped, as if by saying the name she had raised a ghost.

"I think you ought to tell me a little more about the alternative in Dubai, Anna." *Not bad,* he thought.

Her mouth set in a hard line. The arrival of the entranced waiter arrested her reply, and a whole tray of dishes was laid before them. The waiter began to load their plates with samples of each dish, missing no opportunity to lean over her or speak to her. Alan picked up a fork and took a mouthful of perfect basil beef.

She leaned over her food. She smelled like cardamom, but she was hissing mad.

"Did we have sex some time when I wasn't paying attention? Do I have some special relationship with you, that you should question me about whom I may meet?"

Alan reached for his anger at her, just touched it to be sure it was there.

"I have some natural concerns about you meeting the man you described as a 'mole in the CIA.' That's fair, I think."

Again, the angry, quick head movement. And then a sigh.

"So you know."

"Yes."

She switched her attention to her food. She carved through the dishes on the table like a cat with a tin of tuna, but then she paused and dabbed her mouth with her napkin.

"Tell me about your wife."

Something about the way the question was asked put him on his guard. Or more on his guard.

"Why?"

"She is important to you, yes?"

"She's everything to me. She's, oh, beautiful and smart, but that's not . . ." He tapered off. She was considering him again.

"Did you bring me money?"

"Yes. Okay, Anna, we tried music. What do you like?"

"In music? Were you listening?"

"No, in life. Find a new subject."

"I like fine rifles."

"Rifles." Alan flashed on a conversation he had overheard on the boat—worst dates. *I was meeting a spy in Bahrain. . . .*

"Yes! Efremov had a few, and we bought more. A Holland and Holland nitro express. One of those wonderful US Marine rifles with the half-inch bore. We were going to go lion hunting in the mountains, except that we both felt there weren't enough left to justify the hunt."

"Iran has lions?"

She looked at him as if he was an idiot. He hastened to correct the impression.

"I have a 1918 Springfield armory sniper rifle."

"With a star on the muzzle?" She looked impressed.

"Absolutely."

She leaned forward, her food forgotten.

"Have you shot it?"

"Sure. My friend and I tried some long shots."

"You shoot together?"

"We shoot skeet, when we can."

She frowned.

"Efremov and I used to lie in the rocks near an old quarry and shoot for hours. Your friend is Harry O'Neill?"

Alan looked at the liquid eyes and saw that she knew the answer, so he nodded.

"Your friend Harry. He runs a security company. He is a very impressive man."

"Yes, he is."

"Shall we have dessert?" She smiled. "What other rifles do you own?"

NCIS HQ.

Triffler had meant to go home but he found himself in his office. He supposed that there had been some consciousness in getting there, but it was a little eerie, to set out for home on a Sunday morning and wind up here. The office was eerie, too, the corridors empty.

He looked at the room he had shared with Dukas and that was now his again. The wall of plastic crates looked suddenly tacky, the plants and the *tschotchkes* foolish. He made a pot of coffee, whistling, thinking about Moisher and his case. He took a cup of coffee and sat at Dukas's desk because it was actually his own old desk and he felt in charge there.

George Shreed, he thought. *How do we get from George Shreed to Tony Moscowic?* Or how do I get Moisher to go from Tony Moscowic to Shreed without passing Go? *How do I tell Menzes that there's some third party, and the third party may be connected with Tony Moscowic because* *he got five big ones for "entry into S's"? That has to be important to the* *CIA. Has to be. Maybe it's even important to Dukas somehow.*

He could just get on the blower and tell Menzes all about it, but he had liked Menzes when he had met him at the Old Commonwealth with Dukas, and he didn't want to screw him. How could he give this part of the investigation to Menzes and not taint it?

He closed the door so that he could see the chart he had made of Shreed's life. It wasn't quite up to date—he hadn't entered Shreed's running away. If in fact Shreed had run away and hadn't fallen down his cellar stairs or had a stroke while he was in a movie. Triffler looked it all over and then looked it all over again.

And then he saw the letters A, M, and H. Full caps.

Angel of Mercy Hospice.

Tony Moscowic had taken three thousand dollars to bug a *hospice?*

An old phrase from a criminal-justice class rattled through his head: *deathbed confession.* But it was Shreed's wife who had been in there, not Shreed. But she would have known things, wouldn't she? So that somebody who wanted to know Shreed's secrets might have—— He thought it through and was half-ready to believe that Menzes himself had paid Moscowic to bug the AMH, except that that wasn't the way the Agency usually operated. Some other country? *What rinky-dink intelligence service would hire a Tony Moscowic? Yes—North Korea, Sudan—you name it.*

He got out Moisher's card and called him at home. On the phone, Moisher sounded even younger than he did in the flesh. Triffler wanted to ask for his parents.

"Hey, Detective Moisher, Dick Triffler. I had a thought."

"Yeah?" As in *Yeah, yeah, yeah, pant, pant!*

Triffler was leafing through the Northern Virginia phone book, and he didn't speak until he was sure that the Angel of Mercy Hospice was listed in just that way. Then he said, "About that AMH."

"Hey, yeah!"

"You think of looking in the phone book?"

"Yellow Pages?"

"No, the white pages where they list businesses and stuff like that. You said it was a place, not a person, right? It just occurred to me that you could look under the As, and under there find things that also had an M and an H."

"That'd be a lot of looking."

"Well, yeah, because you'd have to do DC and Northern Virginia as well as PG County and maybe Montgomery, right?"

"Boy, that's a lot."

Triffler wanted to reach down the phone and grab his throat. "But it might pay off!"

"How would I know?"

Triffler suppressed a groan. "You'd have to make a list, and then visit every place on the list with a photo of the dead guy and ask if they'd ever seen him or if they knew his name. You might get lucky."

"Gee, that's a lot of places to visit."

"Yeah. I'd get right on it." He heard Moisher sighing, like a man whose Sunday has just been taken away from him. "I'll bet if you worked it right, you could get the Virginia and DC cops to do their areas for you." He was counting the number of AMH businesses. "After all, how many can there be?"

Not so many, actually.

After he hung up, he smiled. If Moisher would get on the stick, it would work—if, that is, somebody at the hospice remembered Tony Moscowic.

If not, maybe he'd have to tell Menzes and let *him* figure how to keep his case from being tainted.

31

HARRY O'NEILL WAS SIPPING A SECOND CUP OF COF-
fee in the restaurant of the Hilton, staring out the enormous windows at
the dhows drawn up along the pier in the last rays of sunset. Most of
them were from Iran, laden with carpets and saffron, opium and mari-
juana. They were at the forefront of Harry's thoughts because he was
trying to judge if Shreed might attempt to use one of the boats to cross
to Iran and disappear. He hadn't heard from Djalik, who was supposed
to be following Shreed, and he didn't know what to do next. His watch
told him that Alan ought to be meeting with Anna at that moment, but
his concern was fixed on Shreed. He knew he ought to call Dukas, but he
was leaving his cellphone free so Djalik could get him.

When his cellphone rang, he had it in his hand and active before it
had a chance to ring a second time.

"Harry?"

"Dave, where the hell are you?"

"I'm driving through the Al Hajar. Shreed crossed into Oman about
an hour ago."

"You sure?"

"Sure as shit. Border guard remembered him. I think he's headed for
Muscat."

"I'm on my way. Get somebody to cover the airport and head for the docks."

"Roger. Call me when you land."

Nicosia.

Khouri, the Palestinian detective, lay in a clean bed in what at first looked to Dukas like a dirty room but was only in need of paint. The equipment was new and sparkling, in fact—oxygen, an IV. The cop himself looked young and gaunt, as if the ordeal had taken both years and pounds off him. Gorzum loomed at the foot of his bed.

Dukas let Wahad talk. Gestures were made in Dukas's direction. A third man, introduced as Mister Almasi, also Palestinian, stood on the other side of the bed—tall, shrewd, older. *Palestine Liberation Organization*, Dukas thought.

"Ask him to tell me what happened," Dukas said, gesturing toward the wounded man.

The story was the one Dukas had already had from Wahad, embellished by Gorzum: the Palestinian detective had interrupted a drug buy, then been attacked by two men he thought were muggers. He had shot one and been shot by the other before any of the three realized that they were all policemen.

"Then what?"

The young cop looked at Mister Almasi before he answered. "The buyer and the seller ran away."

"Ran?"

More eye contact between the two Palestinians. "A manner of speaking."

"Who was the buyer?"

"An American."

"How did you know?"

"We can all tell." Gorzum laughed.

"Did you know the American?"

The detective's eyes went again to Almasi. Then they went briefly to Gorzum and slid away, then locked on Dukas's. Dukas turned to Gorzum. "Can I talk to him alone?"

Gorzum shook his head and widened his stance, announcing immovability.

It was one of those impossible moments that block an investigation: the man wanted to tell him, because he wanted the ten-thousand-dollar reward, but he wouldn't do it in front of Gorzum, because Gorzum might screw up the reward. And Gorzum wouldn't leave. *Check.*

Dukas took three photos out of his pocket, one of Shreed and the other two of men of more or less the same age. He handed them across the bed to Almasi.

Both the wounded detective and Almasi recognized Shreed; Dukas would have gone to court on their reactions. But both denied recognizing any of the three.

Dukas asked some more questions and then Gorzum said they had talked enough, and he held the door open. Dukas and Wahad went to a seating area and huddled together, as people do in hospitals. Dukas pressed the photo of Shreed into Wahad's hand. "Ask Mister Almasi to show this to the detective again and ask if it's the man. Just do it! I'll take care of Gorzum."

Wahad wanted to object; he was a conciliator, not a conspirator. But Gorzum came up then and Wahad excused himself and headed off as if looking for a toilet. Dukas offered to buy Gorzum coffee. When they got it, the caffeine hit him like a sweet blow. "You know this Almasi?" he said.

Gorzum more or less shrugged. "PLO. Big shot." They talked about being cops until Wahad came back and signaled Dukas with his eyes, and Dukas excused himself. Down a corridor and around a corner, Almasi caught up with him. He held out the photo. His English was not very good, but it was good enough to tell Dukas that the young detective had said yes.

"Sharid," the Palestinian said.

Dukas thought it was an Arabic word. He must have looked puzzled, because the Palestinian said it again. Then he tapped the photo and again said, "Sharid."

Then Dukas got it. *Sharid, Shreed.* He nodded his head too vigorously. "Shreed!"

The Palestinian made the universal sign, fingers on thumb, rubbing. "Money."

"Not now. Later." Where was Wahad when he needed him?

"Money?"

Dukas pointed out and down. "Tomorrow. Day after tomorrow." How could he explain that he didn't carry ten thousand dollars around in his pocket? He sighed. Exhaustion weighed on him like an overcoat.

Washington.

The Chief of Naval Operations worked a seven-day week, or at least a six-and-a-half-day week, because he liked to go to church on Sunday. By one o'clock, however, he was in his office, ready to wade through the e-mails and the paper that he often couldn't get to when other people were around. Now, however, an aide poked his head in and said, "Can you see Admiral Pilchard?"

Momentarily annoyed, the CNO forced his face to stay expressionless, then let it rearrange itself into something pleasant. Pilchard was an old friend from flying days. "Five minutes," he said, knowing that Pilchard would understand—one of the compliments that friendship paid to command.

"Dick," he said, standing with his hand out. "What's up?"

"I know your time's tight, so I'll make it short."

The CNO nodded his thanks.

"A female chopper pilot named Rose Siciliano. Top commendations, deep-select for promotion, just finished the War College, then she got blindsided by a false accusation from the CIA, and she's been in purgatory since. Her name's been smeared in the fleet. Now there's confirmation that the whole thing was a put-up job, and I'd like her cleared and commended so that everybody can see she's clean."

"Why today?"

"Because Lieutenant-Commander Siciliano is stretched thin; her husband's at sea; and the guy who smeared her is a CIA biggie who's apparently defected."

The CNO sat up a little straighter. After a glance at a walnut clock on his desk, he said, "You better take ten minutes."

Pilchard laid it out for him. He produced such documents as there were, named names, gave a crisp history of George Shreed and his apparent flight. He ended with the presumption that Rose's ordeal had been caused by Shreed to cover himself.

The CNO leaned back. "I'd already heard that a top CIA guy was gone. I've raised holy hell about it because it wasn't the Agency that told us; it was an NCIS agent. I've got ships out there looking down Chinese gun-barrels, and the Agency can't tell us what the hell the guy took with him!"

"They're probably in denial. They won't admit he's gone."

"What do you want?"

"Exonerate Rose Siciliano. Her husband, too—he's one of the guys who's looking down a Chinese gun-barrel."

The CNO looked again at the clock and tapped a pencil on the desk. "How come I didn't know about any of this, Dick?"

Pilchard's chin went up. He hated gossip, but he didn't blink at laying blame where it belonged. "Your intel people sat on it. Somebody over there is the conduit for the Agency smear. Maybe it was just you-scratch-my-back, I'll-scratch-yours. Whoever it is managed to get her and her husband's orders changed with the authority of your office."

The CNO threw down the pencil. He stabbed a button. "Manion! Get the DNI on the phone—get him off the golf course if you have to. Now!" He stood and began to prowl the room. "What's she want?"

"Reinstatement of her orders to the astronaut program."

"She's got it. How about if I bring her in here until the orders are written—special aide on TAD to my office? That's an endorsement that the fleet will recognize."

Pilchard stood. "More than I had the balls to ask for."

The CNO nodded. "Give Manion her phone number. I want to talk to her directly." He glanced at the door, and Pilchard, taking the cue, headed for it. "And Dick—anything you know about this crap in ONI, you share with me—right? I want a head."

Pilchard paused, then nodded.

Bahrain 1800 GMT (2100L).

Alan and Anna left the restaurant arm in arm. Alan had reached a level of comfort with her that puzzled him, like having a dangerous criminal as an old but untrusted friend. They walked up the street through the humid evening air, and she told him stories from her time in Bahrain and Dubai. They weren't ugly stories, or she censored the ugliness; mostly they were comic stories of men and socialites and parties. She never mentioned how she had moved from the Arab states to Iran. He didn't ask. He told her stories about the boat.

They walked through the lobby at the hotel and Alan took her up to his room. She sat on the bed.

"Money?"

"I have to send for it. What do you have to sell?"

"Is this photo Rose? She is beautiful. Did you place her here to protect yourself from me?"

She crossed her legs and tossed her head and smiled. He suspected that her statement was right, and that left him feeling even more of an adolescent.

"Maybe. Probably. What are we here for, Anna? I know who the mole in the Agency is."

"Perhaps you need to buy my silence, then."

Alan shook his head. He thought he'd done well enough in the small talk; now he was in the real battle.

"I'm not buying your silence. What I want is your help in stopping George Shreed. Do you know his whereabouts?"

"I will. He wants me; or rather, he wants what is left of Efremov. You have no idea where he is now, do you?"

"I know he was in Dubai six hours ago. We'll find him."

"Perhaps, but in twelve hours I'll know where he is. I can sell you that. And I still have all of Efremov's files, Alan. Can I interest you in a white paper on French arms sales to Iran? On North Korean mini-sub construction? Some names of Hezbollah and Republican Guard officers overseas? George Shreed is not the only item on the table."

He walked over to her, from the secure chair to which he had retreated, and he stood close to her and looked her in the eyes. He was so close that she expected him to kiss her, but then she saw it had never entered his mind. His eyes weren't hard, close up, but they were very intense.

"Anna. In thirty-six hours, China will go to war with India. I think China is counting on George Shreed to win the peace, or failing that, the war. He has codes, or something, that the Chinese think will tip the balance and overturn all of the US's vast superiority in technology and training."

"I don't know what he has. What do I care? I'm not a fan of your United States."

"Thousands of people will die, Anna. For nothing. For bad diplomacy and a gambit in Beijing. You can help stop that, Anna. You can control the event."

"I am not a philanthropist, Alan Craik. But I will do my part in saving the world for the agreed price. For one million dollars, I will give you Efremov's files, and throw in whatever I learn in the next few days about George Shreed's whereabouts."

"Let me send for the money, okay?"

He picked up the telephone and called Soleck's room. There was no answer. He took a slip of paper from his wallet and called the pager. She got off the bed and went into the bathroom.

"I've always loved the Gulf," she called over the sound of running water. "Water, endless water. Think what that means to an Arab."

The phone rang.

"Craik."

"Howdy, sir. It's Evan?" Crashing music in the background, and a relentless rhythm machine beat.

"I need the suitcase."

"Wow! Cool. Where are you?"

"In my room. Seven forty-six."

"Wow! So it's going down? On my way!"

Soleck probably thought he was living in a *Miami Vice* episode. Anna came back out wiping her hands on a small towel. "Even the towels here are good. I used to steal one, every time I had the chance."

"The money will be here in a moment."

"I wonder sometimes about you, Alan. Why am I not grabbed and— interrogated? Or why not use your black friend to protect you?"

"I don't get you, Anna. What do you want?"

She shot back, "Absolute control of my life. To never *again* depend on a man for protection." Her hands were clenched for a moment, and then they unclenched. Alan heard Harry whisper *"get her motivation"* at a café in Italy. Well, there it was.

"George Shreed won't give you that, Anna. George Shreed will leave you drained, or dead."

She was quiet for a moment, but when she turned back to him she had recovered her wry smile.

"Poor Shreed. If Allah hath a thousand hands to chastise, most of them must be near Mister Shreed just now."

Alan answered a low knock at the door. Soleck filled the doorway, but from somewhere down the hall there was a giggle. He looked past Alan into the room. Anna had risen from the bed and was standing close behind Alan. Soleck stared at her.

Alan reached out and took the case from his unresisting hand.

"Later," he said, and closed the door.

"Who was he?"

"One of my pilots."

"Very handsome. A little young."

"I think he's already found a friend for the night."

She took the case and laid it on the bed, then popped the cover. It was crammed full of money, stacks in all denominations. It did not look like the slim, well-ordered briefcases of cash that appeared on TV. Anna laughed to herself.

"What did you do, ask for contributions?"

"It's the payroll from my ship. I didn't have a lot of time. It's short, too, by a little less than a hundred thousand dollars."

"I asked for an automatic teller card and an account in a Swiss bank."

"I didn't have time. I can make that happen, if you can wait."

She looked at the money in the case, and a curious look of revulsion passed over her.

"I have sold myself in too many hotel rooms."

"You aren't selling yourself, Anna. And I need that information."

She looked at the picture on the nightstand and at the suitcase. Nothing was as she had planned. She wanted an ally.

She needed some money. *Didn't it always come down to that?*

She sat on the bed and began counting the money. Alan watched and then began to write a receipt. He didn't know what good it would ever do him, but he had signed for the full amount on the ship, and he wasn't simply going to let it go.

"That is a receipt? Make it out for ten thousand dollars," she said.

"Ten thousand? I thought—"

"I can't carry this through customs."

"I brought it in good faith."

"And I'm responding the same way. This," she took a CD from her purse, "should tell you everything you need to know about how he communicated with China. It is all of his messages to them. I'll be honest. I can't read them. Your people will be able to. That's worth ten thousand, I think. And your guarantee that if I provide Shreed's whereabouts before the Chinese ultimatum expires, I get one million dollars."

"Do you know where he is, Anna?"

"No. I told you. But I will in a few hours. Give me an e-mail address."

Alan was at a loss to know where there might be a trap in this, or what e-mail he should provide. He was reasonably sure that the US government would pony up one million for Shreed. He scribbled his private e-mail address on a sheet of the hotel pad.

She took it and looked at him with satisfaction.

"So we finally do business, yes? And you admit that I have the key? Shreed is running for China, and I am the one who knows things. What will you do to learn these things, Alan Craik?"

"I can promise the money." He thought they would honor his promise. Then he caught sight of her in the mirror, and for the second time that evening, he knew that he had said the wrong thing.

"I don't want money." She tossed the disk at him like a blade and scooped ten thousand dollars into her purse. "Does it never occur to you that I might have other needs besides money? Oh, sex. You think I might want sex, and set your wife beside the bed like a virgin with a crucifix."

"Anna—"

"I want a life I control. I want a passport and a name and a deal that I can live with; control of my own life."

"Anna, be fair. I brought what you asked. I can't get you a passport. . . ."

"No, you brought money. You are angry that I should seek to sell my wares elsewhere, but all you offer me is money, yourself. Do you know how familiar this is, to a whore? Why don't you hit me a few times?"

She walked over to his bedside table and scrawled something on his receipt before she walked to the door. She opened it and stopped in the doorway, but she didn't turn her head. Alan wondered what had gone so wrong, so quickly, or whether this was acting.

He thought of the gun in the bag by the door, of forcing her to tell him whatever she knew about George Shreed. It wasn't in him.

"Anna, wait." He took a step toward her and the phone rang. "We're talking about the lives of thousands. . . ."

The phone rang a second time. They were balanced on the edge of a sword, and Alan had to know. He reached for the phone.

"Alan! Harry! He's boarded a boat in Muscat!"

The door slammed like a pistol shot, and she was gone.

ANNA WALKED through the lobby like an aristocrat on her way to the guillotine, her head high, her back straight, without a glance to either side. She was not sure what she had expected from Alan Craik, after the first two meetings, but she always forgot his intensity. Some men would talk about the lives of thousands of people to get her in bed, to impress her, or themselves. Alan Craik meant every word. He was an honorable man.

She smiled a little, as the grandeur of her new plan hit her. She would join the honorable men, win her freedom and the million dollars to keep her new life unsullied.

She already knew where George Shreed was going. She was going to travel to Jolcut, Pakistan, to meet with George Shreed. And kill him. They could pay for the body, and she would be on the side of the angels.

Oak Grove, West Virginia.

Rose was spending the Sunday afternoon with her kids—and with worry about her husband.

Mikey was curled into her on the sofa; the baby was asleep in a chair. They were supposedly watching television, but she was thinking about Alan, and Mikey was simply being with her. Sensing her worry, he had reverted to being a little boy—a scared little boy who wouldn't let his mother out of his sight.

"Is Dad okay?" he said.

She patted his leg. On the other side of him, the black dog stretched and wagged his tail.

"How're you?" she said.

"Fine." He sounded wan.

"How about a treat?"

"I'd rather have Dad here."

She tried to laugh, couldn't manage it, hugged him. "So would I," she said. Then the telephone rang, and when she got up to answer it, Mikey followed her, to stand next to her and put one hand into hers as she listened.

"Lieutenant-Commander Siciliano, please."

"Speaking." She frowned—an official call. *Was it about Alan?*

"This is Commander Ahlbein in the office of the Chief of Naval Operations. Stand by for the Chief, please—he wants to speak to you personally."

Her heart stopped. *If anything has happened to Alan—*

"Lieutenant-Commander Siciliano?"

"Sir."

"This is the Chief of Naval Operations. I had a talk with Admiral Pilchard a while ago, and I want to apologize to you personally for the shabby way you've been treated. I also want you to know I'm mad as hell about our part in it."

"Thank you, sir." Relief flooded over her like a blush, turned to pleasure as she understood what he was really saying.

"Commander, I want to assure you that we're doing everything we can to make sure this ordeal you've gone through is over. Admiral Pilchard suggested, and I agree with him, that you need for us to show you some support. I can offer two things. One, immediate selection for full commander. Two, how'd you like to come TAD to me for a while?"

"That'd be—"

"Preparatory, I mean, to going to Houston for astronaut training."

"That'd be great!"

"Only one thing: I have to ask you to clam up about this guy your lawyer thinks scapegoated you. That's key, I'm afraid. We don't know what he may have taken or where he took it to; if that word gets out, we'll have every two-bit navy in the world testing us. And we'll be wondering who knows things he shouldn't know. So—if I give you my personal assurance that you're going to Houston, can you put a lid on the story?"

"If I have your word that it's over—yes, sir."

"You have my word. You're a damned fine officer." He paused as if he was going to hang up, but he added, "You can put up those silver leaves as of 0600 hours tomorrow." She heard the smile in his voice. "Subject to confirmation by Congress."

"Thank you—sir—" But he was gone. In his place, the younger voice of the commander who had first called came on, and he began to go through details of when she would like to report in Washington. And how soon could she leave West Virginia? If she was coming to DC TAD, would she need an advance? And if—?

If he heard her weeping, he paid no attention.

3 2

Langley.

IN A ROOM IN THE CIA BUILDING, ELEVEN PEOPLE SAT around a conference table. Alone at one end, Carl Menzes was suffering the isolation of failure.

At the far end of the table, an assistant to the Deputy Director presided. Clyde Partlow, Shreed's nominal boss, sat next to him, already in the clear because he had argued successfully that Shreed was his equal, not his underling, and he hadn't dared challenge him. Around the rest of the table sat people from Operations and Public Affairs, men and women in casual clothes who were trying on this Sunday to spin Shreed's absence into an acceptable media presentation for Monday release.

"Finding his car was conclusive for me," Partlow said. Always a congenial man, he was today as warm and giving as a TV evangelist. "His canes in the trunk—that's conclusive. And if the bloodstain checks with his DNA—well, it's clear, isn't it? Poor George is dead."

Far down the table, Menzes cleared his throat. The people nearest him leaned away as if he might be about to emit a communicable disease. "We don't know that. His assistant, Ray Suter, told us—"

The chair pointed a finger, the thumb cocked like a gun. "You fuck up, you shut up. *You fucked up.* Got me?"

Menzes flushed a dark purply red and leaned back. Nobody looked at him.

"Now," the chairman said, "let's explore this line of thinking that Clyde's brought up. Suppose Shreed is dead? What does this do for us?"

Nicosia.

The wounded Turkish cop was in another room in the same Nicosia hospital. Unlike Khouri, the detective, he readily identified the photo of Shreed, but he stonewalled about what he had been doing that day. Gorzum, who seemed now to be on Dukas's side, had shouted at him then, and Dukas, playing a card dealt him by the PLO man, Almasi, said, "What were you doing, sitting in the Topkapi Café with the American earlier in the day?" He felt like an actor reading lines, having no idea if the question had any basis in fact.

Wahad had translated; the cop had looked terrified; Gorzum had shouted something that had to be a threat. After two lies and more shouting, the man in the bed had begun to babble. "He says okay, they were sitting with the American outside the café to protect him. He had hired them, their day off. Just earning some extra money because the police don't pay well."

Dukas looked at Gorzum, but he was wondering how the Palestinian, Almasi, had known about the Topkapi Café. He asked what had happened at the café.

"He says," Wahad said, with one eye on Gorzum, "that the American met with a man. They talked. The other man left."

"What man?"

"Now he says he remembers the American called the man 'Colonel.' Maybe a military man."

Gorzum said something in Turkish, and the wounded policeman muttered to Wahad.

"Now he remembers there were other men with the Colonel. He just remembered it. Four men."

"What did they do?"

"They looked around."

Countersurveillance, Dukas thought. He could see pretty well what had happened—a clandestine meet. "What nationality were the men?"

"He doesn't know."

Gorzum pushed Dukas toward the door. More rested, he might have tried to stay, but his will was mush. Gorzum went back in to scold the policeman some more, and Dukas wandered down the corridor and found himself facing Almasi, who stood there as if to say, *I told you so.* They looked at each other until Wahad joined them, and Dukas said, "Tell him that all the guy'd say is that Shreed met with a man he called 'Colonel.' "

"He says he knows. He says they were Israelis."

Dukas put together *Israelis* and *Colonel.* "Mossad?"

"He says yes, Mossad."

"Is he sure?"

A rapid exchange. "You think we don't know when a Mossad officer flies in?" Wahad, too, looked tired, but he was speaking quickly. "He says his people saw a Mossad colonel with the American and the policemen at the café, but it meant nothing to them until the shooting. They hadn't seen your wanted message at that time—it was Khouri who had seen it."

Dukas chewed it over. If Shreed had met with Mossad, then he was thinking of selling something—himself?—to Mossad. Had they set a second meeting? Had Mossad already picked Shreed up? "Ask him how I can get in touch with Mossad."

The two men spoke in Arabic. Wahad turned cynical eyes on Dukas. "He says, 'Shoot a Jew.' "

Almasi walked away from them and disappeared.

AFTER NINE LOCAL TIME, Dukas made Wahad take him to a cyber-café. He didn't want to talk on an open line; he didn't have a STU; and he didn't want to go to the embassy to use one—too many questions, too many CIA people. E-mail was, so far, fairly safe if you didn't use words that could be keyed on.

He sent Triffler an e-mail:

"Hi Dick: my guy pos id here by two. He also met with King Solomon's Minds and may now be their boy. Report upline urgent and direct to

CNO and let him decide to tell Crystal Palace. DON'T YOU MAKE THIS DECISION YOURSELF. Having wonderful time, wish you were here. Mike."

Then, to Wahad's relief, he had himself driven to his hotel, where he undressed and crawled between the clean sheets and closed his eyes.

And the telephone rang.

Dukas groaned. Nobody could possibly know he was there. Except NCIS, Naples. He picked up the telephone.

"Mike Dukas, please."

"Who wants him?" His voice was so husky he could hardly speak.

"Harold O'Neill of Ethos Security Services."

"Harry, Jesus Christ, I didn't recognize you. How the hell—"

"Cellphone, called NCIS, got no time. This is not a secure call. Here's the dope, Mike: our guy made a meet in Dubai and just blew by us. You there?"

"Dubai?" Yesterday, Shreed had been in Cyprus. Now he was in Dubai. Dukas was having trouble focusing. "I thought you were covering Al in Bahrain."

"This other came up. Valdez caught it."

"What about Al?"

"He's on his own."

Oh, sweet Jesus, Dukas thought. "Holy shit. Okay, I'll catch up with Al. You stay after our friend there."

"Al won't be there. He's—he won't be there."

"Leave messages at NCIS, Bahrain, then. Better there than here." Dukas rubbed his eyes. "You're *sure* this was our guy in Dubai?" *Because if it was, Mossad don't have him.*

"Mike, I *saw* him. Pretty much saw him, anyway. Jesus, he killed one of my guys."

"Positive ID?"

"Close. As good as."

Close is not as good as. "Shit," Dukas said. He was not sure that Harry had ever seen George Shreed, in fact. "Double shit," he growled.

"That about sums it up."

Bahrain. Oh, God, another five hours in the air. Dukas lay back on the pillow. "I'm dying for sleep, man."

"Tell me about it."

"Okay. Okay." He sat up. "I'm on my way." He put the phone down and fell back, sound asleep. Within seconds, his eyes opened, and he groaned, halfway between sleep and waking, and the habit of a lifetime, the habit of duty, forced him to the surface of wakefulness. He reached for the telephone. "Call me a taxi," he mumbled.

Bahrain 1830 GMT (2130L).

"I just want to know where the fuck we're going!" Stevens whined.

"I filed a flight plan for Muscat," Alan said. "That's all I know right now."

"Can I get JP-5 in Muscat?"

"I'll call the *Jefferson* when we're in the air and get it." *In the clear, because we don't have any trustworthy crypto.*

"How about a country clearance?"

"Paul—"

"Right. Shut up and drive the bus." Stevens was back to giving him sullen looks.

Over the Persian Gulf 1949 GMT (2249L).

Alan had to shout into the cellphone to make himself heard above the roar of the engines, and Harry's voice at the other end was fuzzy and indistinct.

"He's on a boat?" Alan shouted for the third time.

"...hour ago!"

"Is he on a boat?"

"...boat!"

Alan gnawed his upper lip in frustration and stared at the image on the screen. Dozens of small boats were in the Strait of Hormuz, and, without a second plane, they couldn't use the off-axis MAFI imaging to classify them. Targets smaller than fifteen meters tended to resolve as amorphous blobs on the screen.

Alan switched to a datalink picture of the Indian Ocean and measured the distance to the *Jefferson* by eye. Then he put up a far-on circle to represent the best speed that Shreed's boat could make, if Shreed had indeed taken a fast boat out of Muscat. *Fifty knots in a cigarette boat? Maybe more. Call it fifty.*

"Harry, I'm going to land at Muscat in one hour, do you copy?"

". . . copy!"

"Meet me."

". . . ger." Sounded like *Roger*, anyway.

He cut the connection and tossed the cellphone on the other seat, where it rested atop the lead weights that balanced the plane when there was no one in the SENSO seat. Then he asked Soleck to get him an encrypted connection to the *Jefferson*.

Rafe came through loud and clear, his voice only slightly distorted by the range and the encryption.

"Rafe, I need the other MARI bird to rendezvous with me at 24N 060E. Do you copy?"

"That's two four North, zero six zero East. I copy. Launch in one five minutes."

"With a buddy store."

"Roger one buddy store."

"Rafe, he's running in a small boat."

"What do you see us doing?"

"We find him and blow him out of the water."

"I don't think so, cowboy. We've got orders."

Alan thought about Rafe, who had overflown Algeria once against orders, to save gas. "Rafe, this might be our last chance."

"Where's he headed?"

"No idea."

"He ain't going to China in a cigarette boat, buddy."

"He might go to Pakistan. By the time we find him, he'll be well up the coast. Dawn, coastal traffic."

"Roger. I'll talk to the admiral, but he's not going to like it much. How will we know we have the right boat?"

"Someone in Muscat saw him board. I think we may even have photos."

"Okay, cowboy. Keep it cool. I'll get the birds in the air and get back to you."

And then Alan was alone with the night and his radar screen. He had an hour until they could get the photos from Harry in Muscat, and he spent some of his time putting vectors on traffic outbound from Muscat. Ten minutes winnowed the possibles down to fourteen. Alan entered them into the datalink in the hope that they would still be in the link after he took off from Muscat, saving him time on his search. If George Shreed was on one of those boats, he was five hours from the Pakistani coast.

He tried to keep his mind off the meeting with Anna. He had failed to win her over, and, worse, he had failed to anticipate that she would simply walk away. He replayed the end of the meeting with Anna over and over, trying to choose the moment he should have acted. Force? Persuasion? When the chips were down, he had ignored Harry's coaching and attempted . . . He hadn't really attempted anything. She had run the meeting, reached a decision, and left.

Had she reached a decision?

He replayed the meeting again. He lacked Harry's cynical view of her psyche, and the more he looked at it, the more he wondered.

He had the CD she had given him. He had time and a laptop, so he unclipped his harness and moved around the tunnel until he had what he wanted, and then, with the tray locked across his knees, he fired up the laptop and put the black plastic disk into his drive and brought it up. It took a long time to load, long enough to worry that she had taken him on this as on everything else.

The CD contained a set of files. When he accessed them, they all came up as cheap, grainy pornographic images.

Washington.

Ray Suter was terrified. He'd thought he knew what fear was when he'd killed Moscowic. That was nothing.

Internal Investigations had kept him at Langley for five hours, going over and over the same questions: Did he know where Shreed was? Had Shreed been acting strangely? What did he make of Shreed's absence on Friday? What were Shreed's plans for the next week? the next month?

On and on and on. Then they would leave him, then suddenly come back and start again. He'd told them the exact truth—except that he hadn't told them the *real* truth.

"Don't leave town. Stay by your phone." Somebody named Menzes had been in and out while they interrogated him, then was lecturing him. "We may want to polygraph you."

Ray Suter sat by his phone and agonized over what George Shreed was doing with what Suter thought of as *his* money *right now*, because if he could get at all that money he wouldn't have to give a shit about what CIA Internal Investigations did or said.

But if he didn't get the money before he was polygraphed, he was dead meat.

Langley.

The meeting to decide the public face of George Shreed's disappearance had gone on and on. They were now in the phase where most of the participants, having got the chair's signals that Partlow's idea was a good one, were chiming in with their own views that the idea was in fact a *great* one: George Shreed was deader than General Franco, so how could any harm have been done, and how could his disappearance be the Agency's fault? They went around the table in order (skipping Menzes), piping up with what they hoped were fresh takes on the greatness of the idea.

Menzes sat silent. He rested his right cheekbone on the base of his right hand. He stared at each of them in turn, his expression morose. He managed not to look contemptuous: after all, he *had* screwed up—Dukas had told him he was moving too slowly on Shreed—and the people he was being forced to listen to were, at least on paper, his betters.

When there were only four more enthusiasts to go, a hand touched Menzes's left shoulder. He turned his head. A middle-aged security guard was beckoning to him. Menzes raised his eyebrows, then brought his left hand to his chest: *me?*

The guard nodded.

"Phone call. Urgent," the guard whispered as Menzes brushed past him. As he left the conference room, Menzes looked back and saw the chairman scowling at him.

The voices went on. They had been three hours figuring out exactly how George Shreed's death was the best thing that could have happened, in the best of all possible worlds. Now, a silver-haired man who had taken off his jacket and rolled up his sleeves was talking about TV news anchors who would listen favorably to CIA spin. "—Haseltine, prime time, *dynamite* anchor, has that cute co-anchorperson with the gap between her front teeth—a real friend of ours. I think that if I feed his to him tonight—I've got his private phone number—we can be assured that an important segment of the American public will hear our side of the story first, namely, that a patriotic American has met his death in the service of his country."

"At the hands of agents—no, let's not say 'agents,' " a nervous blond man broke in, "um, *representatives*—of a foreign government—"

"We don't *know* that," a woman in jeans and a Gap sweatshirt murmured.

"We don't have to know! We're the CIA! We're allowed to speculate!"

"Speculation is dangerous," she all but whispered.

The chairman bent his magnificent head toward them. "Arguing among ourselves won't get us anywhere. Karen, we don't need dissent."

The woman gave the smallest of shrugs.

The chair leaned back. "We're in agreement, then? The play is that we're afraid that Shreed, an Agency official with a long and distinguished record, may—*may*—have met his death through foul play. However, we're able to say that no important American data has been compromised."

The woman smiled at him. "Absent three computers with missing hard drives."

"Goddamit! The computers are privileged information and won't make the story! Agency officials aren't allowed to have classified data on their home computers, therefore Shreed didn't have anything on his home computers!"

Clyde Partlow poured the oil of his voice on these troubled waters. "The missing hard drives could be looked at as confirmation that there was foul play—somebody killing poor George and taking the hard drives in the mistaken belief that there would be something there. Of course, as we all know, George wouldn't break that rule in a million years, but, uh, a foreign power mightn't understand that."

"The Chinese?" the coatless man said. "Can we say the Chinese?"

A middle-aged woman across the table nodded. "They're the buzz right now. They're misbehaving like hell in the Indian Ocean."

"Let's leave details for—" The chairman stopped dead. Menzes had slipped back into the room.

Menzes stood at the corner of the table. The chairman was waiting for him to sit down. Impatient, he jerked his head.

Menzes held up a piece of memo paper. "I've just received a message from the Chief of Naval Operations. I think you'll want to hear it." He paused. He looked around. The chairman scowled and prepared to point his pistol-grip finger again. Menzes, however, ignored him. " 'George Shreed was positively identified in Nicosia, Cyprus, as of yesterday. We have reason to believe that he may have defected to Israel and now be under the protection of Mossad. Refer all questions to this office.' "

The chairman put his face in his hands. "Oh, *shit*!" he moaned.

33

HARRY WAS AT THE HATCH WHEN ALAN GOT IT OPENED, flourishing a digital camera and a cellphone.

"I got three photos of the boat. Let's get him.'

Harry had an enormous black bag sitting on the tarmac. His posture made it clear that he thought he was coming along. Alan opened his mouth to protest: *you're not Navy anymore, you're not air-qualified.*

Harry read Alan's thoughts.

"I saw him board. I might give you an edge in identification. If you want to get a shot at him, you have to be rock-solid in your ID. Damn it, Alan, he killed one of my guys. I want a piece of him!" Alan reached out and put his hand on Harry's shoulder. "Get in!"

"Thanks."

Harry whacked Alan's shoulder and turned back to the Jeep. He shouted something at Djalik, who shook his head ruefully and shouted back. Then Harry ran back to the hatch, lifting the huge bag effortlessly.

"What's that? Airport novels?"

"Precautions."

WHEN HARRY came up through the hatch, Soleck stared open-mouthed, and Stevens pulled off his helmet

"What the hell is he doing here?"

"He's coming with us."

"Like hell he is! He isn't even in the Navy, for Christ's sake. I'm not giving some fuckin' civilian a joyride."

"Paul, I don't have time to argue. He saw the target. He's going with us."

Stevens looked out over the lights of the airfield and back at Harry, whose head and shoulders filled the entry hatch under the TACCO seat. He picked his helmet up off the dash and flipped it like a basketball, twice. Then he pulled it on sharply.

"You're the boss, cowboy."

Three minutes later they were in the air.

THE SECOND MARI BIRD was twenty minutes from the rendezvous when they cleared Muscat air traffic control. Stevens put them into a shallow climb to give the system a wider view of the ocean's surface while Alan reviewed the information in the datalink. Soleck began linking their MARI to that of the second plane. Harry sat staring at the laptop that Alan had handed him as soon as he had strapped in.

"Show me the photos of the boat, Harry."

"Right. Next three images are his boat. Press this—"

Alan looked through the viewport in the camera and tried to memorize the boat. It looked to be ten meters long and apparently had inboard engines. The beaked bow and swept sides looked like every cigarette boat Alan had ever seen. He counted three antennas on the stern.

"Can I have a peek, sir?" Soleck asked from the front seat. Alan handed the camera to him.

"CAG on the radio for you, sir."

Alan pressed the talk switch.

"Ranger One, this is Ranger Two, over?"

"Ranger Two, I copy. What's our status?"

"We have two F-18s within call. They're on a tanker at point Charlie on the datalink."

"I see them, over."

"What we don't have is permission to shoot. If we have solid ID and everything else looks good, we can ask. Do you copy?"

"Roger that, Ranger Two. I took the liberty of bringing an eyewitness who's seen the boat. Thought that might give us an edge."

"I have a feeling I don't want to know. Is this witness air-qualified?"

"I didn't check, but he seems to be adapting. It's Harry O'Neill, Rafe—Prowler AI during the Gulf War—*you* remember!"

"I didn't hear that. Don't repeat it. Have you got link on the MARI?"

"Roger. I've entered contacts one through fourteen. Based on position and vector, one of them should be the target. Which I assume is making for Pakistan."

"Concur."

"Unless he's heading for that Chinese surface action group."

"That's a long way in an open boat, bud. They were last located south of Goa."

"Roger. Let's start looking."

MARI was cranky and the link dropped after every resolution. The first two boats they imaged were fishing boats with masts that showed clearly in the high-resolution mode. As time started to slip away, Alan changed his image strategy and made the targets closest to Pakistan the priority. They got three in a row without dropping the link; better aspect and some change in atmospherics between the planes, probably. None of the boats met the parameters.

Soleck sat in front with the digital camera. He compared each image they gained with the photo on the camera. After they imaged their sixth potential target, he came up on the intercom.

"Sir, you want to look at this thing again? I want a second opinion."

Alan took the camera back and held it to his eye.

"What am I looking for?"

"Look at the bow, sir. See anything?"

"Too dark."

"I don't want to influence you, but is that an antenna right on the point of the bow?"

Alan stared at the photo until his eyes teared up, then put the camera down and closed them. He looked again.

"Can't tell."

Harry turned his head. "There was a whip antenna on the bow. It had a little flag at the top."

"Thanks, Harry. Anything else?"

"There were two men aboard besides Shreed. There were antennas on the windscreen, too."

"Better than nothing, Harry."

"This is some kind of improved ISAR?"

"Better resolution and a 3-D image."

"But it still needs some movement in the target?"

"Not always. We can get land-based contacts, but movement helps."

"Hence the antenna question." Harry relapsed into silence, and Alan went back to the MARI. Image seven was a cigarette boat, her raked sides crisp on his screen, but the length and antenna array on the stern were wrong. Image eight seemed to take forever, as the system dropped link each time Alan hit the image button on his console.

"Paul, give us a little altitude."

"Roger."

It was the first word that Stevens had spoken in an hour. Alan felt the plane climb and noticed that he was wet with cold sweat. His eyes felt swollen. He switched the intercom to limit it to the back end.

"I blew the meeting with Anna."

Harry didn't turn his head.

"What'd you expect?"

"She's going to Shreed. I should have held her."

"For what, shoplifting?"

"Look at the crap she dropped on me for ten thousand."

Harry smiled enigmatically. "I'm not sure it's crap."

Alan stared at the screen in front of him, still dissatisfied, and murmured *should have done something* even as he cued his radio.

"Ranger Two, I need a better aspect on contact eight."

"Roger. Turning to zero four zero."

"We're going to need gas soon." Stevens sounded bored.

"How soon?"

"Thirty minutes."

"You copy that, Ranger Two?"

"I copy."

Alan settled the cursor on the moving dot that represented contact eight and hit the image button again. The image danced on the split screen, a tiny, throbbing blob that bore no resemblance to a boat. It crept around the screen like a creature in a video game.

"Looks like a periscope," muttered Soleck.

"Stern aspect. Heading straight away, or close enough." Alan felt a little rise of hope. If it was a stern aspect, this contact had the required number of antennas on the stern.

"Ranger Two, I need a broadside aspect on contact eight, over?"

"Roger. Wait one."

Alan held the image and watched it rotate slowly as the other MARI bird, fifteen miles to the north and east, gradually gained on the contact.

"Bow antenna!" Soleck shouted. "Bet you that's our guy. Bet anything!"

It would take minutes to get a full, side-on picture and get the computer to measure the length. Alan looked at the coastline on the datalink, put into the system by Soleck while they planned Opera Glass. Alan wished he had Craw in the other seat to spell him or to pull up the electronic detection gear and watch for Pakistani SAM sites on the coast. They were close, now—less than one hundred miles from Pakistan. Contact eight was less than twenty miles from the coast.

"Ranger Two, do you have anything on ESM?"

"Roger, Ranger One. We have multiple radar hits from associated SAM sites around Karachi."

"Ranger Two, contact eight is probably the target."

" 'Probably' won't cut it, Alan."

He knew that. The Indian Ocean was balanced on the fine edge between local violence and all-out war. An American plane shooting at a Pakistani ship would probably push the conflict over the edge.

"He's about thirty minutes from land."

"Ranger Two, we have six more contacts we haven't imaged."

Alan watched the green outline grow on his screen, pixel by pixel. The image was a fair match to the photo, and the length looked as if it would be about right.

"Ranger Two, the antenna count is right."

"Length?"

"I don't have it yet. Ranger Two, if we don't call in the guns now, they won't get to him in time."

"I'm aware of that, Ranger One." *So shut up*, Rafe was saying.

Alan saved the image on his screen and imaged contact nine, which proved to be a fishing boat with an obvious net derrick amidships.

Contact ten had the same configuration and was moving parallel, the two probably dragging a net between them. Then they lost the link for long seconds and Soleck could be heard cursing in the front end until the resync program functioned and lights came back to green.

Ranger Two had a good broadside aspect on contact eleven, a cigarette boat about ten meters in length. The antennas weren't easy to count, but she appeared to have at least one on the bow and several on the stern. Contact eleven was a good deal farther out from the coast than contact eight but appeared to have roughly the same goal. Alan cycled back to contact eight and got a good broadside image. Contact eight seemed a little longer. When he set them side by side on the screen, neither he nor Soleck could find enough points of difference to sort them out. Alan cursed.

"Ranger Two, contact eleven also matches search criteria."

"Roger, Ranger One."

Alan looked over at Harry and pressed his intercom switch.

"Any ideas?"

Bahrain 2045 GMT (2345L).

Dukas landed at Bahrain's Manama airport two hours late. Changing planes at Riyadh had been a mess, with delay piled on delay, but at least it had given him time to check the disk that Sally Baranowski had given him. It seemed years ago that she had put it in his hand at BWI. On the screen of his laptop in the Riyadh business center, George Shreed's comm plans for Chinese Checkers had come up with an almost offensively new crispness—crafted years ago in Washington, now ageless in Saudi Arabia.

There were, as she had told him, three plans—Indonesia, Colombia, and Pakistan. Nothing was there for Dubai, although that was where Shreed had been seen by O'Neill. Shreed had now to be in transit—no matter where he was now, he was in transit until he found a protector and settled somewhere. Dukas figured that it was protection that he had been seeking in Nicosia, hoping to trade a lifetime's knowledge for a new identity in Israel. An odd end for a spy, perhaps, but not necessarily a bad one: he would get a new life in a warm country, and the Israelis would get a fund of information, which they would cajole and bully from him for the rest of his life. They would hoard what they could use, shop the rest around the world for whatever it would bring.

Coming into Bahrain, Dukas's mind was on the chase ahead. Or at least he hoped that there was a chase ahead: if Shreed had been lost, all that they could do was try to cover the three comm plans with NCIS people in the locality and hope that he would turn up. More likely, the CIA and the FBI would recover from the shock of Shreed's flight and take over the investigation, and Dukas and Alan and Harry would be out in the cold. Thinking of being shut out, he realized how much he wanted Shreed: the investigation hadn't been only about Rose, he understood now. It had always been about her betrayer, too. And it had become personal.

The flaps came down and the aircraft turned into its final approach. Dukas, sitting in an aisle seat, merely glanced at the window to see the blue waters of the Gulf for a few seconds; then they straightened, and he looked ahead. He was planning his moves. He had called NCIS Bahrain from Nicosia and told them to meet him and to have an international, satellite-connected cellphone for him. He had asked for the ten thousand dollars for the detective, Khouri, and an additional ten thousand for himself. The duty officer at the other end must have been a stoic; he had said only, "Okay—okay—" and not reacted otherwise. Not his money, seemed to be the attitude.

The wheels banged and the tires screeched and the engines revved. He was on the ground in Bahrain.

He was met first by somebody from a VIP welcoming firm (thirty bucks per greeting—not so *very* VIP) who escorted him through passport control and customs, waving a hand and rapping out terse Arabic at the personnel as if he were a government VIP himself. Then he steered Dukas through a side door into a corridor lined with departure gates, and there was a cheerful, light-skinned African-American named Buse from the local NCIS office. When he saw the VIP guide, Buse shouted, "You got Dukas?" He held up a cellphone. "You got mail!"

Dukas pushed past his escort. He was reaching for the phone before he got to Buse, then pressed it against his ear with both their hands still on it. "I got a car!" Buse whispered. He started to lead Dukas along the corridor.

"Dukas!"

Static, a high-pitched hiss, squeals and glurps as if he was listening to somebody's gut. A voice said thinly, ". . . not very good—"

"Can't hear you! Hello!"

More hissing. Dukas looked at Buse. Buse shrugged. "It was okay a second ago. Somebody named O'Neill—" He was steering Dukas through the passing travelers.

Dukas mashed the little phone against his ear. "Harry? Harry?"

"Mike?" The voice was thin and faint.

"Where are you?"

"Flying in a Navy S-3 . . . Alan. We're over the—"

"What?"

"—Ocean, Indian Ocean. We've got the target on the . . ."

"Target?" *Shreed?*

". . . radar array. Whiz-bang stuff. He's headed for Pakistan, Mike—Pakistan—did you get me?"

It clicked for Dukas. "Harry, listen! He has an old comm plan for—!" Dukas was ready to say *Northern Pakistan! North of Islamabad, a place called Jolcut,* and then he remembered that the line wasn't secure.

Hiss, gurgle. ". . . Pakistan?"

"I'll send it to Valdez. You hear me? Harry, I'll message Valdez. Okay?" *Goddamit, goddam the cellphone, goddam the airplane, goddam Shreed!* He was afraid he was blowing their secrets sky-high if anybody was listening. E-mail was a lot safer than an open cellphone. Harry must have an encrypted link from Valdez; that was the way to go. He glanced at Buse, then looked around them in frustration and backed against a wall between a men's and women's toilet.

"Harry—?"

It was then that he saw her. She was just handing her passport to the gate attendant. Radiantly beautiful, dressed to kill, as seemingly relaxed as if she were heading for a holiday.

Anna!

He didn't need to check the photo Harry had taken at Pompeii. There was no question.

"Harry—!"

Noise, noise, "—to hear you."

"Harry, she's here! She's just boarding a plane for—" He checked the board. "Tashkent. *Tashkent!*" *Jesus, what was she heading to Tashkent for?*

"Her? You've been in touch with *her?*"

Suddenly, the phone was clear, and Dukas could even hear the sound of the engines. "Harry, she's just going down the gangway to an aircraft for Tashkent!" He grabbed his VIP escort. "Get me on that plane. That one—Tashkent—!"

"Mike, what the hell are you saying? Alan lost her last night—you see her?"

"I saw her; now she's gone on board a plane. I'm trying to get on—" The attendant was closing the gate. Dukas looked at the VIP guide, who was standing by the desk, hands spread in the universal sign of resigned helplessness, shaking his head. "Shit! The plane's going—!"

"Mike, she's going to meet *him*. We know she is."

"I gotta follow her—!"

"Mike, no, what'd you say about Pakistan?"

As he told Harry again that he'd e-mail Valdez, Dukas saw what was happening. He knew where Tashkent was; he knew that Anna had been born in one of the Stans. With Shreed heading for Pakistan, the likeliest plan was for her to go there via her home territory, and the likeliest place for them to meet was the comm plan from Chinese Checkers—and at this point, all he could do was play the likelihood. His own best move was to go where the comm plan led. "I'm following."

"You're starting to break up. You're going to Tashkent?"

"No, no—where *he's* going. Where's Alan?"

"He's here . . . me. Are . . . sure . . . -stan?"

"As sure as I am of anything. Harry? Harry?"

But there was only the high hiss and a sound like ticking. Dukas handed the phone to Buse. "Keep that at your ear for one minute and see if he comes up again; if he doesn't, hang up and wait." He turned to the VIP guide, who had joined them. "Get me on a plane to Islamabad. Now. Okay? Go!"

He turned back to Buse. "Anything?"

Buse shook his head.

"Keep listening. Can you listen to me at the same time? Okay, did you get me some money?" Buse nodded and reached inside his golf jacket for a sheaf of papers. He handed them over and followed them with a pen, made a writing motion. The papers were receipts for the ten thousand for Khouri and the ten thousand in cash. Dukas began signing, using the vertical wall as a desk.

"Zip," Buse said. He punched the cellphone off. "I'm Jack Buse. I know who you are."

They shook hands. Dukas was signing papers. "You lay on the VIP guy?"

"Thought it would move the shit faster through the pipe."

"Good man." Dukas found which copies were his and handed the rest to Buse. "You got my money?"

"Kind of a bundle. Would you believe we had some Navy guy leave half a *million* in cash with us last night? Christ, in a suitcase!" He was unfastening a waist wallet, wriggling out of it and dragging the belt from his pants like a snake. "Better count it."

Dukas began to push the thing down inside his own pants. "No time, I hope. That my satellite phone?"

"Yes, sir. Six thousand bucks' worth."

"Want me to sign?"

"From stock."

Dukas pushed the wallet down and dragged it around to the rear so that it rode on the slope of his buttocks. It made him look as if he had an even bigger butt, which he didn't need, but it was pretty well hidden.

"Buse."

"Sir."

"I gotta go to Islamabad. What have we got there?"

"Zip. *Nada.* Pakistan's out of bounds. There's also a State advisory. I don't recommend Islamabad, Mike—that's a war zone. Try Karachi."

Dukas shook his head. "I get to Karachi, the Paks shut down their airlines because there's a war on, I'm stuck. You know anything about getting a gun up there?"

"Just holler. They're up to their ass in guns." He came close, lowered his voice. "Tell you what I'll do. We *might* have a contact in Islamabad. Can't provide any muscle, only information, maybe a little—" He rocked his hand back and forth; he could have meant women, dope, guns. "You call me every hour on the hour until I get there—just press 1 on the cell-phone; it's already programmed in. Okay?" He held up a computer disk. "This is yours, too. It's unclassified, but it's got some stuff on it you might want—contact numbers, e-mail addresses here and DC, stuff like that. Jeez, if I'd known where you were going, I'd have thrown in a dictionary."

"Pakistani?"

"There isn't a Pakistani. They speak a bunch of languages. You're go-ing *north* of Islamabad? Up there, it's Baluch."

Dukas eyed him. "How come you know that?"

Buse shrugged, grinned. "I'm smart."

The VIP man joined them at that point and told Dukas that he was on a flight to Islamabad if he could pay in the next ten minutes. "And I suggest you do, sir—it may be the last one."

Dukas started walking in the direction the man led him. "Can you get me a Baluch dictionary?"

The man frowned. "I can get you a computerized phrase book of lan-guages used on the Indian subcontinent, sir. It would include Baluch. However, a *dictionary*—"

"That'd be great! Do it, okay? Meet me at my gate—you're really super— Hey, Buse!"

"Sir."

"That phone call I got—did they give you a way to call them back?"

"He gave me a number in Dubai, said it was his office—it's 2 on your phone."

Shreed was heading for Pakistan. Anna was heading for Tashkent. Harry and Alan were heading for—where? Could they land a Navy air-craft in Pakistan under current conditions? The way he saw it, Anna would make her way down from Tashkent, probably to Islamabad, by air—between the two cities was the Hindu Kush, mountains towering almost as high as Everest; she wasn't going to walk. Shreed would make his way up from the coast. If the comm plan was followed, they would meet in front of an ancient mosque in a tiny village called Jolcut. In an area that was now a war zone on the border of Kashmir.

Dukas bought the *International Herald-Tribune*. Chinese troops were massed on the Kashmir border, and some Chinese aircraft, including helos capable of carrying special forces, were reported actually over western Kashmir, close to Jolcut.

Well, Dukas said to himself, *that seems to leave it up to me, doesn't it. Thank God I'm a superhero.*

Over the Indian Ocean
0143 GMT (0443L) Monday.

Harry turned off the cellphone and clipped it to his palmtop. "Mike says Shreed's going to Pakistan to meet Anna."

"How the hell does *Mike* know?"

"He's going to message me via Valdez, then we'll know. Valdez already said Shreed and Anna have a meeting set for—twenty-six hours from now." He was pushing buttons on the palmtop. "I'm trying to get Valdez."

"We're fucked. We can't follow him to Pakistan."

Harry looked at the cockpit.

"Your pilot any good?" Alan read his intent in the glance.

"Harry, you're out of your gourd!"

"You want George Shreed, or not?"

"What do you think!"

"I think that we take this plane and we land somewhere. When we get Shreed, we send for the plane. Dukas can't do this, Al."

"Stevens will have a cow."

"He can leave the meter running, for all I care."

Contact eight had merged with the Pakistani coast. If that was Shreed, he was now ashore. Contact eleven was still a few miles out, well into Pakistani territorial waters and moving at an astonishing sixty knots. Alan stared into the simple green geometry on the screen and made his call. He switched his intercom to full cockpit.

"Paul, let's hit the tanker."

"About time."

"Get a full bag, Paul. We're going to Pakistan."

"Like fuck we are!"

"We think we know where Shreed's going. We aren't beaten yet and I'm not going to give up."

"Is getting my ass shot off by a Pak SAM going to save the world?"

"You want to live the rest of your life as a passed-over O-4? Come on, Paul! Soleck knows the Pak radar coverage. *We can do this.* Nobody can do this right now but you. You want to make a difference, Paul? We have one shot, and it's right *now*."

"Are you fuckin' nuts? Look, you said yourself we were in a state of near war with Pakistan. You want to take this giant radar reflector right in there?"

"Yup. And I want you to fly it."

Soleck cut in, his voice pitched high with excitement.

"I say we should go!"

"Fuck, that clears it all up. The teenager wants to go." Stevens sounded a little manic himself.

Alan felt the plane turning toward the tanker. He thought of his failure with Anna, his other failures in a chain that bound him to that moment and Stevens.

Harry was massaging the laptop, making little grunting noises as it did what he wanted. Then he grabbed his GPU and started fingering that. He slapped his leg and shouted, "Got it!"

Alan switched to rear-seat comm. "What's the word?"

"A comm plan, forget the details for now. Jolcut—some two-bit town with an antique mosque where the meeting is. It's north of Islamabad, up in the bad country, man—close to Kashmir. mountainous, I mean, that's *goat* country. We can put down at a little import-export field in the mountains and head north in a truck."

Alan switched back to full comm.

"What's it going to be, Paul?"

"I'm still thinking it over. We have to tank either way. You going to tell the CAG?"

"*I'm* still thinking it over." Alan tried to match Stevens's tone. Stevens laughed without mirth.

Alan switched to communicate with the other S-3. "Ranger Two, this is Ranger One, over?"

"Roger, Ranger One."

"*Play Catch*, Ranger Two, and *Dodge Ball*." The comm card said that *Play Catch* meant they were coming in to tank. *Dodge Ball* meant they were going to go to emissions control, or EMCON. They would no longer talk on the radio or run their radars. They were close enough to the Pakistani coast to make such precautions sensible.

"So you're *not* going to tell him."

"I'm not going to ask him to order you, if that's what you mean. I'm not going to lay this one on him."

"You're laying it on me, instead."

"That's right."

Stevens was quiet while he pulled the flashlight off his flight gear and pulled abreast of the other S-3, a dark bulk against the starlit sky. He cycled the running lights and turned his flashlight on.

"I've never done this before," said Soleck.

"Yeah, I remember my first beer, too," said Stevens, and he throttled down and dropped into trail below the other plane. The basket of the refueling line became visible well above them and began to descend. Stevens handed his flashlight to Soleck and flexed his fingers like a gunfighter preparing to draw.

"We pull alongside and flash our lights. That means we're ready. He flashes back and starts the hose. When we're done, we do the same again so he knows we're clear."

"Cool."

"What the hell do they teach you guys at the RAG, anyway?"

"Tactics," said Soleck with some pride.

"Mostly, in S-3s, we give gas," said Stevens with a sour pride of his own and pushed the throttle forward.

"Paul, have you ever missed the basket?"

"Not that I can remember."

Bang, and they were in.

Alan leaned out into the center aisle and watched the JP-5 pour into their tanks. He had the radar off, but he didn't need it to tell him that contact eleven was well in with the coast, perhaps even in port. When the fuel passed thirteen thousand pounds, he was pretty sure that Stevens had decided to take them to Pakistan. "Evan, do they have their FLIR camera on us?"

"Sure. It's SOP during tanking."

Alan pulled out his kneeboard pad and scribbled, erased, scribbled some more. Then he pushed up into the front cockpit and crouched behind the throttle panel of the central console. He looked up until he could see the nose of the FLIR pod pointed at them. Then he put the red cap on his flashlight and started flashing it.

Stevens's concentration was on the plane and its relationship to the aircraft above him. Soleck was more curious. "What are you doing, sir?"

"Signaling in EMCON, Mister Soleck."

He finished his signal and crawled back into his seat. He switched the intercom to the back. "Harry, where's this airfield?"

"Are we going?"

"I think so."

"Didn't we used to give people orders in the military?"

"Harry, I can't order this guy to do this."

"I know. Just talkin' trash. The field is north of Beta."

Alan fiddled with his keyboard and raised the overlay that showed the coast of Pakistan.

"It's about here," said Harry, leaning over and putting his finger on the screen.

"I'd be happier if you could call it closer than that."

"Sure." He handed his GPS unit across, the readout startlingly clear in the dark. There was a latitude and longitude on the screen, as well as altitude, and range, and bearing.

"Nice."

"Surely you've got a GPS in this thing."

"It's four times the size and works half the time."

Alan felt the plane rise under him, and he watched as they came alongside Rafe's plane. This time Soleck flashed the lights. Rafe waved from the other cockpit, and his landing lights came on and went off. When they began to fall away to the north, Alan could no longer contain himself. "What's it going to be, Paul?"

"Oh, we're going to Pakistan."

Soleck shouted, "Way cool!"

"Paul, I'm giving Evan a GPS unit with the coordinates and altitude of the field where we want to land."

"You have a plan for crossing the coast?"

"I'm looking at the radar coverage now."

"You sent something to the other plane in Morse?"

"Yeah. Chances are they won't even read it for a couple of hours. The TACCO has other things on his mind."

"So you knew I'd go."

"No, I hoped."

"We're going in low, right?"

"Yep."

"Then why don't I call Karachi Air Traffic Control and declare an emergency?" Declaring a false emergency was a crime in international law, but it seemed pretty pale besides violating another nation's airspace.

"And?"

"And we drop like a rock, slip under the coverage, and hope they don't see us. If they do, we claim the old hydraulics leak and say we need an immediate landing. Better than nothing."

"Better than anything I thought of. Do it."

FORTY SECONDS LATER, Rafe heard Stevens's voice calmly announce a total hydraulics failure and declare an emergency on the Guard frequency. He thought through his years in S-3s, their little quirks, and the likelihood that one would lose its hydraulics after a five-hour flight, especially a plane that had so recently had a total hydraulics refit. He looked out over his port wing at the faint line of gray that marked where dawn would soon be coming, and he did not smile, although one of his eyebrows twitched.

"Alan fucking Craik," he muttered.

34

GEORGE SHREED PULLED HIMSELF UP THE PIER WITH his hands, his weak legs barely capable of supporting his weight. He was forcing himself to wait twelve hours between doses now, and the pain kept him focused on his goal. He reached the last rung on the ladder and hauled himself onto the pier, and one of the two men who had brought him over handed him his bag with enviable effortlessness. Then they both clambered up beside him, so close that Shreed could smell their breath in the predawn stillness. They would see him as a weak old man, and probably demand more money. He looked down the pier to the lights of the railway station, just visible through the morning cooking smoke.

"You promised another ten thousand dollars." The man's English was very good, and the old George Shreed would have tried to recruit him on the spot. Unlimited access to the whole Persian Gulf via the boat and command of several languages added up to a natural spy. Probably, he was already working for somebody. Shreed smiled, reached into his bag with unfeigned weariness, and came out holding a large automatic pistol.

"No, I didn't. But if you want to get me to the train station, I'll give you another thousand. Or we can stand here until I get tired and shoot you."

"This is a misunderstanding, surely." The other man pushed the first one aside. "It seems fair that we get more. What if someone saw us in Oman? It may ruin our trade." Neither seemed alarmed by the appearance of the gun in Shreed's hand—respectful, but not frightened. *Probably a regular event on this run.* This seemed like a bargaining tactic, not a direct threat; they didn't strike him as the right kind of men to just kill him for his bag.

"Train station. Okay? Good. Please walk in front of me."

"My brother needs to stay with the boat."

Brother was a term tossed about with some ease in these regions, and Shreed was unsure whether the older man would really do as a hostage to prevent a shot in the back. It was dark, however, and both men seemed satisfied with the thousand-dollar bonus, and Shreed didn't have a lot of options.

"Okay, friends, we'll all walk down to the end of the pier together, and then your brother can walk back while I can see him. You get another thousand. Everybody walks away happy. Ready?"

The two Pakistani smugglers shrugged and began walking down the pier. The set of their shoulders said it all. *Inshallah.*

Vicinity of Bela, Pakistan
0255 GMT (0555L).

They were below one thousand feet, with enormous ridges rising well above them on either side. Alan had the ESM gear up in the back, and, although his stomach lurched every time he got a hit, none of them had proven to be radars. Perhaps the unknown signals were radio-repeating towers or cellphones or microwave dishes; none met the computer's parameters for an air-search radar.

The GPS unit had sounded several alarms, and Harry was now unstrapped, leaning forward between Stevens and Soleck and peering out into the predawn gloom. Somewhere off to the east, beyond the ridge, the sun was rising on Karachi. They were in the foothills of the Pab, according to Harry.

"Khyber Pass up north another three hundred miles. We're on the edge of the hill country. The Brits fought here, Alexander fought here, and the CIA fought the Russians here."

Stevens snorted. "Thanks for the history lesson. I'd rather have an airfield."

"Airfield's about twenty-five miles. Keep following the valley over that range of hills. I have to call ahead."

"Harry, how well do you know these guys?"

"Well enough."

He took his helmet off and tucked his head against his neck, covering his right ear with one hand while his outstretched elbows kept him wedged in the doorway between the cockpit and the after cabin. He kept pulling the cellphone from his ear and staring at the screen, clearly trying to wish a connection into being.

When he got through, he spoke in Arabic for several minutes. Alan had no idea that Harry spoke Arabic—not the touristic mangle that Alan managed in the souk, but real Arabic—although it made sense for a man whose business was in the Middle East. Again, he was reminded how Harry had changed, and how little he really knew him.

"Do we have twenty thousand in cash?" Harry said now.

"Yes." In fact, Alan had several hundred thousand; he had deposited only half the money with the NCIS in Bahrain.

Harry went back to the phone.

"YOU LANDED HERE BEFORE?" Stevens wasn't taking his eyes off the ground, but his voice was level.

"Twice," Harry said.

"What's the approach?"

"Come in from the west and fly down the runway. They'll set fires to mark the approach."

"That's a mighty big chunk of rock for a blown approach." Stevens sounded almost happy.

The airstrip was a tiny ribbon of gravel under a mountain, the first true mountain of the central Makhan. It took up the full length of a valley, with a cluster of huts and a single hangar at the far end. The vegetation was sparse at this altitude, and the first kiss of the sun revealed a

Martian landscape of jagged red rock. Terraced fields showed as wide green steps climbing the shoulders of the ridges, and dots of dark green in the red-gray indicated where trees grew among the rocks.

"Get in your seat and strap in." The cliff had grown to fill the whole windscreen.

Harry tumbled back into the after compartment and fumbled with the toggles until Alan forced them into the seat's harness. They began a sharp turn.

"It's going to be a bumpy night?" Harry's gentle sarcasm stayed with them through a turn as tight as the break on approach to a carrier. The nose lifted and dropped like a bucking horse. The cliff face generated serious wind-shear effects.

"Any problem if I just land now?"

"They won't have the lights on."

"Screw that. I'm here and I don't want to play games with that cliff again. There's enough light to land."

Alan heard the engine noise drop away and felt the loss of altitude. They seemed to be gliding down and down and down. Alan's window showed the first glimmer of sunrise over the eastern ridges, Harry's the blur of the cliff face passing them. From Alan's seat, the cliff seemed to be a few feet beyond the wingtip. That *had* to be an illusion.

Soleck and Stevens had begun to exchange landing checks. It sounded so normal that for a fraction of time Alan imagined they were landing on a carrier. Still the feeling of weightless descent. Each buffet of wind threatened to push them into the cliff, but Stevens's compensations were precise. Alan wondered what their angle of attack would be after such a steep descent, and then he thought of the landing in Sigonella and tried not to worry. Stevens knew what he was doing.

His view of the sunrise was gone, now, blotted out by the last ridge that defined the edge of the valley. They had descended from early morning into the end of night. Alan risked a peek at the windscreen, but all he could see was the ridge at the end of the airstrip. And then he saw Stevens's hand on the throttle, and he snapped upright and into his ejection position. The throttle went forward. The plane roared with life. The rapid descent slowed, slowed, and they met the ground with a hard thump.

The gravel was uneven, and the plane vibrated for several seconds. *It's like landing in Africa,* thought Alan. Then they began to slow, and, well before they ran out of gravel strip, they had made the invisible transition from dumping speed to rolling taxi. They were down.

"Hey, civilian guy, what kind of plane did you bring in here?"

"Call me Harry."

"Okay, Harry. What kind of plane did you bring in here?"

"A Cessna 184."

"That's what I thought. Don't list this as a bingo field for S-3s, okay?" Stevens was high on life, happy in a way that Alan had never seen. Soleck was silent.

"Where do I park?"

"Roll it right into the hangar. We don't want to be seen, and its paid for."

"Gas?"

"They're looking into it."

"Hotels?"

"The best that money can buy. A little above per diem. Alan, we have a four-by-four waiting to take us north. We'll take turns sleeping in the truck."

"How far?"

"Five hundred miles. Maybe twenty hours. Could be more."

Alan unstrapped, found his bag, and started stripping his flight gear. "Money?"

"Leave some for the pilots. We may need the rest."

Alan had changed before the auxiliary power was cut and the pilots had finished their checklists. He took his time, methodically cutting labels from every item of clothing. He made up a packet with one hundred thousand dollars and handed it to Soleck.

"You still got a gun?"

"Yes, sir!"

"You're responsible for that money. Don't spend it all in one place."

"Roger that."

"If Pakistani brass come, you had an emergency declared and you landed at the first field you could find."

Stevens laughed.

"Hell, we only glided three hundred miles."

"Let them worry about that. Don't mention us. Here's my celphone.

If you can charge it, do so. If not, only turn it on every hour on the hour."

"I hear you."

"Thanks for getting us here, Paul."

"No problem. Just don't get your ass shot off. If you guys die, I'll *never* get out of here."

"Paul, I may have to ask you to fly farther into Pakistan and land at another unknown field. Maybe at night."

Stevens smiled, a slow, wicked smile that transformed his face from that of a dopey, overweight jet jock to a Basil Rathbone villain.

"I heard you."

"No argument?"

"Cowboy, I'm in for the whole ride now. Getting this far was worth an Air Medal. Getting you out, if you make it, will be worth a Silver Star. Full commander. Another look at command. Right?"

"Yeah, I expect so." It seemed crass to Alan. But maybe one man's crass was another man's heroic.

Stevens must have seen his expression. "Fuck you, Craik. You think I'm blind to what we're doing?" Stevens shook his head, as if disappointed in Alan again. "We're saving the world. I'm almost happy to be here. Get your ass in the truck before I sing the 'Star-Spangled Banner.' "

Alan stuffed the rest of the cash into his sleeping bag sack and pushed the bag in on top.

"Guns?"

Harry patted his shoulder bag.

"A shotgun for me and an Uzi for you. And some other precautions. Give me some of your cash. I'll need to pay the landing fee up front."

Alan handed him a bundle of bills.

"Get a receipt."

Harry rolled his eye, but when he came back he had a scrap of envelope with writing in Arabic. Alan scrawled the amount, the date, and a countersignature at the top and handed it to Soleck. Ten minutes later, buried in the back of a large, military-looking Toyota truck driven by a hillman named Kamil, they were bouncing into the sunrise on a dirt road headed east.

Karachi, Pakistan 0730 (1130L).

The villages along the track were cubist dreams, long strips of brightly colored boxes set against a landscape of sand and blowing trash. Children stood and watched the trains go by, even the youngest girls swathed from head to toe in printed muslin. They showed only enough interest to raise their heads, their eyes devoid of curiosity, their faces blank.

When he saw that the ticket collector was checking identity cards, Shreed had a moment of panic—which passport was safe here?

He elected to use the one with his own name on it. The power of its American seal should be enough to send the ticket collector on his way. Perhaps an element of unaccustomed fatalism had entered him by osmosis from the country he raced through.

He took the passport out and held it open to the man when he paused at the seat. The ticket collector glanced at the cover without interest, noted the presence of a US five-dollar bill, and moved on.

35

NCIS HQ.

INFORMATION ABOUT THE HUNT FOR GEORGE SHREED reached Washington by trickles and inferences all Sunday night, but it had immediate consequences on Monday morning. Ray Suter was told to stay at his desk and "keep himself available." At NCIS, the halls were full of rumors that heads were rolling at the Office of Naval Intelligence. Triffler, to his astonishment, was in the midst of everything: he had a face-to-face meeting with the CNO, and he encountered a Rose Siciliano who had gone from accused outcast to CNO staffer and was suddenly a full commander.

Triffler was summoned early to the CNO's office to make an unprepared brief, a surprise that didn't terrify him but one that didn't impress him with his own worth, either: he knew that he was there as a stand-in for Dukas. The brief—a summary of his and Dukas's work on the interagency balls-up that had ruined Rose's career—was not done in the Pentagon briefing suite but in the Chief's office, with nobody else present but Rose and a captain who proved to be the CNO's intel staffer.

"So you don't know precisely how somebody at the Agency got somebody in this office to implicate Commander Siciliano?"

"No, sir."

"And you don't know who was responsible?"

"Dukas thought he knew, sir."

"Do *you* know?"

"No, sir."

"Why not?"

Triffler knew that there was a time to swallow hard and a time to say you've been screwed. He took a deep breath. "Agent Dukas got a direct order to concentrate on Commander Siciliano's case and forget the inter-agency thing."

"A direct order from who?"

Triffler had read it in a file in the twenty minutes he had had in a cab coming over. "It was passed to him by our boss from CNI. The signature was a Captain Veering."

The CNO looked at the intel captain, who nodded almost imperceptibly. Triffler could hear Veering's head start to roll. The CNO's face was dark with anger, but he kept his voice even as he said to Triffler, "Agent Dukas believed that the source of the lie that implicated Commander Siciliano was this guy Shreed?"

"Definitely."

"Where is this Shreed now?"

Triffler was not afraid to say he didn't know.

The captain spoke up. "Agent Dukas appears to be pursuing him to Pakistan—did you know that?"

Triffler admitted that he didn't know that, either. The CNO looked at the captain, who said, "NCIS Bahrain reported him in Bahrain at six-thirty last night our time, and off about eight-thirty, destination Islamabad."

Triffler sank deeper into confessions of ignorance. "I don't know about that, either, I'm afraid. Dukas doesn't have a secure link with me."

"Or with anybody," the captain growled.

The CNO turned to Rose. "Your husband's in on this, too, is he?"

"He's a designated agent of Dukas's in this business with the woman he calls Anna. They were supposed to have a meeting yesterday in Bahrain."

The captain smiled. "Her husband put half a million *in cash* into the NCIS, Bahrain, office safe. She'd turned it down. Then Dukas reported he'd seen her at Manama and she was headed for Tashkent."

The CNO's voice showed his irritation at this complexity. "*Tashkent!* How the hell does this relate to Shreed?"

"She and Shreed have been in touch, apparently with an eye to hooking up. We get this from an independent contractor who's, uh, surveilling Shreed's Internet use."

"That legal?"

The captain cocked a skeptical eyebrow. "I'm having it looked at."

"Make sure the answer is 'yes.' "

It was Rose's turn to smile. "The contractor is a man named Harry O'Neill, sir. Ex-Navy. Maybe you heard of him when my husband flew him out of Uganda and landed a Cessna on the *Rangoon*."

"Another friend?"

"Close friend, sir."

"Where is *he* now?"

The captain cleared his throat. He, too, it seemed, was having trouble keeping up with the tangle of Rose's pals. "He seems to be aboard the S-3 that was pursuing Shreed in the IO, sir. With Lieutenant-Commander Craik—Commander Siciliano's husband."

"How do we know that? The *Jefferson*?"

"The *Jeff*, plus this O'Neill seems to have an encrypted link with his office here in DC, so we also got a message that way. Via an ex–Navy man named Valdez who is, uh—" He looked sheepish. "Another friend of Commander Siciliano's."

The CNO looked hard at her. "Trustworthy?"

"I'd take him anywhere, any task. He was with me on the Peacemaker project as an EM."

"Okay." The CNO rubbed his hands together as he thought. "Nail down some sort of contract with O'Neill and his firm. Use his Internet link as comm when you have to. *If* this bastard Shreed hasn't compromised our codes, we're still safe to communicate with Craik via the *Jefferson*, but stay alert for a change there if we find that Shreed has bitched us. The real problem is Agent Dukas, who's out there on a shoeshine and a smile, as far as I can tell. He kind of a loner, Triffler?"

"Well—he does things his own way, sir."

"So he hasn't got a STU and he hasn't got codes, and God knows what he's doing. How's he going to communicate with Craik and the S-3?"

"He picked up a satellite cellphone in Bahrain," the captain said. "We think he's got e-mail capability that way; otherwise, he's got to find a place to connect his laptop. Ordinarily, that wouldn't be a problem in a big city like Islamabad, but that's a war zone now."

"Do we know what he plans to do in Islamabad?"

The captain shook his head.

"And Craik and his crew?"

The captain's eyebrows semaphored again. "They gassed outside Pakistani territorial waters eight hours ago and went EMCON. If they headed for Islamabad, they should be there by now—but they didn't file a flight plan and we haven't heard zip from the Paks. We've got the naval attaché nosing around for word of them."

The CNO eyed Rose. "Would your husband take an S-3 into a war zone without a country clearance?"

"He, uh—it's my understanding, sir, that his admiral gave him a lot of leeway in, um, pursuing Shreed."

"I like yes or no answers. Would he take his aircraft into a war zone without a country clearance?"

"Yes, sir."

The CNO exchanged a look with his intel captain and sat back. "Folks, I've got two battle groups cooling their heels because we don't know how bad Shreed's spying has been. I want this sonofabitch caught, and I want him caught *now*." He looked up at them. "And I want him caught by *us*. The Agency and the Bureau will take twenty-four to thirty-six hours to gear up, and that'll be too late; besides, as you said, Gil, it's a war zone now. So—comm support for everybody, number one; number two, what's the combat situation up there? Gil, we got anybody over at Combined HUMINT now? If we have, I want them here pronto, and I want to know every agent they can scrape out of the files in Pakistan. And tell them that if they blab, it's their career. We got anything like marines within striking distance?"

The captain shook his head.

The CNO looked grim. He nodded at Triffler. "Thank you."

Meaning, *Get to work.* Except that Triffler didn't see what he could do.

After Triffler was gone, the CNO's face turned grim and he said to the captain, "Get me Admiral Kessler. I want to know what the hell he thinks he's doing." His look moved on to Rose, and the scowl he gave her said, *And I want to know what the hell your husband thinks he's doing, too.*

A DEFINITE AIR of us-vs-them prevailed at both NCIS and ONI, with the Navy the *us* and the CIA *them*. Nonetheless, Triffler tried to keep a back channel open to the Agency through their Inter-Agency Liaison Office, hoping that Menzes would know of it and would be receptive to any news coming from the police investigation into the murder of Tony Moscowic.

All morning, no such news came. Triffler almost had to hold back his own hands from picking up the telephone to call Moisher. He was afraid that the young detective would give up on the search for "AMH" too early, that the allure of Monday Night Football or an early visit to his favorite bar would make it easy to give up the boring round of checks against businesses culled from the Yellow Pages. When, at noon on Monday, no news had come, Triffler was tense and angry, telling himself that any rookie cop could have found the Angel of Mercy Hospice by now. *He ought to have it!* he screamed inwardly. Then he realized that he was starting to act like Dukas.

If it walks like a duck and it talks like a duck— At lunchtime, he phoned out for pizza. He made coffee, spilled some on his immaculate desk, and didn't bother to wipe it up. He was practicing sympathetic magic: if he behaved like Dukas, maybe things would turn his way.

And the telephone rang.

"Guess what?" a voice said.

"Moisher?"

"Guess what!"

Triffler felt a surge of anger. "I told you, I don't like guessing games! What, already?"

"Jeez." The terribly young voice sounded let down. "I thought you'd be surprised. I found AMH."

"You're kidding!" Now it was Triffler's turn to sound young and excited. "Where? What is it? Did they know Moscowic?"

So Moisher told him the whole story from the beginning—not just how he found AMH, but *the whole story.* How he called the Montgomery and PG and Virginia police. How much help he got and how much he hadn't. How many names he pulled from four phone books. How many calls he had made on Sunday. How many calls—

"Moisher!"

"I'm getting to it, I'm getting to it! Just listen to this—at ten o'clock, I call—"

"Moisher, get to the point, will you? I appreciate all this detail, and it'll make a piss-elegant report, but just give me the facts, okay?"

"These are the facts."

"The *salient* facts."

"What's 'salient'?"

"Important."

"That's what I'm doing. Anyways, okay, I'm going into too much detail, I know; I'm excited, okay? So here's the bottom line: right this minute as I speak, I'm sitting in the office of the manager of the Angel of Mercy Hospice in Falls Church, Virginia, and *this is the place!*"

Triffler let out a huge, satisfied sigh. "No shit! A hospice!"

"Truly! It's a place where people come to die. You know that?"

"Uh, yeah—but, hey, what a great piece of work!"

"Man, my feet hurt. My buns hurt from driving. My fingers hurt from writing! Did I tell you about the Korean laundry in Kensington?"

"So—what'd you find at this hospice?"

"Where I am as we speak? Oh, at first, nothing. No hits. I was ready to leave. Then I think, no, wait—if this guy was planting a bug, he didn't talk to the receptionist or the manager. He talked to the guys in the trenches, right? So I go to the nurses and I go, 'Who does the scut work here? Who's around with bedpans and shit like that?' So they go, 'The practicals and the orderlies and *staff*,' and I talk to some of them and hey, Triffler! I hit pay dirt!"

"They recognized him."

"Absolutely! One woman, she's black but very bright, she'd seen him *twice*! Even reported him the second time to the manager, so I check, and the manager wants to cover her ass because now she knows this is not about Aunt Annie's false teeth disappearing from the nightstand, so she's cagey and says 'Well, maybe, I'm a very busy person.' So I go, 'Well, we're talking murder here, so I hope you're really recollecting everything important,' and she gets her ass in gear and in about fifteen minutes she can tell me which goddam *room* this Moscowic was in. No kidding."

Triffler hadn't even blinked at Moisher's "black but very bright." He was resigned to whites, and he didn't distract them when they were on a roll. "That's great. Great work."

"Well—I got lucky." Moisher was beaming over the phone. "Then guess what?"

"I can't guess."

"I found the bug."

Triffler felt it like an ice cube down his back. This was definitely new. "How?"

"Guy who's dying here actually talked to Moscowic. The deceased gave him some cock-and-bull story about being in the wrong room, but the guy—a gay, I think, but observant—didn't really buy it, and he re-members that Moscowic was heading straight from the door toward the bedside light when he barged in. So I go, 'Toward the light?' and he goes, 'No, he was bending over, like down toward the floor.' So I look, and what d'you think I see?"

"Shoes?"

"Nah, shoes! My ass, Triffler—the wall plate! I mean, check it out—nightstand, lamp, cord, wall socket. We're talking a bug, right? because that's what's in his notebook, the Xerox pages. Okay. So I look all over the lamp and the nightstand, I don't see anything."

"You trained to look for bugs?"

"Hell no, what you think I am, the FBI? Nah, I just looked and used my head. Then I borrow a screwdriver and take off the wall plate and there it is."

Triffler's stomach dropped into his shorts. He hated to ask the obvi-ous question, afraid of what Moisher had done to the bug. "You took it out?" he said.

"Jeez, what d'you think I am? No! I called in an expert, a guy I know in PG police. Triffler, don't you know *anything*? You never touch a thing like that. Never!"

Triffler felt weak. "Good for you."

"Yeah, he's having a look at it now, and what I think is, if I'm lucky, it's got prints on it, or the wall plate has, which I handled with Kleenex from the gay. Right? Moscowic's prints. Just icing on the cake, because I al-ready got a positive ID, and the guy in the room, although he won't live long enough to testify at trial, I can depose him and I'm golden, right?"

"Right." Triffler cleared his throat. He was looking at the chart of Shreed's life. "What's next?"

"Guess whose room this was before the dying gay moves in?"

Triffler wanted to shout *George Shreed's wife!* but he bit the words off. "Whose?"

"The wife of a guy at the CIA. Get it? The *Central Intelligence Agency!* This is a fucking espionage murder!"

"Oh, now—" Triffler could see Moisher going off on brilliant tangents. "Don't jump at conclusions. Hey, listen, I just had a thought. I *know* somebody at the CIA."

"I was going to go to the FBI. Except they'll take over my investigation, won't they?"

"They have that reputation. No, listen, I got this acquaintance, he's in Internal Investigations, a really stand-up guy. Moisher—call this guy, I bet he'd be grateful. You know, it helps to make contacts like this."

"How?"

"Future reference. Suppose you want to leave the police department some day? Good to have a contact at a place like the Agency."

"I don't feel comfortable with spying and all that stuff."

"This guy is in Internal. No spying. He's like a cop."

"They'll blow me away. I'll be this dumb local dick and they're the God-Almighty CIA."

"His name's Carl Menzes. You can mention my name. Just tell him you were following this lead in a murder investigation, and it led to the wife of a CIA employee named—what was the name?"

"Shreed. Mrs. George Shreed. Name of Jane."

"Well, you could call Menzes and say something like, 'Hi, I'm a friend of Dick Triffler's, I'm investigating a murder and the trail has led me to the wife of a CIA employee named George Shreed.' I think he'd be very grateful."

"Well—"

"Moisher, you gotta do it sometime. See? You don't want to be perceived as suppressing evidence."

"How could they perceive that?"

"Well—they're the CIA—"

"Oh, shit! You think this guy would still be in his office?"

"Try him. It'd be a really good idea to try him. And Moisher—you done good, no kidding. Brilliant!"

The pizza had arrived by then, and Triffler tore into it, being messy in honor of Mike Dukas. He was sitting at his old desk, not his new one, and he allowed tomato sauce and cheese to drip on the desktop and a couple of files. He saw that he had already dripped coffee on some of the papers. He finished the pizza and was thinking of doughnuts when Carl Menzes telephoned.

Triffler listened to him, sucking bits of cheese and anchovy through his teeth, wiping grease from his fingers on the drawer pulls. He said, "No kidding," and "Unh-*unh*!" several times. When Menzes was done, Triffler said, "That's amazing."

"Somehow I think you're not amazed. This detective mentioned your name—how close are you to this investigation of his?"

"Not close."

"Funny you should be working on Shreed because of Siciliano, and here he pops up in a completely different context, and your name gets mentioned."

Triffler thought of Dukas and how Dukas would handle it, and he became his own real self and said, "Keep me at arm's length. Understand? I've kept Moisher at arm's length. Anything I know about this is tainted and you can't use it in court. Get me?"

"So you already knew."

"No comment."

"Okay, I get you. Moisher's going to send me everything he's got. He says that this bugging of Shreed's wife's room was done for 'Hotshot,' who is somebody he hasn't identified. That your view of it?"

"Sounds right."

"He says that there's a log for 'entry into S's.' You got any ideas there?"

"None."

"S is for Shreed?"

"No comment."

"Well, Moisher says that the entry into S's was apparently worth five thousand dollars. Any comment?"

"None."

"I thought it was a big fee for a locksmith."

Triffler was silent, thinking, *Go, go—go for it!*

"So, I ask myself, why does it cost five thousand bucks to get into a house? And all I can think of is a bribe. Correct me if you don't agree."

Triffler said nothing.

"So, I'm wondering who's worth five thousand and can get into

Shreed's house, and except for Mrs. Shreed, who was already in the hospice and dying, I can't think of anybody. However, if I call Shreed's local police, I can find if there are other people who have authorized entry, and guess what: the Shreeds had a cleaning woman with a key. What d'you make of that?"

"You're telling the story."

Menzes actually laughed. "Triffler, if you ever think of leaving NCIS, keep me in mind. I can always use a guy who understands an evidence trail." Menzes was still laughing when he hung up.

Triffler drove to a Dunkin' Donuts and bought a mixed dozen. Back at the office, he passed the box around and bit into one of the forbidden fruits.

"Jeez, Triffler," a female agent said, "what's going on? *You?*"

Triffler let red jelly run down his chin. "I'm awarding myself the Mike Dukas Prize for Biting Your Tongue in Aid of Jurisprudence."

36

Jolcut, Pakistan 1430 GMT (1830L) Monday.

LONG AGO, IN BASIC COUNTERINTELLIGENCE TRAINING, an instructor had told Mike Dukas that the ideal clandestine meeting site had multiple entrances and exits, terrain to screen the meeting from prying eyes, and a logical proximity to the agent's daily routine. At first glance, Jolcut lacked all the requirements.

It was no different from dozens of other little hamlets at the edge of the war zone. Its strategic position at the top of a long hill suggested that its inhabitants must be familiar with violence, must have endured it for hundreds of years—but there is a difference between endurance and acceptance. Caught between the northern plains of India to the east and the Khyber Pass to the west, the region had been a highway for invaders since well before Alexander's phalanx had rolled to the Indus River, and the villagers here had suffered them all.

The sun cast long shadows on the trash-strewn road as Dukas trudged up the hill toward the town. He had left his taxi miles away in another hilltop village and had taken a weirdly painted local bus to a turn in the highway. When he raised his head now, he could just see the smooth column of a minaret silhouetted against the sunset sky. He shifted the duffel bag in his hand and kept walking.

The same strategic position that made life in Jolcut historically precarious gave it utility as a meeting place for spies. The Gilgit entrance to the Karakoram highway to China was two hundred miles to the north. Afghanistan and India were closer still. The main east-west highway ran flat and straight along the base of the hill below him. A watcher in the village could see movement on all the roads in the area, yet, even three-quarters of the way up the hill, Dukas still couldn't see into the village. He wondered if there was a watcher now, but it was too late to go back. He kept walking. His leg muscles burned as if his heart was pumping acid instead of blood.

He crested the hill and got his first look into the town. The whole thing wasn't more than a hundred yards square; the main street was only a row of false-fronted rectangular buildings painted in contrasting pastels, the false fronts giving the place the look of Hollywood's notion of the Old West tarted up for Easter. Behind the main drag the roofs sloped away at random angles, a crazy quilt of alleys and narrow streets.

At the far end of the main street sat the mosque, which the Chinese Checkers comm plan used as its meeting site. It was smaller than he had expected, with the minaret set in a corner and the square block of a low tower behind it.

The mosque was in ruins. And that was *not* in the comm plan.

Oh, shit, he thought. Even at a distance, he could see that the place had been bombed, and recently enough so that the rubble hadn't been cleared away.

He walked down the deserted street, his nostrils assaulted by a combination of rot and spice. Scraps of trash muffled his footsteps. Twice he saw furtive movement in doorways, flashes of color that suggested observation, and then the smell of wood fires began to overwhelm the perfume and the rot.

It was dinnertime in Jolcut.

When in Rome, he thought, and he sat on a detached block of stone and began to eat the pakora he had bought at a bus stop.

HE HAD CALLED Buse every hour, as he had promised in Bahrain, and the smart NCIS man had come through for him. Half an hour out of Islamabad, he had said, "You'll be met. Look for a sign. He'll give you your mother's maiden name and the make and year of your car. Good luck, man." He was good, Dukas had thought—no crypto, no time, so he had waited until it was too late for anybody to look up that shit before the plane landed and had given it in clear. And there was a short, very dark man waiting at the airport with a sign that said "MIKE!" When Dukas had looked at him, the man had shouted, like a child reciting a poem fast before he forgets it, "Maranlis! Subaru! Eighty-seven!"

He never gave a name. He said he was a VIP greeter, but what he did for Dukas was not very VIP: local clothes, a big thirty-eight special, and a duffel bag with a knocked-down AK in it. And a taxi driver who knew how to get around roadblocks and didn't ask questions. And why would he, with a thousand American dollars of Mike's money in his pocket?

And now here he was in a minuscule village, an American in a country that no longer liked Americans, a Christian in an Islamic nation, a cop in a place that had no local cops. He wiped his greasy fingers on his pants and hoped that the pakora didn't give him the crud. That would be the last straw.

He looked around. A tourist? Sure, he was a tourist. He took out his cellphone and, hoping that it looked at a distance like a camera, pretended to take pictures of the ruined mosque and then of the tower behind it. Pretending to get just the right light, just the right positioning, he studied out a route up the rubble to the tower. It could be done.

But could it be done in the dark?

In the west, the last gleams of the sun disappeared behind the magnificent peaks of Afghanistan, where, not so long ago, American weapons had helped to a fuel a war against an enemy who now no longer mattered.

BEFORE THE STREETS WERE DARK, he found a hostel, which was really only a shed for truck drivers who got stuck on the highway below. English speakers, if they existed in Jolcut, weren't on order that night; Dukas conned a few words of Baluch from his computer—*bed, sleep, traveler*—and was pointed to what might have been intended as a mattress. *Toilet?* More like a privy, but big enough to assemble the AK in, which he then propped against the outside wall before he showed himself once more inside before disappearing as if to bed.

Then it was dark, and he got the rifle and found his way back to the ruined mosque and the pile of stones he had picked as his route up the tower. With the rifle slung on his back—*romantic, very romantic, Lawrence of Arabia goes rock-climbing*—he scrambled up. Rocks fell with noises like an avalanche. Small animals scuttled. A dog barked. Dukas, cowering on the stones, waited for the village elders to come with torches and guns. When they didn't, he scrambled higher, put his left foot on a stone ledge, and hoisted his out-of-shape body to the top.

As housing, it wasn't much. There was a low wall and a rotting wood floor, and, in the light of his pocket torch, a trapdoor. That was bad news, because he could smell cooking, and he had an idea that the tower, or at least its lower floor, was occupied. The best he could do was move fallen rock from the wall to the trap and hope that if anybody came visiting, at least the rocks would make a racket.

Then he sat down to wait. For what, he was not sure. The woman and Shreed were to meet below him where the front of the mosque had been, perhaps, and he would climb down with his badge in his hand and arrest the traitor and take him home. Clean and fast. A dream.

He wondered how Triffler was doing without him. Better, probably. And Menzes? Dukas shook his head. It was as if that had been a hundred years ago. He crawled to the wall and looked into the warm night and saw the highest peaks of the Hindu Kush glowing white in a full moon to the west, one of the most beautiful views he had ever seen. Little fires burned in a walled market beyond the square, human and almost domestic; they enhanced the breadth of the view beyond the village. The road to the south was a sharp line across the foot of the hill.

And then vehicles were moving down there. He could see a small convoy moving fast along the road, their headlamps blacked down to slits. The roar of their distant passage rose slowly behind them like the passage of a jet plane in a clouded sky. The first vehicle slowed at the foot of the hill, and, after it turned, the sound of clashing gears lingered a little.

Oh, shit, he thought. *They're coming here.*

He had expected that Shreed would have a local agent to watch his back. But not truckloads.

Pakistani army setting up an outpost? The Indians, invading?

Three vehicles pulled into the rubble-strewn square with a roar and a shriek of brakes. Men jumped down from the first two; one man, taller than the rest and older, shouted orders. They had stubby machine pistols; two had sniper rifles, another man a heavy radio. They were dressed in a complex camouflage pattern he had never seen, and one of them started arguing with the older man as soon as they got off the trucks.

Dukas looked at their faces in the moonlight and listened to their language with a sinking feeling in his gut. He thought of Sally sitting at her computer. *"Chinese Checkers—it was such a funny name for him to pick."*

The soldiers in the square weren't Pakistani or Indian. They were Chinese.

He dug out his cellphone.

Kashmor, Pakistan 1430 GMT (1830L) Monday.

Harry had pulled the Toyota in between two international relief agency trucks. The traffic jam that blocked their four-by-four looked endless in both directions. Vehicles from the north were fleeing the fighting, and the refugees already had the blank, slack look of refugees everywhere. Vehicles from the south were taking aid and military supplies to the war zone.

"Let me do the talking," Harry said.

"Shouldn't we have kept Kamil? Do you speak the language?"

"I speak Arabic. Kamil is a hill man—he'd just make trouble, now. These guys will speak Urdu or Baluch. Anyway, somebody will speak English, and I'll stick out a lot less if I do, too. The guys in the truck ahead are Canadian."

"When did you learn Arabic?"

"Last couple of years."

"Probably important in your business, now."

"I learned it to read the Koran." He looked at Alan with a wry grin. "I converted to Islam."

They pulled forward a few feet and stopped again. One of the Canadians hopped out of the truck ahead, pissed by the side of the road, and strolled up to Harry's window. He was a tall, heavy man, his face burned red by the sun. A hardass.

"Who you guys with?"

Harry pulled a business card out of his pocket.

"I'm Harry O'Neill. I run a private security firm."

"Oh, sure. Doesn't everybody?" He came well up the side of the Toyota. "Who do you really work for? And why'd you cut into our convoy?"

"I really do run a private security firm. Mostly, I work for the UN."

"Look, I don't really care who you work for, okay? I just want to know that you aren't running drugs. That could get us stopped for hours, okay?"

"No drugs. Who you with?"

"IRC. We got about twenty trucks."

"You know this checkpoint?"

"It's new. I've only made this run twice, but there's never been a check before the desert."

"I do work for the IRC in Mombasa."

"Yeah?" The man looked disbelieving, but interested. "You can prove it, eh?"

"Yeah, but why should I?"

"Because if you don't want me to point you out to the checkpoint, I want to know, okay? I'm not losing four hours here because some drug dealer decided to use me as cover."

Harry smiled and pulled out his phone. The truck ahead rolled forward and Harry nudged the Toyota along a few more feet. The checkpoint became visible to the north. To the east, a passenger train moved slowly into the desert. The big Canadian kept pace on foot.

"Call your headquarters and ask if they know Echos Security. Call the United Nations High Council for Refugees, if you know the number. I'd give it to you, but you wouldn't trust me."

Somebody was shouting at the Canadian from the truck ahead. He looked them both over and shrugged.

"No time. I won't tell them you're part of our convoy, but if they don't ask, I won't say different."

"Fair enough."

Alan looked over at Harry. "Are we screwed?"

"Just let me do the talking."

The truck ahead rolled into the checkpoint. Soldiers raised the canvas in the back with their rifles, but the inspection was perfunctory and the truck was halted less than a minute.

Harry rolled the Toyota forward and halted next to the officer.

"Where are you going?"

"Islamabad."

"This highway is closed except for required traffic."

"I understand that, sir."

"Are you with the Red Cross?" Asked with deceptive mildness, the question made Alan cringe inwardly. This was not an ignorant man.

"I provide security for UNHCR sites."

"You are American?"

"I live in Dubai."

"Really? You don't have a newspaper, do you?"

"I don't. You want to know about the cricket?"

The officer nodded, his whole demeanor changed. Dubai had been a right answer. So had the word "cricket."

"It was a very close game, but Inzamam-ul-Haq attacked the Australian bowling and in the end Pakistan won by ten runs."

"*Allah ahkbar!* The game was starting when we were sent here."

Harry handed over a UN passport. *Where had Harry come up with a UN passport?*

"Do you need something to read?" Harry burrowed in his bag and pulled out a thick yellow book. The cover said "Wisden." The officer took it with reverence—the bible of international cricket.

"This year's!"

"I have another. Take it."

The man held it on his palm, weighing his duty to look at Alan's passport against the book.

"Drive carefully. The desert road is full of refugees."

"Good luck to Pakistan. I hope they make the final."

"*Inshallah.* Go on, please."

Alan breathed again, and the Toyota rolled forward. He didn't even notice the last cars of the passenger train passing beyond Harry's window. Aboard the train, a man raised his head from the computer on his dinner table to glance at the endless traffic jam. It was George Shreed.

SHREED GLANCED UP from his screen because a flash of light distracted him, but his thoughts were far away. The screen showed the encrypted commands that would begin the drain of Chinese intelligence money from their secure accounts in Hong Kong and Malaysia. He thought that when he showed Chen the empty bank accounts, Chen would defect to save his skin—what old East German hands called an "induced defection." And if he didn't, Shreed would shoot him. He thought Chen would more likely defect.

He would have in his pocket the first high-level Chinese intelligence in American history. China's intelligence service would be bankrupt and impotent. China would be caught in the middle of a public attempt at military adventurism, and she would have to back down on CNN. Shreed could see the ships turning away in his mind's eye. They wouldn't raise their heads out of the middle kingdom for a generation.

And then?

And then America would have no enemies with any power for a generation, and he would have been proven right. That would be his triumph. Even if he never went back, even if he never *made it* back, it would be his triumph. They would talk about him for generation after generation. Teach his great coup at the Ranch. He would be a legend.

Or a piece of shit, you egotistical bastard. He grinned at his reflection in the train window. But, like all grins, it faded. For the cynic, there is no triumph, even in triumph. *What were you expecting, God's finger to come down from the sky and tickle you under the chin?* Still, he was glad that he hadn't been able to get to Belgrade, unable to kill Chen. This was going to be better, no matter how it ended.

He waited until the signal on his laptop indicated that he had a strong link to the Web. Then he put a finger on the key that would start the process, and, to his astonishment, the finger was trembling. *So long getting here—so much effort—* He thought of Janey. Had she forgiven him?

He pressed the Send button, sat back, and sipped his coffee.

His project had begun its final phase.

I'm so lonely, baby.

I'm so lonely I could . . .

Jolcut 1830 GMT (2230L).

The village at the top of the ridge above her appeared deserted. It reminded Anna of the hilltop village where she had spent her childhood, except that her village had had ancient stone walls and the graceful line of an aqueduct sweeping away to much less dramatic mountains. But her village had had much the same smell, and it was the smell that awakened her feelings: cedarwood fires, the perfume of strong spices, the dung of goats and sheep and horses.

She did not look like a daughter of this village, or of the one where she had been born, for that matter. She was dressed in ancient jeans and a flannel shirt, and her bright hair was covered in a local wool hat. Over the flannel shirt she wore the shell of an ancient army coat, and over both she wore a loose black cotton robe, unbelted, and a heavy internal frame pack on her back. She looked like any of the Western students who came to the mountains seeking enlightenment and a good climb.

She had no intention of walking up the road to the village. She knew that Shreed wouldn't play fair, but this time she intended to be early and be ahead. He had given her signals, alternates, routes—all irrelevant in her present mood. George Shreed, whether deserving or not, had become the archetype of every human being who had ever used her.

She had been on her own—without a protector, without an *owner*—for three weeks. To preserve her freedom, she had killed, betrayed, stolen, lied, and kept her bed empty. She raised her head, looked at the village on the height, and smiled her feral smile. By one simple act of revenge against a man who had tried repeatedly to kill her, she would win security and, just maybe, some friends. Alan Craik would know that she was something . . . she didn't like that thought much and didn't follow it.

The scree at the bottom of the slope was the hardest part of the climb up the hill. She had to move around boulders through the shards of other rocks, with the weight on her back making movement difficult. Once free of the rubble field, she was able to move up the steep western slope with more speed and confidence. The moonlight made stark shadows among the rocks, lighting handholds and footholds in the lateral outcrops that made the west slope look like giant steps climbing into the moon.

After half an hour, she pulled herself over an outcrop and rested, panting, with her pack braced against the next ledge. A stronger smell of goat registered through her fatigue. There were goat droppings here on the outcrop; she was sitting in a tiny trail that led up to her left around the hill. When she stood, her sandal-clad feet could follow the gritty sand and gravel mix that marked the path by feel. She became cautious, expecting a sentry or a night herder.

Anna stopped. In a village without electricity, the last rays of the sun usually marked the end of the day, but the silence from above her was too total. She missed the sounds of animals, the occasional bang of a pot, the little night noises that proclaimed the health of a village. It was not yet late. In the time she had been on the slope, not a baby had cried, not a single couple had engaged in a late-night shouting match. Perhaps Pakistanis were quieter than her own people, but she felt uneasy.

More than a hundred feet below her, she caught a movement in her peripheral vision. When she turned her head, she thought for some moments that she was watching an animal, but as she squatted in the trail, the movement resolved into two man-shapes moving warily. The moon provided her with a gleam of metal—a gun. *Shreed's people.*

With muscle-aching care, she wriggled out of her pack, heedless of the old goat droppings in the trail. It took her more than a minute, and she cursed the American notion of "quick release." Lighter by fifty pounds, she unzipped the top pocket of the pack and extracted a Walther pistol, fitted a clip into the butt, and winced at the click as it slid home. She slipped the pistol into the waistband of her jeans, rolled on her stomach, and got a drink from the water pack strapped to the pack frame. The men were still there. They seemed to be examining the base of the scree where she had started her climb. That was not a good sign.

The silencer and the second clip for the Walther F88 had slipped from the top pocket all the way to the bottom of the pack, and she thought that she must sound like an avalanche as she wormed her arm through the clothes looking for them. She put them in a pocket with her cellphone, took another drink of water, and started crawling up the trail.

Anna was the descendant of a hundred generations of practiced hill thieves. Childhood play for both sexes had involved hours of just this sort of pastime: crawling up a track covered in goat shit to surprise one of her brothers. They were all dead, but their arts lived in her, and she wriggled along like a snake, ten yards at a time until she reached the edge of the plateau, where centuries of feet had cut a path in the final outcrop of rock. She leaned against the rock and raised her head above it, her heart crashing against her chest, rivers of sweat and grime running down between her breasts and down her back. Her head came up by inches, until one eye could just see over the lip.

The ground between her and the first square building appeared empty. She waited, motionless, for more than a minute. Stillness was how she had always caught her brothers. *Patience.* The patience that had enabled her to hide inside herself for five years as a prostitute in Riyadh and Dubai.

While she was motionless at the top of the ridge, it came to her forcefully that she *would* kill George Shreed. Up until that point it was an idea, an ambition. Now it was her sole focus. She had endured things that had destroyed other women. She could endure more to be free. She crouched, filthy from the crawl, at the top of a hill with enemies behind her and ahead and thought, *This is life. I will succeed or fail by my own hands.*

She began to crawl across a patch of open ground. She made it to the edge of the first building unseen, close to the base of a trash heap that served several houses. It wasn't bad, after the goats; at the moment it smelled of lemons. She crawled around the rubbish with care, the soft base of the mulch muffling her movements completely. When she thought she might have a sight line into the village, she raised her head again with great care. She was between an outbuilding, probably a set of stalls for animals, and two houses at the western edge of the village. She guessed that the gray moonlit puzzle ahead represented a little maze of alleys, every window shuttered against the dark. The village sloped down from where she lay, and she thought she could see a minaret against the moonlight. Its base was hidden by another shape, and it took her seconds to realize that there was some sort of tower rising between her and the minaret. High in the tower, a single light burned, either a candle or a kerosene lamp. It seemed to be the only light in the village.

She rose slowly to her feet and flattened herself against the second house, then crabwalked along the wall of the building until she reached the alley. She moved her head out at waist height and looked both ways. Again she was patient.

A man's boots sounded on a stone. He did not bother much with stealth—a villager? He moved quickly, almost violently along the alley until he reached the intersection so close that she could have slapped his back. He looked confident. He also looked *Chinese.*

His attention was on a building across the alley, a low, square building with a flat roof and the sort of decorative wall that often meant a roof garden in an Asian village. After a moment's hesitation, he stepped forward, leaped, and caught the wall with his hands. With muscular grace, he used his arms to pull his weight up and then swung his hips over the wall to land on the roof. It was the maneuver of an athlete.

The athlete had a sniper rifle on his back.

She listened. He had moved to the other corner of the roof, the one facing the rest of the village. The roof was high, and with the slight slope of the village, it probably afforded a view right to the base of the tower. The sniper was not there to watch the approaches to the village. He was there to cover the mosque.

What a viper Shreed was. *He had sold her to the Chinese.*

Anna took a long time over her options, and she shivered a little with the cool air and the sweat. Her retreat was blocked. If they had followed her trail up, they would be almost at the top by now.

If she had seen three of them, there must be at least a squad, perhaps a platoon. The sniper had had the muscles and agility of a hard man, a paratrooper or a commando. She needed a place. Would they search the houses if she didn't show up at Shreed's meeting place?

The sniper had a good spot. He was probably lying down, his rifle already set up, waiting for the action to begin. From the noise, he was fiddling with something. A tool? And he almost certainly had a radio. But who would call him? As she reckoned the odds, the sniper had the virtue of immediate action and comparative safety. He had a good rifle, too, a weapon she could use. He was the devil she knew. She drew the heavy silencer from her breast pocket and screwed it on the barrel, easing the threads back and forth to get a perfect fit as Efremov had taught her. Then she ejected the clip into her palm, easing the clip past the catch to muffle its sharp metallic noise. Then she wiped the sweat from her face and reversed the operation, inserting the other, the whisperloac bullets from the stall in Dushanbe—subsonic bullets that made a silencer really effective. The clip still made a tiny *click* as it seated home, and again she waited, utterly silent, immobile.

She moved her head out into the alley again, this time at a different height, and waited, counting slowly to one hundred. Nothing moved but the man on the roof, who was making little metallic sounds. Now, too, she could hear the animal noises that had been hidden by the last rock outcrop on the hill. Up here, the village sounded more alive, although the human noises were still absent. Every mother must be huddled in a cellar with her children gathered round her as the foreign soldiers prowled the village.

Now she was alive in the night with a gun, and the thought of terrified mothers and her own mother with her throat cut on the dirt floor of the cellar enraged her, pulled at her, and with one surge of adrenaline she crossed the alley and leaped higher than the man had done, her left hand catching the edge of the wall and her body swinging, right knee over, and the man was turning, his mouth a little open, his right hand scrabbling at his belt, and still she was patient the extra half a second, and she settled her right foot on the roof and dragged the left in next to it, crouched on her haunches, both hands coming together, and his eyes were huge in his round face and her hands came together with the gun. She shot him twice in the face. His body spasmed, his kicking feet making more noise than her whole sweeping attack, and she smelled his body's surrender of control. She sank to the roof and shook, the sweet high of adrenaline screaming in her veins in contrast to the silent village. Then she started to examine the body and the rifle.

NCIS HQ.

Triffler's workday was nearing its end, and he was tired and let down after his high of the morning. He hadn't heard a word more about Dukas, and the rest of the case seemed frozen. And then the phone rang.

"Hey, Triffler, Carl Menzes." Menzes was almost giggling. "Want to go on a bust?"

"What the hell?"

"I thought you might like to be in at the finish of something. We ID'd a kid who was in Shreed's house and we're getting the guy who put him up to it. We're going to scoop them both in half an hour."

"Four hours ago you didn't have zip!"

"Yeah, well, something of this importance, we *move*. Plus, with the Bureau, local cops, and my own folks, I got sixty people on this since noon."

Sixty! Dukas would have killed for six!

Menzes was going on. "We got the cleaning woman; she started crying as soon as my man showed his badge. Moscowic, the dead guy, bribed a cop to get her kid on a dope charge—she lets him into Shreed's house, the kid goes free, so of course she did it. *That's what cost five Gs. So she* tells us that it wasn't Moscowic who went into the house; it was a kid, punk hairdo, the whole nine yards. And he goes in, and what do you think he does? He sits at Shreed's computers for two hours!"

"No shit."

"He's a hacker, what else could he be? So I get to the Bureau, they have a file of these guys, and they fan some photos in front of the cleaning woman, she goes, 'That one.' Nick Groski—did juvenile time for computer crime, isn't supposed to go near one for three years, ha-ha. So the local cops call his parole officer, and he's got an address for him in College Park. You know Carnivore?"

"What the hell is that, a game?"

"It's an FBI program to bug e-mail, come on! This is where it helps to have sixty people working on a case, I kid you not! By three this afternoon, they had the hacker's Internet providers and a warrant and they're into his e-mail, so half an hour ago, they caught their first message. It says, 'It's going down.' Nice?"

"I don't get it."

"I don't get it, either, but guess who it was sent to."

Triffler started to say, *I don't like guessing games* but he remembered that this wasn't Moisher and said, "Who?" instead.

"You ready? *Ray Suter.* Familiar name?"

Pause, then a lightbulb. "I just interviewed him. Shreed's assistant."

"The very man. Sent the e-mail to his office here at the Agency. Suter left the office twenty minutes ago and we're trying to locate him, but we know he turned toward the Beltway and we think he's heading for the hacker's place in College Park. You want to go?"

"You're going to bust them *now*?"

"I got a search warrant that's still warm from the judge's hand; I don't want to let it get cold. Local cops have a warrant for the kid because of the cleaning woman's testimony—illegal entry, plus violation of parole. If Suter's with him when we go in, it's conspiring with a felon, at least as a charge until we get something better. And if there's one partial of Moscowic's in that apartment or in Suter's car, we've got suspicion of murder. Want to come along?"

Triffler wanted to, but he knew what was the right thing to do. "If my name's on an arrest sheet or even a report, you could be tainted. Thanks for thinking of me."

Menzes started to protest, then caught himself. "You're a hell of a guy, Dick. Hang in there."

Washington 1430L (1830GMT).

Suter drove through rain-wet streets with hatred in his heart for every other driver on the road. The Beltway had been nightmarish; the streets inside it were worse. Delays, near accidents, real accidents. *Asshole!* he thought as he almost rear-ended a Honda that had braked suddenly. Ahead, a young woman was climbing out of a car, laughing, flirting with somebody inside—it was for her that the Honda had had to stop. Suter leaned on the horn. The woman looked down the street at the line of stopped cars, her face uncomprehending. Other horns began to sound.

"Jesus!" Suter shrieked at his windshield. He pounded on the steering wheel.

Five slow minutes later he pulled into the parking lot of Nickie's apartment building. Suter's hands were trembling. The message—*It's going down*—meant only one thing: Shreed had initiated the program to pull the plug on the Chinese intelligence money. If Suter got into that money now, he'd be out of the country before morning, and then let Internal Investigations try to polygraph him!

Lots of money. Which Nickie was going to track to its destination and then redirect to an offshore bank account.

Suter dodged through the rain. By the time he got to the apartment house doorway, his feet were sopped to the ankles, and he could feel water soaking through his suit jacket. His mood was foul, worsened by the weather and tension and the fear that something, somehow, would go wrong.

One thing at a time, he thought. He had had to tell himself that all day. He had come close to panic several times, and he had had to tell himself to hold on, to go slowly, to look only at the next step. He never should have killed Moscowic. The horror of the killing, the sheer messiness of it, had spooked him. *To have done it so badly!* Next time, he would pay to have it done.

He climbed the stairs to Nickie's apartment because he couldn't bear to wait for the elevator. At the top, breathing a little hard, he turned right and walked along the ugly corridor, hating the smells of cigarettes, cooking dinners, babies, disinfectant. Somebody was laughing. A television played. *Assholes!* he thought. He wanted the world, his world, emptied of all the people who got in his way, who impinged on his consciousness. Shreed's money—*his* money—would do that for him.

"Hey, Nickie," he said when he had let himself in.

Nickie looked up from the computer and said, "Yeah." He had never asked about Moscowic after Moscowic had disappeared. He never asked about much of anything, in fact. Nickie lived in the computer.

"So—it's going down?"

Nickie had already turned back to the screen. Suter stood behind him. Incomprehensible numbers and words were parading across the screen.

"What's happening?" Suter said. He couldn't keep the tension out of his voice.

Nickie drank from a tall plastic cup and gestured toward the screen as if to say, *See for yourself.* Suter wanted to grab his thin neck from behind, right now, and squeeze. To get some response from Nickie.

"Nickie—what the fuck is *happening*?"

Nickie shrugged. "It's going down." He was eating a Big Mac. He chewed noisily. The apartment stank of food and dirt. Suter wanted to scream.

OUTSIDE IN THE PARKING LOT, Carl Menzes sat in his car and watched the rain splashing in the puddles. He had a headset on, and he was listening to a report from an FBI agent in the apartment lobby. When the man was done, he switched his mike and talked to all his people at once. "Suter's in the apartment. We're going in now, and please, will the local jurisdiction double-check that you have officers in place on the stairs and near the windows, because one or both of these guys may try to leave. Confirm, please."

A minute later, he was out of the car and in the rain, his coat collar up. Moisher, the gee-whiz detective who had the murder case, was hanging near the apartment entrance. Inside, two FBI agents waited.

"You Menzes?"

He turned. A black policeman was coming through the rain as if it was a dry day. He stuck out a hand. "Renfrew, PG police. Yeah, they call me Renfrew of the Mounties, so I heard the jokes."

"You got the search warrant?"

Renfrew held up a document in a plastic cover.

"Okay, you serve it. This is Detective Moisher; he's going to do 'suspicion of murder' if we turn up any prints. You got a crew here?"

"They've already started on his car."

Menzes led the way into the lobby. "We'll take the stairs; Renfrew and Moisher take the elevator, if you will. And one thing, gentlemen—this guy Suter is a CIA employee. That means he signed a paper that allows his employer to interrogate him in matters of security. *Don't* Miranda him." He looked at each one. "Let's go."

SUTER WAS WATCHING the numbers fall down the screen like confetti. The numbers changed, but he didn't know what the change meant, except that Nickie started to laugh.

"Shut up."

But Nickie kept laughing. And then he saw something that made him laugh even harder.

"I said shut up!" Suter's right arm twitched, as if he was going to hit the kid. "What the fuck are you laughing at?"

"Your money, man. Your money—it's going!"

"I know it's going, asshole, that's the idea! Your job is to find where it's going!"

Nickie laughed some more. He was almost on the floor, it was so funny. "Man, I know—I know—" He was laughing so hard he couldn't say it. "I know where it's going!"

"Then shut the fuck up and tell me where. Where?"

Nickie made a gesture, fingers fluttering, down, down. "It's *going,* man—going, going, *gone.*" He hiccuped, laughed, gasped. "Your guy there didn't send—didn't send the money to a fucking *bank*! He sent it to—to—" He roared again. "Cyberspace!"

Suter grabbed him. "What d'you mean? It's *money!* Where'd he send it?"

He was shaking Nickie, and the kid went limp and hung from his hands, staring up and gulping his laughter. "It isn't money, you dick— it's digitals. It's just *signals.* It isn't money until somebody sends the signals to a bank and then asks the bank to turn them into money. And this guy didn't send it to a bank! He sent it to—nowhere. Cyberspace. He *destroyed* it, man!" Then he kicked Suter in the crotch and tore himself free and grabbed a glass ashtray from a table.

And the doorbell rang.

The two looked at each other and then at the door.

A loud knocking sounded. "Police. Open up!"

Nickie dropped the ashtray, which fell on the carpet with a thud. Suter was fiddling with his tie, his eyes too open, hyperventilating.

"Open the door, please! Police!"

Suter crossed the gray-brown carpet, looking back once at Nickie as if to see if he was still there. There was no back door, and the windows were three stories above the street. Where would Nickie go?

Suter opened the door. He saw what struck him first as a crowd, too many people, faces, men.

"I'm Officer Renfrew of the PG police, and we got a warrant to search these premises. This is Detective Moisher of the Bladensburg police, Special Agent Dillick of the FBI—" He had pushed his way in as he spoke, moving Suter backward. Somebody moved past Suter, and he heard Nickie cry out, and a voice began to read Nickie his Miranda rights.

Suter would have gone on moving backward, but a hand closed around his left arm and a voice said, close to his left ear, "You're *mine.*"

Suter recognized Menzes then.

37

DUKAS COULDN'T RAISE ALAN AND HARRY ON THEIR phone, and, after an hour of trying, he called the number in Dubai and left a message. He'd have to hope that Harry checked in.

"Harry, this is Mike. I'm at the location. Listen up, man—we got trouble.

"The village sits at the top of a steep ridge next to the highway. There's one good gravel road up from the highway and it's marked, but if you come that way we're fucked, because there's a dozen Chinese military all over this place like fleas on a dog. You can't come in by car, you get me? I think the best way is up behind, the steep side.

"The town itself is roughly square. At the center, from, um, east to west, are a small open square, the mosque where the meet is, and a tower. The mosque is a ruin, I think a bomb, and I haven't seen the caretaker, who's our friend's contact and advance man, so maybe he's under the thing someplace. But that means another screwup, because he's supposed to leave signals and I haven't seen him and there wasn't any signal when I came by the place in daylight. What we got here is Screwup City.

"You'll be able to see the minaret of the mosque from the road, and the top of the tower. Use those to orient yourselves.

"I'm on the tower.

"There's eleven troops and an officer and I'm sure they're Chinese. That makes no sense, unless China has invaded Kashmir while I wasn't looking. What I think is, this is a special unit that infiltrated or parachuted and they're here because of Shreed. Maybe to back him up, maybe to take him—Shreed hasn't been behaving like a guy who was running happily to Beijing, after all. But it may not matter—these guys aren't going to like us, no matter what they're here for.

"They're covering the road in and the square to the east of the mosque. I don't think they're covering the rest of the ridge, but I can't tell. There isn't enough of them to do it very well. I do know that. They've been sneaking up and down, scoping out the town—looking for Shreed's backup, I think. Except there isn't any, that I can see. The locals have battened down the hatches, and if they know what's going down, they're just letting it happen."

Dukas sighed.

"A guy could get real lonely in a place like this.

" 'Bye."

North of Jand, Pakistan 2155 GMT
Monday (0155L Tuesday).

Alan handed the cellphone back to Harry and shifted down for another sharp curve.

"We have to send for the plane."

"Why?"

"Because if I send for it any later than right now, we can't get out of Pakistan in the dark. You sense what we've been seeing at those last road-blocks?"

"Yeah. A lot of military buildup."

"Right. I think Pakistan is getting ready to punch over the border on a wide front with a lot of guys and some Chinese air. Once that happens, it's war. Not just another border clash. And we won't get to drive out through it, Harry. If we get Shreed, we have to fly out."

"Al, this may come as a shock, but have you considered that we may have to shoot Shreed?"

"Yes."

"Can Stevens get an S-3 up here?"

"Short of Rafe, he's about the best I've seen. And the Pakistanis are all looking east, Harry. That might not be true tomorrow."

"Okay, cowboy. But this is going to be messy. Chinese, villagers, Shreed, maybe the woman."

"One way or another, it'll be over by dawn. Shreed either shows by then or he doesn't. I'll ask Stevens to buzz the road then."

"Give him a signal?"

"Headlights on the car?"

"Good enough."

North of Rawalpindi, Pakistan 2240 GMT Monday (0240L Tuesday).

George Shreed pulled the car to the wide gravel shoulder, driving carefully to avoid the deep strips torn by trucks. Despite a fresh dose of morphine, he was too keyed up to sleep. *The Chinese money must be running out of their accounts like water,* he thought—*no, like an invisible gas, escaping into the atmosphere.*

He had two tickets for a flight out of Islamabad at 0830. For him and Chen. It would take them to Athens, if the plan went that way. He had another, a single, for Thailand.

He rummaged in his flight bag and took out a big automatic pistol and a shoulder rig. If he had to shoot, the game would be over anyway. Then it would just be a matter of professional pride to take as many with him as he could. The big Desert Eagle automatic had a ten-round clip, and every round had an armor-piercing bullet, what Americans called "cop killers."

He knew the route to the mosque, but he looked at the map one more time, anyway, relieved himself beyond the gravel, where a stink of urine told him that other drivers had had the same idea, and looked at the moonlit mountains in the far distance. It was damned cold, and he didn't linger. His legs obeyed him well enough. *Close enough for government work, as they say.* He rested with his weight against the car and looked at the mountains again. Then he got back in his car.

"On to glory," he said aloud, and turned the key.

Jolcut, Pakistan 2320 GMT
Monday (0320L Tuesday).

The moon was going down. Dukas was cold. Around him, the Chinese had settled into positions and were silent. Below him in the tower, a slamming door had startled him, and, when he had looked over the wall, he had seen the family file out one after the other to a privy—a teenage girl, a younger boy, two women, a man. Then silence.

After another hour, his cellphone buzzed.

"Mike! Harry."

"Jesus, at last! Did you get my message?"

"Roger."

"Situation's unchanged."

"Where are you now?"

"On my ass on top of this tower. It's cold here, man."

He could hear Harry repeating it to Alan, who must have been driving. Then Harry's voice came back. "We're about twenty klicks away. Maybe forty minutes if we don't hit another roadblock."

"Meeting's going down in an hour."

"We're doing our best, guy! The plane's coming in to pick us up in two hours."

"And the Chinese?"

"If they're hostile, we'll deal with them as hostiles. What kind of weapons have you got?"

"A big revolver and an AK."

"How many of them can you see?"

"I can't *see* anybody; it's fucking dark! But I know where six or seven are."

"Can we climb the ridge?"

"Yeah. Yeah, I think so. Tricky in the dark."

"Where are the snipers?"

"One's below me. The other is off in the town."

"Where?"

"Fuck, I don't know! He headed off west of the market."

"So he's west."

"Yeah. It makes sense. The town rises to the west. Some of those roofs may give a line of sight to the square."

"Or he's covering the ridge. Okay, road is east and sniper's west. Locals still quiet?"

"It gives new meaning to 'dead town.' "

"No sign of Shreed."

"Zip."

"Okay, Mike, turn your phone from 'ring' to 'vibrate.' You got that option?"

"Christ, I'll look. Yeah, it could be a bear having it ring at the wrong moment. Okay, menu, options, ring. Yup. Good to go."

"This may change, but I'm going after the sniper to the west and Alan's going toward the square. When you hear us, take the sniper in the mosque."

"In cold blood?" He heard Harry's silence. "I'm a cop, Harry; I'm not used to killing that way!"

"Got a better idea?"

Dukas was silent.

"Stay close to the phone, Mike."

Dukas didn't want to let him go. "Those your headlights on the road?"

"No way."

"Somebody coming."

"Him?"

"Slowing at the turn. Stopped. Coming up. Now I can't see him."

"Hang on, Mike. We're coming."

"Yeah."

To himself, he said, *But I'm here.*

38

CHEN RUBBED HIS HAND OVER HIS HEAD FOR THE SEC-
ond time in as many minutes, being careful not to disturb his headset. A
radioman huddled over his box in a corner of the ruined mosque, his
face twisted in frustration.

"Nothing, sir. Number four just won't come up."

Chen clenched his hands at his sides to avoid rubbing them together.
The wait had been long and cold. The moment of decision was close,
but in the final communications check, one of his snipers had failed
to report. Top Hook was capable of anything, as far as Chen was concerned, but he had assumed that with crippled legs Shreed would be unable to climb the ridge. Now Chen was chilled by a doubt—was Top
Hook in fact already among them? If so, did he already guess Chen's in-
tentions?

I'm being a fool, he thought. Top Hook was a cripple and couldn't
climb the ridge. The missing sniper had fallen or damaged his headset.
This was not the time to lose his nerve.

Chen put his hand against the cold metal in his right ear. "Two, report."

"Ready."

"Number Two, Four has failed to report."

"And?" The sergeant was a peasant with a chip on his shoulder. Chen wanted his advice but did not want to have to ask for it.

"I want him found."

"Who do you want me to send? We don't have a reserve—as you requested."

Chen was too keyed up to worry about the eternal war of precedence between the soldiers and the spies.

"Send whomever you think best. Just do it."

The sergeant's voice snapped out in his southern dialect. "Seven and Twelve!" They were the roving patrol at the base of the slope. "Work your way up the west slope and find Four. He's someplace in the west end of the market."

"Affirmative."

Chen couldn't see the valley and the highway below, but he kept peering into the darkness at the end of the short street that led to the bottom of the hill. He wished that he still smoked, and then remembered that he had ordered the soldiers not to smoke. He glanced at his wristwatch, then had to raise it to his eyes again. Four minutes until the meeting time.

He had expected Top Hook to arrive early, but here, only four minutes remained, and then the real worry would start. What if Top Hook didn't come? That was worse than the idea that he might be loose in the dark at the top of the ridge. *He couldn't have spotted the cars, could he?* Chen had had the cars hidden, two in the market, one far off down the valley.

Nothing to worry about yet, he told himself.

"One? This is Seven." The voice was a whisper even with the amplification of the headset.

"Go ahead, Seven."

"We've found a backpack on the west slope. Civilian. We're investigating."

A new voice entered the net. "One, this is Five. A car has just turned off the highway toward the village. It is a white four-door sedan. Lights are on."

"How many passengers?"

"Only the driver."

"All soldiers, prepare to execute Sword."

"All soldiers, or all soldiers except Seven and Eleven?" The sergeant's tone was abrasive.

"Seven and Eleven to continue their search."

Chen breathed in deeply, then exhaled slowly to calm himself. Everything was all right. Top Hook was coming: of course, a lone man in a car would be the crippled American; the missing sniper was no longer important. Top Hook was coming up the hill. Alone, as Chen had hoped. Once he stopped his car and got out, the rest would be easy. Of course, little things like the sniper's failure to respond could go wrong. But the biggest obstacle was passed. Top Hook was coming.

Still, Chen worried about the backpack. *Could Top Hook have protectors?*

Headlights rose like a small white dawn over the crow of the hill, and their light filled the square and cast long shadows from the chunks of rubble.

Jolcut, Pakistan 2357 GMT (0357L).

No one had come close to the house where she waited. The dead man's radio had crackled three times, each burst of tinny gibberish raising her adrenaline. She thought about moving but couldn't see how she could find a better position—from where she was, she could see in all directions for at least a few meters.

Anna lay on the cold tile of the roof and did isometric exercises to keep warm. The duffel coat under her black robe was thick enough, but her hands and feet were cold. Her breath came out in silent little clouds.

It had taken her half an hour to find the sniper's scope, nestled in a tiny leather case in a corner of the roof. The soldier had been fitting it when she had killed him. She had wasted time looking for a heavy scope like those on Efremov's hunting rifles, but the scope she ultimately found was scarcely five inches long, with a soft, rubbery covering. Fitting it to the rifle took more time and froze her fingers again; clearly, the Chinese hadn't mastered the idea of the quick-release. And she worried that it might not be centered.

The feel of the gun was alien to her, its cheekpiece too high and the magazine exactly where she wanted to place her off hand. She practiced pointing it at doorways and shadows in the marketplace and at the two men she had spotted there. It provided a little light amplification but was barely creditable with a full moon. On a darker night, it would have been useless. Even with the bright moonlight, she worried that she would lose things if people started moving.

She began to look at things over the iron sights. She really didn't trust the scope. She would only get one or two shots.

And it had begun to dawn on her that if she took them, she would die.

A rock, tumbling down the ridge behind her, snapped her back. She moved across the roof, keeping away from the dead soldier. The corpse disturbed her, awakened fears best left unexamined. She raised her head slowly over the edge of the roof wall and looked back along the alley. She heard the soft bleat of a goat.

No one in her home village left a goat out at night. The sound had come from the byre behind the house, the byre with the refuse heap. She stared at the stark shadows thrown by the moon, unable to decide if she had seen a movement. She was seized by an urge to scramble across the roof and check the other side. They could be moving all around her, the dropped rock a deliberate ploy. Then she heard a car's engine roar in the square behind her, and the headlight beams splashed over her for a moment and on the roof across the street.

A man's head and shoulders appeared so slowly at the back of the alley that at first she didn't fully register the motion, but the man twitched at the brief illumination above his head and a meaningless crisscross of shadow suddenly resolved into a man. Her rifle was just where she had left it, on the other side of the roof, its bipod already set, its barrel aligned with the center of the square. She reached into the back of her jeans and pulled her pistol out, turning the weapon's receiver to avoid catching the silencer.

The man was moving, bent well forward, along the alley toward her. A second man was emerging in the shadow thrown by the first, one hand on his partner's back. She froze as the second man raised his head and scanned the rooftops. They didn't have night-vision goggles. But they did have submachine guns.

Without moving the rest of her body, Anna pressed the automatic against her jeans and worked the slide, rubbing her thumb along the safety until she was sure it was off. The perfect coordination of the two men in the alley indicated expertise, but their caution suggested that something had alarmed them—had they found her pack? She cursed again having left it.

The two men moved forward a step at a time. The front man had his machine pistol raised slightly above horizontal. The second man's head moved, looking everywhere. She strained her neck muscles to stay immobile, while her left hand moved slowly up her body to change her balance, because the crenellations along the edge of the roof would cover her for only a few more feet of their approach.

The goat bleated again, and the rear man of the pair twitched toward the noise. An opportunity missed: she hadn't had her balance changed yet.

Now she had her weight on her left hand. The pair moved forward another few feet, their heads swiveling like radars. Anna no longer felt cold. Her heart was pounding so heavily she could feel it in her head. She was wet with sweat. Adrenaline warred in her veins with the need to stay still.

Every few seconds, the rear man glanced behind him. She watched him do it once, then a second time, trying to catch the rhythm. Then she brought the pistol in line with the target in one motion, as Efremov had taught her, letting her index finger point at the man in front, now only a few feet away, and she fired. The pistol spat, the flash almost swallowed by the silencer, and then she was rolling on her right shoulder and along the roof, clipping her head against the wall. She had no idea if she'd hit him. A burst of shots tore at the wall, the roar of the gun filling the village and the night.

Jolcut, Pakistan 0000 GMT (0400L).

Dukas watched the car roll to a stop well before it reached the rubble pile and the fallen pillar. The driver left the headlights on and the engine running. Dukas closed one eye to keep some of his night vision and continued to stare at the driver's-side door. A long moment passed before it opened, and then the driver emerged as if the car was too small to hold him, wriggling a little to get clear of the seat. One hand reached up and grabbed the top of the door and hauled him erect. He had a coat over his other arm.

It was George Shreed.

"Chen?" he called.

A balding man in camos emerged from the entrance to the ruined mosque below Dukas.

"I am glad you made it. I was worried. Did you come by way of India?"

"The border was closed." The voices seemed too loud in the darkness, as if amplified. Dukas recognized the sign and response from the Chinese Checkers plan. The bald man, then, was Shreed's Chinese control. He came out warily, a surprising nervousness visible in his posture and his stiff walk.

Have they not met before?

"Perhaps you could turn out your lights?"

"I thought I'd take you for a little drive. The mosque looks like it's had it."

Chen stopped well in front of the car and off to the left, out of the main splash of the beams.

"I don't want to hold this conversation in the public street," Chen said.

"You're going bald!" Shreed said from the dark behind the lights.

They have met before.

"Time has various unpleasant surprises. I would rather you turned off the lights and we talked here."

"Afraid I'm going to run off with you?"

"Could we stop shouting across the street in English and meet in the mosque?"

The headlights went out and the engine noise stopped. For a moment, even with both eyes opened, Dukas was completely blind. Then he caught a flicker of movement—Shreed limping across the tiny square. The bastard didn't have any crutches. Dukas gripped the AK-47 so hard his hands hurt.

Shreed stopped a few feet from Chen and held out his hand. "Good to see you, Chen."

Chen. Like Smith, for God's sake.

Chen took the hand. Shreed, despite a slump caused by fatigue or pain, was half a head taller. He put the arm with the overcoat gently over Chen's shoulders and started forward as if guiding the smaller man toward the mosque. Chen stiffened and then moved beside him.

Metal gleamed in the hand that held the coat.

Shreed has a gun under the coat.

If the Chinese officer had noticed, he gave no sign, but after a few steps he shrugged himself free of Shreed's arm. They picked parallel ways across the rubble. They were almost to the door of the mosque when a short, loud burst of gunfire cracked through the village, echoing off the walls and the street.

Shreed and Chen had separated by half a dozen feet. At the first shot, Chen dove inside the entrance to the mosque; Shreed threw himself against the wall, where, Dukas knew, the sniper in the mosque's ruin couldn't see him. Another man ran to the corner of an alley that entered from the north and raised his weapon to his cheek and fired. The flash dazzled Dukas's eyes, and then he saw that Shreed was down. He lay on the littered pavement, a black shape like a shadow. And then he moved.

Shreed rolled on his back and fired, twice, loud, sharp cracks that resounded around the square. The man at the corner was flung back as if punched by a giant hand. Shreed rolled into the rubble at the base of the wall and disappeared.

THE FIRST GUNFIRE caught Alan and Harry well up the ridgeline, moving up the tiny path by inches. The fire was above them. Both cringed. Alan reached back and handed Harry up the outcrop he had just climbed, and then there was another set of shots, a short beat punctuated by two sharp reports.

Alan's eyes sought Harry's eyes in the starlight. Harry nodded. They began to scramble for the top, all caution gone. Harry made it first and rolled over the last lip, Alan well off to his left by the time he hurled himself on the flat at the top. Another burst of small-caliber fire sounded off to the right, well away from the center of the town. Harry could see the minaret and the bulky shoulder of the tower against the sky, and he put his head down and sprinted across the trash-strewn open ground to the shelter of the first houses. He stripped the automatic shotgun over his head and cocked it.

Alan was already gone: they had agreed to separate, hoping to seem a larger force than they were. Harry glanced around the corner of a house and then sprinted to the next one. Another shot crashed from his right. He flung himself across the street. No shots answered.

A Navy SEAL had told him, *Once the music starts, speed is life.*

The tower was off to his left, now. He was trying to get into the back of the square, but the two bursts of fire had come from this direction. Another loud shot came from the square. Then he caught a flicker of movement on a rooftop forty feet away, higher than the rest.

Harry rolled to his right to put a screen of low shacks between himself and the movement, his lungs gasping for more air, his heart shaking his ribs. He raced for the next corner and threw himself on his chest like a runner sliding for first. Up the alley now revealed he saw a man firing around the next corner, using a house for cover. He was firing at the roof of the building where Harry had just seen movement. Another man in a Chinese uniform lay kicking in agony behind the first. *They were both in Chinese uniforms.*

Harry took a long moment to aim and blew the top of his head off.

ANNA HEARD the roar of the big shotgun from *behind* her assailants. It didn't matter; they would be all around her in a moment. She rolled up into the corner of a new crenellation and aimed.

Nothing but two bodies.

She rolled back out of their line of sight and waited, her whole body shaking. No one had fired. Someone had killed the second man. The reaction was as great as if they had been alive and fired at her. But her brain was still in charge and she rode it out, waiting until her limbs were under control. It took thirty seconds.

Then she looked again.

HARRY'S FIRST THOUGHT was that the man on the roof was Dukas; it *almost* fit his description. But it was wrong, and a second's observation proved it; Dukas was over there, six streets away, by the minaret. It wasn't Alan. It *was* someone who had killed a Chinese soldier. Harry smiled unconsciously, like a man with a really good and unexpected birthday gift.

"Don't shoot, Anna," he called, and rolled out of his cover.

ALAN STOPPED in the shadow of the first building he reached to press the Send button on his cellphone. Then he moved, racing up the opening between two houses. The stench told him it was a midden, not an alley, and he could now see that the opening ended in a wall. He leaped for the top and tumbled over, landing without grace on the other side. He had screwed up, was exposed in the open, off-balance, but no shots came. A two-story house with a high wall at the back loomed ahead of him, and again he jumped, his arms finding just enough purchase on the top to get one leg up. Broken glass bit into his gloves and raked his right knee, but he kept going, right over the wall and down the roof of the little outbuilding beyond, feeling an ooze of blood down his leg.

The layout of the town reminded him of the houses in Mombasa's Old Town—walled gardens behind continuous street-facing houses. If he kept to the walled yards he'd be safe from anybody covering the alleys.

A rooster crowed behind him, startling him with its raucous call. The glass cuts burned through the haze of adrenaline. He was twenty-five yards into the town and the minaret was dead ahead, its middle height silhouetted against the square tower beyond. He scrambled up the trash heap at the corner of a courtyard and leaped over the next wall landing softly on more trash beyond it, trying not to think of what was getting into the deep cuts on his knee. The minaret looked close enough to touch now. Its far wall ought to give on the square.

He flinched as a burst of fire blew holes in a gate to his right, showering him with splinters. Somewhere, a man screamed, but Alan's attention was riveted on the muzzle flash that he had seen above the gate. He took two steps to the gated wall and got up on a crate without raising his head, then rolled his gun out over the wall in one motion. There was a helmeted man inches below him, another one six feet away and facing the gate, and Alan pulled the little machine pistol up and shot wildly, on instinct, actually missing the first man for a split second and then hitting him and walking the shots to the other.

He dropped back below the wall and heard more shooting to the west. The scream of a wounded man rang out again, hoarser from repetition. Alan wiped his arm across his face to clear the grit and the crap from the trash heaps he'd jumped through and noticed that his sleeve was in shreds, probably from the glass.

Then there was the clear, long crack of a large-caliber rifle from the tower, and Alan knew that Mike had got the message of the open Send button on his cellphone.

DUKAS FELT the phone vibrate and pressed the button, but for some seconds the noises he heard were a mystery.

"Hey!" he whispered.

Then he realized he was listening to footsteps running: Alan and Harry were in the town. He set the phone next to his flashlight on the low bench beside him and raised his rifle. Shreed had fired two more times, both at targets that Dukas couldn't see, so he knew his quarry was still down there and alive.

Dukas had never been a killer, and for a moment he hesitated as the iron sights crossed the hazy shape of a second sniper, prone in the moonlight at the back of the mosque where a corner of old stone supported a triangle of roof. But the man was focused on the dark to the north of the square, and for all Dukas knew he had Alan in his sights, or Harry.

Then fire broke out just across the square, out of Dukas's field of view, and the muzzle flashes lit the tops of the alleys in pulses of yellow and white as if a fire was burning. A man screamed. Dukas wrenched his attention back to the sniper, held the sight picture, and fired.

He missed.

The man rolled on his back and over the lip of the roof as Dukas shot again. He hadn't aimed. Really aimed. *Buck fever.* Dukas knew that if he put his head down he'd never get it up again to look, and he forced himself to scan the rubble of the mosque. He kept the rifle pointed down and moved it as he changed lines of vision, just as they had taught him long ago at Quantico.

The cellphone was making human sounds on the bench behind him now. He ducked down without thinking and pulled it to his ear.

"Yeah?"

"Mike. What the hell's happening?"

"Shreed's down at the base of the mosque. He's hit. I missed a goddam sniper."

"I can see the tower. I'm at the—fuck. I'm about fifty yards away, almost due north of you. I just shot two guys." Alan sounded a little high. Dukas remembered Alan eight years before, in Sudan—an adrenaline junkie.

"Shreed's control and a radioman are in the mosque," Dukas growled. "The sniper's off north of the mosque in another ruined building."

A shotgun roared behind Dukas and his tower—west, he reminded himself.

"That's Harry," he heard Alan say.

"Grenade launcher?"

"Shotgun. Watch the north of the square. I'm going to move. If anyone tries to get me, they have to cross your line of sight, right?"

"Not everywhere."

"Try, Mike."

Dukas moved along the parapet several meters and raised his head.

CHEN NEVER lost his nerve—not when the shooting started, not when his men began to fall, and not when the sergeant tried to seize control. His mind became beautifully clear, his doubts erased by the need to act. He focused on his sketch map of the village as he struggled to organize a counterattack against what he thought were Shreed's forces—US Marines? Rangers? It was clear to him that he had walked into a trap, and, if he survived, he knew that he would reexamine his failure to secure the village over and over. And he would not be alone in the reexamination: his superiors—

Perhaps Shreed's men had been waiting in the houses. Perhaps—

At least four of his men were down or not responding. Shreed was on the other side of the mosque wall, wounded and perhaps dying, and his forces had a sniper in the tower above him. Chen ordered his men on the south side of the square to cover the tower while the two men immediately under his hand secured Shreed. Shooters at the base of the tower would be able to hit the sniper or at least keep his head down. When he had Shreed, he would take the tower. He sent the sergeant to get around into the market and find the tower's entrance.

He turned to the radioman and the sniper who were clinging to the wall behind them.

"Have you sent the message?" He was trying to reach the command in Szhinjiang.

"Yes, sir."

"Any reply?"

"They're putting a response together."

Hours. He had to get into the tower and hope that Pakistan was still friendly to China.

He explained how he wanted them to move to capture Shreed. "I want him *alive!*"

The two soldiers were scared, determined, and young. Chen didn't think he would last as a platoon leader in a war. They were all too *young.* "Ready?"

They both nodded.

He gave the word.

ALAN STRIPPED the clip out of the machine pistol. He looked at his watch. Eleven minutes ago, they had started up the slope. While he thought, his right hand, as if it had its own brain, reached back into the pack at his hip, took out another clip, and tilted it into the receiver. His mouth was dry, his knee wet with blood, and his whole frame seemed to shake with the beat of his heart.

He jumped down from the crate and was shocked to feel his knees sag a little, as if the joints were stiff. He flexed them, twice, gritting his teeth at the pain from his right knee. *Probably why SWAT guys wore kneepads.* Then he moved to the bullet-riddled gate and lifted the bar. No one fired, and he pushed the gate open until it shielded him from the square. Then he threw a can from the rubbish heap into the street. Nothing. He glanced around the gate and saw the edge of the square for the first time. Another body lay at the mouth of the alley.

A brief storm of fire struck the gate and ricocheted around the alley. Alan flung himself back and flattened at the gateway, peering through the dark under the gate itself. Another burst buzzed by him. He saw two shapes move out into the open, firing as they came, and he fired without hitting either, the gap between gate and earth too narrow to let him get a sight picture.

They were going for Shreed.

A blast like a cannon shot echoed through the town, and one of the men sprawled backward, rotating like a broken gymnast. *Harry or Mike?* The other leaped, fell flat. Alan saw a third man firing steadily almost straight up, and he realized the man was shooting for Dukas. Somebody else was spraying the alley with fire from the south. Alan took an instant, working himself up to it, then leaned out with the machine pistol and fired left-handed.

His first thought was that the machine pistol had detonated. It was gone, down the alley. So were two fingers from his left hand.

IT WAS IRONIC, Shreed thought, that his wounds had robbed him of the use of his legs. Yet he had been used to getting by without them, and now he dragged himself about the rubble as fast as he could, the ache in his back sealed away by morphine. The shots had gone in below his body armor, he knew that, probably kissed his spine.

He was down, but he wasn't out.

He thought he had got one Chinese with his first shots. Then he had wasted ammo, firing at every movement he could see. For the first few seconds he had assumed that all fire was directed at him, and he hadn't allowed himself even a flicker of hope until he saw one of the Chinese cut down by fire from another position. He couldn't understand who might be out there or why they were shooting the Chinese. He didn't really care, and he was unaware that he was screaming sometimes. He simply wanted Chen. He held tight to that thought whenever he moved and felt the grating, the almost audible crack from his lower back. *Chen. Tell him and then kill him.*

Things were getting gray around the edges when the two Chinese soldiers charged him. He got the big pistol up and shot on reflex, center of mass, but the other man came down on top of him and his gun was gone. Then he stopped trying to make sense of it. He felt himself floating a little, bouncing, and he thought it was over. Then he was slammed back to earth, the blow to his ribs shooting the first real pain in several minutes through every nerve ending, and he screamed.

THE RADIOMAN was dead and another soldier was down at the base of the tower, but Chen had Top Hook at his feet. He still looked big, and American, even as he screamed. Chen wanted to give the sniper a medal on the spot.

"That was—incredible."

"Thank you, sir."

"Because of you, we may win this yet."

The square was silent for the first time in what seemed like hours. There was no more firing from the north side, where he had had men; now Chen counted them as casualties. He should have five left.

He took a shaped charge out of his pack and checked the firing mechanism. He'd planned to use it on Shreed's car, back in the other world where his plan worked and he scooped Shreed up cleanly. *A little distraction to make the forced defection look like a terrorist bomb.* Now he thought that it would probably be powerful enough to punch through the wall of the tower. The sergeant could go after the tower's door. Chen acknowledged to himself that it wasn't much of a plan, but he had become focused on the tower, because there was somebody up there who was killing them; and because unless the Americans had a big team, he thought his survivors could hold the tower until the Pakistanis or his own service came.

He took the charge and wriggled forward to the base of the tower wall. "Two?"

"In position."

"When I blow the charge, take the tower. That goes for everybody. Acknowledge!"

Numbers counted off, leaving telltale spaces. Eight men silent.

Chen punched the charge on the wall and set the timer, pushing rubble over the charge to give it the best possible chance, then tumbled back behind the remains of the mosque wall. His mind registered the surprising observation that the wall had been inlaid with places of Chinese porcelain.

He clapped his hands to his ears and rolled into a ball.

DUKAS HEARD Alan cursing and went back to the cellphone. He was covered in stone chips from the volley that had greeted his attempt to peer out over the edge; several were embedded in his cheek. He had fired two shots. His hands were shaking.

"Alan!"

"Fuck fuck fuck FUCK!"

"Alan!"

"Hurts like a son of a bitch. Mike, they're trying to get around the tower. I caught some movement to your, uh, east and west."

"You okay?"

"Just go! Look!"

Dukas steeled himself before looking out the low arches on the south. Three men were moving along the edge of the rubble. The first disappeared to the west into the market even as Dukas raised his rifle.

Bang.

The last one dropped. The second one whirled and fired, a blaze of light and angry hornets all around him. Dukas stood his ground and the other man fired again and so did Dukas, simultaneous roars, and then the man was gone and the rifle was empty, its bolt back. *Short magazine.* He didn't have reloads. He put the rifle down on the stone roof carefully, as though it was something very valuable, and then he reached into his jacket for the revolver, and the tower moved.

ALAN HAD HIS HAND WRAPPED in lint and roughly taped. There was blood everywhere and he couldn't seem to get enough pressure on the hand to stop the spurts until he put a tourniquet on the brachial artery on the inside of the upper arm just above the elbow. That seemed to take forever. He heard Dukas fire from the building.

He had retreated into the shelter of the yard. When the blast came, it struck the open gate full on and crashed it back against its stops, the sound lost in the explosion. The slamming gate stopped within inches of his face, and the wave of smoke and noise dazed him. He shook his head, his ears ringing, and reached in the holster at his waist for his pistol. Then he worked the slide against his thigh. Alan had never been hit before, and he felt leaden with shock and fear. And worry: he hadn't heard Harry's gun for long minutes.

The Chinese had Shreed. The Chinese were trying to storm Dukas's tower.

He had reached a state where his muscles seemed to be making decisions for him. While his mind was still thinking that he didn't have the energy or the will to find Harry, his legs had levered him to his feet and pushed him to the gate, which still hung straight. He shouldered it open to keep it between him and the square and ran the other way down the street. At the first crossway, he turned left without pausing to look up the alley. He could hear his feet distinctly, slapping on the packed earth in rhythm, even though his ears were still ringing. He wasn't even looking around and he thought, very clearly, *"I'm dead."*

He passed an opening to the left, back toward the square, and kept going west, trying to keep parallel to the men moving behind the tower. At the second turning, he stopped, straining for air, and looked to the south. This lane turned slightly to the west. It appeared to be empty in the moonlight. He moved off, jogging slowly along the left margin of the street, his mouth half-open in an attempt to quiet his breathing. His left hand hurt at every heartbeat and every step, and blood continued to pulse out of the bandage, drops falling to the ground as he went.

He thought this route would take him to the area behind the tower. If it didn't, he wasn't sure he'd make it back.

Ahead of him, the street suddenly opened into a wider space, and a small truck blocked his way. He crouched by the wheel and gasped for only a moment; then he leaned out around the hood. The tower was clear in the moonlight, rising from a row of market stalls at its base. Silent shapes were climbing through the stalls.

THE BLAST extinguished sound, and the pillar of powdered rock and smoke that leaped up the north face of the tower was answered by a second column of smoke that followed the trapdoor into the air. Dukas was thrown flat, and when he gained his knees he saw that the whole north wall of the top of the tower was gone. The big pistol was still in his hand. He swayed and thought of Shreed, still down in the dark at the base of the tower if the explosion hadn't killed him. He crabwalked across the roof to the empty hole that had been a trapdoor. Dust still rose through it, and with the dust, a sort of mewling like a young cat wanting food. It was dark down there.

Dukas gritted his teeth and lowered himself into the empty space by his hands, his feet kicking out for a ladder that was no longer there. It seemed easier to take his chances on the drop than to pull himself back on the exposed roof; he lowered himself to the full reach of his arms, tried not to think of how tall the tower was, and dropped into the dark.

It was farther and more disorienting than he had expected, and he landed clumsily, his right foot on something yielding, and he sprawled. Nothing broken. The little sound came to him again. The stairs in the wall were over to the left. He felt for the wall, didn't find it where he expected, and stumbled again. *He had a flashlight in his pocket.* The thought came to him from a distance, as if he had just remembered where his keys were in the midst of a frantic search. He pulled it out and turned the head until the beam illuminated the dark.

He wished he hadn't.

It didn't take a forensic expert to understand that the charge had blown a large piece off the inside of the tower, scattering shrapnel from the ancient stones in a concentrated cone. One body had its head severed just at the neck. The sound was coming from a boy, who was lying at the head of the stairs with both of his feet gone, his blood flowing down a set of stone cataracts to pool at the bottom.

The child might live. Dukas whispered to him while he grabbed at stray bits of wreckage and came up with curtain cords that he used to bind his legs. His attempts seemed feeble and useless, his tourniquets like Band-Aids compared to the damage. The boy made inhuman sounds from his chest.

I brought this here.

He avoided the blood at the foot of the steps and turned the light on the door just as the shooting started again.

THE SHOTGUN roared to Alan's right, throwing one of the shapes back into a stall. A burst of return fire from the base of the tower gave him a target and he shot at the flashes, aiming low. The shotgun went off again, a sound like ripping canvas, and Alan's target crossed a beam of moonlight right in front of his sights and he fired, his right hand propped on the hood of the vehicle. Harry was methodically firing low into the lightly built stalls, forcing them to move.

The central stall was sturdier. It looked like a shed built of corrugated iron, and its roof ran back to the tower. At least one survivor was under it, firing steadily in short, disciplined bursts. Alan could see the light of the muzzle flash but not the shooter. He began to move out from behind the truck, his gun hand fully extended toward the target. Harry was silent, either hit or reloading. Alan moved to his left, toward the corner of the tower, keeping the corrugated iron stall between him and the shooter. When he reached the line of stalls, mangled by repeated hits, he began to move along them toward the entrance to the iron stall. Then, to his relief, Harry fired again, this time at something on the other side of the market. Alan saw his flash as the shotgun roared. He waved his pistol and pointed at the central stall.

"I see you." Harry's voice sounded clear across the market. The shooter in the stall fired at the voice. Harry fired again.

"There's another one at the other end," he shouted. Alan froze, pointing his pistol into the moonshadows fifty feet away. He heard movement inside the main stall, which went all the way back to the tower. The shooter there was moving.

Alan moved too, first to his left again to get cover from the south end of the market, then straight to the wall of the warehouse. He heard scrabbling sounds, a wooden thud, and a single roaring shot, followed by silence. He moved as quietly as he could back down the warehouse toward its dark mouth. Then he looked around the corner with his right eye, toward the south end of the market. He lowered himself to his haunches and crouched, perfectly still, watching the darkness to his front. The shotgun roared again, and the thin fabric at the front of one of the south-side stalls shredded.

"Harry!" *That was Dukas's voice in the warehouse.*

"Mike! There's a guy in there!"

"Not anymore."

Alan flung a bolt of cotton out from his hiding place and it spun, unrolling a little, across the market. No fire greeted it.

Harry fired twice, aimed shots at the base of stalls.

Dukas stayed where he was.

"I think we're shooting at shadows," called Harry.

Alan watched the dark.

"I'm crossing the square. Cover me."

Alan pointed his pistol at the other side of the square, and Dukas materialized at the corner of the warehouse.

"Where's Harry?"

Alan's speech was slurred, and he spoke slowly.

"He's crossing the square. Maybe—shooter over here—"

Dukas held the big revolver in both hands and pointed it where Alan had indicated. Harry moved very quickly from cover to cover. Nobody fired.

THE EXPLOSION had deafened Chen and half-buried him in debris. It took him time to extricate himself from the new wreckage piled on the old, and more time to clear his head. The sniper, however, was already up and moving. Shreed, lying behind the stone of the prayer screen, seemed untouched. He'd stopped screaming. Now he was talking to himself.

Chen raised his head, half expecting to be shot.

At first glance in the moonlight, the tower appeared untouched. Chen had to focus to see that the whole facade sagged in the middle. A deep gouge like a thumb mark in clay disappeared into shadows at the base. If the charge had blown a hole, however, it was too small for entry.

There was a burst of flickering light from the far side of the tower, like hidden fireworks. The noise of the firing took a moment to register.

"Sergeant! Report!"

"I'm at the door to the tower. They're all over the square."

"Get inside!"

"—door."

The sound of the shot and the noise from his headset told him the story.

"Sergeant!"

Chen looked back at the sniper, who was prone in a rubble pile, covering Chen's back.

"Report!" he demanded on the command channel.

Only silence responded.

Shreed was talking again. He said Chen's name several times. He started to talk about money, and Chen thought for a moment about how typical Shreed was of his kind. Dying, he didn't talk about God or revolution; he talked about money.

Then Chen began to understand what Shreed was saying.

THE THREE MEN picked their way along the edge of the tower. Harry stopped to check the body at the corner, the one Dukas had shot from the tower. Dead. Harry took the dead man's machine pistol, searched him for ammunition, and handed it to Dukas, who looked over the gun, fitted a clip, and hung the sling over his shoulder. Alan stayed silent, leaning against the wall of the tower. He had refused to stay behind, and they had re-bound his wrist and bandaged the wreck of his hand more carefully. While Harry took his time over the hand, Dukas kept looking to the east beyond the tower.

"Don't worry, Mike. They won't get away." He had sounded very sure. Dukas hadn't asked any questions. He looked shellshocked.

Harry came to the southeast corner and stopped, looking south. Then he got down on hands and knees and looked carefully around the corner. He watched what little he could see of the square down the wall. Dukas thought that he was going to wait forever. Alan merely leaned against the wall, stolid as an animal heading for slaughter.

Harry turned the corner quickly and then moved close to the wall, still covered from the mosque by the tower's jutting corner. Dukas followed him closely, one hand on his back, Alan a little farther behind.

When they stopped at the last corner, Harry could hear Shreed talking, and a voice, higher in pitch, shouting in English. Harry froze and then sank into a crouch.

"Where! Where is the money?"

"All—gone. All gone."

"What did you do with it?"

"I think—you'll be . . . happier—U.S. of A." Shreed's voice was weak, fading into murmurs, but it sounded happy.

"Bastard!"

Harry crept the last few feet and looked around the corner. He could see nothing but rubble. He kept moving. He could feel Dukas's hand on his back. He could hear Alan, another step behind. He was afraid that Alan was too far gone to bend over, that he would walk into a bullet like a zombie. He turned to look, and Dukas stepped right past him, half crouched, his whole attention focused on the voice.

"They'll kill—go . . . home."

"I'll kill you right now! Traitor!"

"Fuck you, Chen." Shreed's words were slow and distinct, as if they had been practiced many times. Harry had scrambled to keep up with Dukas, who stepped straight out of the shadow of the wall.

THE SNIPER had heard the movement. His commander was oblivious, prattling in English, and he twisted as quietly as possible to change his front. He rolled to a crouch and moved in a long glide away from the northwest corner, where he had waited so long. In one motion he raised his rifle to his eye and raised his body so that the muzzle appeared a few feet from Dukas.

When a shot from the darkness severed the sniper's spine, Dukas was sprayed with his blood. The sound of the shot lingered and echoed. Dukas crouched, stunned, and Chen spun and fired from a few meters away, knocking Dukas back into Harry. The shot hit his collarbone and turned in, plowing through the soft tissue and exiting at the back.

Alan raised his right arm like a duelist and brought the sight down one-handed. He leaned forward a little as Dukas fell. He shot once and Chen stumbled back, stepping on Shreed, and caught himself against the prayer screen. Chen raised his gun again and then flew forward as if kicked between the shoulders, to fall just in front of Shreed's head. There was a gaping hole in the back of his jacket and the body armor beneath.

Alan hugged one side of the doorway and looked over at Harry, flat against the opposite wall.

"Where did that come from?"

"Anna, bud. I met . . ."

Dukas staggered up and forward even as Harry tried to restrain him. He fell to his knees beside Shreed, who was still watching Chen, his eyes open and unglazed.

"George Shreed, I arrest you for the crime of high treason—"

"Who—shot—Chen—?"

"—against the people and nation of the United States—"

"Who the—fuck are—you—!"

"—crimes of murder, attempted murder, conspiracy to commit treason—"

"Partlow—fucking parade—"

"You have the right to remain silent—"

Alan watched it with his vision tunneling, and it seemed as if Mike Dukas was a priest saying last rites over a dying man. Harry had moved next to Dukas, trying to tend his wound, but Dukas knelt there, his badge out, blood running down over his belt in back. Alan tottered forward, unsure, confused, losing blood.

Then Dukas had completed his rites. He let Harry reach a hand down his back, winced when Harry came to the exit wound, and slumped.

"Hey, buddy, you up to slapping a compress on Mike while I apply pressure?"

Alan tried to cross the distance back to Harry. Harry was right there and needed help. He focused himself. *Compress.* In the little pack on his hip. His good hand went there, moved around, found something wrapped in paper, emerged. Harry had the wound bare, the whole track of the bullet's course around the neck clear under the skin. Blood flowed at both ends of the wound where the collarbone had split the bullet. Alan slapped the compress on, and his smart hand, the right, went back for tape. Harry cut pieces off the roll and they managed to stuff the ends of the wound with gauze. The focus helped. Alan emerged a little from the tunnel of his own wound.

"How's Shreed?"

"Who cares?" Harry looked over at the man by the prayer screen. "If I thought he might live, I'd shoot him myself."

"We have to get out of here."

Harry paused, cut lengths of tape all down his arm, and looked at his watch.

"Plane comes by in twenty minutes."

"Need to get a car down—to the road."

"Give me a minute here." He was putting tape over the other tape ends, running tape all the way over the compress and around Mike's neck and down his back.

"Mick?" Shreed asked with perfect clarity. "That you, buddy?"

Mick? Alan's father's name. Alan thought of the George Shreed who had been shot down in 1972 in Nam, and of Alan's father, Mick Craik, flying top cover for him beyond the point of no return, until the choppers came and his dad had had to land an A-6 on a dirt road. George Shreed, who had been part of his life since he was a child. Who had tried to help him, in a twisted way, when his father had died, and who had betrayed them all. Harry, Rose, Alan himself.

There were things he had to know.

He fell on his knees beside Shreed, as close as Dukas had been.

"It's Alan, not Mick."

"Alan Craik." Shreed smiled, the old smile, malevolent, bitter. "Here?"

"Why? I want to know *why*. Why did you do it?"

"Do what?" Still the smile.

Betray your country, Alan wanted to shout. He wasn't sure what to say. The man was probably dying, and all Alan felt was rage, rage that pushed him out of the tunnel and on to the cold plane of reality.

"*This.*"

"This op? *Because I could.* None of those other dickheads had— intestinal—" Shreed rolled a little as if to rise on his elbow and gasped, falling back so hard his head hit the rock.

"You weren't running an op. You betrayed people. *People died!*"

"China—won't trouble—us—"

"What the hell—China—!"

"Dickheads. Idiots." His lips moved, and he pushed his head up. "Like Partlow! Bureaucrats!"

"My wife. You framed Rose."

"What?" Shreed was weak. Whatever lift he had got from talking to Chen, seeing Chen die, was going. Still, he had the strength to laugh. "Your wife!" It was real laughter. Then the laughter ended, and he muttered, "She bought me some—time."

"What did you bring the Chinese?"

Shreed looked at him, struggling to concentrate.

"Chinese?"

"You ran to the Chinese. *What did you take them?*"

Shreed gurgled, turned his head, and spat against the wall. The saliva had red in it. His eyes lost their focus; behind Alan, Harry and Mike were as concentrated on Shreed as he was. Dukas began to rifle through Shreed's pockets. Harry searched Chen.

"Poison."

"What about poison?"

"Brought Chen—poison—"

"Isn't he your control? He's running you?"

"Bastard—never—"

Dukas leaned over. "Never what? Never controlled you? Tell me another one."

Then Shreed almost shouted, with sudden clarity, "How'd you get here, boy?"

"We followed you."

Shreed closed his eyes. His chest moved up and down rapidly, and it came to Alan that he was laughing again. He wheezed and coughed. His eyes sprang open, focused, a clear blue untouched by frost, staring right into Alan.

"You taking me home?"

"If we make it."

Shreed said something too quietly for Alan to hear. He bent over and noticed that blood was again spurting from the wreckage of his hand. It seemed to be happening a long way away. Shreed tried to push him away and spoke clearly.

"You think you're heroes, but you don't—understand—"

Harry leaned in, his dark head between Alan and Shreed.

"You'll hang."

"I'll have—monument like—Casey. You'll see—who the hero—is—"

Shreed's mouth worked a little, but no more sound came out. It was as if Harry's voice had broken a spell. Alan stood slowly, the almost forgotten rip across his knee springing to new pain.

"I'm going to get a car down to the road to signal the plane," he said. "Harry—take care of—"

"I'll watch Mike. And I want to find . . . . . . the other shooter."

Dukas looked up at him, his lips white.

"He doesn't have anything." He looked dazed. "Maybe—maybe in the car. . . ."

Alan nodded.

ALAN DROVE Shreed's white sedan down the dark track, feeling the first hit of a morphine injection and its false security as it crept through his system. He looked at his watch and drove the car out on the road, shifted hard and pushed the pedal down until he was flying past the ridge, past the turn where their own abandoned vehicle sat off the road, on and on for more than a mile until a bright red-and-yellow sign flashed past. The wind was from the south, right in his face. It would make a landing easier. He slowed the car with the gears and the brake and backed it in a K turn until he had it pointed north, his left hand smearing the wheel with blood. Then he turned it off, rolled the window down, and waited. He could see headlights shining at the top of the hill. Harry would be getting Dukas and Shreed into one of the Chinese trucks up there.

Alan pulled Harry's cellphone out of his pack and wedged it between his knees while he turned it on, waited for a signal, and pressed the auto-dial for Harry's computer office in DC. It was answered on the third ring.

"Ethos Security."

"Valdez?"

"Who's this?"

He had to brace himself. "Alan Craik."

"Jeez, Mister Craik, you don't sound too good."

"Valdez, I need you to pass a message—"

"You guys okay? Where are you?"

"Tell the Navy, Valdez. Get to the highest level you—can and tell them—we got him."

"The guy you were after."

"And *I don't think he had time to pass anything.* That part is—very important—" He had trouble keeping his voice loud enough.

"You got the guy, he didn't pass anything."

"I can't swear to that, Valdez. But we got him meeting the Chinese . . ."

His voice faded a moment, and he rallied himself. "And no one left that meeting alive. You got that? Do it now. *Now.* Very important—"

"Mister Craik, you sound like shit, pardon my French."

"Just—do it—"

Alan pressed the cutoff switch.

He heard the vacuum cleaner noise first. It sounded intermittent and far away, and he was surprised by the flash of the landing lights in front of him, only a mile distant. He flicked the car lights three times, a long pulse each time. The engine noise dwindled away to a whine, and then he saw the plane clearly, lined up and only a few meters above the road. It passed over his head in a rush and was gone, and then he heard the engines go to full power and it turned west, out over the valley, and came around. He lost the engine noise then and watched Harry stop where the village road met the highway. Harry's lights did a good job of marking the start of a runway, and Harry probably didn't want to risk running down the road when the plane was on approach.

The landing lights came on again to the north, and Alan thought that Stevens looked too low, too early, but the plane came on and on, past Harry's lights, and it was down, and the engines roared as it braked itself, taxiing, and rolled out. The S-3 stopped well north of him. He cut his lights, cranked the engine, and turned them back on, and then, his vision coming and going as if a light was being turned on and off, drove to the edge of the jetwash, rolled the car to the shoulder, and parked it.

Harry was already strapping Dukas into the SENSO seat. The front of the cockpit was illuminated red and green by the gauges, the back end darker with both tactical screens down. Soleck unstrapped and bounded past him, pausing to try to shake his hand, then seeing him stagger.

"Jesus—Commander—"

"Shreed's in the truck," Harry said. "He's still alive."

Alan put his good hand on Harry. "You'll have to ride in the tunnel."

"I'm not coming with you."

"I'm not leaving you here!" Leaning back against the aircraft, not able to bear his own weight, Harry fading—

Harry held him up. "I'll be long gone in an hour."

"Harry—no way you can hide. Never make it on your own."

"I won't be on my own, old boy. I'm going over the mountains to Tashkent."

Alan tried to see him.

"Anna," Harry said. He smiled and tapped gently on Alan's shoulder. "Who do you think shot Shreed's control? God?"

Alan thought of the Chinese officer's reeling back and then snapping forward. It all seemed unlikely and far away, as if Harry was telling him a fairy tale. Harry put a hand on his neck and slipped past him. When he returned, he and Soleck had a makeshift stretcher. It took all five available arms to get Shreed up through the hatch and back into the tunnel, and then Soleck wove parachute cord between tiedowns until Shreed looked like the victim of a giant spider. Alan leaned against the frame of the hatch with Harry. He wanted to lie down, and blood loss had taken the edges off his peripheral vision.

"Anna—" He was trying to think it through. "Do you—trust her?"

"Ask me in five days, Al." Harry was rewrapping Alan's hand.

"When—I don't get—?"

"In the village. She needed professional help. I'm the help. I think she's looking for a side to be on. I'm willing to be the side. Tell you more at home, over a beer."

Alan couldn't think of anything to say, so he took Harry's hand and they embraced. In the cockpit, Soleck was already strapping in.

"You know how to close the hatch from outside, Harry?"

Harry nodded. Alan picked up his helmet. Stevens was shouting something at him from the front, and Alan could guess that it was about fuel and darkness. It was important, but what mattered to Alan was his friend Harry, filling the hatch. Harry, who was grinning like a maniac. Alan strapped himself in and bent down before attaching the shoulder straps. *Long time since Harry grinned like that.*

"Take care, man. Watch—yourself."

"You're the one traveling with the viper, Al. Good luck."

They held each other's eyes. The hatch started to close and then popped back. Harry's head came in.

"Tell them the price for Anna's stuff is now two million, bud." He slapped Alan's knee and the hatch slammed shut, cutting off Alan's reply. Forty seconds later, the plane was rolling.

39

Above southwestern Pakistan
0230 GMT (0630L).

"MISTER CRAIK'S NOT RESPONDING." SOLECK HADN'T spoken in an hour, and his voice was rough.

Stevens was groggy, waking disoriented, then stretching to ease muscles cramped by hours in an ejection seat.

"Not a lot we can do about that, Soleck."

Soleck looked out the windscreen at the undulating landscape revealed by the first gleams of morning sun. He had the ESM system up and running on his tiny front-seat screen. He wanted Alan Craik back. The ESM took art to run and understand, and Soleck had to look up every hit on his kneeboard cards. Craik would have known most of the signals by heart.

"Tall King radar active at, uh, wait. That's west of Karachi; it's Sonmiah."

"I'm not an intel geek, Soleck. What's a Tall King?"

"Air search radar. If I saw it, it saw us."

"If we go lower, we run out of gas before we cross the coast."

"I know."

Stevens was wearier than he had ever been in his life. He felt stretched, somehow, his mind expanded to fit circumstances too wide for ordinary thought. He'd been flying for days, almost all of it at low altitude and a great deal of it in mountains. They'd been challenged twice so far on the return flight, both times by local air traffic control. Stevens had talked gibberish the first time and not responded the second. If either of them had had any adrenaline left to give they'd have used it anticipating the surface-to-air missile that should have followed, but the S-3 had survived. They had no way of knowing how busy the Pakistani operators were that night, watching India.

Soleck had spelled him twice, each time for an hour, once on the flight north, once south. Soleck piloted the plane well, keeping them low, climbing ridges within hundreds of meters of the stony surface. He could do the job, but he couldn't keep the plane right down against the ground the way Stevens could. That kind of talent came with thousands of hours of practice.

Somewhere in Soleck's second hour, Alan Craik had ceased to communicate. Stevens had been asleep. Soleck hadn't been able to take his attention off the plane. Now that Stevens was coming back to life, Soleck wanted to go to the back end and check everybody there. He gave Stevens a minute to orient himself and then spoke.

"Ready to take her?"

"I've got her."

"I'm going to check the back."

Soleck unclipped the top of his harness, flipped the buckle on the center and stood, stooped by the cockpit's low overhead but still able to take a luxurious stretch after an hour of immobility. Below them the Porali River unrolled in the dawn light to the west, the first sunlight sending a dazzle of sparkles off the surface.

The back end smelled of blood. Alan Craik's maimed left hand had a trail of dried blood that ran down the armrest and his knee and pooled in the steps to the hatch under his feet. His face was an unnatural white in the dawn light filtering past Soleck from the cockpit. Even his lips appeared drained of color. Soleck laid his thumb along the carotid artery and felt the pulse. A bare flicker.

The NCIS agent, Dukas, was far down. He had a lot of morphine in him, and he was out cold. His dressing appeared to be holding. Soleck thought that he probably ought to try and get water into him or something, but he had no idea how serious the wounds were. He might have been gut shot. Best to let him be dehydrated.

The body in the back was still breathing. That was all the attention

Soleck intended to pay it. Soleck stood over Shreed's bound body, held a plastic bottle to urinate, and then stowed the bottle back with the computers. He looked around at the three wounded men and shook his head. Soleck was a very young man. He had a vivid imagination, but the events of the last hours surpassed it. He was part of this, not an observer but a participant, and somehow that was wonderful, in spite of the blood and the pain.

Soleck went back and squatted by his commander, looking into his face. Craik was farther gone than Soleck, who had never been in combat, had ever seen. He chewed his upper lip, feeling a bubble rise in his throat.

"He dead?" Stevens sounded matter-of-fact.

"No. Lost a lot of blood."

"He's full of surprises. He'll live."

Soleck sat down in his seat and started to do up the straps.

"I just wish there was something I could *do*."

"Flying the plane isn't enough for you?"

"He's going to die."

"What's on the ESM?"

"Nothing. The Tall King hasn't radiated again, or we're back below its coverage. I think we're too low to have it see us."

"Seventy miles to feet wet."

"How far to the carrier?"

"No idea. If they moved into the box they planned on Sunday, another hour after we get gas. I'm going to break radio silence in three minutes."

"We'll still be over Pakistan."

"Yeah, but if there isn't a tanker waiting when we cross the coast, we're going to have to swim for the boat."

"The tanker will be there."

"It had better be."

Soleck looked down at the little green screen, its characters obscured by the sunlight now washing across it. He held his hand to shade it. He looked away and then looked back to make sure he wasn't wrong. The information stayed the same, and, as he watched, the long vector changed and resolved into a diamond. The radar had a signature that he knew without reference to his kneeboard cards.

"Slot Back."

"Where?"

Soleck pushed buttons and put his face right down on the screen. Passive sensors in the S-3 didn't give altitude and they weren't really accurate about range. The bearing was almost directly astern.

"At least one Su-27, astern. It has a search range of about one-fifty miles, so if we just detected them, let's call it between one five zero and two zero zero miles."

"Does he see us?"

"We won't know until we see his radar lock."

Stevens didn't take his eyes off the ground in front of the airplane.

"Call the boat."

SOLECK HAD a comm card three days out of date; the frequencies and call signs would have been changed. He'd have to start on the Guard frequency and hope that he wasn't alerting every Pakistani site within radio range to their presence.

"USS *Thomas Jefferson,* this is AH 902, over." He watched the green diamond on his screen leap forward almost a centimeter. He keyed his mike again.

"USS *Thomas Jefferson,* this is AH 902, over."

"AH 902, this is *Jefferson,* go ahead."

"*Jefferson,* this is, ah, Ranger One. We need gas ASAP and have a—" Soleck read down the old comm card quickly, "Vampire, that's a Vampire, in close pursuit." He remembered that the crypto might be no good; that he was talking in the clear.

"Ranger One, this is *Jefferson,* I copy need gas and Vampire in pursuit. Wait one."

They'd be scrambling for the old comm card. Or maybe they were ready. The Su-27 moved again and this time the new diamond formed while leaving the old one still glowing a little behind. So there were two.

"Make that two Vampires."

"Copy. Ranger One, go up to number four on your old card."

"Copy. Roger." Soleck tore his eyes off the little screen and read digits off his old comm card while pressing them into the radio.

"Ranger One, this is Tarheel One. Do you read me?"

"Loud and clear, Tarheel One."

"Give me your location, Ranger One."

Soleck read coordinates off the GPS and passed their altitude as well. He watched the ESM screen and then spoke to Stevens and the distant voice of Tarheel One at the same time. "I think Vampires have just gone to burner."

"Roger."

Stevens snapped his head around and looked at the sky above and behind them. Soleck did the same. Neither saw anything.

Stevens got his eyes down to an instrument scan and then up out of the cockpit, made a minute adjustment and watched the ground blur by beneath them.

"Ranger One, fly one eight zero. Texaco is waiting." The voice sounded utterly calm, almost happy. "Stay in the clear and don't try going encrypted, Ranger One."

Stevens smiled. Soleck measured the map by eye. Forty miles to the coast. Eleven miles past that to international water. The gas was going to be really, really close. The gauge wasn't accurate below two thousand pounds, and they were well below two thousand pounds.

"He's going to have to meet us low."

"Roger, Ranger One. I'll pass. He'll come up when you start to close."

The two Su-27s, invisible somewhere behind them, continued to close the gap on ESM, their range accurate to a margin that meant that they could be flying alongside or fifty miles behind.

"Tarheel, those Vampires are breathing down our necks."

SEVENTY MILES AHEAD, Chris Donitz turned slightly so his nose was pointed directly at the S-3 somewhere to his north. His wingman followed him through the turn. He called the air wing commander on Strike Common and hoped the new crypto was good.

"Permission to go nose hot?"

"Granted." That was Captain Rafehausen on the S-3 tanker.

Donitz's RIO fired up the AWG-9, kept in standby for the duration of the flight to hide their activity. The S-3 appeared low, a big radar reflector. The two hostile contacts, tracked passively until now, leaped to the screen. They were twenty miles astern of the S-3 and pressing fast.

"Big Eagle, this is Tarheel One. Twenty miles and closing. Permission to press?"

Big Eagle looked at his watch. 0303 GMT. He smiled grimly under his oxygen mask.

"Players, this is Big Eagle. Open your envelopes." Throughout his strike package, pilots or their navigators would be fumbling through the process of loading the new crypto. It should, according to the CNO, work now. It was a new set of codes. He waited a moment and then hit his "ENCRYP" button on his comms and then watched his ops display to see who was in the new crypto link. He watched planes appear like fireflies on a summer evening, and the second he had Tarheel One, he made the call.

"Tarheel One, this is Big Eagle. Go get 'em."

"MISSILE FIRING!" Soleck thumbed the chaff/flare trigger and started to spray the sky with decoys. Stevens pulled hard on the stick and rolled the plane into a tight turn, adding power and spending their precious fuel like a prodigal. He turned east, straight into the rising sun.

The first missile, diving from high above them, lost track against the ground clutter and missed them by hundreds of feet. The second missile didn't buy the first chaff cloud, was misled by the second, and detonated. A giant fist slammed the underside of the plane. Soleck scanned the instruments, felt the new vibration in the yoke, and looked at Stevens.

"We're still here!"

Lots of new experiences for Soleck.

DONITZ CROSSED the coast on full burner, above twenty thousand feet and descending slowly. The Su-27s were below ten thousand, still well north. Donitz wanted to focus their attention on his F-14 Tomcats immediately. Beyond-visual-range engagement would at least break up their formation, giving his flight the possibility of engaging the newer, faster Flankers one at a time.

He got a firing solution with his "Buffalo" AIM 54C and fired one.

"Fox One."

The half-ton missile dropped off the wing and then leaped forward with a roar that vibrated through the Tomcat even at full speed. After five seconds he fired a second missile.

"Fox Two."

The range was not extreme; under ideal conditions, the AIM 54 could score a kill at one hundred nautical miles, and, given the front aspect and the altitude advantage, conditions were approaching the ideal.

Then he called his wingman.

"Tarheel Two. Snot, bracket left." How a lieutenant named Breslau had earned the nickname "Snot" was lost in history.

"Roger."

"Commit. Take the guy to the east."

"Roger."

The approaching fighters were now turning away from the AIM 54s and probably jinking. The Tomcats had their opponents in their front quarter and needed only minor maneuvers to keep their AWG-9 radars on the targets. The AIM 54 does not go into self-guidance mode until the last few miles of an intercept, but given the range and altitude difference, the Su-27s had limited maneuver options and couldn't break lock with a simple turn. The long-range shots and the surprise of coming under fire while hunting a lone S-3 had wrecked their formation.

Donitz thought that at least one of them was very new. Now they were down around four thousand feet, several miles apart and forty miles away. The S-3 was off to his left, so low that he'd be invisible to their radars. Snot, Donitz's wingman in Tarheel Two, had rolled to the left and separated the two Tomcats by over a mile. Tarheel Two was adding to the confusion with his own long-range missile at the eastern Flanker.

"Fox One."

AIM 54Cs cost the taxpayer one million dollars a round. They'd just bought the S-3 a new lease on life for three million dollars.

"OUR TOMCATS! They're firing. No lock from the Slot Back."

"They'll never see us again!" Stevens sounded as if he was swearing a vow. He pulled the nose back to the south and throttled down as far as he dared. They descended a few feet lower, so that Stevens's flying began to seem like a roller-coaster ride. He was low enough to make surface effect winds an issue. His face was covered in sweat.

The fuel gauge dropped below a thousand pounds and the numbers started to reel off.

"SNOT, BREAK LEFT!"

The two Su-27s were well separated coming out of their maneuvers to avoid the AIM 54s. None of the three missiles had hit, but the two Flankers were miles apart and the engagement could now develop as a series of two-on-one engagements rather than a heads-up two-on-two fight. Donitz didn't want to test the Su-27s in a dogfight; he wanted to beat them with tactics before their superior design and newer, stronger airframes could tell.

The lead Flanker was just visible and turning to get his radar on Snot, now extending off to the west. Donitz throttled down and turned in on the lead. The lead plane seemed to hesitate and then fired a missile and turned away, the missile losing lock immediately as the radar came off its target.

New guy.

"Take the trailer."

"Got him."

Donitz turned, conserving speed by losing altitude without pushing his throttle. He wanted the other pilot to beat him around the circle. The lead Flanker was turning away from Snot, turning hard to the east. He already seemed to have forgotten that Donitz was there, above him and covering Snot's backside. His own turn was to the west, just far enough to get a tone on Donitz's AIM 7 Sparrow missile. Donitz fired one and then followed the Flanker, turning back to the north as the other's hard turn away from Snot leveled off. At the end of his turn, his opponent was low on speed and low on options, and Donitz's S-turn had kept the radar-guided missile in aspect all the way home. Way late, the enemy pilot woke up to his danger and pumped chaff, breaking back to the east and diving to get the speed he had wasted in the turn. Donitz gave his plane more power and followed him down, now almost perfectly behind him and four miles away. The Sidewinder growl told him that he had an ideal IR missile shot. He let it growl.

The enemy pilot never got enough angle of separation between his plane and the chaff to matter. The AIM 7 blew a chunk out of the starboard engine nacelle and shredded the starboard vertical stabilizer. Donitz watched the enemy plane shudder, stand on its nose for a second, and then begin a tumbling fall. He saw the pilot eject.

"Scratch one Flanker."

Snot had passed through a merge with the second Flanker in a hail of missile fire that left both planes intact, each turning and dropping chaff and flares against his adversary. Donitz, higher and with energy and time, thought he still owned the second guy. He turned west and descended. Snot turned left, across the sun, and reached for altitude.

"They're Chinese!" Snot barked as he turned.

The second enemy pilot was not a neophyte. He didn't follow Snot across the sun and into Donitz's waiting missiles. He didn't waste IR missiles on a target backlit by the rising sun. He completed his turn to the east and immediately went to full power as he pulled his nose up and back to the west, leaving a perfect S-shaped contrail behind him as he gained speed and left Snot right out of the fight. Snot continued his turn, looking for a long-range tail-on engagement, his head snapping back and forth trying to get a visual, his RIO calling out the range, but by the time he had the tone his opponent had passed the range limit.

Donitz still had the altitude and the energy. Always the patient hunter, he waited until the second Flanker was fully committed to the second half of his S-turn and followed, again killing his speed to stay above and behind the other plane. His nose was too high to have the tone, but, having gained the position he wanted, he pulled back on the stick, pushed forward on the throttle, and felt the rush as the gravity rose like a wave of epoxy to trap his body, and his vision tunneled.

He began to see stars. He could only guess what the other plane was doing. Snot's RIO was calling numbers to him, guessing that he was graying out.

Donitz held the turn. He wanted to pass behind the guy and surprise him, turning back hard and catching him as he ended his turn. He passed some invisible line in his mind and changed the angle of his turn. He should now be approaching the other's port quarter.

Tone. *Grrrrooowllll.*

"Fox Two." Spoken with enormous effort.

With afterburners like solar flares against the cold western sky, the Sidewinder had no difficulty tracking. The second Flanker went up in a single white flash, her fuel or another weapon ignited by the little IR missile. There was no parachute.

"Hey, that guy was mine!" Snot sounded indignant.

Donitz slowed his turn and pushed in the throttle, letting his vision return to normal while his RIO searched the sky to the north for more planes. They were low on both fuel and missiles, and a second flight of Flankers would be a catastrophe. He thought of the second guy's perfect S-turn and the blinding flash as his plane went up. A real pilot.

Dead.

"Shut up, Snot."

RAFE HEARD the engagement develop, followed it with body English until it ended, and realized he had turned his own plane slightly north while his attention was focused on the fight. The coast was only a few miles away.

"Ranger One, what is your fuel status?"

"Below one thousand."

"Coming to you."

Rafe completed the inadvertent turn to the north and went to full power, diving slightly to lose altitude and gain speed. The other S-3 had only a few minutes to reach him, and Rafe had to effect a join-up without making the other plane maneuver or climb. And Stevens would have to hit the basket the first time.

Somewhere above him and well to the south, the E-2C updated the datalink and gave him the picture. No apparent enemy aircraft. Ranger One was twenty miles to the north and crawling toward him, very low. He continued his dive, aiming a mile to the east of the other S-3 to give him space for a single sharp turn to match direction and speed. He'd use the tight turn to dump velocity. At the same time, he was registering that the Tarheel flight had to be low on gas and munitions and that he needed more shooters to cover the refueling. He was also aware that he was now over Pakistan and thus in defiance of orders and international law, and that bringing up more Tomcats and Hornets could be viewed as escalation. The admiral was a long way away.

"Contacts bearing 005, one hundred eighty miles." The E-2 was on the ball. A hundred and eighty miles was beyond the AWG-9 radar range.

"Tarheel, break off. Gunslingers, cover our refueling."

Forty miles behind him, two more F-14s turned out of their combat air patrol position and raced for the coast of Pakistan. Donitz's flight turned away from the oncoming contacts, well beyond their range, and headed for the tankers. And all along the Pakistani coast, surface-to-air missile sites began to come on line. Campbell, Rafe's TACCO, began to reel off numbers.

Rafe had an EA-6B and a flight of F-18 Hornets ready to suppress the SAM sites, but, once they started shooting at Pakistan, there would be no hope of avoiding war.

SOLECK SAW the SAM site come up off to his left and put the MARI radar on it. Mister Craik had told him that surface ships often mistook the high-intensity beam for targeting radar; it seemed possible that a SAM operator would make the same mistake.

He hit the button for image mode. The fuel fell below five hundred pounds.

RAFE REACHED the point he had mentally designated for his turn.

"Hang on!"

He pulled the plane as if he was entering the break over the carrier and going for a shithot okay on his landing. He kept his hand steady on the throttle, watching his airspeed all the way. He was looking to exit the turn at one hundred eighty knots, just fast enough to pass over the other S-3 and then slow to match speeds. Stevens was right there, right where Rafe wanted him to be, and steady as a rock.

"Extend the hose."

Alan's S-3 had a scorch mark running up the fuselage from the tail section, and a wiring harness trailing like the tail on a kite. Then they were gone, hidden under Rafe's wing. Rafe sideslipped a fraction toward the other plane and throttled down.

———

STEVENS WATCHED the tanker from a mile away: the beautiful turn to join, the fractional sideslip to gain the perfect position. He flashed a glance at the fuel. Effectively, empty. One shot at the basket, which was coming, coming, *there.*

Stevens added a fraction of power, pulled the nose up a hair, added a little more power, and slipped a foot to the left. It looked right. It was right. He nudged the throttle, the plane gave one leap like the last surge of a wounded animal, and the probe slammed into the basket and caught. JP-5 streamed down the line. Soleck was looking at him with enough adoration to soothe any ego ever formed. Stevens's hands were steady as a rock, but his left knee had developed a tendency to tremble. The fuel gauge started to register the new gas.

The SAM site had gone offline. The Indian Ocean was visible even from their fraction of altitude. They had fighter cover and they had gas, and, suddenly, Stevens realized that they were going to make it.

Washington 0300 GMT (2200L).

In the CNO's map room, Rose watched the two new contacts turn away on the big screen. Behind her, there was a babble of voices; the CNO talking to the President, various cockpit voices from the air far away, the low murmur of aides dealing with other crises. The CNO put his phone in its cradle and avoided her eye.

"Package is back over international water," a short, stocky woman with gold wings and full commander's stripes announced. The sound levels increased, like applause at a game heard on a radio in a distant room. It didn't touch her. She got to her feet and moved toward the CNO, who was standing with the DNI and another admiral she didn't recognize. The stocky woman pushed a cup of coffee into her hand.

"Drink that. He'll be okay."

"Thanks, ma'am." Rose had forgotten that she, too, wore the three broad strips of gold that marked a full commander. She sipped the coffee. *The universal Navy cure.* It tasted like ship's coffee; bitter and old. Her husband was, she knew, "weak and not responding due to loss of blood." That much had come from the S-3. And that was all she knew. The voice that had reported it had sounded very young.

The big blue screen that had held the drama of the fight over Pakistan was empty now. Everyone else had lost interest. The crisis was over, or rather, it had given way to a new set of crises: the Chinese reaction, the justifiable squawks from Pakistan.

When the screen became active again, her coffee cup was empty, and the screen showed another battle group, this one in the Taiwan Straits. There, surface ships were holding contact on a submarine that was too close to the carrier. There, that same carrier had a strike package on deck to deal with the Chinese missile sites that were poised to fire on Taiwan. There, a Chinese surface action group seemed ready to exchange missiles with the American carrier and her escorts, an incredibly one-sided exchange. China would lose every exchange on the map, but had, until now, behaved as if she could prevail by willpower alone. And once the missiles started to fly in the Taiwan Straits, the world would never be the same. It was twenty minutes until the expiry of the Chinese ultimatum to India.

George Shreed had brought them to this: her husband bleeding in the back of an S-3, her country at the brink of a war that would devastate continents. They were to the point that a single bad turn by a pilot, a single missile launch over Taiwan, would act like the first particle slamming into an atom. The reaction would be nuclear.

She stood apart, small but perfectly straight, the empty cup forgotten in her left hand. Her eyes followed the action in the Taiwan Straits on the screen, but her whole being was focused on a single plane far to the east, now throttling down from a straight-in approach to a steep angle of descent. She couldn't see the trailing wiring harness, or hear the crash as the whole weight of the battered plane hit the deck. She couldn't feel the scorched tail hook grabbing at the three wire, the rush of the engines as they went to full power and then, as if grudging their voice, dying away slowly. The press of medics and crash crews who rushed the plane were invisible to her, too insignificant to be featured on the CNO's command display. She imagined it all, several times, and she imagined different endings, some with fire, some without.

Cheering woke her from her trance. The stocky commander hugged her and was replaced by another aide, who pumped her hand. Someone in front of her was pounding a table with his fist and laughing. She looked around. Whatever they were applauding, it wasn't the landing of one S-3. She looked up automatically at the big clock; it was one minute until the ultimatum expired.

"Pakistan's asking for a truce!" someone shouted in the passageway outside. "China blinked!"

ROSE CRAIK wondered that the avoidance of a possible world war left her with so little response, but she fixed a smile on her face and continued to watch the screen. She knew, remotely, that Pakistan's request for a truce meant that China's ultimatum no longer had any teeth. China would be forced to back down on every television in the world. Inasmuch as her country and her service were safe, she was happy, in a detached way, but her soul was elsewhere.

Twice, she tried to sip from the empty cup. A tall figure moved into her peripheral vision, just to her right, and there was a hand on her shoulder.

"They're on the deck," the CNO said. "Everybody on board is alive." He was smiling, and the rest of what he said was lost in the rushing sound in her ears.

PART

THREE

Last Words

St. Anselm's Cemetery,
Washington, DC.

ON ONE OF THOSE HAZY, MUGGY SUMMER DAYS THAT
make Washington a tropical-duty post for some foreign countries, Alan
Craik and Mike Dukas stood on a green slope that looked down over
gray monuments and gravestones toward a flower-covered mound. Alan
had his left arm in a sling; Dukas, his throat covered by a clavicle brace,
had both wrists supported by a thin plastic harness.

Neither spoke. They were watching the dispersal of the cluster of people, mostly men, who had stood at the grave. There hadn't been many,
perhaps twenty, but more than half of them had stayed until the grave
had been filled and the flowers laid down, and then some of them had
leaned close and added things to the pile. Now, they were drifting away
at last.

Alan watched a lean figure in a dark suit climb the slope toward them.
He didn't recognize the man, nor did he think he had been among the
mourners.

"Menzes," Dukas muttered. It was the first word either had spoken in
half an hour. "Agency Internals."

Menzes came on slowly through the heat. When he was a few feet
away, he stopped and nodded at Dukas as if confirming something that
Dukas had said. He and Dukas looked at each other.

"Menzes," he said, putting out a hand to Alan.

"Al Craik."

"Yeah, I thought so." Menzes cleared his throat. "I sent my personal apologies to your wife, but I'll say it to you, too." He stood straight. "I'm sorry."

Alan nodded.

Menzes moved to stand next to Dukas, and the three of them looked down at the new grave. Only four figures stood there now.

"What were they putting on the grave?" Alan said.

"Medals." Menzes straightened his back again. "Their intelligence medals." He was silent as the group below them broke up. One figure began to climb toward them. He was quite an old man and moved painfully through the heat. " 'The best intelligence officer of his generation,' " Menzes quoted. "That's what the one who gave the eulogy said. 'The greatest American patriot since William Casey.' "

Slowly, slowly, the dark figure came closer.

"None of the big shots came. I thought Partlow might come, but he didn't have the balls. Only the Old Guard."

The old man was close enough now so that they could see that tears had streamed down his face, which was red from the heat and the climb. He was puffing. He stopped twenty feet away, head low like a bull's, getting his breath. He never took his eyes off the three of them. When he could breathe, he started shouting.

"You bastards killed him! We know who you are. You killed him! You hunted him down like a fucking dog, a man you weren't fit to lick his shoes! You *bastards*!"

White foam gathered in the corners of his mouth. One of the other mourners had followed him, and now he turned the old man and, with one hateful glance at them, shepherded him down the slope and led him away. He was still shouting.

"The *Times* said he was a loyal American with a long and distinguished career."

"That's the public position."

"What'd they get from him?" Dukas said.

"Nothing. He never woke up." Menzes stared at the grave. "The disk you got from the woman, though—it had enough treason embedded in the porn to have hanged him. Many times."

ALAN STARTED forward, and the other two were pulled into his wake. They walked down to the grave, moving carefully around stones, black, gray, white, forgotten names chiseled with loving care. Alan stood by the flower-covered mound. "Are we sure he's in there?" he said.

"Are we ever sure of anything?"

This time it was Menzes who moved first, heading for the gate, and the other two who followed. As if separation from the grave released them, they began to talk of other things. Menzes, who seemed to know a lot, asked Dukas about Sally Baranowski. She was in rehab, Dukas said, trying to get her daughter back. He didn't say that whatever might have happened between the two of them hadn't happened; he had been in a hospital, and her life had gone off on its own course.

"Nice woman," Menzes said. "We interrogated her. She was clear, but the old boys had it in for her because of—" He jerked his head back toward the grave.

"She got reassigned," Dukas said.

"I know."

"You?"

Menzes laughed. "Not yet. But they're trying." They walked on. "How about you?"

"I'm off to Holland as soon as I get out of this fucking contraption. You wanta come work for the War Crimes Tribunal? I can always use a straight shooter."

Menzes laughed again. "Seems like yesterday I was saying that to your man Triffler. Good guy."

"We're all good guys," Alan growled. "It's just that nobody else thinks so."

They stopped by Alan's car. He jingled his keys in his good hand. "Was he the best intelligence officer of his generation?"

Menzes's lean face was grim. "He was a traitor. He may have been crazy; he may have been well-meaning; but he was a traitor. *We won!*"

"I don't seem to hear the brass band."

Menzes shrugged. Dukas smiled. Alan shook his head.